FOOTSTEPS

IN

THE

DEW

Titles in the Rookery Rally Series:

In The Early Morning Light
A New Day Dawning
Footsteps in The Dew

FOOTSTEPS IN THE DEW

Tales from the chimney corner

EDWARD FORDE HICKEY

Matador
9 Priory Business Park,
Wistow Road, Kibworth Beauchamp,
Leicestershire. LE8 0RX
Tel: 0116 279 2299
Email: books@troubador.co.uk
Web: www.troubador.co.uk/matador
Twitter: @matadorbooks

ISBN 978 1788035 606

British Library Cataloguing in Publication Data.
A catalogue record for this book is available from the British Library.

Printed and bound by CPI Group (UK) Ltd, Croydon, CR0 4YY
Typeset in 11pt Aldine401 BT by Troubador Publishing Ltd, Leicester, UK

Matador is an imprint of Troubador Publishing Ltd

www.edwardfordehickey.co.uk

Frontispiece *Days in Olde Tipp'rary*

For Bedelia and Jack with gratitude

Author's Note

I have tried to leave my footsteps carefully down on a literary journey – a journey similar to a laughing child attempting to make matching long strides behind a farmer as the two of them go out to fetch the cows in a field where the silver dewfall has clearly indicated the big man's wellington footsteps. *Footsteps in the Dew* endeavours likewise to match the strides of a previous generation of oral storytellers, who frequented the evening cardplaying fireside during the late 1940s in north Tipperary.

Of course the written word will always be somewhat of a mongrel – in that it cannot record a pictorial image of those old storytellers – whether at the fireside or during their harvesting breaks in the meadow or the bog or on their daily journeys to the creamery with a child sitting next to them on the lace of the ass-and-car. Nor can a book of tales include the wondrous pauses within those stories of old or the facial, hand and shoulder mannerisms of the teller – not to mention the occasional spit at a fly. An author can but make an honest attempt to follow in these storytellers' footsteps and it is left to the reader to gauge the extent to which I have succeeded.

E.F.H
December 2016

A superb collection delivered by a natural storyteller . . . charming, poignant and thoroughly entertaining.

from Addison and Cole's senior editor, Ben Evans

Stories that are unnervingly impressive . . . the language highly evocative . . . the emotions powerful.

from The London School of Journalism

Introduction

It was Wednesday evening on Tipperary's Rookery Rally hillside. As usual the two candles were lit reflectively on the back and front tables. The glass globe of the oil-lamp had been cleaned of its brown stains for this special occasion and it shone its flame all round the Welcoming Room, making huge spectral shadows across the back wall.

Suddenly the rhythm of hobnail boots could be heard echoing across the stream's flagstones in front of Dowager's cabin. The poachers (led by Ayres 'n' Graces) opened the door and they took off their hats. The house-light sparkled out behind them onto the yard and on towards the stream in a long silver ribbon.

"God save all here!" they said and into the warmth of the Welcoming Room they brought a pair of fat rabbits for Dowager's pot. They hung them on the nail behind the door so as to bring her good luck.

The card-table was then pulled out onto the middle of the floor for the game to begin. The players sat round, waiting for the deck of cards to be cut and dealt out. They lit their pipes and soon sent clouds of smoke spiraling up to the rafters. The silence of the cardgame was marred only by the ticking of the clock on the dresser.

An hour later and it was time for the last hand of cards. Blue-eyed Jack gave a polite little cough as he leaned back on his chair. Then his eyes glittered and he rapped the table with his knuckles, getting a woebegone look from the rest of the players at the sight of his big trump – the Ace-of-hearts. Showers of pennies were sent flying round the table and he quickly scooped the money up in his fists. With the games at an end it was time for the evening story to begin.

"Who will tell this evening's tale?" said Dowager, her eyes scanning the men.

The players turned their chairs away from the table and they made a little scurry for the hearthstone, forming a semicircle beneath the hob.

By this time Blue-eyed Jack had managed to heap half-a-dozen whitethorn logs and a bucketful of turf on top of the fire, causing the flames to flicker fiercely and the sparks to fly straight up the chimney. It wasn't long before the six players were roasting their shins red-raw from the tremendous heat of the blaze.

They knew of course whose turn it would be this Wednesday to tell the latest historical tale of events. Ayres 'n' Graces beckoned Rambling Jack to take the place of honour on the cushioned bench in the depths of the chimney corner.

There followed a delicious pause of childish expectation among the listeners. It was always the same thing of a Wednesday once the cards were over and done with – a time for one tale or another to while away the rest of the evening before the door was closed and the latch bolted for the rest of the night.

Rambling Jack now leaned forward towards his friends across the firelight. He spat into the midst of the sizzling flames. This was the signal and they each waited breathlessly. Then without further ado he began the evening's tale.

ONE

The Black and Tan War Days
and how a young girl called Soolah Patricia
saw heaven above and beyond the stars.

We Had Our Anti-heroes

And now it's my own turn to spin the tales and I have to tell you this: there were among us not only genuine heroes worthy of posterity, but also a list of what you'd call anti-heroes here, whose names we should hastily scrub from the book of celebrations. Formost of these was that old slyboots-of-a-fox (Renardine). Unlike the weasel, he'd prefer to snap a henhouse of chickens into a million feathers rather than select a single hen for his supper – at least until By-Jiggery and Taedspaddy put an end to his life.

The ferret too was a rascal that needed a good deal of our attention. The older children (as soon as their parents were abroad at the woodpile cutting logs) might be seen opening the hasp of the little creature's cage and letting him loose round the room. Spotting his chance for freedom, the wily little devil (if you tried to trap him with the yardbrush) would sink his teeth into your fingers till the blood came squirting out onto the floor and the bone broke with a painful crack. There was but one answer: to stick a burning sod-of-turf up into his arse and send him howling out the half-door – never to be seen again. The hawk or the fox would soon make bits of him.

We also had our unfriendly badger on the upper side of The Bull-Paddock. And though we knew that he (like the ferret) would hold onto your leg till he heard the bone crack, Brandy (Old Sam's dog) failed to heed this valuable lesson the day he came to tangle with that old curmudgeon below at the rotten tree near John's Gate. The poor dog was seen walking with a distinctive limp for the rest of his days – his right paw having been snapped asunder by Badger. If we had been there to witness this fierce battle we would never have allowed such a fate to happen to him; for our years of training had taught us that if one of our dogs was ever faced with the enclosed teeth of any badger we'd only to reach for a stout stick and crack it in two across our knee – the sound of the stick's crack being enough to distract the rascal and make him dislodge his teeth from any poor dogs' leg – thinking (the old fool) that the crack of the stick had broken it.

There were times, however, when our dogs were so badly damaged in conflicts with a family of badgers that we were forced to forget our hedging, fishing and shooting and go off and look for the sett where these particular villains had set up home. Each of us took hold of a crowbar and a shovel from behind the half-door. As soon as we arrived (man and boy alike) we dug out the entire family – Badger's wife as well as himself and all their innocent children. Then we gave each of them the quick death with our shovels, belting them into their pig-like snouts and chastising them once and for all.

The Little Children

Apart from the day-to-day torment of these animal anti-heroes, we had one or two other worries to think about – worries about our children and their childish fears. For, like little children of former days, they were full of a rich and (at times) unwanted imagination. As a result of this they spent many a sleepless night preoccupied with a list of hallucinations as long as your arm – dreams of slimy, scaly serpents crawling round the yard and sitting on the windowsills and looking in at them in their beds, causing them to screw up their eyes and close the flaps of their ears with their fingers – as though that was the way to send these cruel fiends away.

And if such vivid illuminations weren't enough to put them in a trance and make them wet themselves, then the older boys (the minute their parents were abroad milking the morning cows) took a mischievous joy in frightening them with further gruesome tales – tales (it might be) of some imaginary horseman from The Bog Wood, straddling his horse and cracking his whip and ready with a blast of his bluderbuss to pounce out and snatch a few helpless babes up onto his saddle and sail away with them to his grotto in the far reaches of hell.

The Card-Players

Finally there were those sly old cardplayers introducing our children to a host of popular villains before the little dears had a chance to kneel by the fire and say their night prayers and run off to bed – tales about Old Malignity from out near Growl River and the roar of his trumpet which these innocent-eyed card-players swore they heard whilst making their way home after the card-games were finished – tales about Warts The Journeyman and he stamping his nightly boots round Shy Dennis's haunted shack and he ready to carry off unsuspecting children down under the surface of The Green Pool where Sammy-the-twin had gotten himself sadly drowned. And of course there were the tales about The Wreck of The Hesperus from The Valley of The Black Cattle and he seen rising up out of the misty half-hidden stiles that edged our fields and he swinging his fierce hammer at the sight of any child going down to the well for a bucket of water: 'I'm looking for a stray child to nail to a tree like mee friend, Jesus.' To the merriment of our cardplayers this was the final straw for the saintly Dowager – causing her to drop her hand-of-cards onto the floor and utter the severest of curses: 'If that filthy basthard were shitting gold abroad in the haggart, ye'd not see me within an inch of him – he'd fitter go and wipe his bogied nose.' And (to the laughter of Blue-eyed Jack) she'd hit the table a savage belt of her fist. Enough said.

The Children's Heroine

On a cheerful day like today, however, we can forget about these miserable old articles – human or otherwise; for there were many happier occasions in the lives of our children (especially the girls) – days when they were seen putting on a man's Sunday shirt and pretending they were saying their saintly Mass like the recent missioner (Canon Eloquence) – days when they were seen strutting ladylike in the haggart and aping the manners of Lady Demurely from The Big House with their cups of pretend tea and their prized mud-cakes and they wearing jewelled necklaces and bangols of fresh daisies. That's when you'd see our women scratching their heads and hear their voices ringing out across the yard: 'Will ye look at the gymp of our dreamy children – and they putting on their airs and graces as though they were Soolah Patricia herself?' For (unlike our list of anti-heroes) this young girl had long become a name revered amongst us and stored forever in our hearts – ever since the time when that dreadful war with The Tans was being waged hot and heavy round the countryside – the day that her devotion showed itself in an act of unimaginable bravado – an act driven by an insatiable love for her dear father, news of which didn't leak out among us till after her untimely death a few years later over in the next county – Kilkenny.

It Was Springtime

It was back in the year 1920 when springtime was already murmuring with new life and the skies were blue after all the snows. The morning was hot and drowsy and the sun had evaporated the dew from the ditches and fields. The low-flying blackbirds and sparrows were beginning to shake the music from their throats and mesmerise everyone with their chirruping chorus. As if that wasn't enough – out from Dowager's henhouse came the hens, ducks and geese to add their own bit of an orchestra. Exploding from the pighouse came the big fat sow – to put in a snort or two in a most complimentary fashion. They were all waiting to be fed from the galavanize tray behind Dowager's ass-and-car. As for the men – they were thinking of ploughing and rolling the soil for their future crops of spuds, cabbages, turnips and oats. And the old ladies in nearby Lisnagorna were saying their long list of prayers and twiddling with their rosary-beads for the sake of the war that was being fiercely fought against The Tan Soldiers from across the water and asking God that these foreign gentlemen might go back across the sea and rot themselves inside the four walls of hell since they were the ruin of our poor lives all over Tipperary.

It Seemed A Glorious Morning

It seemed a glorious spring morning just like every other morning – with the rest of the week lying ahead of us and the message of Father Honesty's sermon fixed firmly in our heads to keep our souls safely on the heavenward journey. But events can change quickly and take the daylight away from the course of our lives in one great big flash. This was to prove true for Red Scissors's uncle (Old Tim), who until now had lived without a care in the world above on The Little Bald Plain near Sheeps' Cross. There he was – sitting in his yard, sibilantly whistling to himself the way he always did and teetering back and forth on his rockingchair. Onto his hair shone the sun that had just peeped round the corner of the pighouse. He stooped down to pick up another hazel-wand from his basket. With his penknife he went on whittling into shape the rest of his hazel-spikes for the rabbit-snares that would help him catch a few fat rabbits for the weekend pot. All in all he was as contented as the hens and geese around his feet as he listened to the silver-coloured stream into whose depths the ducks were solemnly gazing, pecking at their feathers and grooming themselves.

Just A Stonethrow Away

Whilst Old Tim was contemplating the beauties of his yard, matters couldn't be more different a stonethrow away where the peace and quiet of Dowager's yard had been suddenly broken by the arrival of a heavy tender-van and its unwelcome occupants – The Tan Soldiers. She began cursing these rowdy fellows under her breath ('foreign jailbait basthards – that's what ye are!') when she recognised them leaping down from their van. They had left their barracks an hour or two earlier and had already been warming their gills with a few mouthfuls of Curl'n'Stripes' best whiskey (the rawgut potheen). With their bellies welloiled and their heads aflame they were bent on doing as much damage as they could across the hillslopes of our once-happy Rookery Rally.

They knew that Dowager's Welcoming Room was a safe haven for the odd renegade lad, who might be on the run from them. And so – in spite of the protests of herself and her sound man (Handsome Johnnie – he was still alive in those days) – you'd find a band of these wretched fellows every blessed night of the week bursting into The Welcoming Room, their faces long-practised in bullying sneers and they pushing husband and wife out of the way up against the press-cupboard with their rifle-butts and furiously rousing the sleeping children out of their beds. These brave little soldier-boys would then start ripping and shredding their way through the mattresses with their fixed bayonets and tossing the few bits of furniture all over the floor – as though a rebel or two might be hiding in a shoebox or underneath the piss-pots or the settlebeds. Then, stamping out the half-door, you'd see them racing off down the yard to frighten the screaming hens as they began searching the henhouse and the pighouse for munitions and grenades.

Any Diehards Here?

This particular morning (the morning of Old Tim and his rocking chair and his whittles) was to prove no exception: 'Any *diehards* here?' they roared as they paraded themselves and their bayonets through The Big Cave room behind the hob. The starry-eyed children cringed behind the apron-folds of Dowager, not knowing if they were going to be shot dead in a minute or two. Once more they saw The Tans stabbing at the mattresses where Dowager and Handsome Johnnie slept. And when this unseemly inspection was finally finished Dowager saw them casting a lustful eye (oh, the heathens) at her little daughters, not one of them old enough to be an object of plunder and lust for their hot Tan bodies. Then the blackguards roared out of the yard and headed uphill towards The Valley of The Black Cattle.

Perilous Joe

Of course they had a motive for their morning's playfulness for they had been sent out by their colonel-in-chief (Perilous Joe) to look out for Old Tim's son (Tippity) and put a bullet in his chest the minute they cast an eye on him. Tippity was a lad of no more than twenty years of age and sleeping rough with six of his comrades abroad in the hidden valleys at the back of Bog Boundless. He had made himself the thorn-of-all-thorns in The Tans' flesh of late and they couldn't get a wink of sleep from thinking about him and what they were going to do to young puppydogs as brazen as him. Needless to say – these townies from England hadn't a hope in hell of finding their way into the more remote places in the hills and tracking him down. Indeed we ourselves would have had to find a well-trained horse (or better still a young mule that could twist and turn its way in and out of the heather) to find a route through the treacherous bogholes out near The Eagles' Nest. We couldn't help smiling to ourselves. There wasn't a man jack of us who would raise his little finger to help these foreign scholars in their search for our young hero.

In Recent Weeks

In recent weeks Tippity had been working his way down from the hills and had made himself an outpost in the pineforests on the far side of Lisnagorna. From his chosen vantage point he spent a day or two watching The Tans driving proudly by in their tender-vans and they sitting back-to-back with their rifles pointed towards the ditch in case a little leprechaun might leap out and attack them. To see them parading the countryside as though they owned the damned place filled him with anger and he couldn't wait to send them off to a quick death.

The next Tuesday he and his band crept down to a hiding-place near the bridge across River Laughter. As soon as The Tans and their tender-vans arrived on the scene Tippity and his friends loosened the pins on their hand-grenades and lobbed several of them from inside the ditch, killing at least half-a-dozen Tans and leaving their limbs all round the road for us all to see. That's when Perilous Joe showed that he wasn't a pure fool altogether and he ordered The Tans to put wire cages round their vans so that the grenades would simply bounce off of the roof and explode harmlessly on the roadway behind them. So much for Tippity's villainy (he thought) and The Tans laughed to themselves.

Our young rebel was quick to give them the laugh back: 'I'll take the smile from the faces of these bleddy eejits and teach them a few Irish manners,' said he to his friends; for he knew only too well how to chastise their hides. He spent the next few nights fixing long steel hooks onto his grenades – a handy invention that was soon admired by the rest of us. The next time he and his comrades began pelting their grenades out from over the ditch, the hooks fixed themselves firmly onto the nets that protected the vans, preventing the grenades from rolling off onto the road. Once more the grenades split the air in two, blowing The Tans back to the hell they'd come from (thought Tippity with a smile).

Rage! Rage! Rage!

Rage! Rage! Rage! What was Rage up until now? We didn't know the meaning of the word till a few days after Tippity's outrage with his grenade-hooks. That was when foreign anger turned into nothing less than a tornado. From that moment on not one of us was going to be left a moment's peace. With a ferocity that we'd never seen before (and at any hour of the day or night) The Tans rattled their boots round the depths of every yard and haggart – our henhouses, pighouses and cowsheds. They charged into every room in every cabin, destroying what bits of furniture we had. We saw the insatiable hatred in their eyes – their frustration at not being able to get hold of Tippity and put a stop to his wickedness. Each morning we were left picking up the broken bits of our tables and chairs. We spent hours on end trying to glue them back together.

It didn't need a mind-reader to see that, even without the orders of Perilous Joe, The Tans were not going to leave us alone till they'd given Tippity an unmerciful death and left him to rot abroad in Bog Boundless for the two eagles to dine on. However, after days and nights searching for him they realised (it was that devil-of-a-colonel's own crafty idea) that they'd have to resort to a much more sinister tactic than wasting every minute of the day tracing Tippity's footsteps across those cursed bogholes.

Like Angry Bulls

And so – on this fine spring morning we heard them clattering the wheels of their van up towards Sheeps' Cross and testing the strength of their lungs as though they were a crowd of angry bulls fresh in from Spain. They went out passed the crossroads and then we lost sight of them as they went on towards The Little Bald Plain. They reached the farmhouse where they saw Old Tim innocently whittling a smart finish to the last of his basket of snare-sticks.

That's when Pandemonium and her dark fairies (The Black Fates) came swooping in across Tim's stream. The Tans jumped down from the van and made a rush across the yard. Cursing the old man to perdition they pounced on him and his frailty, ignoring his feeble protests. A deadly fear filled his sweaty face and in a single second he saw that his world was about to get turned upside-down. They dragged him out of his chair. They tied him to his ass-and-car. They stretched out his legs in the hope that he'd squeal for mercy like one of our cornered pigs. They stripped the shirt from off of his back. Then they flogged him mercilessly on the boards of his cart. Resting him on the cobbles they unbuttoned his trousers and grimly threatened his privacies with their penknives: 'Look at this fine specimen of manhood,' they sniggered to the mountainy children who had come out searching for nettles to dress their mother's bacon and who were peeping out at them from behind the frightened haystack. But the children's throats were frozen in shock and they daren't utter any of the savage curses taught to them by their mothers during their nightly prayers.

Fair play to him! Old Tim had the same lion-hearted courage as his renegade son. Not a word of betrayal as to Tippity's whereabouts was about to come from his proud lips on this the cruellest of all days – no matter what price he'd have to pay with his tortured body. What sort of father would he be if he told them which soldiers' barracks his son was responsible for burning to the ground a few weeks back? What sort of father would he be if he told them the careful plans that Tippity and his comrades had in store for the destruction of the rest of those hated foreign barracks round the hills of north Tipperary?

Everything Now Moved With Speed

Everything now moved with lightning speed. Remembering the recent deaths of their friends and the fierce rebuke of their colonel still ringing in their ears, The Tans steered their tender-van up as far as the half-door. They kicked the chair and Old Tim's basket of snare-whittles out of the way. They dragged him to the back of the van. They lashed his two ankles unceremoniously to the van's tailboard.

Raining down curses and scorn on the fields of Tipperary and on all Old Tim's forebears and with the old man strapped down and unable to defend himself, they steered the van out over the cobbled yard and thundered across the stream. They headed for the unmade road where they picked up a good bit of speed. At every turn of the wheels they hopped Old Tim's skull off of the stony road. Had the wicked whelps no fathers of their own back in their own country?

A Dark And Dismal Light

A dark and dismal light fell on the children as they ran out from the haggart and stood on the flagstones to see what was happening. Their morning was about to be turned into a cruel fantasy as soon as they heard the roar of the van coming down passed the bend at Sheep's Cross. Their bewildered eyes saw the savage carnage and the blood dripping from Old Tim's crushed head ('mee head! mee head! sweet suffering Jaysus, mee feckin' head!'), splashing behind him off of the dusty road and spattering the bark of the trees and bellflowers. The shouts of the soldiers re-echoed round the children's ears, scattering the dosing ducks and fading away passed Old Sam's grove where children for years had played happily in secret. They could scarcely breathe as they saw the poor man's head bouncing like a hurling-ball off of the road with the van continuing to pick up speed, dragging Old Tim and his glazed eyes behind them as though he were a fallen tree-trunk. The very stones must have risen up at the sight of what was happening. Would the children ever forget the old man's dying screams? – and all because The Tans couldn't get their filthy hands on Tippity.

A pig in his gore, having been led onto the horse-and-cart for an uninvited meeting with his slaughterers, had been a sight all our children knew only too well, having seen from time to time the sad pig's blood spattered on the straw of the cart as they waited to get their eager hands on the pig's bladder and play with it. But to witness the murder of an old man who had never put a single bad word passed his lips – that was something else. And after witnessing such unbelievable savagery for the first time in their young lives they were filled not only with Sorrow and Pain but with a fierce Anger against these soldiers who had come from abroad – an anger that would never again leave their hearts or minds.

'We'd give the world to set just one of our two eyes on your fighting Tippity,' laughed The Tans as the van disappeared down the hill and they pointed back at the young rebel's dying father. But with the last feeble breath in his body he told them to go and feck themselves and put their filthy noses up the miserable arses of the mothers who had given them birth. And then his soul fled away over the hills and on towards The Beyond – to a far better place where his troubles would be gone from him forever.

They Wheeled The Van Around

The Tans turned the van round. Back up by Moll-the-Man's stile they wheeled Old Tim. They entered his yard. They unharnessed his ankles. Their anger was now sated and they laid his battered corpse down in the yard almost reverently. The hens, ducks and geese (weren't they the wise ones?) scurried away into the silent haggart. Lancy (Old Tim's sheepdog) was utterly bewildered and sat beside his dead master, frantically howling and licking the bloodstains from his face. The sow hurried away and hid herself in the depths of the haggart dock-leaves. Her turn might well be next.

The Tans and their hollow boots went out passed the pighouse gap. They found the horse's tackling and harness inside the stable-door. They made a hurried fire from the twigs and kindling round the woodpile. They brought out dead ferns from the side of the cowshed. The wind rose up around them and soon a blazing fire was heard rustling. It filled the yard with thickening smoke before turning red and blue on itself. They threw the tackling (the collar, then the winkers and haymes) into the fire. For a minute or two they halted and thought about putting a torch to the thatch of the sturdy old cabin. However, even their black hearts protested at doing the likes of that. Instead they crossed the haggart singletree where they set fire to the two cocks of hay. Its blaze would be seen below in the valley round Abbey Cross and in the top windows of Lord Demurely's elegant mansion – if not as far as the distant streets away in The Roaring Town.

This was the day that Rookery Rally was shaken to its boots. The burnt hay would be a salutary lesson to any other young revolutionaries and would knock any vague plans out of their patriotic little heads. Of course the news of Old Tim's murder was now going to spread far and wide – up through The Hills-of-the-Past – out through Bog Boundless – as far as The Mighty Mountain and Diddledy-doo – maybe even into the ears of God Himself above in his heaven.

The Day Was Drawing On

The day was drawing on. The Tans seemed to regret their recent action and to lose their wild excitement. They began to sober up a bit. After all, they were only youths from inside English jails or else out-of-work labourers, looking for excitement and anxious to earn a shilling or two in support of their wives and young ladyfriends back home. There was now a mood of hollow foreboding in their midst and they sat on their haunches round the dead body of the old man. Their hats rambled sluggishly over their faces as though to hide their guilt. Each soldier seemed locked inside in his own lonely isolation in that strange luminosity of the day's twilight. They made Old Tim's trousers decent and they covered him with a blanket from the house. After a while they took out their fags and began to put smoke to the heavens in an effort to calm their nerves. Their brows were furrowed and they began to talk thoughtfully to one another and to recollect the morning's events. They could get no peace of mind. Their voices took on a hushed and subdued tone. 'What have we done? What on earth have we done?' Somehow it seemed as if they knew that a black serpent from hell had winged its way in among them and taken hold of their souls. The sun was now beginning to go down, tinting the clouds with bright hues so that the late afternoon seemed to glow around the dead man with a hazy lemony light. The ditches too seemed to take on a delicate blue from the sky and the mountains. Already the evening flies were gathering in around the body and were waiting to lay their eggs.

At last, blessing themselves to ward off the wrath of God, the soldiers hauled themselves into their van. The van clattered out of the farmyard, the wheels chattering heavily on the gravel and The Tans resting their chins reluctantly on their guns as they passed down The Creamery Road towards River Laughter's wooden bridge before vanishing towards their barracks. The children stood dumbfounded on the flagstones and watched them pass by for the second time that day.

That Evening

That evening (the saddest day in our history) everyone kept themselves indoors by the fireside and we shuddered to think what would happen when we called upon Handsome Johnnie to go up into the hills with the devil's own news and tell Tippity how The Tans had murdered his saintly father – and the way the horses' tackling and his year's hay had been burnt to the ground. We knew it would destroy the heart in him – that his rage would be unprintable – that if he got the chance he'd see Perilous Joe in hell. Meanwhile he couldn't show his face or come down from the hills to lay siege to the soldiers' barracks: they'd be expecting him to do that very thing and their eager guns would be welloiled for slaughtering him. It all seemed a hopeless case. There was nothing for us to do but wait and wait. And so we waited. The men sighed and the women prayed.

That Same Afternoon

The afternoon of Old Tim's destruction saw Soolah Particia (she was fifteen years old at the time and the youngest of the old man's children still left at home) returning to her father's cabin. She had spent the morning going over to the church in Copperstone Hollow. She was a girl of apple-bloom with bright cornflower eyes – *the smiley one* we used to call her for she usually had a smile on her as big as a watermelon. Her mother (Noonie) was still in The Roaring Town Hospital after a neck operation to remove a goitre and had ordered her daughter to go across the fields and bring back the two gallons of holywater from the church barrels so as to give her father's farm the blessings of a new life. Blessings for the cows and the sheep, for the ass and the horses too, who would soon be going out to plough the seventh field. Blessings that would bring good fortune to her family (little did the poor girl know what had just happened) and good fortune to her own small patch of cabbage-shoots which one day soon would sprout up sturdily in the hot sun.

By the time it got to late afternoon there was a stream of other girls walking home alongside her, it being women's work to lumber along with two heavy gallons of holywater apiece. The younger children stopped their play on the flagstones as soon as they saw Soolah Patricia coming up The Creamery Road and heading in the direction of the mountain path that would lead her to her own half-door. Not one of them had the heart to confront her and tell her the miserable news about the horrendous scene they'd witnessed with their own eyes a few hours earlier.

Not A Care In The World – Till Then

Soolah Patricia had left the schoolhouse three years before this blasted war had ever entered our lives. She had just been given The Sacrament of Confirmation, the sacrament that would make her a strong and perfect soldier to stand up for Jesus (so she'd been told). In those days – like her brother (Tippity) – she had not yet been fatigued with the cares of this life and was as free in spirit as any young starling. You'd see her parading round The Creamery Road in her bare feet and humming one tune after another as if to compete with the birds. Indeed her dearest wish was to mimic those little birds and it was said she could hum birds clean out of their nests (though none of us had ever seen her do it). Such was her love for all living creatures, however, that her grandmother (Thimble) had given her the present of a pet goat on the day of her Confirmation and she spent hours humming her music into the goat's ear.

Up till now her life and that of Tippity remained innocent and uncomplicated. Indeed we said that the gift of Pure Romance was surely in the two of them – to see them roaming the roads while everybody else spent their hours chasing after the ass, felling timber, sawing up logs, mending fences and cutting back rushes to make a cowshed bedding for the cattle. Of course their playfulness couldn't go on the livelong day and there were times when you'd see Soolah Patricia at her wool and her spindle-wheel as she sat on a chair in the yard and followed her mother's instructions and scrutinous eye.

That might be the time for Tippity to go off gallivanting instead of looking after his father's sheep over on The Heights. Yes, Tippity – passing the entire afternoon riding his father's stallion through the forests and out by The Valley of The Pig where his ancestors must have rambled when hunting the wild boar and the swift-footed deer. He was a perfect little nuisance – to see him emerging from the trees and winding his way in and out amongst us turf-gatherers and we toiling away in the melting heat and the sweat hopping off of our noses as we planked up our weary bit of turf – to see him with his father's unlicensed gun cocked on his shoulder and he dressed in his best brown suit as though he were Lord Demurely and he splitting his sides with laughter at the rest of us poor scholars. And as though that wasn't enough to torment us with – the next day the little demon would appear at noon while the lizards were all asleep – to see him seated on the highest bank of turf beyond in Currywhibble and he mischievously tapping his toe and again vexing everybody – his blasted flute-playing pervading the air as he coaxed those haunting airs out of his grandfather's flute (Old Silver Lips) – tunes as sweet as a grape that he'd heard (some said) from the wilderness fairies of late afternoon and the mesmerising leprechauns that dwelled inside Fort Dangerous. I tell you this – not a single billygoat dared crop a blade of grass on those dreamy afternoons – so enchanted were they by Tippity's fluteplaying. It was then that the rest of us invented a new sets of angry curses ('will ye look at the little whoor') and poured them down on his head – to see us slaving away and the little devil not rolling up his sleeves to give us a helping hand with the turf. And yet we all admitted that the violets would grow thorns before our ears ever heard such wondrous music as Tippity's again.

Dancing Round The Crossroads

To add to this little saga there were days when Soolah Patricia was seen dancing round the crossroads to her brother's jiggy tunes – then throwing herself up behind him on the back of the stallion and meandering the length of Bog Boundless – the two of them with the sun's glow on their foreheads – she with a book in her hands and he with the flute to his lips and everyone groaning all over again at the way they were spinning their young lives away. Ah, wasn't Envy and Jealousy a fine thing? And oh – to be so young and to be living their youthful days to the full. Pure Romance indeed!

But Now We Were Shaking Our Heads

With the death of their father the rest of us were now left shaking our heads, realising that those had been the last happy days of a young boy and his soft-hearted sister – halcyon days of two fairylike creatures – days of picturebook poetry inside in their childish souls as they clung on to the final vestiges of youth – days of quaintness never to be seen again. Sadly they were about to realise the true meaning of this cruel war against The Tans – about to learn from one source or another that their beloved father was stretched out dead in a pool of his blood in the yard.

As Soon As Soolah Patricia Came Home

As soon as Soolah Patricia came across the flagstones she felt an unusual quietness in the air – a ghostly creepiness all round the yard. She heard no bird singing. She saw no leaf moving. And then her nostrils were filled with the pungent stench of the burnt haystack in the haggart. Behind the pighouse she saw the horse's tackling – just a few small bits of sad burnt leather – and she gave a roar out of her that almost caused the dead spirits to rise up from their tombs below in Abbey Acres Graveyard.

She ran to the half-door and entered The Welcoming Room. The neighbours in their cloud of sadness had beaten her to it. They had straightened out whatever few sticks of furniture they could so as to make the place decent enough. What did she see? She saw a crowd of tearful elderly folk and they sitting on their chairs like ancient statues all along the whitewashed walls. They held their rosary-beads reverently in their fists. They had pulled the settlebed out into the middle of the floor. On it they had laid the body of poor Old Tim beneath the white sheets. They gazed down wretchedly at his cruelly battered head. In spite of this he was now as peaceful as a sleeping child, with a crucifix in his clasped fingers. If his young daughter were to die this very minute nothing could be worse and Soolah Patricia felt that in the next second her heart would burst asunder and come out in bits through her ears. She threw herself across the settlebed before falling like a shattered dish in a faint on the ground.

Morning Sunlight

When morning sunlight broke through the clouds Bishop High-Hat and half-a-dozen clergymen came on the scene. They led our sad procession in along the gravelly pathway that arched towards the cemetery gates in Abbey Acres Graveyard. The funeral bells peeled mournfully. There wasn't a soul that didn't attend and draw comfort from fervently reciting their rosaries for the soul of the old man – that is if you forget about Tippity, who didn't dare set foot amongst us, and his saintly mother, who was still strapped to her bed inside in the hospital. None of us had the heart to ride into town and give her the sad news about Old Tim. Even Soolah Patricia had recovered her spirits seemingly enough to get herself in as far as the graveside. But to our surprise and astonishment the poor girl was as silent as the grave and never shed a single tear – not one.

Old Tim's mournful coffin was held aloft. Then it was paraded three or four times round the graveyard before being rested gently on top of the boards at the graveside. The obsequies for his soul were solemnly recited and not a dry eye was seen amongst any of us (except for Soolah Patricia). The Bishop was a wise man and he took this opportunity to remind us of Jesus on his cross. He said how Our Blessed Saviour forgave his murderers. He said that if it was good enough for Jesus to do so fine a thing it was surely goods enough for the likes of us and that we were to try and follow in his footsteps. He then roused our spirits and said that we were to forget despair and that a new day was dawning and that Hope and Freedom were fast on their way to our downtrodden land. Meanwhile above in the clouds Old Tim was looking down at us and smiling to himself at the grand and holy show being staged in his honour among his friends in Rookery Rally. A few minutes later we took our silent boots and our rosary-beads home with us. In spite of the bishop and his fine words we felt that a fierce cauldron of hatred was about to bubble up all over Rookery Rally and not one of us knew where it would lead or where it would end up.

Two Days Later

Two days later (the Sunday following the murder of Old Tim) we had finally finished blessing the animals and crops. It was three o'clock in the afternoon. Tippity and his band of renegades found themselves sitting silently in ambush among the pinetrees above Lisnagorna. Before long the evening would be creeping in on them and the sky would lose its rich blueness and the clouds their cottony whiteness. Indeed the sun was already beginning to slope its way down the sky beyond Corcoran's Well when up along the hillslopes that led to Saddleback Village (what Tippity was half-expecting) came a troup of twenty-six tired-looking mules. They were carrying a load of bren-guns and several sacks of munitions bound for the barracks in Tipperary Town. The news of his father's savage death had by now reached his ears and had left him as sad-looking as an old woman struggling home with a bad ass on a wet night. His eyes kept filling up with blindingly bitter tears and he felt his heart would break into a thousand pieces and fly away through the pinetrees. His comrades ached at the sight of their young leader's suffering and each of them made sure to keep a good distance away from him – away from the blazing anger, which they saw written all over his devastated face.

Strange – Very Strange

There are moments in a man's life which none of us can explain. As Tippity looked down the hillslope he saw spread out in front of him the first of the mules and foreign soldiers. Behind them he saw the long procession of guns. And now before the judgement of God stood this young rebel and in his hands his eager gun and it more than ready to send these devils down to hell for the unspeakable things they had done to his father.

The first rosy-cheeked soldier drew ever closer, rounding the bend of the bluff we called Tomb Ridge. This lad was an easy target for Tippity's gun. He could see him clearly. He wasn't a day older than himself. Suddenly the invisible hand of an angel seemed to swoop down out of the clouds, holding back his trigger-finger and overpowering him. Itchy sweat began to roll down his back. His legs went limp and his belly turned as sick as a cat. Inexplicably his desire for the blood of this young soldier left him and he no longer had any desire to kill him. Instead, his eyes went on passed the young man and took in the rest of the line of soldiers. And again he was filled with a similar spasm of unearthly panic and indecision. What on earth was happening to him? Was he to let this procession of guns march passed him and roll their way on into Tipperary Town? What would his comrades think of him – that he had finally lost his mind?

In a flash he understood what was taking place: that it wasn't the hand of an angel holding him back: it was the presence of his father's compassionate ghost. It was unbelievable. He could almost reach out his hands and feel the shadow of the old man standing next to him – breathing into the very heart of him and stifling the hatred clean out of him. He could hear his father whispering in his ear. 'Hold back! Hold back, my son! For the sweet love of Jesus-on-his-cross, hold back. Do not destroy the threads of a man's life as young as yourself. What's the use? What's the use?' And as a result the bloodthirsty gunshot that was meant for the first young soldier was never fired.

Nevertheless – a few seconds later Tippity's gun began to make the sweetest of music. And just as when his welloiled rifle had once laid low the springing hare and the fluffy-tailed rabbits out in The Valley of The Black Cattle so now he continued to fire dementedly – not at the young

Tan soldiers – they too had mothers who loved each of them (whispered his father) – but at the bemused bellies of the mules. To the astonishment of his comrades the blood-spattered bodies of all twenty-six mules soon lay strewn around the road. And as he blazed away Tippity thought to himself: 'Ye soldierboys haven't a clue how lucky ye are to have escaped with yeer lives this blessed day – fools that ye were to have pawned yeer souls to the Devil in the killing of mee father.'

He Looked At The Carnage

Tippity looked at the carnage in front of him. It was strange – what he had done – or rather what he had failed to do. Good son that he'd always been to his father, he had obeyed Old Tim's ghostly whispers and had saved his bullets for the mules. And what of the procession of The Tans? They looked the very same as a herd of cattle stung by a hive of angry wasps. They retreated out over the hillside and vanished into the Lisnagorna forest, losing themselves in the early evening mists, not knowing (nor would they have believed it) that their lives had been saved by Old Tim's murdered ghost. For, as soon as he had soared his way up through the clouds to meet his Maker he found himself being sent back (just this once) as a messenger – to warn Tippity that his soul would sweat in hell's everlasting flames were he to lay any of the young soldiers low when there was another way of gaining hold of the procession of arms – namely the killing of the mules.

He and his band of rebels ran down the slope. They proceeded to take command of The Saddleback Road and gathered in the bren-guns. With the rest of the munitions the guns were soon heading in the opposite direction – into the hands of the young Irish lads above in The Rebels' Den on the Mureeny mountainside.

The Following Sunday

The following Sunday, after she'd heard of her brother's capture of the guns near Saddleback Village, was the day that Soolah Patricia (not to be outdone) left her childhood behind her and made an immediate leap into womanhood. Though still aching from the pain in her heart, these last few days had given her a little bit of time to think clearly not only about the tragic death of her father but to compose plans in her head as to what she might do. Tearfully she knelt in the yard and made a solemn vow to her sacred father's memory: 'Perilous Joe may have the brains of a Pope (she thought) but it won't do him one bit of good. As sure as I'm mee father's daughter, that foreign devil will find himself rotting in hell before tomorrow's sun goes down. This I vow.'

She climbed on top of the galavanize sheeting over the pighouse where Old Tim had hidden his double-barrel gun. She knew he used to keep a box of red cartridges in the press cupboard when he was alive. With the gun and cartridges in her hands she was like a hen about to lay an egg. That night she couldn't sleep a wink. When all was quiet she stole out the back window. She headed out across the fields. She hid the gun in the depths of the groves surrounding The Big House in Abbey Acres before returning home.

Next Day

Next day she put on her dead father's boots in honour of him. She stepped out the door and took her leave of the yard. Shivering with fear and excitement she ran through the woodbines and the tangled undergrowth. When she came to the alley of tall trees in the woodlands bordering the estates of Lord Demurely she lay down low and she waited. By now she was aware of the colonel's impending arrival at Lord Demurely's mansion – aware too that it was this blackguard that had ordered the torture and death of her father. She knew where to position herself – where to wait for the approach of the great soldier – him and his fine motorcar. She'd give him a welcome none of us would ever forget. But in spite of herself she started shivering and she asked God to forgive the evil that was in her heart.

It'd Soon Be Dark

The afternoon light was beginning to fade into the dewy evening. It would soon be dark – darker still for Perilous Joe (she thought). In a minute or two he'd be at the gates of The Lodge. She could picture it: he'd get out of his car: he'd ring the bell at the gates, requesting admission. He would never get the chance to enter the gates or steer his car down the sandy drive winding through the avenue of elm-trees – would never get the chance to circle the lake in front of Lord Demurely's mansion. Her double-barrel gun would make sure of that. She made the sign-of-the-cross on her forehead and continued to finger her mother's rosary-beads. In her pockets were the two waxy red apples that her father had given her the previous week for the journey to the church to fetch the gallons of holywater. To steady her nerves she chewed them till there was nothing left, not even the core.

She Cocked An Ear

Her soul was now empty. Her heart was aflame. She continued to picture The Tans and the disfigured body of her murdered father and the bloodstains on his jaw. She could see the howling face of Lancy, the sheepdog. She could see Noonie, her heartbroken mother, who had at last been told the sad news – could see her throwing off the blankets inside in The Roaring Town's Hospital and bewailing her lovely man. And now she longed more than anything to see the blood of the colonel reeking the ground at her feet.

She cocked an ear. The crows above looked on silently and helplessly. She listened desperately for the great man's arrival – just like the lion listens for the nearness of the gazelle. She heard the purr of the car's engine. It finally came to a halt at the gates in front of The Lodge. The fear and anger pounding in her childish chest was almost too much to bear. She realised she'd have to act quickly.

The tragic scene was set. She knew where her duty was: she'd do whatever she had to do – one death for another death – and would exact a terrible vengeance for the sake of her beloved father. Not a wink would she sleep (for Decency's sake) till it was over and done with. Meanwhile the six black swans, indifferent to the outcome of warfare, glided carelessly down Lord Demurely's wrinkly lake as the colonel finally drove his motorcar up to the gateway.

He Stepped Down From The Car

Perilous Joe stepped down from the car. Ever the gentleman, he went round and opened the passenger door for his attractive young ladyfriend, a certain Miss Raffles from faraway Bow. From her hiding-place in the undergrowth Soolah Patricia looked at this stylish young girl – a girl no more than a year older than herself. She was as slim as a yardbrush and had a dash of red paint on her lips and white powder on her jaws.

A Time For Tea

It was now dusky evening, a sort of quiet and unworldly time – a time for tea – a time for fine conversation and gentle drollery inside in the mansion of Lord Demurely but not out here on the roadway. She quickly bestirred herself, her big boots shaking the earth from under her feet.

In the blink of an eye the rifle and the strange and confused madness that was Soolah Patricia leapt forth in front of the colonel – as though she was about to greet him. But a blizzard of scalding hate shone out of her eyes as she pointed the gun at him: 'Let you run,' she gestured, motioning the rifle towards the hapless young English girl. 'Run for yeer life!' But such fear had gripped the misfortunate Miss Raffles that her limbs had become as soft as sugar. She stood there speechless and transfixed by the side of the car, clinging to the handsome colonel's jacket. Perilous Joe tried to protect her, his arms round her shoulders.

Soolah Patricia thrust the heel of her rifle into his chest. He bravely spat his contemptuous spit back into her face: 'So – ye'd give the world to set just one of yeer two eyes on Tippity, would ye?' said she, wiping the spit from her jaw. In a girl as young as this such rage was unheard of. Perilous Joe could see it – stretching across the void from her heaving shoulders and from the fierce gun in her fist.

'I'm his flesh-and-blood sister,' cried Old Tim's daughter and her eyes were full of tears. 'And now – for the first and last time in yeer miserable life ye can set not *one* of yeer handsome eyes but *two* of them on me and mee rifle. Ye'll set yeer sights on the light of the blessed sun for the last time this day – the sun which my poor dead father can never see again.'

Too Late! Too Late!

Too late! Too late! Perilous Joe knew it was his final hour. He hadn't time to think or utter a word or say even a prayer. And the ghost of Soolah Patricia's father, who had come down so readily and had stayed the hands of Tippity from shooting the young Tan soldiers, now remained hidden in the clouds – unable to intercede a second time or hold back the hand and the gun of his bloodthirsty daughter.

Even then – the colonel's young girlfriend didn't make a run for the trees but remained frozen to the side of Perilous Joe. Like the rabbit before the weasel her body shivered in terror: there was no escape from the eye of the fierce gun in the crazed Irish girl's hand: she was on her way to meet her Maker. For a split second Time was as still as the tombstones in Abbey Acres Graveyard.

As Yellow As A Quince

The apple-redness of Soolah Patricia's cheeks turned as yellow as a quince. She discharged her bullets – CRACK! CRACK! – into the man responsible for her father's murder – into himself and his young mistress. The rifle-crack shook the forest pheasants from their reverie in John-Joe's potato-field nearby. And no bird sang or called to another bird. The simple Irish girl had blown out both their temples, her rifle singing their slumping bodies into feathery-heeled eternity in front of the gravel drive of Lord Demurely. The smoky stench of blood and burning cordite filled the air and bits of the colonel's skull clung to the wheels of his car. And now the sun above the clouds refused to shine. The chilly sky turned into gloomy greyness. The winds brought down angry raindrops round Soolah Patricia and Old Tim wept bitterly from beyond the skies.

She Wiped Her Blood-stained Fingers

Ceremoniously Soolah Patricia wiped her bloody fingers across her cheeks. She had dreamed about this moment the minute she'd imagined her father's skull hopping off of The Creamery Road, killing him. Before the gatekeeper could raise the alarm she threw the gun into the lake, leaving just the echo of her self-satisfied whisperings behind her as she darted away and mingled her shadow into the mauve tints of the evening, her skirts crackling through the undergrowth. It wouldn't be long (she thought) before the news got round that Perilous Joe was dead. And what would Tippity do then? For it'd be on him that all would turn their suspicious eyes.

She continued on her homeward journey. She came to the river where she halted – our own childhood River Laughter. She wiped the blood from her cheeks and her clothing. She removed her dress and in her knickers stepped into the heart of the shivering river. She could feel it welcoming her – could feel it wrapping itself round her and cleansing her of her sin.

Then she ran on home and melted in over the yard stream. She entered her cabin in a pure daze. She knelt beside the settlebed where her poor father had recently been laid, bowing her head in serene contemplation as though he were still by her side. And only then did she shed tears by the bucketload.

By this time the yard outside was chattering with the last of the blackbird songsters scurrying to their roost as the daylight got sucked from the sky. The solemn trees waved their branches in the early-night breeze. Dark clouds began to spiral slowly across the moon. All nature seemed to peer down into Old Tim's yard. Soolah Patricia got up off her knees and looked out the half-door. In spite of her tears she was in a state of blissful Ecstasy. Blindingly she hopped out over the singletree and into the haggart. She headed for the ploughed fields. With the last of the holywater she blessed the sacred soil and she gave a final fist of it to the ass leaning in over the gate.

Days And Months Passed By

Days and months passed by. The Tans continued to hunt for Tippity. In the dead of a moonless night they surprised a few of his comrades abroad in

Bog Boundless – a small triumph. They didn't bother to torture or half-drown them in the bogholes. They shot them there and then without a jot of remorse or sympathy and left them on the lonely heather for the two wild eagles to come down from The Mighty Mountain and chew on. Ned-of-The-Hill was second-in-command to Tippity. Without a thought for his own survival he had knelt down to perform the last rites and say The Act of Contrition into the ear of his dying comrade (Bill-the-Bear's son). The Tans gave him the kicking of his young life – the kicking of his death. To treat his head like a football – was there nothing on earth to be held sacred? Was there no shred of dignity to be allowed – even at this most solemn moment?

Tippity Made A Decision

Seeing how the exploits of his little band were going so poorly, Tippity became desperate. He saw that Tipperary and his country at large were soon to be bitterly divided as Irishmen started arguing and fighting amongst themselves. It'd take the miserable Irish to do that (he thought to himself). There was something else: in spite of his mother's novenas and her rosaries for his safety and for his success in the struggle for our land's freedom, The Dark Avengers from John Bull's Secret Service were drawing nearer to him every blessed day: their breath was almost on him: he could feel it: he could almost smell it. More than anyone else it was he that had caused so much havoc to The Tans. And what was it all for? They had killed his best friends instead of killing himself. Even his innocent father had been sacrificed for the sake of himself. It was too much to bear.

A Cold And Frosty Morning

One cold frosty morning, with childlike tears dripping down the side of his nose, he bade farewell to the land and the sky he had so well loved since the days of his boyhood. His mother gave him her last few shillings from the jug on the press-cupboard. She wrapped his flute in brown paper for him. The place would be lonely without the breath of him near her – heartbreakingly so.

Two days later and sleeping rough, the coastline of Cork found him and his heavy heart walking down towards the pier. He hailed a ship that would lead him to the streets of Baltimore in The Land of The Silver Dollar.

The Sowing Of The Crops

That same year and the year thereafter came and went. The shooting and the killing continued with the seasons. Though she was too young for the farm's backbreaking work, Soolah Patricia (herself and her dark secret) went on with doing the work of a man for her mother – the ploughing and the rolling and the harrowing. Once more she and her gallons of holywater went forth across the fields and sprinkled each of the crops (the spuds, cabbages and mangols) with God's blessing. And later in the year she tended to the harvesting of the hay, the timber, turf, spuds and turnips. It was a miracle the way a girl like her could work. We all said it. You'd never know that anything unusual had happened in the life of herself and her gun and that she was still driving the anger away from her body with her work.

A Change Came Over Her

But then – a change came over her. Everyone could see it. It was a gradual mental collapse – nothing short of an impending madness for what she had done with the gun. It seemed to her as though The Avenging Furies, having chased her brother out of the country, were now coming back to catch a hold of her – that God in his heaven was looking deep into her soul – that he was shaking his angry fist at her.

Her mind grew more and more disturbed. Sometimes she was seen walking up the hillslope and out towards the bog with her shopping-bag when she should have been going down the hill to get her messages from the shop. For the first time in early springtime she took to wearing her grandmother's red calico blouse and her green-spotted skirts. You'd see her and her confused boots leaping stag-like across the ditches bordering her mother's farm – see her stepping across the hill and up towards The Valley of The Pig. Hanging down from her hair was a flowing stream of red and yellow ribbons, purchased from Fanny Farthingale's Dress-Shop in The Roaring Town. Along with her she took a sweet-gallon. She vigorously flailed into it like a drum, beating away the fierce anger that was still in her body for the loss of her father – beating away her loneliness after the exile of her beloved brother. At some hallowed spot where a rebel had once fallen she'd kneel in prayer and say her Act of Contrition for the repose of his soul. Before quenching the fire at night she'd gaze on the locket she wore: it had a few spare locks of her father's grey hair inside in it. She would stroke the two fatal cartridges, which she had pumped into the skull of the colonel and his young mistress. And then she'd go off rambling and roaming the lanes and listening to the bawls of the nightly foxes and the squeals of the little weasels.

Three Years Later

Three years went by. Her mother (Noonie) caught a fever and was laid low for a fortnight. And then she lost her battle and she died and was quietly buried in Abbey Acres Graveyard. Soolah Patricia was on her own now – herself and the ghosts of her mother and father and the sound of their eerie boots walking round The Welcoming Room in the middle of the night.

In the evening she'd place the happy-death candles all round the vacant settlebed and more candles among the rose-coloured wedding glasses on the windowsill. The flames were everywhere, like the setting for a churchday wedding. At night she slept in the bed of her parents as though she was trying to get nearer to them. At three in the morning and not able to sleep, she'd gaze out the window at the stars and the speckled moon, higher than ever in the heavens (it seemed) and at the white clouds in a great halo round it. The moon seemed to be looking back at her. It was as though the wild girl was hoping to see the ghost of Old Tim up there with a smile on his face as of old. She would shudder and finger the heavy blankets and pray fervently for his soul and that of Nonie before quenching out the last candle on the side of the teachest. And as soon as she was warm enough she'd start dreaming of the green fields of Kilkenny – the spot that her father had often talked about – the place where he was born and had spent his happy childhood days.

Her Anger Was Gone

The years rolled on and at last her anger for her dead father and her lost brother was gone from her. Besides – she was sick of farming the land. She sold the farm to Jack-the-Herd for the princely sum of four hundred pounds. 'To hell with it – let him and his likes turn over the furrows from now on. After all, it's good brown clay.'

In the dead of night she put pen to paper and wrote Jack a hurried note: 'Welcome, Jack, to yeer new farm – and to the devil with all foreign settlers. May ye have better luck than me with it – for it brought me nothing but the creeping horrors.'

One Dark Morning

It was half-past-three one dark and windy morning. With hushed breath she scraped out the cake of ashes from the ash-hole. In a religious sort of ritual she threw them to the four winds. She was full of mixed feelings as she gazed round her home-place for the very last time. To her surprise, however, a new peace swept down from the hills, enveloping her and she began to drink it into her chest.

Watched only by the ghosts of her ancestors she packed her few belongings and quietly closed the cabin door. With Bonny the ass and her ass-and-car she crossed the chequered yard-stream and rumbled out over the flagstones, the black cardboard trees swaying whisperingly to and fro on either side of her.

She set sail for Old Tim's birthplace, leaving for good the hills of Rookery Rally and the rest of us far behind her. Not once did she think of regret or take a look back. The sky above her was sprinkled with soft sparkling stars and the breezes' music was calling to her to keep on going – herself and the ass – as though in a fairytale. She could smell the scent of the warm pinetrees of Lisnagorna. She could see the worn yellow lights of The Roaring Town winking sadly and dismally in the black valley below her. Once out from the lane she gave a stern whip to Bonny's back and he stretched out his bony legs. The two of them plunged down the silent road and on towards the town.

Next Morning

Next morning when we awoke we realised that her little cabin was empty and that she had disappeared from view: here yesterday and gone today – like her father and mother and brother before her. We were left scratching our heads over what was to remain a mystery till a future day when she came to die.

In County Kilkenny

In County Kilkenny the dew-whitened mists of a new day's dawning came slowly in and beheld Soolah Patricia driving Bonny and the ass-and-car up the main street of a town with a stone bridge across it – a crazed vision from out of nowhere. She pulled up at the doors of the Convent of Mercy. The legs of the distressed old Bonny were worn to a shred after such a long journey. Soolah Patricia knocked on the convent door's brass knocker and stumbled in, her mind sizzling with confusion after such a long journey.

'I have come home.

I have brought ye mee money.

I have brought ye mee soul,' she said to the nuns.

And she held out her fists of money towards them. Who was she? Where had she come from? None of this mattered. With words of mercy the holy women led her across the threshold – now that their eager hands were clasped onto the money. They took her down to the kitchen and fed her with a hearty good breakfast. It was to prove her last good meal once they had the four hundred pounds stowed away in The Reverend Mother's locked desk. From that day forwards – never to be seen again – Soolah Patricia joined forces with other young girls (*the fallen angels*) in the depths of the nunnery's Laundry Room.

In the years to come she'd work at the washing, ironing and darning of the nuns' garments. Those other sad girls never raised a smile. They had even more sorrowful hearts than she had and many a sad tale they could have told her. their Confessors and The Guards (their fathers and mothers too) had sentenced them to slave for the rest of their miserable lives in the stifling heat of the laundry – the result of the stain of illegitimacy that they'd brought on their family and having had their babies snatched away from them after loving their young men too passionately and at the wrong and unspecified time in the eyes of Mother Church. Jesus must have wept above. Enough said.

Battered Crows

There were a few old battered crows in the rookery around this wretched place in Kilkenny – a place most unlike our own Rookery Rally with our childish laughter and our songs and the dance-steps that Soolah Patricia had been well-used to – especially on those days when she and Tippity used to ride the stallion round the bog and the rest of us listening to his haunting flute-tunes during our breaks from farming the turf.

As The Years Rolled On

And as the years rolled on there wasn't a day that Soolah Patricia didn't look out over the trees. There were no tears of sorrow or anger left in her anymore. Now and then she'd heave a sigh (when no-one else was looking), wanting to fly away up there into the sky – wanting to be as free as those raucous crows – wanting to be far away from her world of self-inflicted Penance. Unknown to anyone she would spent her days trying to look even further beyond the transparency of the sky. It was her everlasting secret – she and her eyes still full of gladness, full of moisture – wanting to be far from the earth and looking into the ghostly faces of old Tim and Noonie, those she had loved so well.

And in spite of the crazed madness in her – her mind and heart (may God forgive her) was forever dizzy with the terrible beauty of what she'd once done – herself and her dreams – the big gun that took away the pain of her father's ghost and his bloodied head – the big gun and the murder of the haughty Perilous Joe in revenge for poor Old Tim and the way he and she and Tippity had been forced to finish up their days.

TWO

How Big Red became the greatest of all our heroes.

Big Red

In Rookery Rally men were on the small size: five feet and eight inches would be good. The women were even smaller, usually a shade over five feet tall. Men and women alike, they were all neat and tidy in their bodily frame but their hands were invariably as big as shovels from snatching at bales of hay, twisting wire fencing and a thousand other tasks requiring the use of firm hands and wrists.

However, Big Red (the son of Saddle-the-Pony and the grandson of Swally-Tails, who had once been a shop-boy inside in The Roaring Town) was a rare one among us. For a start – at birth he was as pink as a foxglove and already had a fine shock of crisp ginger hair unlike the rest of us who all had hair the colour of tar.

As the years of his childhood progressed this hair of his grew increasingly red and there were little curls of ginger hair at his shirt-cuffs and his eyelashes were a deep sandy colour like a ripe field of wheat. Nor did his distinction among us end there: for by the time he was about to leave school he had turned into a most healthy specimen – as strong as an ox and square-shouldered with a perfect jawline on him. What's more – he weighed in at twelve-and-a-half stone.

By this time the thickness of his hair was a Samson-like forest that lay down over his forehead and ears and covered half his back as well, like the ruffled crest of a shiny cockerel. We marvelled to look at it for it bobbed all over the place as though he were surrounded by a strong wind.

And another thing – the young lad was six-and-a-half feet high in his bare feet, a foot-and-a-half higher than his treacherous little schoolmistrees (Big Screech). As the saying goes – if the anger ever took hold of him he could put her in his pocket. Indeed Big Red was the only man in Rookery Rally who could more than equal the Clare men in height for they were all a shade over six feet: this we knew for a solid fact.

Our One And Only Real Giant

The children in Rookery Rally were tired of reading about giants in their school storybooks. Big Red, however, was the one and only real giant that they had seen in the flesh. Inside in Dang-the-skin-of-it's schoolhouse our young scholars told the other children, who had come down to the school from the opposite direction (namely from The Gap of The Two Goats and The Valley of The Hollows) that they were the proud owners of a real-life giant – that he was very big and was very red from all the blood he had scattered. They even grew a little poetic (the scamps) – telling these other children how Big Red's powerful muscles rippled like wet cowdung and (quoting their parents) that he was as strong as the two ends of a sheaf.

Of course like any of our traditional storytellers they soon began to exaggerate their tales, boasting that their giant was as tall as the gable-end of the schoolhouse – that he was at least eight feet in height – that he always started out the day by eating a whole sackful of spuds and half-a-gallon of milk to wash the spuds down. With open mouths the other simpletons were only too ready to believe everything that they heard. This led our children into more and more fantastical explanations about their giant – that he was forty-stone weight with legs to match – that he could carry a sixteen-stone sack of cowshit across the yard on his back – that he could pull a cart down as far as the bridge with a ton-and-a-half of hay on it – that he could eat a whole sheep if he wanted to – that his stride was four times their own and that he could reach their schoolhouse (a distance of three miles) in less time than it took to skin a cat. Oh, the little liars! Would they ever have the nerve to enter Father Sensibly's confession-box again?

Armed with the possession of this giant ('we have him in the palm of our hands,' they smirked) our little mischief-makers found themselves ready to do battle with the rest of the children, were they so much as to blink an eye in their direction. They'd only to snap their fingers and whisper the name of Big Red and see the other children scuttling for the ditch and trying to squirm themselves into sheer invisibility in hiding-places behind the briars. But of such a fine parental upbringing were children in Rookery Rally that it never entered their cracked little heads that they could have done much more – could have demanded half the school's snacks of bread-and-blackcurrant jam or a barrow-load of Matty's stolen turnips if they'd only been barefaced enough to use the threat of Big Red putting his fist down on top of the other childrens' heads. Ah, what a fine chance that was – one that was greatly missed by our young simpletons.

Less Than A Decade Later

Less than a decade later you'd hear Rambling Jack and Red Scissors discussing Big Red's towering gifts as they sat on the singletree outside the flagstones. Dowager as usual had her ears cocked back like an ass, listening to the two of them as she went on cleaning out the two creamery tanks nearby: 'Isn't his mother (Halfpenny-Gret) a tiny drop-of-a-thing?' she said.

'True for you,' said Red Scissors. 'And didn't his grandmother go by the name of The Little Midget and die very young – in her early thirties – so frail of nature was she, poor thing?'

'So where the hell did Halfpenny-Gret get Big Red from? Was it out of one of Lady Demurely's Christmas crackers?' laughed Blue-eyed Jack, coming out the half-door.

Halfpenny-Gret

Halfpenny-Gret was as thin as a hayrake all her life. Small and frail though she was, she had her own gifts but in other ways was the same as the rest of us. Every one of our women baked their own soda-bread. So did Halfpenny-Gret. And here we may mention that our men baked nothing whatsoever – unless their mother was dead or there was no sister left to take over the house and only one or two brothers still at home to support one another. In which case one of the men had to forgo tending to the cattle and horses and had to steep himself in a new set of skills – the boiling of the spuds and the baking of the soda-bread and the washing and darning of the clothes. The two brothers then became like a husband-and-wife team – one working on the land and one at home in the house.

Anyway – in addition to the making of her soda-bread Halfpenny-Gret did a great deal more – she baked cakes in all their variety: cakes for the priests: cakes for the nuns: cakes for anyone mean enough to demand a cake – be it Easter or Christmas, at a christening or one of the feast-days for Our Blessed Lady. Jams and marmalades she would make in like measure – dripping them from her muslin bags into the largest pan you ever did see. Of course she wasn't a pure fool altogether and she didn't produce all these little gifts for nothing: a weekday Mass in return was always acceptable from her priest and a few shilling from the rest of us ensured that she was usually not short of a shilling or two in the pockets of her bib. Her *bits of snow* she called it.

The Four Girls

She gave birth to four girls – all small and handy-sized like herself. Her husband (Saddle-the-Pony) was so called because he had half-a-dozen mules to pick from when he went off hunting in the hills with his dog and gun. And another thing – Halfpenny-Gret was forever calling him *dear this* and *dear that* and even *darling old Saddle*. This was more than strange among us. For as far back as we could remember nobody had ever heard a word of affection coming out of anybody's mouth: such slobbery talk was a foreign sort of politeness used only by Lord and Lady Demurely, the big softies. Enough said.

Saddle-the-Pony

Saddle-the-Pony had been a smart man and knew what he was doing when he married into Halfpenny-Gret's farm. 'It's just a few acres thrown up against the side of a hill,' said the Weeping Mollys sneeringly. Small though the farm was, seemingly it was able to inspire jealousy in the hearts of some of us. 'Isn't Saddle-the-Pony the lucky devil to have landed himself with Halfpenny-Gret and those few old raggy acres?' said the smirky drinkers down in Curl 'n' Stripes' drinking-shop. And the rest of us shook our heads sadly, not knowing why we weren't so fortunate as to get ourselves something for nothing.

And now there came another chance for the old gossips. Whereas women were generally giving birth to between ten and fifteen children apiece, Halfpenny-Gret had just the four girls and that giant son of hers (Big Red). To have deliverd a mere five children was seen as almost a disgrace. Even Saddle-the-Pony was saddened by the lack of more children to his good name. He knew that behind his back some of us were laughing up our sleeves at him and criticising him for the weak manliness in his lower body and his poor performance in the marriage-bed. There was no worse insult amongst us than to criticise a man for his inability to father at least a dozen children by the time his wife reached forty: farmers all over Rookery Rally knew the price of a fine bull in the engendering stakes.

The Apple Of Her Eye

Being the one and only son, Big Red was the absolute apple of Halfpenny-Gret's eye. And though she had to chastise him once or twice in his earlier years for profaning the name of Jesus and had to tie him to the well-bucket and leave him unfed for half the morning, this was not her usual rule-of-thumb for bringing up this lovely son of hers. Indeed it was no wonder that Big Red grew to his giant's height for this good woman was in the habit of feeding him five huge meals a day to the consternation of her four daughters. You'd think she was fattening a pig for the market (they cried). Big Red would eat a dozen cuts of bread-and-jam before Saddle-the-Pony had time to finish saying the Grace-before-meals or even placed his spud on his upturned fork. 'I'm thinking that our young son has worms in his belly,' said he one bright summer's morning. So himself and his wife saddled up the ass-and-car and, together with their startled son, headed into Copperstone Hollow to see Doctor Glasses, a young doctor fresh in among us from Cork at the time.

The doctor twirled his moustache. He took one look at Big Red. He shone his pencil-torch into both the boy's eyes. This was a very strange thing for him to be doing. He invited the perplexed parents to take the torch and see for themselves the unusual shine glistening out of their son's eyes. Damn the bit – couldn't the pair of them see that no greyhound or newborn calf had such a shine as this in their eyeballs: 'Thank the good God-in-heaven for the prize of this fine child,' said Doctor Glasses. 'He's in savage health. I'm pleased to tell ye there'll be no examination-fee this day or any other day: ye'll never have to give me a shilling out of yeer arse-pocket.'

With that he laughed out loud and then Halfpenny-Gret and Saddle-the-Pony laughed also. They almost bowed before him as they scuttled out the hall door. With what strength he had left in his old body Saddle-the-Pony threw Big Red up in the air and let a roar out of him: 'Thanks-be-to-Jesus for the gift of our lovely son.'

The Schoolhouse

But joy can be followed at times by a counter-balancing sorrow. This came upon Big Red when, armed with his new satchel, a few apples and a slice of brac-and-butter, he trudged his boots into the schoolhouse of Dang-the-skin-of-it and met up with that miserable old sourpuss, the master's sister (Big Screech).

Though his body was growing like a beanstalk, over the next few years the child found himself left behind at the bottom of the schoolroom alongside the six year old children, who had just started school. Even before the class had time to bless themselves the poor lad was seen cringing in the far corner, unable to get to grips with the new learning and his brain was all a-fumble. It was as though he had the flaps of his ears closed and never opened. He had a permanent frown stamped across his forehead.

Of course he wasn't born to be a donkey or a gatepost. But no matter how hard he tried he couldn't read and he couldn't spell the simplest of words like the rest of the children – even though Halfpenny-Gret could spell rocks of words from here to the bridge across River Laughter (twas said). Nor could he write his name or copy out the daily news from the blackboard. What a terrible thing it was to be straddled with the label of *numbskull* on one day and *leatherhead* the very next. And as a result Big Screech was often seen putting the hay-sugan ring around his neck and standing him on a chair in the corner as though he were some stray rabbit at the edge of a cornfield. To the other children this was a very strange thing to behold, for within a year or two Big Red had grown higher not only than the sour little mistress but a good deal higher than the master, Dang-the-skin-of-it.

A Victim

Each day he became the victim of Big Screech and her squints of black temper. At the best of times she was not a delicate lady to be seen wasting seconds on morning pleasantries. You'd hear the tremor of her silk dress vibrating as she puffed and panted all round the room as though she was an old bellows. And then she'd go to work on Big Red – whaling into him with her savage point-to-the-map stick or her brother's sally-switch.

At other times the children saw him frog-marched out the door, armed with the black-handled knife and the commands of Big Screech ringing in his ears: 'Go down to the river and cut yeerself a sally-switch – a good one that's bendable and a yard long.'

Dutifully Big Red brought back his new sally-switch. Big Screech would then inspect it, giving it a bit of thought as though it were some sort of rare beast. She'd make a few dainty roundabout turns like a practising sword-fighter, swishing it threateningly round over her head in front of the children's awestruck faces. After that little escapade she proceeded to teach Big Red his lessons by belting him a good few times across his extended hands or (if the humour was on her) battering him on the seat of his britches.

How sad it was to see Big Red – his dangling arms and his sombre-looking eyes – and not a single twitch out of him as he took the belts she proudly bestowed on him. He collected more and more of these belts each day and the marks on his legs were often as big as a duck-egg.

However – to see Big Screech laying into Big Red and bringing him down to size helped make the day go smoothly enough – the rest of the children having escaped the lash. The sound of her switch on the seat of his britches was to become a regular bit of entertainment – a distraction from the otherwise dreary monotony of the school lessons. You might well ask yourself – what cruel witnesses these children had become as they looked on in amusement at Big Red's pain. When they thought of it in later years they must have bowed their heads in shame.

The Unfair Distribution Of Heights

When she heard of these chastisements, Dowager had the answer: it wasn't Big Red's dull wits that were causing Big Screech to beat him so often and mercilessly: it was his sheer size. At the dinner table she'd point her fork at the table: 'And who – tell me this – can blame our lively little schoolmistress for being so ungracious with her switch? God (it can be seen by us all) has given this woman a mere four-and-a-half feet of height in her stocking-vamps: to Big Red he has given more than six feet of height – and the lad's not yet fully grown.'

Such an unfair distribution of heights was Dowager's excuse for Big Screech's acts of cruelty to the child: 'Wouldn't such unfairness in the distribution of heights anger The Devil himself and cause him to leap round the classroom and go whaling the arse off of Big Red each morning the very minute the school-prayers were said?' Blue-eyed Jack had to nod his head in agreement with his mother' subtle explanation and we were all left wholeheartedly bemoaning the loss of Dang-the-skin-of-it's kindly wife (Gracious Mary), who had always taught the children (unlike Big Screech) in the politest of ways before meeting with an untimely death two years previously.

The Two Times Table

When it came to answering the Two-Times-Table (a simple task, since every child recited it on their way to school) Big Red got into a sweaty panic all over again. His dry mouth was so uninspired that he was unable to give even the simplest of answers. As a consequence of this supposed outrage the little vixen could be seen dancing a new set of jigsteps round the huge child.

In a fit of desperation she took upon herself a new means of teaching him wisdom – one that she had learnt back in her own schooldays in the far west country, namely a few tidy cuffs to the poor boy's jaw. So unusual a tactic was this that some children thought it might do the trick and bring the Two-Times-Table spilling out from Big Red's mouth. Their wise old parents could have told them that it'd knock far more sense out of his brain than into it.

This New Method

From her own schooldays in Copperstone Hollow even Dowager had heard of other masters and mistresses attempting to provide the feeblest of scholars with extra brains by giving their jaws a few similar cuffs with an upturned fist. Indeed Big Screech was becoming such an expert in the use of this method of teaching that she added a few little trimmings to it that were all her own. For when Big Red went cowering back to his bench she made a rush after him like a hissing snake and administered a well-aimed kick to the seat of his britches to help him on his way, driving him headlong in amongst the startled six year-olds on the bench.

Poor Big Red – he lacked even the smallest morsel of tact. For, had he howled with the pain of his chastisements, he might have seen the intervention of Dang-the-skin-of-it from the room next door. But, like any boxer in a scrap, he wouldn't give in to this mad old woman and uttered not one cry of pain. This was enough to incense Big Screech all the more and to such an extent that she'd stop only to get herself a drink of water from the bucket before getting at him with her sally-switch all over again. By this time the entire classroom had begun to marvel at the antics of her. If she – a small frail woman of four-and-a-half feet in height – could belt this huge giant-of-a-child like this, what wonderful powers she must have been given by her Heavenly Maker the time she was born.

Enough Was Enough

However – enough was enough. It was clear that the schoolmistress had her own well-defined brand of intelligence. Big Red was to find his own intelligence too. He'd grown sick-and-tired of the daily beatings from this little beauty-of-a-schoolmistress. And then – one fine morning after the children had drunk their mugs of cocoa the lively one made a singular mistake. It was a fatal one. She insulted Big Red's saintly mother for having been such a born fool as to have given birth to a numbskull like this giant-of-a-child and bring shame on herself – on her family and race – on the entire schoolhouse – on the whole of Tipperary – on the world. It was a long list.

Through the mists in his feeble brain Big Red could see that such an insult was unbearable. The recent kickings from Big Screech's boots – these he'd been able to withstand. When she'd prodded him up against the wall and kicked at him till the soles of her boots were exhausted – this too he had been able to withdstand. Even her cuffs to his jaw and the sally-switch on his arse – whatever the shape and size of the delivery – these too he could bear. But the sudden insult to his mother – this was to put an end to one brief chapter in his life and start another one.

For the first time in the annals of Rookery Rally the children saw Big Red blinking back his tears and wiping them away from his jaw. To see him crying was a new one on the class. More was to follow when they witnessed his particular new brand of intelligence. It was as though a big drum had started to beat a tattoo inside in his head – as though the blood had suddenly started to boil inside in his veins. He walked blindly to the front of the room and snapped the sally-switch of Big Screech into several pieces. Then he caught hold of her and wrapped his big fist around her dainty wrist – almost gently like any gentleman would do. Then, dropping his own wrist, he took hold of her by the seat of her black dress and held onto the heel of her left boot so there'd be not an inch of room left for her to start kicking out at him. After that (remember how later in life he was able to carry a sixteen-stone sack of cowshit on his back across the yard) he gingerly lifted the coy little mistress into the air as though she was a bird's feather. He took her out into the yard where the children heard the squeals of her ('Put me down, put me down – you little fecker!') – so loud you'd think a pig was being killed. And with the strength of our previous blacksmith (Old Titan, Hammer-the-Smith's father) Big Red then let a roar out of him that could surely be heard above in heaven. After that he pelted her fair and square ('ye ould bitch' said he) into the middle of the dungheap at the end of the schoolhouse where you could see nothing more than her neck and chin sticking out from the dung. Would she ever rise up again? The children wondered.

Poor Dang-the-skin-of-it – he who had always bemoaned the use of a teacher's fists on a scholar's jaw – was next to receive the wrath of Big Red. For this was to be a day when he'd not be parting the flaps of his coat and warming his gable-end at the fire. There was a six-foot-high locker where he kept his greatcoat and his silver-handled walking-cane for the lunchtime parade with Big Screech up and down the avenue.

Big Red rushed in the door and before the master could blink an eye he lifted him up (as though he were a cabbage) and placed him on top of the locker. There sat Dang-the-skin-of-it – himself and his stiff white collar, looking down on his pupils like an ass staring out over a wall. He'd never be able to get down. The children would never forget the sight – the mistress in the middle of the dungheap – the master sitting cosily on top of his locker. It was a dream of pure delight – a dream that they'd never forget for the rest of their lives. There and then they beatified – almost canonised – Big Red for the job he'd done that day.

The Children Began To Fear A Great Fear

Suddenly it dawned on them what had happened and they began to feel a great fear. After all, they had all been sniggering and jeering at the stupidity of Big Red not being able to read his letters, not being able to write his name, not being able to do the sums. Would Big Red turn on them next? Might he take it into his head to take them out one-at-a-time and kill them all? For the remainder of the morning, however, they went unscathed (thank God).

That was only for a short while. The afternoon came around before anyone knew it and a fine drizzle began to fall mournfully on the schoolhouse. The children knew their weather. This was a bad sign – almost prophetic. For that was when they found themselves lucky to escape with their lives, realising that Big Red hadn't quite finished the job he'd started. He made a smart excursion over to the nearby Yellowstone Quarry and hurried back with a wheelbarrow full of rocks. By that time the children had somehow managed to drag Dang-the-skin-of-it down from his embarrassing perch on top of the locker. They had wiped the dung fairly well from Big Screech's black dress. Both of them had recovered a little of their previous composure.

All of a sudden the entire building shook. The Sacred Heart picture on the wall was sent dancing about from a new and unreal vibration as Big Red took an armful of rocks and sent them *(boom! boom! boom!)* hopping off of the slate roof. 'Mee mother! Ye basthards from hell! Oh, mee mother! How could ye do such a thing as to call her a fool?' Listening to the hammering of the rocks and almost dead with fright, the master and his dainty-toed mistress were getting the worst of it all over again. At hometime would they ever be able to get to their pony 'n' trap under the trees and get back alive to their house above the school?

The two of them cowered behind their desks – 'Get down, lads! For the love of Jesus-on-his-cross, get down!' – and bade everyone hide themselves behind the benches. There they all crouched like a flock of sheep beneath a ditch when the rain comes on. It was now as though a jeep-load of Tan soldiers were entering the fray – open warfare between Big Red and his captives inside in the schoolhouse. Decades later many of the children could still conjure up the immense scenario that was to remain stamped on their minds forever. If only one of them was a painter – to capture the animal rage of Big Red and the sight of the terrified master and mistress cowering behind their desks – what a museum piece it would have been. And to conclude this lively little sketch, Big Red broke every goddamn window in the two schoolrooms and with a battered look and his nose flattened from all his tears, he cast the school aside forever and wiped his eyes and jaws and went home and put his arms around his tearful mother. What need had he of meeting the bishop in May and getting his Confirmation-ticket (said he): 'Give me a reins, mother (he sobbed) till I go back and hang Big Screech from the rafters for calling you nothing but an old fool.'

Later that evening the weary lad took a pile of furze bushes from the cowshed. He laid them at Big Screech's front door in a vain attempt to set fire to her. However, in a week or two matters began to cool down a good bit and the rest of Rookery Rally wore a great heap of smiles on hearing of Big Red's rage and his own particular method of punishing anyone who transgressed against his saintly mother. Before the summer was over he was the hero-of-the-hour and (as with the children) he was almost canonised in everybody's eyes, for we all hated the dastardly punishments often handed out inside school walls up and down the country.

In The Years That Followed

In the years that followed, Big Red's one and only talent (apart from his brute strength) was his double-quick athleticism. He was so lithe and agile for a huge man and he loved our national game of hurling, his hurleystick ever ready to see the colour of another hurler's blood. At the age of sixteen he was a fully-grown man and had been shaving with Saddle-the-Pony's cut-throat razor since the age of fifteen. Our priest (it was Father Sensibly at the time) had long forgiven him for his angry outburst and his use of The Yellowstone Quarry wheelbarrow-load of stones against the innocent windows of our schoolhouse. In his heart-of-hearts the holy man was tickled to death by this former child's chastisement of the teachers – not so much Dang-the-skin-of-it as the master's sister (Big Screech), that cumbersome old vixen. Oh how he wished (didn't we all?) that Gracious Mary were still alive and teaching the children alongside her husband!

The Hurling

Big Red was now living on feeds of good beef and plates of mutton-stew together with raw steak and milk. His mother couldn't take her eyes off of him. Indeed his size was the talk of the entire parish. Father Sensibly summoned him to get ready to hurl at the hurling training-session with the men's team (The Abbey Cross Rovers). You can imagine the big lad's excitement as he cleaned his boots with his mother's black polish the night before training and went about inspecting his togs and oiling his hurleystick with the drop of paraffin.

It wasn't long before this robust young hurler came to our attention from these training evenings. So needlefine and honest was his puck-on-the-ball that he could whip it further along the ground or hit it higher in the air than anybody else. On top of this he was so strong that he was able to greet his opponent by pushing him with his hurley-stick. ('stick into yer man – shove into him!') half the length of the hurling-field. He was like a tick on a cow's udder and could take the skin off of the other lad's back if needs be.

In those longtailed evenings the game would start simple enough. You couldn't mistake Big Red and the thick sandy curls wobbling on top of his head. What he lacked in grace he made up for in guile. And another thing – he always had that feigned look of simple innocence in his childish eyes. But as soon as the opening whistle was blown and the priest threw the ball in among the hurlers, he found the blood dancing round in his veins. Straightaway he gave his opponent the finest cut across the arse with the boss of his hurleystick – to set the other lad's spirits boiling with rage. He followed this up with a sharp dig into the startled lad's ribcage with the heel of his hurleystick – leaving him in a state of unnatural dread and his unfortunate ribs sore enough to prevent him coughing for the rest of the week.

This bullying and jostling style of Big Red soon had Father Sensibly grinning from ear to ear. It was plain to see that from the first resounding clash of the hurleysticks Big Red was able to prevent even the trickstiest hurler from getting a score off of him. If a barn door (said Father Sensibly) could stop a runaway horse Big Red was the man that'd put a stop to an opponent's mazy dancesteps. And as a result the lad became an obvious choice for playing at the centre of the defence in the season's first official engagement.

The Peak Of His Stardom

The peak of Big Red's stardom came at the very first match. It was scheduled to take place against The Mountainy Streamers. Their ground was pitched in a shelterless spot – just a few old spindly trees and a river (The Crown River) that was full of salmon at various times of the year. It'd be a festival occasion – to raise funds for the new pump recently rigged up by the water-diviner (Divinity Blue) and his hazel-wand and to pay for the new hurling-jerseys of the Mountainy Streamers.

The evening before the match was a wretchedly stormy event.

Everybody stayed indoors by the side of their fire. Big Red stayed indoors too – inside in Lepping Guinness's drinking-shop where he lowered half-a-dozen *twins* – a well-known combination of whiskey followed by a glass of The Black Doctor. Though just sixteen he was well able to handle all the drinks that came his way.

The stormy night was proving a bit of a problem for next day's match. Of late there had been many wet days such as this and the grass of the hurling-field was long and uncut since the sheep had not been let in the gate to keep it well shorn. The ground would be as heavy as lead and we knew that next day would be a bad day for striking the slither-ball – that there'd be parts of the field turned into oozy mud before the match was well into the second half. Worse still – the ball itself would be a ton weight – thanks to the heaviness of the water sinking into it as the match wore on: it'd be nothing but a wet rag.

Next Day

Next day proved to be sunny and cool. The red leaves would soon be falling – you could feel it in the air. Big Red felt on top of the world as he cycled towards the gound, his hurling-boots proudly tied to his hurleystick, which was belted onto the bike's crossbar. The blue-coloured mountains lay mistily ahead of him – mile after mile – and the bogland's solitude lay over to his left, all covered in windy heather and ferns and scarce a bush to be seen.

He finally arrived and (God bless the mark) everything was grand. The afternoon came on. The match was about to get going. A merry crowd (mainly men from an earlier generation) had gathered and were seated on either ditch alongside the pitch. They had come on bikes or on horseback or driving their ass-and-cars and traps – tying everything to the ditch once they were close to the hurling-pitch.

The ground was now well-packed. The tricolour flag could be seen rippling in the breezy weather. Everyone was pulling on their fags and waiting excitedly to see the new white hurleysticks and admire the whizz-whizz of our ground-striking hurlers, who could cut the ball like a pat of butter. There were a fair number of women there as well and they were as excited as hell at the sight of the towering hurlers. This was a fine chance to gaze on the manly bodies of their heroes – as sleek as a snake's skin and not a pick on them – a chance for one or two of the older ones (the hussies) to dream of that unknown article hidden inside the hurling-togs ('ah, the fine dacent byze that ye are!')

Out They Stepped

Out stepped the two teams, their coloured jerseys embroidering the green of the grass in a dazzling patchwork. They were like a flock of geese as they flapped their hurleysticks left and right in a cutting action against the grass. Among our own men we could see Tasty (the son of Leatherbelly, who had once owned the only red ass we'd ever known). There was Bohir (the son of Dowager's older brother, Gooseberry-the-Pony). In the opposing team there were men like Mull-it-over and Swerve (his cousin) – men rich in heart and the best-natured fellows in all Tipperary (what you'd expect from the mountainy men). Their play was renowned: it was as feathery and light as the gas in a pig's bladder.

The Ball Was Thrown In

As soon as the hurlers had drained the juice from their oranges, the priest threw the slither-ball in between their legs. He made an immediate beeline for the side of the pitch as though he was expecting a shower of hailstones to follow behind him. The teams commenced battle and the hurleysticks cleaved the air. Straightaway the field turned as lively as a hive of bees. The hurlers' faces were soon as red as the blood in the overhead sun from the seething fierceness rising up in them. It was as if the lid of a cauldron had been lifted from off the fire as the slither-ball went zing-zing-zinging off the ground. It wasn't long before one or two hurleysticks were smashed into smithereens and hurlers were waving them round and round – shouting *a hurl! a hurl!* and looking for rapid replacements.

And Then . . . The Second Half

At halftime the players dug into their oranges again and listened to a thousand pieces of conflicting advice, which left them more confused than ever when they came out for the second half.

The play commenced before we knew it had even started. Both teams went at it like gnats, setting the grass aflame. The rowdy uproar continued to spin along nice and handy till it reached the die-away minutes of the game. Up until then the teams had been evenly matched: no-one could foretell which side would win the day and walk home with the green laurels. Men started looking at their pocket-watches. And then – a sideline puck was given in favour of our own Abbey Cross Rovers.

The Meddler

As you might suppose – there were among the spectators some grand and respected hurlers (real ones and imagined ones) from the days of old. Brilliance burned also in the wrists of one of our own men, namely The Meddler (the son of the famous Dazzler) – a foxy devil always darting here and there as though he were a young ferret. He was as elusive as a wizard-on-wheels and you might as well try stopping Rambling Jack's runaway pig when you saw him gliding down the touchline with the ball stuck to his hurleystick on one of his famed solo-runs. He was always looking for a chance to score and had scored many great points for us in recent years. Best of all – he would often send the ball curling in triumph over the crossbar from the narrowest of angles with the crisp beauty of his sideline strokes.

All Eyes Were On Him

All eyes were on him to see what he would do. He was, however, too far down the field – three-quarters the length of the pitch from The Mountainy Streamer's goalmouth. No matter how kindly he caressed the ball there was devil-a-fear that his sideline puck would reach such an immense distance and bring home the winning score for our Abbey Cross Rovers. Once more men started looking at their pocket-watches. The referee began to look at his own watch and it seemed as though he was about to blow the final whistle.

The Sublime Moment Came

The Meddler stepped up to take his sideline puck-of-the-ball. He swung his hurleystick threateningly round and round avove his head – his chest stuck out like a young turkeycock and he eyeing the forwards of his own team some eighty yards nearer to the rival goalmouth than himself.

The black crowd jutted out their chins. They craned their eyes on the great man. A breathless suspense had settled over the whole place: the hush was dreamlike. Suddenly the crafty rogue gave Big Red the wink and slipped the ball squarely across the field into the young lad's outstretched fist.

There followed an inspired moment to be forever captured in Time. It was as though our young giant and his anger had never forgotten Big Screech's insults to his saintly mother. He turned himself into the biblical Samson and an unnatural energy found its way into his huge body – a creeping sensation right down his spine and a source of strength far greater than anything he'd ever felt before. You know it yourself – in every man's life there comes a high point, a peak and a glory from somewhere on high and this was to prove the most sublime moment in Big Red's life – a joy that could never again be matched anywhere: he was about to shine his name into the annals of all the mighty Tipperary hurlers.

He hadn't a second to think.

With the ball in his fist he could see only the opposing goalposts – the breadth of a church door. They were calling out to him. And that was when The Fairy-Godmother of The High Winds flew down and sang sweetly in his ear: 'Come to me, Red! Come to me, Red!'

He Tossed The Ball

The silence was broken as our hero tossed the ball (the ball that was soggy and greasy and as heavy as a lump of lead) forwards and into the air. He raised his hurleystick as though it were a weapon of war. As cool as ice he sent it on its rasping ninety-yard journey across the aching sky . . . sailing high and with the feathery-heeled speed of a black hawk that flies to its nest . . . not only over The Mountainy Streamers's startled crossbar but clean out of the hurling-ground.

We all could see it – as if the clock had stood still – as if all human motion had slowed down. The ball seemed to hover above in the clouds for a split second. Then it disappeared – lost and gone forever – never to be found again – or else it would have been enshrined in the four walls of our Copperstone Hollows Church as a sight more rare than wintertime swallows.

The Winning Score

Big Red's score proved to be the winning point and we heard the referee's whistle warbling to end the game. And another thing – from that day to this it was said by the smartest men among us that Big Red struck the ball not only the unbelievable distance of ninety yards but a further twenty yards in excess of it. Not only that – but the whimsical drinkers below at Curl 'n' Stripes' drinking-shop (forever the humourous wags) professed that by the time our giant's ball finished its devastating journey it was completely covered in snow!

From Gold To Rust, The Sun

And now the sun's golden light turned into rust as the exhausted hurlers from both teams left the field. It were as if they'd been thinning turnips or tramming hay all day. It was time for their thirsty throats to fill the drinking-shop and empty it of its barrels of The Black Doctor. Oh, the hullabaloo as our supporters disgorged themselves from the side of the ditch and followed the hurlers out the gate. They slapped them on their sore backs and pelted their caps into the air in celebration of an insurpassable puck-of-a-ball that would never again to be seen on the green fields of Tipperary – a puck that was diamond-true (said some of the poets amongst us) – sweet as honey (said others) – like manna in the skies (said more of our poets). Indeed the hoarse cries from a thousand tongues could be heard in Mureeny ten miles away, outmatching any chorus put together by ducks, geese or hens in the presence of a hungry fox. And Big Red was not only beatified all over again but some said he ought to be thoroughly canonised as a pure miracle-of-a-man should The Pope in his goodness allow it.

Like A Flock Of Billygoats

Like a flock of billygoats the crowd made their way into the drinking-shop of Joe Tornado – himself a once-great hurler, who (twas said) would have sold his mother's boots for the price of good booze, though he was now an avid teetotaller. All were determined to shake off the drooth and oil their throats for they were as dry as parchment – indeed you'd think it was they that'd been doing all the fine hurling. The shop was soon full to the gills with men's good cheer and jubilation. Some clinked their whiskey-glasses and swallowed them in a single mouthful ('give us another slug of yeer best whiskey') to sting their veins. Others gulped their pints of The Black Doctor greedily to rattle inside their bellies, their whiskers full of frothy foam. They smacked their lips.

The older fellows puffed blissfully on their pipes of tobacco, enveloping us in a cloud and sipping their booze speculatively. Many were the tearstained eyes as they re-enacted Big Red's great puck and compared it with other past scores. These older fellows felt transfused back to the days of their agile youth. It was a sight to melt the heart of a stone when one of these old pensioners made a quick run at Big Red as he was seated at the fire and planted a wet slobbery kiss on his lips with a faraway look ('I love you') of admiration in his eyes.

Sunset

Finally the sunset came in. The hills started to lose their orange colour, turning the whole place into a mystery-land. Only a small wedge of sunlight remained in the shadowy corners of a hurling-field that had offered us so much joy. Still steeped in the game's excitement the bleary-eyed crowd straggled out the door and made their way to their bikes, their ass-and-cars and their traps.

Our Abbey Cross hurlers slowly made their way down the hills and into Rookery Rally in a drove of sauntering horse-and-carts. In the dusk crowds of happy-faced children ran up the road to welcome home their victorious team – as though they were storybook heroes come back from The Land of The Moon. All would be talking about it for weeks to come.

Later That Evening

Late in the evening the true distance of the flight of Big Red's hurling-ball was discussed among the remaining drinkers. It was The Meddler himself (and he still nuzzling his glass of stout), who found the answer to it all. He called the men ('follow me, lads, till I measure it') out from the barrel-planks where they were seated. He put a dab of white paint on the twenty-six-inch wheel of his bike. Accompanied by the bemused drinkers and making as straight a line as though he were ploughing a field, he wheeled his bike from the rivals' goalmouth to the spot near the sideline where Big Red's strike had been taken. He counted the number of spins of the painted wheel and confirmed the distance to be ninety yards to the inch. What a marvellous bleddy man Big Red was (said everyone). What a bleddy marvellous man too was The Medler (someone else laughed). He'd the brains of a pure pope, hadn't he? That story was told again and again and a bike with white paint became part and parcel of Dang-the-skin-of-it's Euclid Lesson from that day forth.

Hailed As A Genius

In days to come (indeed for the rest of his young life) Big Red was hailed as a genius. What did it matter if he couldn't read or couldn't write his own name? The rawgut whiskey and The Black Doctor were repeatedly poured down his throat as time after time he was led into one drinking-shop or another to recall the day of his gigantic ninety-yard puck. And soon this puck went into the annals of our folklore – to be trotted out in our tales at winter firesides until (with the odd embellishment) Big Red became not only a saint everywhere but an entire god.

His Restlessness

Restlessness, however, finally began to couple itself with Big Red's heavy drinking. Such a restlessness was buried in the bones of us all – an urge to get away from the drudgery of the farm and the cattle – from the wind and the rain – to go and cross the wide ocean to The Land of The Silver Dollar where money lay in piles on the streets or to venture any place on earth before the dampness took hold of our lungs and bones. In this respect Big Red was no different from the rest of us: he found himself in the grip of our natural fidgetiness – anxious to bestir himself and catch the next boat.

A Sad Farewell

Halfpenny-Gret was heartbroken as any mother would be. Saddle-the-Pony had long ago resigned himself to the fact that Big Red would leave home one day and go abroad to fill his pockets with gold – that there'd be no-one left to help him plough the few acres and sow the spuds and cabbage shoots – no one left for the thinning of the turnips and building the hayreek.

He took down three straws from the thatch outside the half-door: it was the usual ritual. The first one was short, the second was middle-sized and the third was long. He held them in his closed fist for Big Red to pick out one of them: the short one for travelling near at hand to The Land of John Bull: the middle-sized one for The Land of The Silver Dollar: the third one for Van Diemen's Land, the furthest away by miles.

He Arrived In Wolverhampton

The day of Big Red's departure came round. The pink shafts of sunshine fell on him and his suitcase. After a tearful goodbye and the waving of our red handkerchiefs he finally crossed the sea and made his way to Wolverhampton in England's midlands. As with any new adventurer it was as if he'd landed on the surface of a foreign planet. But he shook himself out of his mists of loneliness and went to look for work next day.

He met a man as tall as himself standing outside the gate of a building-site. The stranger looked him up and down with a look of derision. He had seen Irishmen before. Nevertheless he beckoned Big Red to follow him in. This giant was every bit as strong as Big Red and went by the charming name of *The Bell-Horse* – a timekeeper who measured the work-efficiency of a man. He wanted to see if Big Red was fit for carrying the double-hod-of-bricks up the two flights of ladders – wanted to see if he could slide down the ladders for the next load – like a playful cat would do from the bark of a slippery tree. This was how the fastest men worked – at lightning speed, without time to wipe the sweat from their forehead or lick the salt from their lips.

The two men spat on their fists and The Bell-Horse proceeded to match himself against Big Red for the next hour. The task was as easy for Big Red as peeling a spud: up and down – up and down – filling the bricklayers' boards with new loads of bricks – himself and The Bell-Horse matching each other stride for stride. Was there ever anything like it? There wasn't a gasp or a drop of sweat on either faces The astonished onlookers applauded the muscle-strains of the pair and there and then Big Red was given his first-ever paid job.

On this selfsame morning, however, he saw that The Bell-Horse behaved in a most unfriendly way to other Irish lads, who found themselves unable to match him with a burst of speed similar to Big Red's: he saw how the big man handed them a single hour's pay for their work and followed this up with a demeaning kick-in-the-arse as he bid them an impolite good-day at the building-site's gateway.

Dangerous Jobs

Thereafter Big Red got himself several jobs, all of which required brawn rather than brains – dangerous jobs that no other man was likely to step forward for or had the strength or stomach to do. Few were the men that had the steely nerves to climb to the top of the highest cranes overlooking the city streets. On sleepy Sunday mornings when men were nursing their sick heads after a night's feed of strong booze Big Red cut a fearsome sight as he crawled along the lofty jib of a crane with a bag of hammers and other tools strapped to his back. For a perilous hour or two he hung out there – a studious lone figure – as he went about repairing the damaged jib and cleaning and oiling its parts so that they'd be in proper working order for the crane-driver next day. In this way he earned fistfuls of good money, travelling as much as twenty miles a day. He never missed a single day's work. Fair play to him!

He Missed His Home

It seemed a long time since he'd left his parents' fireside and had said those sad goodbyes to the rest of us. From time to time he reflected on his days in Rookery Rally and wondered what his mother and father were doing back on the little farm. With an aching heart he recalled that sad morning when Saddle-the-Pony and Halfpenny-Gret had made him kneel before The Sacred Heart picture to receive their blessing – how they had dinned into his head some sound advice: stay away from the women: renounce the cursed drink. Big Red was only too glad to take to heart several other pieces of his parent's wise advice but not these two sage warnings. However, good son that he was, each Friday he posted the day's unopened pay-packet home to his mother. It arrived as regular as the clock and was delivered into her hands by Herald-the-Post.

Good To Find Money

This left him with no money to call his own. He wasn't slow to deal with this problem and found an additional job as an evening barman – a job that helped keep him in some sort of style with a few new shirts and a brown suit and matching tie for Mass and a pair of brown shoes to go with it. With the extra money from these evenings he was able to keep hunger away from the door. But his belly was in less good shape than before – what with the fine drinking he was pouring down his throat every blessed night of the week.

His Second Vice

On these occasions he comforted himself: 'I can drink mee money at mee ease or I can throw it away in the gambling dens or at the side of the racetrack.' As for the women, whom he'd been warned to keep away from, they soon became his second vice and went very cosily with the drinking. Being the owner of a fine physique our giant had always been a bit vainglorious since the days of his hurling prowess. And so he spent Saturday nights (often Sunday nights too) losing his timidity and inexperience in the arms of his favourite whore and bruising his thighs in the powerful amusements of lust.

Three Years Later

After three long years of work and lechery Big Red found himself dissatisfied and anxious to pack his suitcase and return home to us. The soft-hearted fellow ached for those glorious days in Rookery Rally with the hills and the valleys and the little birds flying languidly across the sky – where his fame and popularity from his ninety-yard puck had raised his star and adulation to the very skies. Even with his dull wit he realised that in Wolverhampton (in spite of all the money he was earning) he would always remain a mere speck of dust amidst the throngs of workers pounding the daily streets – that crowded streets were no place for a mighty man like himself. The lonesomeness was cutting him to the quick.

He Came Home

We heard him coming up the road and we gave a yelp of delight. He had brought back to us his lovely ice-blue eyes and he was sporting a new wavy ginger moustache. Halfpenny-Gret had heaped up a roasting log fire and she almost grabbed the coat from off of his back. The Welcoming Room shone with a bright light all round him and in the fibre of his being he was back in his heaven. Then she ladled into this giant of hers a few overflowing mugs of rabbit-soup and a plateful of spuds, cabbage and bacon fit for a king.

However – we were saddened to see that his body was a bit on the weaker side from all the fine carousing he'd been doing beyond in John Bull. Father Sensibly sadly shook his head and didn't bother calling on him for the season's hurling training-sessions. The news went round: Big Red was not going to be picked for the Abbey Cross Rovers team.

The constant jeering was the much-needed spur for our giant to rouse himself and get himself back in harness. As the days went by he avoided the whiskey and The Black Doctor as though they were The Plague, realising that they had been the cause of him squandering his hard-earned money as a barman across the sea. Many men had done the same thing – had squandered away their money before returning to Rookery Rally like prodigal sons and with their trouser-pockets empty as sin.

A Fine Catch

Big Red was still a fine catch for any young woman, should she and her silvery laughter wish to come dallying in an effort to harness herself to him in marriage. But he knew there wasn't a single woman who could match the physical lovemaking of his Wolverhampton whores amid the tossed weekend sheets. Those scandalous hussies had taught him a trick or two that could never be imagined by our own budding damsels: these little missies would be far too bashful for the exhausting bouts of degrading lechery he'd recently enjoyed or might have in store for them if ever they got themselves in his clutches. Their startled mothers (and every young lady knew this only too well) would have whipped the legs out from under them with the yardbrush and Father Sensibly would have cursed them into the fires of hell from his altarsteps had they anticipated a round or two of unholy lovemaking with the likes of Big Red. All this was an established truth.

It was made clear to all these young charmers that Big Red had no time for them and that they were never going to catch his eye or get themselves a fine old time from him and his supposed pocket-loads of newfound wealth. And so – they pretended they weren't a bit put out by his lack of attention to them. After all – he hadn't an acre of land to his name and they shrugged their shoulders and gave up admiring the sight of his muscles and cast their nets elsewhere.

New Feats Of Athleticism

As a substitute for walking the flowery fields with one of these fair damsels Big Red put his energies into the wrestling and the lifting of weights and the pelting of the sheaf. In all these sports (as in the hurling) he proved himself a studious fellow. The following August he became the toast of the Show-Fair when time after time he won the green laurels handsomely. Fair play to him – he had returned to the peak of his physical fitness: we could see the muscles bulging out all over him – his chest, his arms and thighs. His admiring mother and father couldn't get enough of looking out over the geraniums on the window-sill and seeing the stamp of their lovely son when he went marching out from the yard and disappeared with his bike across the stream and the flagstones.

The Weeping Mollys

But because everything was going so smoothly for him the oily tongues of those old gossips (The Weeping Mollys) started wagging again. Wasn't it a shame, if not a mystery altogether, that no young damsel could put a ring through Big Red's nose and lead him up the altarsteps and warm his nightly bed for him in matrimony? We could have educated these old beldames. Didn't they know how hoity-toity these pretty little missies could be – especially if they thought themselves spurned by Big Red? Surely they'd seen it before – how a young damsel in the prime of her girlhood and with apples for cheeks and marbles for eyes and the envy of every woman in sight – how the same spoilt girl wouldn't allow herself to stoop so low as to get herself entangled with any of our young men – even if it was Big

Red and his newfound money? Couldn't they see how no man was good enough for the likes of this misguided young madam and her stuck-up nose – how the years would roll on – how she'd end up living out her days as a forlorn and lonely old spinster? The men round the fire in the drinking-shop would nod their wise old heads and spit their tobacco juice distainfully into the fire: 'She was always so bleddy choosy and now we see the fine mess she's gotten herself into – not a man to keep her in style or to warm her cold old arse in the bed she now finds herself lying in.'

He Was A Shy Man For The Courting

However – not only had The Weeping Mollys misread matters as to whether it was Big Red or some of our young girls who were at fault in not getting him up to the church rails – all the rest of us had missed the mark as well. It wasn't the fussiness and the oh-so-choosy-nature of our young damsels that was stopping one of them getting our giant into bed: it was Big Red himself. The poor lad was in a total flummox when it came to the art of courting a woman. He was no longer in Wolverhampton where he had paid good money for the embraces of one or two strange women and he hadn't the courage (what with his small brain) to approach any of our innocent girls. The simple truth was that he didn't know what he'd say to them if they trapped him on the side of the road for he hadn't a tongue in his head or a notion of charm in his entire body. He'd never been blessed with the gift of other men's lyrical wit and their lying tales. He rarely laughed or smiled. All this (it seemed) was the will of God and there was nothing that could be done about it. Enough said.

He Gazed Into The Crystal Ball

And so – there were long hours in which he had nothing to do but think out matters for himself. Dull though his brain had always been, he was clever enough to gaze into the misty crystal ball and see what sort of life lay ahead of him: long stretches of loneliness once the day came for his mother and father to die and with his four sisters already married far up country and miles away from home. He had seen it before in the lives of other men when old age began to creep up and snap at their heels before wrapping itself unexpectedly round their aging limbs. There'd be nothing to look forward to in the long winter evenings – just an old dog to bring cheer to his cold fireside and no-one to warm either his heart or his bed. It was enough to make a man take the razor to his throat and he almost envied those who had died young. No amount of whiskey or The Black Doctor would be able to drown out the bitterness that was beginningn to seep into his confused soul.

A Final Flourish

However, such a huge attraction as Big Red – a man who could point a greasy slither-ball from ninety yards outfield on the wettest day of the year – was not going to be left without a final flourish to his bow. And it came sooner than any of us expected. The following summer his father (Saddle-the-Pony) went sadly to his grave, having died suddenly from an inward pain. Big Red was filled with a sadness that was almost too much to bear. To escape from his grief he took his big boots off to The Regatta in Kindy-Wells beside The Mighty Shannon River – a spot where a stretch of the river was known for its swift currents and squally storms.

Amongst the swimmers for The Challenge Cup there was a young priest from Clare. He had stripped off to race in the two-hundred-yard-dash to the red marker out at the island. The saintly man was gifted above all other swimmers in the yearly regattas up and down the rivers of Ireland. His father (Old Dinny) had been a fine swimmer too – hadn't he outswam the great Billy Hayseeds? And now – huge crowds had come to see him put on a bit of a show. It was strange to see his lily-white body shivering alongside the other fellows on the bank, for it was unusual to see a holy man stripping off his togs and showing us his chest and ignobly involving himself in a regatta swimming-race: priests as a rule were seen propping up the counter in The Big Tent of The Regatta – with a large brandy in the heel of their fist and another one at the ready beside their elbow.

Big Red Looked Down

From his perch on the spectators' bridge Big Red looked down at the colourful scene and the crowds gathering to see the start of the swimming-race. He took it all in – the fine swimmers in their costumes and the Clare priest among them. He saw the combatants stepping out and lining up at the starting-tape. The expectations were high.

The swimmers looked up to the skies and blessed themselves. The starting-pistol was fired. The race was on. Big Red heard the freezing gasps as the swimmers splashed into the cold water like horses dashing across a river. He heard the mighty cheers of the excited crowd in the glory of it all. A minute later he saw the priest out in front of the other swimmers and making a beeline for the red marker.

Suddenly – as though a huge black cloud had sailed in across the sun – he heard the groans of the crowd when they saw what was taking place in front of their eyes. Following the great man's breakfast a cramp came on him out of nowhere – freezing his legs and taking him down beneath the grasping waves.

A Split Second Of Silence

There followed a split second of silence – a silence when a piece of our history was to be written all over again. For in this singular moment Big Red was to be marked out for Posterity a second time. He found himself in a strange dreamworld amongst a thousand slowcoaches, whose brains were all too addled as to know what next to do. His father's recent ghost came down in a flutter from the clouds and poured his wraith into him. He whispered sharp words into his ear – father and son twinned into one. It was now up to Big Red to show the other poor scholars (the miserable Big Screech included) that he wasn't so dumb and slow-witted after all. He couldn't (whispered his father) stand there like a simpleton on the bridge – a bewildered spectator like the rest of the stupified crowd gazing out helplessly on the tragic scene unfolding before his eyes.

Not A Moment To Think

His father's spirit seemed accompanied by an army of spirits from Big Red's forebears, surrounding him like ivy to the oak – stifling him – breathing into the heart of him – urging him to do the right thing for the sake of his family – for the sake of his race. He hadn't a moment to contemplate the dangers to his life and limb and perhaps at this stage of his life – and with nothing better to think upon but those persistent images of a lonely old age in front of him – his every impulse was to take up this great challenge in the battle between his own life and the priest's cruel death.

He Threw Off His Boots And Coat

He threw off his boots and coat. In a blur he burst out from the throng in a glorious effort to get to the holy man. Like the day of the long puck, an unearthly strength rushed into his every sinew. He took an aristocratic leap out into the air and down from the top of the bridge. He was seen thrashing around in the water and swimming far out. We didn't even know whether he had learnt to swim a stroke whilst abroad in Wolverhampton. Maybe Big Red himself didn't know if he could swim so far out and then double up on the distance so as to get back in again.

The crowds craned their eyes down from the bridge and blessed themselves one and all. They saw Big Red attempting to frighten the life out of the river. They saw how he reached the side of the priest – how he held the priest's terrified head above the waters of The Mighty Shannon River – how he brought him back into the land of the living. They saw him swimming back towards the bank with the holy man's head held high in his hands.

Nearer and nearer to the shore he came – all the way towards the spectators and the prayers being uttered on this side of the river. In one moment Big Red's head appeared above the waters. The next minute he was down underneath them. The priest struggled away from his grip and, living another day to tell the tale of it, he forced himself as far as the outstretched arms on the bank and was dragged safely ashore.

His Final Hurrah

It was Big Red's final hurrah. He was never the man to earn his fame as a swimmer. Hurling, yes. Whoring, yes. Exhausted and to the everlasting groans of us all when we saw what was happening to our young giant, he sank beneath the waves some thirty yards out from our helpless eyes. He drifted away with the current. And as with the beltings from Big Screech's fists and her boots and her sally-switch, the poor misfortunate lad never gave so much as a cry or a cough but was swept away by the force of the river – downstream (ah, no!) towards The Ocean and Oblivion.

Next Morning

Next morning – even before the sun had risen in the sky – Bishop High-Hat came running from his palace in Ennis to do the ceremony. The dismal crowd followed him along the bridge. He solemnly blessed the waters and informed his flock that Big Red was finally at peace at the bottom of The Mighty Shannon River. He called for a bale of straw. He blessed the straw. He threw it over the bridge and into the river. The bale of straw swam away downstream towards the river's right-hand bend. The crowd ran along the bank. The straw came to the bend in the river and there it stopped: 'A man's body will follow certain currents,' said the worthy bishop. 'So will the bale of straw if given an equal weight.'

Bishop High-Hat was not only a holy man, he was also a wise man. The bale of straw was trapped in a mass of underwater briars at the bend of the river. The men and their excitement ('Down here, lads! Down here!) all rallied round. They found Big Red and his puffy face trapped in those same underwater briars – with two fists of weeds in his grasp.

His mother, Halfpenny-Gret, went and brought him home in the horse-and-cart. There was no wake. There'd be no complacency. She'd let nobody near him. After the recent death of Saddle-the-Pony her sorrow was far too great and she locked herself in the bedroom and stretched herself out beside the once-athletic form of Big Red's corpse for the next day-and-a-half.

Full Honours

Next day the cold rainclouds blotted out the sunlight from the snivelling sky. We heard the church bells ring as we crunched our boots into the graveyard. Our hearts leapt up in our throats as we vividly reflected on our giant and poured out our sobs of farewell to him. Then we took him in the hearse and we buried him in his early grave (his mother always knew he'd die early) below in Abbey Acres Graveyard beside Saddle-the-Pony. We gave him full honours with the hurleystick and the blue-and-gold colours of Tipperary wrapped around his coffin. He had been a man that in the end proved he could hurl a ball as good as any man in Ireland. At sixteen years of age he had brought himself fame with his ninety yards puck of a greasy ball on a wet day above in the mountains. He had tested and tasted the charms of many a Wolverhampton temptress (if only the rest of us had had the fine chance) – lying all night in their dusky arms. But now – at two-and-twenty the poor lad was dead and gone forever to The Beyond – just the bright stars of the night and the cold midnight airs to guard his spirit. We thank our God for the gift of our one and only true giant. May the Lord have mercy on your soul, Big Red, for as long as our rivers flow out to The Ocean your name will be remembered with pride. Rest assured of that.

THREE

How we all learnt the lesson that God is everywhere.

Names, Names, Names

Names, names, names. We each had our own names: there was Ned-the-Smoker, Tim-the-Bear, Hammer-the-Smith, Jack-the-Herd and so on. These were the family names that had put their stamp on us over the years and had little or nothing to do with our baptismal names the day we were christened.

Then you had those other names. Within a few miles of us there was Lord and Lady Plus-Fours from The Big House. There was Lord and Lady Elegance, Lord and Lady Demurely – and don't forget Lady Posh-Frock. They were people of high degree and you'd see a stream of them flouncing about arm-in-arm all over the wide open spaces of their lands – them and their imperious looks and their gold watches and chains and their grey tailored suits and a shine on their boots. They had nothing to do but wrap their delicate wrists round their hunting guns. The differences were all too clear: the foreign settlers (as we still liked to call them, no matter how long it had been since they set foot among us) always had these lordly names – Lord This and Lady That. We ladled out the friendly names only to our own Irish brothers and sisters – we and our crushed faces and hardworking vigour that did all the hard work with the plough and the hayfork.

We Poor Scholars

It didn't matter what squabble our men got into over the flow of the water in their streams or what fights they got into over land divides, dykes and ditches. Many a raging battle with pitchfork and cudgel had we had among ourselves in the past. But when it came down to it we poor scholars were all joined together at the hip. We knew that we were the true Irish and that those high and mighty lords were still a bunch of trespassers from the pastures of John Bull. At least that's what you'd hear the likes of Handsome Johnnie and other men like him saying. The quicker Lord Plus-Fours and his crew marched themselves off – the quicker they hopped onto the cattle-boat – the better it would be for all of us including themselves. We could then live our lives in peace with our own little bit of pride left in us. It was the same talk below in Curl 'n' Stripes' drinking-shop and in Merrymouth's drinking-shop and in Lapping-Guinness's drinking-shop where there'd be no need of a few glasses of whiskey to addle the brains of the drinkers and make them tell you they were merely echoing the views shared by all true Irishmen across the land. Their talk was often accompanied by a not-so-charming use of foul oaths and imaginative swearwords when they recollected the most recent battles such as the one above at Mureeny Church. That was the day when the big guns of The Tan Soldiers were seen pounding down on our own young lads, some of whom were but a day out of school and still looking for work. The fighting went on from nine in the morning till four in the afternoon, eventually leaving six spattered corpses lying in the yard outside the church door. The children stood in the nearby field and looked at the dead youths through the bars of the haggart-gate. The mothers came running down the lane. With hushed breath they crossed the churchyard. They looked at the carnage – at the bodies of their sons and their youthful idealism, fighting for Ireland's freedom they had been told. It was a sad sight and there was nothing glorious in it. The mothers took off their aprons and threw them on top of the bloody bodies to cover them. Then with feelings of pure distain and cold fury (as well as utter heartbreak) they took their miserable way back home and only then did they tear out their hair and cry like a pack of sick donkeys. They never got out of bed for the next week-and-a-half. And then they put on their long black robes for another year. They were grey-haired for the rest of their lives.

The following day the children ran round collecting the spent cartridges. They got the hammer and proceeded to hammer them into the church flowerbed, making a reverent circle of them in honour of where our fighters had died. There wasn't one of the men who now hadn't thoughts of sheer murder on their minds. They'd have liked nothing better than to find a few stray Tans and take them out behind a rock and cut their throats for them with the nearest reaping-hook.

With The Women It Was Different

But enough of this sad old talk. The women rarely possessed so sharp a dose of hatred as the men. Of course Soolah Patricia (as we know by now) had been the exception to the rule, having had more than enough reason to turn vengeful following The Tans' cruel murder of her father (Old Tim). And another thing – you'd never see any of our women setting foot inside the door of a drinking-shop to get their mind poisoned with hate. You wouldn't find them sitting in groups outside the church door and arguing how the country should be run. It was the men who gathered at the gates of the creamery – the men who stood in The Market-Square when selling their cattle and pigs – the men who had the time and opportunity to spout hatred and spin it along whenever they chose.

Their wives (the dear souls) had enough on their plates to get through the day-to-day grind of scratching out a living for themselves and their brood of chicks. Often they didn't know where the next day's bit of bread would come from. As mothers they were certain what should always be first on their list: their children had to be clothed – they had to be fed – their brains had to be nourished with more than a watery bowl of stirrabout if they were ever to make a name for themselves in the schoolhouse of Dang-the-skin-of it. They'd tell you that it was the gentry-folk who had the means of providing for our wellbeing. And they'd warn you (if their men gave them a chance to get a word in edgeways) that we should keep our mouths shut tight and should tolerate (if not love) these rich landowners in spite of their foreign ways and titles. Only a mother could have such feelings as this. Without the gentry (they'd say) where would we have been up till now? Dead and buried long ago – that's where. Hadn't men like Lord Manners, Lord Damocles and Lord Dungarees always behaved scrupulously – saving our forefathers from starvation during the merciless Famine by opening their granaries of oats – always supporting the poor like ourselves, who would never have been able to turn our hands to a brown ten-shilling-note without their help? Ah, the romantic women – they could see those fine rich lords stepping out from their grand mansions and reaching out their hands to our people – giving the men part-time seasonal work at ploughing and harvest-time and during the pheasant and partridge shoots. They could see their rosy-cheeked daughters given work in the kitchens and bedrooms of The Big House and serving at mealtimes – ensuring that they had the odd few shillings at the end of the week to bring home for the table and feed the younger children – ensuring that both our sons and daughters were getting an extended education – learning new skills in field-husbandry and gardening (the sons) or in cooking and dressmaking (the daughters). That was how the world had always been organised and Dowager's wise old head would remind Handsome Johnnie of this fact and throw it back in his face. It was a pure disgrace – all this patriotic nonsense in the men's heads. Would this simpleton-of-a-husband-of-hers ever get a stem of sense?

Those Foreign Settlers

On the other side of the coin – Lord Plus-Fours or Lord Manners would never have thought of themselves as foreign settlers, their families having lived in Tipperary for longer than our memories could count. Their forefathers had taken the plunge and crossed the sea from John Bull – had been given Irish land by their monarch over the last few hundred years. It was a grand life for them here on the fertile fields of Tipperary. Indeed Lord Plus-Fours had the best of it all – more than a thousand fat juicy acres. He owned all of Bog Boundless. He had the deep forests that lay up passed Lisnagorna and Currywhibble. His fires would never go short of a log of wood. This made a number of Rookery Rally's men sick in their stomach and Handsome Johnnie would remind Dowager that men like Lord Plus-Fours had reached their high position as a result of some ancestor of his putting his hand in the hand of that unprintable scoundrel, Cromwell, whose army had crossed the sea and laid fierce siege to our towns, slaughtering men, women and children in their thousands throughout the country. Would hell itself be good enough for the likes of that article? That's what he said.

The Big House and Service

Dowager's mother and her mother before her had served in The Big House below in Abbey Acres – a house that had often been a fortress for foreign soldiers during periods of unrest (and there had been many of these). They went there when they were eleven or twelve – the day after they left school. They started out with a brief apprenticeship of cleaning out the ashes and lighting the fires with the big buckets of fuel which the men brought in. They then graduated to serving tea to the lady of the house in her drawing-room. Soon they were able to polish the coal-skuttle and all the brass-work and silverware – not to mention the lovely glass chandeliers. They did the laundry and the ironing. They made the beds. From the very first day they entered The Big House they followed their mother's advice – kept their heads down and minded their manners. They knew their place in the presence of their better.

There was the odd skirmish amongst the grooms and the maids, forcing one or two of them into an early marriage. This was no fault of the lady of the house for the morals of The Big House were as immaculate as The Blessed Virgin's. Though the lord and his lady were not of our faith, they insisted that the servant-girls knelt down and said their rosary each night and kept up their traditional prayers on their knees beside their bed before hopping into it. They made sure that the steward took them to their monthly Confession in the church in Copperstone Hollow. They saw to it that they kept up their reception of the blessed host in Holy Communion. Fair play to them – what more could any of us have wished for? And whilst these good creatures were guarding the spiritual souls of the girls they were also introducing them to the use of the handkerchief on their noses – to the cleanliness of their nails – to the grooming of their hair. They were teaching them the laying-out of the cutlery and the delicate arts of needlework and embroidery. Better still – they were introducing them to fine speech and manners, teaching them a better use of grammar and how to address one another politely and avoid using coarse words like 'feck it!' and 'shite' whenever they burnt their fingers in the fire.

As for Dowager – before she was sixteen she had written out her own copperplate book of baking recipes (meals by the score that Lady Plus-Fours had given her) – to pass on to her children when the need came for them to spread their wings and travel abroad to foreign shores and no man (not even Handsome Johnnie) would persuade her to change her opinion: the lady of the house was generosity itself, possessing a kindliness that she could never forget. And hadn't Handsome Johnnie felt the benefits of The Big House? To be sure he had. The foreign stewards had taught him the delicate skills of grooming and training the young horses in the stable-block – had taught him how to handle the plough with a team of horses for ploughing the gentry's wide acres – so well indeed that he had taken his boots to Galway to win the laurels at the ploughing-match. And had he forgotten his brother (Murty-with-the-greenfingers)? It was in the glasshouses of Lord Manners that Murty had learnt his trade. There wasn't a gardening skill that he hadn't acquired – so much so that he could take a bag of Lord Manner's strawberries to town and sell them in Sally Pink-Frock's shop without her bothering to unwrap and inspect them, knowing that Murty's strawberries would be without a blemish. Enough said

But The Dark Clouds Were Always Looming

You'd often see the women and men working together in the fields and woods, beating the flax and rising up the pheasants with the pointer dogs. They were like a little family of happy songthrushes (the men as well as the women) and you could write a poem or paint a picture about them. The Big House was their home-from-home on these occasions. That was the bright side of the sky. But life wasn't that simple and Dowager would shake her head for she knew that this was only half the story – knew where the dark clouds lay and where other even darker clouds were looming. The Devil (she'd say) had never left the hearts of the more hostile men in our midst – especially those cold-eyed articles with no sons and daughters working for The Big House. She'd heard them say that acts of kindness from the hands of the high-and-mighty gentry had always been done to further their own interests – even during The Famine Days when they needed a constant workforce to keep their estates alive and well. Oh, the miserable lowborn heathens (she'd tell you) to be saying such awful things! And she'd insist that all of us (men, women and children) ought to get down on our bended knees and thank God that our sons and daughters were so well fed – with a shine in their eyes and hair. And though Handsome Johnnie couldn't keep her quiet all the time, there were occasions when she felt she was as helpless as the rest of the women, who were never allowed to make a political statement of any sort and knew they'd always be in second place to their men. It was a constant tug-of-war: the hearts of the men and the hearts of the women pulling in opposite directions.

If You Were A Magician

If you were a magician – if you could look inside our men's head or see deep into their hearts, they'd tell you that they had inherited neither education or wealth – that they'd always felt inferior to the foreign settlers with their mighty estates and their lofty ways, their long tweed overcoats, their smart farting-jackets and their plus-four trousers. Dowager half-guessed the truth. She could see why Handsome Johnnie and his fellow-men sometimes behaved like those heavy storm clouds gathering in across Bog Boundless – whilst she and the women went on twisting their way like a scampering stream through each day as best they could. Nothing would change (she felt) because intimate conversation was rarely if ever a part of everyday life between a husband and wife: they were always too tired at the end of the day. The women, therefore, kept their innermost thoughts and feelings locked inside their hearts until they stepped into the confession-box where they could let Father Sensibly know what was troubling them. God forbid (they told him) that they'd ever get their men's rancour into their souls. All they wanted from the day their children entered the services of The Big House and curtsied before the lord and his lady was a genuine respect for themselves and their families – a recognition that they were part of a noble race – the Irish. That was one thing (they told their priest) that they had in common with their men: they were proud of their race.

Imagine

And now we come to Imagine and the freshness she brought in among us with her unexpected arrival. It was as if an incredibly bright sunbeam had come round the corner and met us full in the face. Her true name was Imogen and she was the daughter of Lord Politely. It's no exaggeration to say she was as lovely as the sweetest apple in Old Sam's orchard. She had a shoulder-length mane of saddle-coloured hair, parted in the middle and gathered in a neat little chignon above the nape of her neck – with a knot of tiny wispy curls in it. These she'd let loose at times to hang down her back. Soft were her cheeks and (unlike the rest of us) her teeth were as white as milk. She'd remind you of a swan with her classical long neck and her arms and fingers as slender as grass. She had the voice of a nightingale that might be compared to the merriment of our own River Laughter. Indeed with those deep brown eyes of hers (moist like a wet sod of turf) she seemed forever cheerful and lighthearted – always smiling on the rich and poor alike from the day she arrived here in Rookery Rally. And if that wasn't enough she had a natural warmth in her fluttery heart and a genuine sense of God's goodness, believing that all mankind (be they from the native sod or elsewhere) were equal to one another in the eyes of The Lord for they were born in his own image and likeness, weren't they?

The Children First Noticed Her

It was the children who first noticed her – not long after her arrival and her wedding to Lord Plus-Fours. Whenever they saw her riding up passed Old Sam's stile on her spanking white pony (Rosetta), they'd run out into the road to get the smell of the new leather on her boots and on the pony's saddle and the warm cloud of fragrant perfume wafting in the air behind this new fairy-woman. They clapped their little hands ('If only we could grow up to be like Imagine!') when they saw her trotting up to the flagstones and stopping to greet them.

The Mountainy Breezes

Whereas we had our own well-trained horses for going to the creamery or fetching back the turf from Bog Boundless or yoking them up to the plough, it was simply for recreation and pleasure that Imagine rode her young pony passed our windows – going off for a day's adventure into The Hills-of-The-Past. Like the children we too found her a sight to behold: in her long red cloak, her green skirts and her blouse the colour of a pigeon's throat: her hair streaming back behind her and her gloved hands expertly mastering the reins. It soon became a daily routine to see the two of them passing by (herself and the pony) for she loved nothing better than taking in the mountainy breezes – contemplating the rivers and woods and the harmonious haunts of our Irish fairy-folk, those spirits of the wild places that we all knew so well.

Soon After Her Arrival

She became so engrossed and entangled in our daily lives that our women treated her as though she was one of their own. So well was she thought of that they soon forgot to call her Lady Plus-Fours. Nor did they dare call her by her first name (Imogen), which was far too familiar a way of talking to any member of the gentry. Instead – they found themselves going further down the hill and labelled her with a well-meaning but slightly outrageous derivative of her Christian name, addressing her simply as *Imagine*. And whenever women like Dowager stopped her in her riding and gave her the traditional little curtsy they'd always follow this up with a bit of daily news like 'Timmy's Kerry-blue cow fell into the drain' or 'Fatty-Matty lost his pocket-watch in the potato-field.' This seemed to entrance her and she'd cock her head to the side and listen to each new bit of daily gossip – seemingly captivated by the long-winded embroidery of our women's speech and the musical accents of their words and phrasing. She'd place her gloved fingers thoughtfully to her lips and murmur: 'Imagine that! Imagine that!'

It was as if she was signalling her utter disbelief that such-and-such a mundane pronouncement could ever be true. And anxious to stay as long as she could, she'd draw on the reins in case the charming Rosetta might be getting a bit tired from listening to all this human chattering. Indeed the poor animal sometimes lost all patience with her and could be seen tossing her creamy mane and pawing at the ground and getting ready to make a bolt for the hills at any minute.

As a result of this quaint little habit of hers ('Imagine that! Imagine that!') our women began answering her good-naturedly as the weeks went by: 'Yes, it is indeed a grand morning, Imagine,' or 'No, I didn't see your father with his shotgun out this morning, Imagine.' She may well have mistaken such talk as another example of our broad-vowelled way of saying her name. However, we began to believe that she liked this friendly misnomer and so – *Imagine* became her name and *Imagine* it was going to stay.

Perhaps she realised how privileged she was to be the only rich lady in our midst ever to have been given this personal honour of the friendly name (like Jack-the-Herd, Moll-the-Man or anyone else we knew). And thereafter this fine young lady took to her new name with an undisguised amusement and even wore it (we felt) with a good deal of pride.

Us And The Likes Of Them

As far as anyone could recall this was the first time that any of us had spent more than a few seconds familiarising ourselves with any member of the established gentry. For there wasn't one of us who hadn't had it drummed into our skulls since childhood that there was a mighty big difference between Tipperary's rich folk and ourselves: it had always been the custom to speak only when spoken to by the high and the mighty. However, we soon heard from Father Sensibly and Doctor Glasses that Imagine had her fine manners and delicate touches brushed into her from an aristocratic school in far-off France as well as The Ladies' Academy in Cheltenham Spa across the sea – all topped off with a season of regattas and balls amongst the rich folk in Dublin's rich suburb of Rathlofty.

'Who would have thought it (whispered our Weeping Mollys) – for us to have taken a shine to a young lady from Cheltenham Spa and Rathlofty?' But (we could have interjected) the reason was because she was a young girl not above inspecting our pighouse or helping an old lady with an armful of sticks for the fire. Of course we sooon learnt that (though very young) she had been married off by her father (Lord Politely) to Lord Plus-Fours, and he thirty years older than herself, simply for his vast acres of land rather than his handsome bearing or courtly manner: he had neither of these and was indeed a rough sort of diamond.

Dowager And Imagine

Dowager thought it a blessed day to have met Imagine and it wasn't long before she began to open her heart to her. She felt sure that with her fresh and genuine airiness this harmless young girl would be capable (given time) of melting even the most savage hearts in our men. It might be a puzzle for them at first to grasp how a stranger like her could admire a wild place like our own when compared to the grandeur of The Big City. They might be somewhat confused to see how her good-natured spirit was marked with a constancy that outshone even our own renowned generosity towards one another's needs – especially as we all could be far from generous when the mood suited us. However, they'd eventually realise that in spite of her polite foreign ways and natural grace she was just a simple and uncomplicated girl, who carried herself no differently from the rest of us – a girl who'd be capable of wiping out all their fears – all their contempt for Lord Plus-Four and what a cantankerous old goat he was; for before Imagine's arrival they'd have loved (even the women) to set fire to his tail.

Talking With The Women

When she'd halt Rosetta and allow her to snatch a bit of grass from the ditch, Imagine would spend hours talking to women like Dowager. It seemed as though her tongue would ramble on forever and would never stop. That's when you'd notice the difference between our men and women. The women found it easy to admire and fall in love with anyone who was a step or two above them. This was an established fact and could be seen every Sunday at Mass when the front pews of the church were full of women and they making sheep's eyes up at their betters, namely the holy saints represented in our statues. You'd never see our men getting up to this sort of tomfoolery – casting gloomy eyes up at mere statues. Indeed it was as natural as a rainy day for the women to start holding polite little conversations with Imagine, who in some ways was like those church saints and a fine noble lady – one they could look up to and (as with the saints) see as better than themselves.

Our Tongue-tied Men

In contrast – you'd have to laugh when you saw how our tongue-tied men with their inbred shyness didn't know what to do with the ladylike Imagine except to shuffle their hobnail boots, bury their nervous chins in their topcoats and take off their coy caps before giving her a stuttery cough and making her a confused little bow when they'd rather be making a quick dash for the hills. It would make you sick to look at the carry-on of these old hypocrites. On the surface they appeared well-mannered and polite when they met her but with their ingrained hurt and their longterm anger – with their animosity against those whom they thought too grand or far higher up the ladder than themselves – what they'd like to be doing was giving her the spit from their mouths, the snot from their nose and a kick up the arse. Of course Imagine and her innocence hadn't a notion of all this bitterness in our men, having never spent time talking to any of them.

Herself And Blue-eyed Jack

There was one exception to all this: Imagine found she had a special affinity with Blue-eyed Jack. The bond between herself and Dowager's eldest son went back a few months earlier – back to a day in springtime when his star was set to rise sky-high in her eyes. A storm came on suddenly like a glowering rash from beyond Corcoran's Well and there were several bolts of lightning followed by drum-rolling thunder above The Creamery Road. Straightaway the whinnying Rosetta turned into a lather of sweat, forcing her to make a sudden bolt so as to get away from the lashing rain and reach safety. At that same moment Blue-eyed Jack was bringing in an armful of logs from behind the pighouse. His eyes nearly fell out of his head when he saw the distress Rosetta was in and how Imagine was getting thrown indelicately around the bushes. He pelted the logs inside the half-door and, heedless of the downpour, raced out across the yardstream to tackle the deadly danger that faced the helpless girl and her pony. In a flash he was at her side and snatching at the reins. Bravely he fought with the pony and, knowing (as he did) the nature of any stressed creature, he managed to restore her to a state of calmness. It was something of a miracle when into his arms the senseless Imagine fell from off the pony's back – when into his cornflower-blue eyes (hence his name) she found herself looking once she came back to the world of the living with her peace restored. From that day onwards she felt that this young man, unlike those other aristocratic toadies above in The Big City, was the sort of man who could take on the world for her if she ever asked him. She knew it. Maybe he did too.

She Couldn't Keep Away

After that she couldn't keep away from Dowager's door. When she'd stop her pony at the flagstones before making her way on up to Sheep's Cross, the younger children would stop playing in The Bluebutton Field. They'd run excitedly across the haggart and over the singletree – just to get a look at the latest fine clothes she was wearing (their lovely warm colours) and the beautiful pony she was riding. For a lady of youthful years Imagine was discretion itself on these occasions and had the good sense never to put her foot inside the half-door and embarrass Dowager. It was as if she knew (though how she had learnt it, we couldn't fathom) that a little cabin with a pile of children in it would often be dirty with an untidy jumble of boots and coats all round the floor: 'Are you decent?' she'd say, waiting politely on the flagstones until Dowager smoothed down her hair and undid the straps of her apron so that she'd come out to greet her politely and mannerly. Imagine then tied Rosetta to the grove's singletree over the road and began cleaning the mud from her boots in the yard-stream.

The Soul Of Patience

These days were endless for Imagine. Dowager was the soul of patience – telling her one little tale after another as if she hadn't a hundred and one things better to be doing this blessed day. None could tell a tale better than Dowager. She would paint in vivid colours the lives of Lord Plus-Four's grandfather and his great-grandfather before him. She told Imagine about the costumes they used to wear – the half-caroline hats and brass-buttoned leggings of the men and the crinoline dresses of the women – and the fine balls and hunts that they attended. She told her how she herself (when she wasn't long finished school and a servant-girl at The Big House) had seen the fine carriages with their white horses coming up the gravel drive. In those afternoons of yesterday she would press her nose (she said) against the glass of the ballroom doors, gazing at the lovely men and their whiskers – admiring the slender women's gaiety – their ringletted hair with the ribbons and the jewels round their tapered necks and wrists and the sweep of their flouncy silk dresses as they flitted and drifted through their waltzes and quadrilles like hummingbirds out of Fairyland. 'If only . . . if only for a single day (she would think to herself) I could become Cinderella and fulfil my dreams of becoming a rich lady before the night vanished into daylight.' Then she'd run away before getting caught and sent back to work. And while she was racing on with her tales Imagine sat rigid and transfixed. There'd come a pause for Dowager to catch her breath and then she'd heave a little sigh when she thought of this picture of pure silver printed forever on her mind.

And then she'd change her tune and tell Imagine the way the rebellious Ribbon-Men attacked the stewards and baillifs all round Tipperary and yet left the nearby gentry in peace – thanks to the natural kindliness in the ancestors of Imagine's husband (the men whom the rest of us referred to as those blasted foreign settlers) and how their granaries of wheat and oats had always been plentifully stored so as to feed those poorer than themselves – especially through the merciless years of The Famine.

'Imagine that!' sighed Imagine. 'Imagine that!'

Slow To Leave The Yard

An hour later and Imagine would be slow indeed to leave the yard and go trotting up towards Sheep's Cross. When she got there she'd spend another hour with Moll-the-Man's mother (Sadie Scissors) or some of the other women. And you could see how these women too (it wasn't just Dowager) had the power to hold Imagine in the palm of their hands with their long list of stories. Her heart (her ears too) seemed to be warmed by the musical tones of the women's ringing voices and the way they put colour and shape into their speech – speech that had been passed on to them during fireside chats in childhood or chats with farmers going to the creamery or the cattle-fair. It was this (rather than the truth of the stories) that gripped Imagine and held her back most mornings – even though the giddy Rosetta should have been eating the coarse grass above in The Valley of The Pig by that hour of the day.

Very Fine Days Indeed

Those days (God be good to us) were very fine indeed for a short while – that is, on the surface they seemed good enough. If one left the men to one side the spirit of Imagine was at one with the rest of us. We were at one with her – like the two sides of a windowpane. Each day she was able to go off on her peaceful rambles up through the mountains, hunting the woods in search of wild birds – especially the small greenfinch, the linnet and the corncrake. She was able to sit for hours amid the wildflowers and the rare species of butterflies – examining all sorts of mushrooms and faunae. And just before the sun lowered itself and the chorus of grasshoppers took its place the children would see her returning with her arms full of Nature's treasures – unusual flowers for her presses and various leaves for her scrapbook. It was clear to their mothers that this gentle soul had the same love and appreciation of the beautiful countryside that we all had in our hearts – even the coarsest of our men. If time allowed, we might see a lump of fresh cowdung hardening in the noonday sunlight. We'd stop a while and gaze at a wily old crow standing alongside the new dung. He was patience itself. He was waiting – waiting for the dung to harden. Then he'd lift it up with his beak. He'd turn it over and then (what he had been waiting for all along) there appeared before his eager eyes his next dinnertime banquet – all the little pink and blue maggots underneath the cooked lump of dung.

That old crow had patience. Imagine had patience too in her search for rare plants. The rest of us in Rookery Rally had patience as well – either in catching the little birds in our cage-traps or in setting out our snares for the rabbits. We were full to the gills with patience – all of us.

Patience Was Not Enough

But even that old fairy-woman, Patience, was soon seen not to be satisfied. Talk was one thing. Action was another thing. And some of our men said that it was high time for a change in our country – time to bite back and wave the green flag of Ireland above our heads. Above in The Big City there were men who had already run out of patience and were preparing to strike a blow for the freedom of our land. The streets of the city were soon to be turned upside-down. It was the holy season of Easter – a time when the world was saddened as it recalled the events that led to poor Jesus being strung up on his cruel cross. And just as Jesus had risen up from the dead it was now their own time (said the rebels in The Big City) to have a bit of guts and rise up and show their manly faces.

When a cow strays into a neighbouring field we hunt it back to where it came from (that's what they said). And the foreign settlers were in the wrong field (they said). And many of our own men in Rookery Rally had to agree with them. And some of our young men already began to make little escapades out into the hills where they started marching and drilling and preparing for the skirmishes that they knew would come. The Weeping Mollys reported what was already happening above in Currywhibble – not a mile from Rookery Rally. They had heard how Patsy Boon was daily leading his bands of young men as they came out from the church gates after Sunday Mass – leading them out passed The Valley of The Pig for the gun practising. Why on earth hadn't his mother been able to put a stop to him? For without proper army training he'd be of little use or no use at all when the call to take up arms was sounded. And indeed that same poor wretch was soon to be chased up into the hills at the foot of The Mighty Mountain where he starved to death beyond in Mureeny. May God be good to his soul – a youth with a heart and a love of his land and he dying at the tender age of thirty-three from neglect and consumption.

Whatever Would Happen Next?

Once more the women shook their heads and sighed – now that the fighting began to spread around The Big City and was soon to travel like an escaped fire down towards our countryside they could see that Rookery Rally was going to get a few licks of it before long and they were filled with worry – thinking which son of theirs might be killed in a battle before the year was out. Oh, the stupidity of our men (said they to one another). It was always the men (they said). It wasn't the women that forced themselves to lift the pitchfork or the pike in days gone by. It wasn't the women (they said) that went off to do the fighting to regain our land and suffer the dire consequences of even greater repressions against them and their race.

The Foreign Settlers

There was no need of a few gossipy women to keep the information flowing. The men were experts in passing choice bits of history onto their children as they sat on the lace of the ass-and-car on the road to the creamery. It was these bleddy foreign settlers (they said), who had forbidden us to speak our native tongue or dress in our traditional clothes – not even allowing us a chimney on our cabins so as to let the smoke out. It was the foreign settlers (they said), who had forced our ancestors to knock down their wretched cabins after the villains had set fire to the thatch and swathed the countryside in flames when the poor men hadn't the breath left in their bodies to pay the increased rent that the absentee landlord demanded from them. It was the foreign settlers who had forced them to walk the roads till they nearly dropped down dead – but not until they had been whipped back to the remains of their cabins and forced to collect the stones from the outside walls of their cabin so as to make a fine high tower for the foreign settlers to sit in and look out over their wide domain. Such was the picture that our men painted before the startled eyes of their children – such the way they poured their miserable hatred into their children's ears whilst they were trapped on the lace of the ass-and-car on their way to the creamery. And by the time they reached the creamery gates these bewildered children began to feel some of the men's hatred – a hatred that would soon be big enough to fill The Mighty Shannon River herself!

The Dam Was Broken

And now the dam of patience was broken and the haunting hour had come. There wasn't a man (even amongst those that were earning their keep below at The Big House) who wouldn't relish taking up the gun to destroy the presence of the foreign settlers for once and for all. For, when all the unravelling was done (and in spite of the kindly ways in which The Big House had always treated us) our men felt themselves tainted by the way the fat of our land had always come to belong to the rich oppressors alone.

Oppressors? Few grown men knew the meaning of this word. But, sitting on the upturned ass-and-car and playing with the cat and her kittens, even the children came to understand what their fathers' hearts were telling them: there'd be no satisfaction – not till the last of the foreign settlers had gone back over to John Bull could Rookery Rally and the rest of Ireland wash its hands in the River Laughter and perform the cleansing ritual.

Dowager Cursed Them

Dowager cursed out loud when she heard the men using such outrageous talk. She couldn't forgive them for their thoughts. In her as in many of the women who had worked in the service of The Big House there was stamped that little bit of light-hearted girlishness – that womanly feelings of Romance when she thought of the fine carriages and the fine men and women and they dancing their lives away. Handsome Johnnie, when he heard her whispering these thoughts into his ears in the marriage-bed would turn his back on her in disgust: 'Women and their dreamery (he'd say).' A stop would have to be put to it all.

It Was Not Going To Be Easy

But thanks to Imagine it was not going to be easy for the men to have it all their own way – despite the way they were nurturing their children in the school of hatred. The women's young friend had the manners and the means to counteract some of the rebelliousness growing in our midst. She was almost a big sister to our children. She allowed them to pat her pony. Then they ran back into The Welcoming Room and came back to feed Rosetta with generous handfuls of their mother's stolen icing sugar. Imagine handed them out sweets and gave them the odd little present such as the spinning top or the penny go-cart or even the wind-up clockwork car. The Christmas after her arrival she lit the little fairylights on her firtree in her yard. She put out a rich display of cakes and jellies and rice puddings for all the children. She gave them brightly-coloured parcels, one for each child.

Imagine that! Imagine that!

Delirious Leprechauns

The men stamped their feet like delirious little leprechauns:

Imagine was this!

Imagine was that!

Imagine was a right royal pain in the arse (they said).

She had become a goddess (they said) in the midst of the women and their children. She had flown down (they scoffed), from the heavens as though she was a pure angel. They could see (couldn't any fool) that it was into Imagine's face that the children spent their mornings gazing. They loved her. They took a pride in her that no man could fathom. It sickened them to death. For godsake, had their own children forgotten to love the land they were born and bred in?

The Time Came – It Had To

Then the time came (it had to come) – the time for Rookery Rally to take swift action and get back the land. The men knew that the British barracks above Lisnagorna had a dozen armed soldiers inside them to keep us poor scholars in our place. One fine morning the creamery carts were making a final push along The Saddleback Road from this side of The Limerick Glen. The men had chosen the older children to drive the procession of ass-and-cars on this last bit of the homeward jog. They would be unmolested by the soldiers. Amongst the milk tanks they were smuggling up to the rebels several rounds of gelignite.

When they reached the chosen spot in the pineforest the children handed the sticks of gelignite out among the men. By now it was noon. The men piled themselves and their sharp-shooting guns inside the ditch at the four sides of the barracks. A few of them ran out from the ditches and threw the gelignite in through the windows of the barracks. A few seconds later the barracks went up in shimmering flames. The eyes of the sharpshooters were fixed on the door and on the roof of the barracks. The young Tan soldiers staggered out helplessly onto the roof. They were like little bunny-rabbits that wait to be gunned down above in The Valley of The Black Cattle. The shrieks of them – they were shot to pieces and their bodies were left there to fall down into the flames. The men of resistance were seen to wipe the spit on their trouser-legs. They were shaking hands with a hatred that their women wouldn't have been able to comprehend or believe. And God in his heaven bowed down his head and wept.

The Priests

The church began to vilify these men and to excommunicate some of the more vicious ones and bar them from receiving the host in Holy Communion. The rebels sent the children with messages to the clergy house, which they posted through the door. The priests were being threatened and marked out for a bullet or two (said some of our fighting men) if they didn't guard their tongues on the altar and stick to their rosary-beads. No pope, no church would prevent the course of progress and quieten the urge to fight and restore the ownership of our land. Thus spoke the voice of the freedom fighters.

She Continued To Wander

As though nothing strange had occurred, Imagine continued to wander through the hills, the little poetess that she was. To give them their due, the rebels avoided confronting her. For even they were afraid of their own mothers and knew that the famed yardbrush would redden their arses if they so much as looked crooked at Imagine.

An Evening Came On

An evening came on, rosy and pink and with the setting sun covering the valleys of Rookery Rally. A haycart rolled along the mountain road from Slack-and-Tack. It drove in through the gates of The Big House. Tied together on the haycart were twelve mattresses to be delivered by way of the servant's back door: 'These are for the bedrooms,' said the haycart's driver. Inside the mattresses were a number of guns and ammunition for the hands of the rebels, who had staked themselves inside the back corridors of the servants' quarters or had hidden in the stables during the course of the night. The rebels had filled a bucket with gelignite and this was accompanied by a fuse and detonator – to be ignited during the night from a hundrd yards away behind the stableblock.

Boom! Boom! Boom!

And now events turned bleak. It was a windy night and during the early hours of the morning (heaven help us) The Big House – *BOOM! BOOM! BOOM!* – was shook with a mighty explosion and went up in iridescent bubbles of flame and heat, leaving nothing but a smouldering thirty-foot crater behind it. In their nightdresses the delirious servant-girls (and the sweat coming out of their foreheads) ran out onto the lawn with the fear that a rabbit feels before the eyes of the weasel. The sky was just a bruised orange fire with swirls of roaring grey and black clouds of ash and dust all around it. The curious cattle had come up onto the lawn to study the burning house. Miraculously (we later heard) there wasn't a headless beast amongst them. Curl 'n' Strpies' mischievous sheepdog (Swanky) was out chasing lambs and had run onto the lawn and scattered the entire herd. Not another soul (including Imagine) was hurt either – not one of the servants was hurt – not a stray cat or dog was hurt. However – Lord Plus-Fours, the old sourpuss, had had his tail well and truly singed (said the rebels) by the exploding bucket of gelignite. The Big House – symbol of the foreign settlers and of overseas rule – had vanished from view and lay in bits in the yard. Not a wrinkle of its former glory had the rebels left behind.

She Brought Out A Bag Of Straw

After setting Rosetta and the rest of the mares free from the stables, the bewildered Imagine came out in her jewelled slippers and her father's greatcoat. She brought out a bag of straw that had not yet been burnt. She placed it in the unscorched grass next to the lake where she had so often sat and fed her carp fishes. By now the wind had bundled the clouds of ash up high in the dappled moonlight. Limply and for a long while she sat on the bale of straw, silent and absorbed in the deepest shock. A slight rain (just a mist) was falling round her in the blackness. She leaned forward with her finger on her lips, shaking her head from left to right, demented.

'Imagine, oh imagine, that it should have come to this!' she cried as she tried to hold back her desperate sorrow and her salty tears flowed down the furrows of her nose and into the lake. Like Zachary in The Temple, Imagine began to stammer and stutter. She began to lose her powers of speech as she gazed at the destruction of her home . . . the unrecognisable bits of her furniture in the devastated rooms . . . the gilded pictures, the broken porcelain and her mother's grandfather clock – a gift to herself on her wedding day – now in sad pieces in the former hallway.

Before utterly losing her voice, she bawled out a last wailing cry – the final words the rest of the household would ever hear from her, as she lifted up her eyes to her ancestors beyond the clouds: 'I will stay here. I will die here in the flames of this fine house. Go on, you wicked cowards, shoot me down like a wild dog. Make an end to it all.'

What kind of a rape was this? It was as though she herself had been gotten hold of and utterly destroyed. How could the men of Rookery Rally have stooped so close to the gates of hell and dragged the heart out of her body? She might as well have been consumed in the flames?

The Women Hurried Down

When Dowager and Moll-the-Man came down they saw the place like a burial pall. They saw poor Imagine sitting beside the lake – shivering like a lost lamb – her once-stately face full of distressed tears and blackened with soot. They couldn't believe what had happened: their hearts couldn't swallow it and it made them shudder to see the state of Imagine. And as they cradled her in their arms and tried to whisper soft words of comfort to her, they heard the last croaky whispers she was ever to make: that as far as this world was concerned she was as good as gone from it – as good as dead. With the drizzle now thickening round them, they headed off home, the rest of the grey countryside again asleep and hushed. They knew that their young friend from over the water no longer wished to live. And it was then that the two women sat down and began to cry heart-achingly like two sick donkeys.

Imagine that! Can you imagine that!

Lord Plus-Fours

A drooping Lord Plus-Fours came out from the coach-house with the horse and carriage and took Imagine away. The next day The Creamery Road was full of dark shadow when the news got out that Imagine was gone. The children sat mournfully on the wobbly singletree and for once in their lives they didn't have a single word to say to one another.

The Heart-rending Journey

From Tipperary to the Big City was the most heart-rending journey that Imagine could have ever made. The reunion with her parents, when her husband drove her into the yard of The Big City mansion in Rathlofty, was a vale of heavy tears – almost as bad as when the women of Jerusalem cried their hearts out on meeting their beloved Jesus and he so utterly damaged and destroyed. What a difference a year had made. What a difference this journey was from the one Imagine once travelled with lightness of heart into Abbey Acres – herself and her grandfather clock and she coming here on her merry tippy-toes to celebrate her happy nuptials with Lord Plus-Fours. She would never recover from her grief and all her former beauty would disappear in the cloudy mists of a war-torn land.

Rathlofty

Imagine spent the rest of her days in Rathlofty. Within a short time she became a tired and withered old lady. Had it all been a dream, a nightmare? Who would have believed that her friends – the old Irish – would turn out to be so heartlessly cruel? Weeping a good deal each day, she could be seen gazing for long hours at a picture of her mother and her father on their wedding day where it hung on the dining room wall. Or else you'd find her sitting by the fire and pretending to read a newspaper though her disbelieving parents could see that the poor girl was plainly holding it upside-down.

The Dream

But maybe she still remembered (as Dowager hoped and prayed she would) the sweet kindness that Blue-eyed Jack had once bestowed on her. Maybe she'd remember the day when he rescued her pony, Rosetta, in the lightning storm and how she looked up into the charm of his cornflower blue Irish eyes.

The Children

A day or two later the children were sitting near the stream. In their dreamy little heads they began to compose a fairy-tale. They started to draw it on the flagstones with their pink and lavender stones from River Laughter. They drew pictures of a princess. And her name was Imagine. Beside her they drew her handsome prince. And his name was Blue-eyed Jack. What came next? They said that the happy couple leaped up onto the back of Rosetta-the-Pony. They said that Blue-eyed Jack clung onto her creamy mane. They said that Imagine clung onto her prince's waist. Then together they road away at top speed, up passed Sheeps Cross and off into the red sunset and out over The Mighty Mountain and away into the fluffy clouds.

They would draw these same pictures in their copybooks when they got to the schoolhouse. But, being young, they'd ask their master, Dang-the-skin-of-it, to write down their exact words for them. Yes – they would write of a poor Irish boy and a rich English lady. It would be a good fairytale, if only they could get the words down from their heads and into their hands and written down properly on paper.

Oh imagine it! Imagine the thought!

FOUR

How Bazeen took the world of Rookery Rally by storm.

His Ancestry

Let me tell you about Bazeen or rather (to give him his full credentials) Young Bazeen. He was a jocular old rogue whose years of laughter had left a hundred scaly wrinkles round his eyes – eyes that were always full of mischief. And this mischief (it was said) he'd inherited from his old grandmother (High Falootin'). His mother was Do-Little, who (as her name implied) had been as lazy as sin – never having had the energy to get out of bed and snag a few turnips or bring home a cartload of turf from the bog (Bazeen would tell you). His father was Old Bazeen and both himself and Do-Little had been dead since the time of Noah's Flood for nobody could remember either of them. The old fella had come back from The Indies – a place our ancestors knew as The Land of Phantoms and Mysteries wherein his own father (Aristotle, the harness-maker's son) – a man that lacked the vulgarities of his fellow Irishmen (he'd have told you) – had been stamping his army boots for many a year.

Aristotle himself had died abroad in those hot Indies and had never had the honour of getting back to us. For one fine day saw him and a host of army boys kicking a football round the army yard when the ball had the sad misfortune to fly into a lake. Aristotle proved himself the man-of-the-hour and bravely dived in to fetch it out so that he and his comrades could get on and finish the game. Sad to say he never rose up from the depths of the lake but got himself drowned. It was an unfortunate but appropriate ending for him (said his colleagues) for he had always been a terrible drunkard and it wasn't long after that when his wife (High-Falootin') came to an untimely end herself after a bite from a gnat.

Old Bazeen Came Home

So Old Bazeen came home. His likes were not to be forgotten for he brought back with him three huge blowpipes or whistles ranging from an inch to a yard in length. These he played night, noon and morning, frightening out of their lives the nearby fishes in Growl River. He became a sort of hermit for a while, spending most of his days hunting rabbits and fishing in Growl River for the wild salmon when the season allowed him to.

In some ways he proved no better than his father. There was a particular day when himself and his ass-and-car and the bags of messages that were heaped beneath the straw bag got damn near drowned abroad at The Furze-bush Bridge. His old ass (Jimmy) shied up into the air as the storm attacked him and he stuck the two jambs of the cart firmly across the road and into the ditch among the several furze-bushes that grew thereon. Whereupon the six pan-loaves and the two dozen sausages were pelted into the dyke and Old Bazeen (much to his surprise) was pelted into five feet of icy water in the river, leaving behind on the cart a dozen bottles of The Black Doctor safe and sound in a box for some honest traveller to come along and consume.

His Residence

And now, having dealt with his famed forebears, we must attend to Bazeen (Young Bazeen), the hero of our tale. There were times when he seemed at odds with the rest of the world – never happier than when he was riding his horse around the hills at any hour of the day or night, a sack on his shoulders against the wind and the damp. In this way he was a unique individual – with that bit of wildness in him which is a part of all mankind, but coming alive in only a few of us. He was sixty years old if a day and he spent his life in a ramshackle shack made out of grey quarrystones with a rusty bit of galavanize sheeting on it to make some sort of a roof. He lived (he'd proudly tell you) five miles from Anywhere-and-Nowhere – at any rate far away from any other habitation on God's earth – his house being in a deep hollow on the far side of The Mighty Mountain. Our children got a glimpse of it in the far distance when they were planking turf abroad in the bog. In their eyes it looked like the only house outside their known world. It was said that this old fellow lived halfways to heaven and halfways to hell. He had seven collie sheepdogs, five growing pups and their mother and father. They would tear the leg off of you if you dared cross over Bog Boundless and into the ten rushy fields that made up Bazeen's farm. We called his farm The Black Banks and we had a name for his shack – The Wild Domain.

Whenever he came home from The Roaring Town with his monthly supplies of flour and paraffin his patient little ass (Jimmy) knew the way damn near as good as Bazeen himself and didn't need a stick's prompt to his back as he led him up onto the far side of The Hills-of-The-Past and on through the heather of Bog Boundless before reaching Growl River. The two of them still wouldn't have reached there for there was still a small bit further before the ass would see a tiny red-coloured speck in the distance – Bazeen's palatial residence. Above and to the left of Bazeen was a hill shaped like the top of an egg. In the mists between day and evening it looked an almost magical place for the mists and the hill seemed to be fighting with each other so as to catch Bazeen's eye – and the red of the dying sun seemed to be forever above both the mists and the hill and trying to subdue the two of them.

Snug In His Nest

Most nights (and with nothing else to do) he spent his time listening to the north wind when it came roaring across from The Eagles' Nest and slapping the ivyclad hawthorn boughs off of the henhouse roof. On these occasions the windows shivered and the door shook and the horse's chains rattled on the nail on the partition. But little did he care about the vagaries of the stormy weather going on outside for he was bolted safely inside in his comfortable little nest by the fire. And that same fire was forever running like a steam-engine halfways up the chimney and holding him in its spell. He was as comfortable as the crickets in under the turf in the box – as snug as the two pet cats in under the rickety stool beneath the hob and he cared not a fig for the outside world or the cold or the ice or the winds or the river when in spate – as long as he had his blazing turf fire and a box full of logs and a constant supply of smoke belching out from the chimney. Indeed he'd tell you (and he often told the rest of us) that he was as content in mind and body as the sad-looking king seated on his throne beyond in The Land of John Bull.

His Horses At The Show-Fair

Apart from his dogs Bazeen had a fine herd of black cattle. He also kept a dozen black horses and had been schooled in horsefare since his earliest childhood under the scrutinous eye of Old Bazeen. How often had he taken one of the old man's young mares to the stallion and after the stallion had finished his work and climbed down off of the mare – how often had he spent the rest of the morning petting her and rubbing his neck against her jaw and all the time whispering his childish words of comfort into her ear and wiping the saliva from her heated lips and nostrils. And ah – what fine foals he used to get!

Come The Fifteenth Of August

Every year, come the fifteenth of August, he came across Growl River and entered his finest mare for The Big Cup at the County Show-Fair in The Roaring Town. He returned home most years empty-handed but there were times when he (poor farmer though the townies sneeringly thought him to be) won the blue rosette against the rich gentlemen farmers who used The Show-Fair as a shop-window for displaying their successful horse-breeding.

The Show-Fair

The Show-Fair was a day of carnival – a day of merrymaking – with crowds from all over the countryside and they more plentiful than buttercups in

May – and they brimful of vigour – and they all jostling and roistering and frightening the hens and geese out of the road as they dropped down from the hills, the bushes beckoning them on towards the town. It was better than a travelling circus. There'd be fortunetellers dressed in their coloured brilliance of shawls and scalves – their arms and ears jingling with golden ornaments. There'd be young lads trying to climb out along the greasy pole to snatch the fletch of bacon before slipping into the nearby stream or else trying to pelt the wheatsheaf over the high crossbar or vault over the five-bar gate. All the priests and the big-wigs would be there with their tall hats and their brilliantined hair. Nobody would do a hand's turn of work and the hay-making could go to hell with every man reaching for his well-angled cap and his Sunday suit and his boots greased with lard and he shaved clean like a new saucepan. And throughout the long day (need I tell you) every man-jack-of-us would help himself to at least a dozen glasses of The Black Doctor or the firewater that was our own rawgut whiskey.

Bazeen Got Ready

The morning of The Show-Fair came on. It found Bazeen full of new life and happiness as he rubbed the sleep out of his eyes. He dressed himself up like a colourful maypole – nothing less than a wedding-day look about him with all the preparations and the pompadouring – his best brown suit on him, his boots as polished as a cherry, his hat cocked cheekily on his poll. He glanced out from the half-door to where the sun had swept in through a wedge-like gap in the hills. It was splendid weather (as you'd expect in August) and not a cloud shadow to be seen. He crossed his yard where the same sun was already burning the feathers on the backs of his ducks and hens. He climbed over the gate and into the haggart and went on towards the misty hill to inspect his cattle and horses before setting out for town. The grass had shot up everywhere – great days for his animals.

He was ready for the road and he pondered to himself: wasn't he the man with the finest of cattle and with horses blacker than soot? Then he had another little thought. He was getting no younger. There was no-one that he could pass on his good fortune to. The Show-Fair, however, was his one good chance of introducing himself to that oft-dreamed-of schoolteacher or nurse, whose good nature might not forbid her coming out the hill and helping him clean off the maggots from the wool of his sheep – whose ladylike nose mightn't object to a bit of horseshit here and there.

Beauty

You'd give your two eyes to see his lean-legged mare this festival day – Beauty – to see the sharply-pointed face of her and her inky black eyes shining like winter berries, so well had Bazeen been feeding her. Her chest was a picture of knotted muscles and he had plaited her thick tail and mane the night before. He had brushed and currycombed her hide till you'd see your face in it, smudging her all over with the paraffin rag to keep the flies off of her. Her hooves and fetlocks he had polished till they shone like a new pin.

He Prepared To Mount

At last he tightened up the saddlegirth and prepared to mount his horse-and-cart, his spanking Beauty high-stepping gently along behind him. 'Ah! (he thought) we'll show those feckin townies a thing or two – them and their grand and haughty ways and not one of them fit to set eyes on me and mee Beauty'. Then Beauty herself pricked up her ears and fanned out her nostrils as though she had to agree with him.

The Town At Last

By now the sun was high in the sky and spotlighting Beauty's fine hooves. They passed The Halfway Pump and Bazeen could see ahead of him the town's church steeple stabbing at the sky. There was a great deal of commotion and merriment when the townies beheld him waving his stick of salutation at them and with his high-legged Beauty skelping sparks off of the road and he himself standing up jauntily in his cart and uttering words of endearment to his flawless mare ('No harsh horsewhip for you, mee Beauty – you know the way to the arena as good as meeself'). As they neared the outskirts you'd think that The Daffy-Duck Circus was on its way – so great were the shouts of the raucous, red-faced townies (especially the women) when they met Bazeen at The Sheep Fields to accompany him in over The Limerick Bridge on the final stage of his journey.

By now the children from the town had left their houses and had run down Jinnet Street to greet him. They were dressed up for The Show-Fair in their best corduroy britches and their pretty coloured frocks with flowers like wallpaper on them. They had never seen Bazeen before and, joining in with the crowd, they followed him on till he came out over the railway. He'd arrived. The stupendous roars of everyone echoed off of the railings behind him, frightened the moody sheep on the other side of the ditch. The very bricks of the houses seemed to re-echo with laughter at the sight of Bazeen. 'If it's mee coat ye want, ye can have it,' he screamed. He threw off his long ginger coat and stamped on it in mock rage, letting the townies know how rich a man he was – a man who owned seven dogs and a dozen horses, not to mention the black cattle that kept the green rushes down in his fields along The Black Banks.

There was ample reason for all the hullabaloo for Bazeen (in spite of his lovely brown suit) was in sharp contrast to his wondrous mare. He was as thin as a shadow from living on meager lentils and nettles. His skin was gaunt – the colour of mouldy grass and he was wearing his father's cheap green-pea shirt (three sizes too big for him). His broken teeth were the colour of mustard and matched his long ginger greatcoat to perfection.

'Will ye look at the dandified spindleshanks and he dressed up like a wild tinker,' smiled Goggles (the Town Clerk) when he saw Bazeen passing by Cash's Sawmill with those thin spindly legs of his and his arms like two matchsticks and not a muscle on him. Unlike the other handsome Show-Fair entrants (among them the debutantes with the stamp of John Bull written all over them) he had no colourful uniform to his name, no hard collar for so grand an occasion – just his greasy cap (though he wore it with the peak-button undone and at a gallant angle so as to put on a bit of a show). However – hadn't he a head of hair that was truly beautiful? Of course you never saw it – unless the townie damsels took a notion to toss off his cap and pelt it to one another.

When he heard that Bazeen had arrived and had taken off his cap and was waving it at all and sundry Tom Slappity (the town barber) left his customers staring into space and came rushing out to inspect the famed head of hair. It was as black as the ace of spades – with the blue sheen in it that you saw on a carrion crow or a jackdaw. The fleas, (if what Bazeen said was true) had made a noble shine in his hair with their spittle and grease. Wasn't he the lying hound?

The Laughter Increased

The laughter increased as Bazeen and his cart (and Beauty following behind) came into the centre of the elegant town itself – its little houses with their wrought-iron railings and well-clipt box hedges and the sidepaths all lined with chestnut trees. And for Bazeen the excitement increased with each stride – the brightness of the other high-stepping horses and the thud of their hooves and not a single trace of horsedung on any of them. To think that he, a man that lived a stonethrow from the doors of heaven and hell, was about to mix with such townie hobnobs. And no horse or man (said he to himself) was going to stand in his way this blessed day. We heard his lofty voice ringing in our ears: 'In with ye, mee Beauty, and show what ye're made of in front of this shower of dungheap townies who know not a horse's head from its arse.' This outrageous outburst was met with even more uproarious laughter and loud applause.

He reached Bank Cross and stopped: 'Stand back, ye halfbaked articles from the town,' shouted the wild man. 'Stand back, I say. And ye that have mares, let ye bring them out to the hill and we'll give ye the finest of foals out of mee best black stallion (Midnight).' There followed a bout – this time – of honest cheering rather than jeering and the odd cap was thrown into the air out of muted respect.

Bazen paid them little or no heed: 'Here I am,' he shouted as he warmed to his theme and saw the sudden good nature of the townies: 'Ye see before ye the wild man, Bazeen – himself in the flesh – the old fairyman and his ramshackle bit-of-a-mare – the man from outside yeer world – the man that never washes his body and lives on the hairy meat of his many horses.'

Goosey-Goosey-Gander's Yard

A few yards further up the road he entered Goosey-Goosey-Gander's yard and left the cart there. Taking a long reins and the halter from under the latboard, he fixed them on Beauty. They were ready to parade in high fashion along the route leading to Summer Hills and The Show-Fair. They snailed their way through the crowd and on towards the end of Jinnet Street and The Market-Square. Then they turned right towards the field that had been set aside for the show.

Two young Guards, merely a day or two away from their recent schooldays, leaned out over the balustraded balcony at Mount Monastery Hotel. Taking off their peaked caps they pointed at Bazeen: 'Is this the same old scarecrow as last year,' they shouted, 'the mountainy man with the same green shirt on him (or so it's rumoured) night and day these last forty years – the shirt that he never washes?' They scratched their heads. It was a grand title for a song (they thought) and they shared a bout of sniggery laughter. Bazeen merely showed them his teeth, which were as yellow as his mare's: 'The fleas keep me company at mee daily work and warm me in mee bed at night,' he roared. This was followed up with cackling screams-of-alarm from the surrounding women (the little devils). You'd think our wild man had tried to raise their skirts!

He Lumbered On

Gnashing what remained of his teeth, Bazeen turned away from The Guards and nudged along till he and his beautiful mare came to Bacon Street where they'd have to turn right again towards the white gates and the loudspeakers in The Show-Fair. Enjoying the limelight, he made a few mock attempts (the little show-off) to control Beauty's high-stepping prancing as she danced her giddy way up towards what remained of the former army barracks (they were nothing but a pile of rubble these days). And again came the roars of the townie children that were following him: 'Stand back, lads! Stand back! Here comes the man from beyond the world'. Their red-faced mothers laughed and sniggered behind their cuffs with no attempt to admire either Bazeen or his fine-looking mare: 'Isn't this the man,' said Tenderfoot when he saw Bazeen struggling to hold back his mare with the long reins, 'who was lately the inventor of new tricks at The Kindy-Wells Regatta – the man that went about showing us how to water-ski the length of the lake?'

And now – hemmed in as he was by the growing crowds – Bazeen found himself occasionally thrown hither and thither amidst the swirling mass. At times he was seen tumbling headlong through a forest of legs, his embarrassed boots suspended in the air. At other times his mare doubled back on him indecisively when the roar of the crowd got her too excited. On these occasions and to everyone's joy Bazeen had to lean back on the heels of his boots at an almost impossible angle in case Beauty might bolt outright from him. Merciful God – would he ever reach The Show-Fair? Would he ever get through the dense throng of people who were rushing full tilt all round him?

The Spiteful Fairies

Woe and alas – The Spiteful Fairies were about to come into town and a small catastrophe was already lurking behind Bazeen and ready to waylay the poor man: 'Keep back! Keep Back, let ye!' said the crowd. 'Can't ye see that the little man wants to get through?' How moods can change. Once more there was jealousy – almost mockery – in their eyes – in their voices – to think that a nonentity-of-a-farmer from the hills would have the nerve to enter his mare among the classical beasts of the rich lowlanders. But the jaunty Bazeen proudly held up his head as he endeavoured to walk on. He let out the long reins on its halter so as to clear a pathway for himself. It was surely forty-feet long and it showed off his mare to full advantage.

Himself and Beauty had arrived at The Old Bakery at the end of Jinnet Street. That's where misfortune in the shape of those Spiteful Fairies came out to greet him. For Beauty, on seeing a well-endowed stallion ahead of her, flaired up her nostrils and raced off smartly in the direction of this fine-looking beast: it was as though she suddenly had ten legs on her. There followed an embarrassing tug-of-war between herself and Bazeen as our wild man dug in his heels a second time in a desperate effort to control her: 'Sight (blasht ye)! Sight! – for the love of Jaysus will ye sight?'

Sensing the occasion, the crowd dug in behind him and endeavoured to haul Beauty back on the reins. But, feeling the fun and the playfulness – the tension of the crowd – and forgetting her own natural shyness, she increased her pace and (by her very strength) rolled the crowd along in her wake – dragging them whersoever she wished in a bid to reach the stallion and introduce herself to him. The sweating Bazeen – the overheated Beauty – the laughing crowd, whose earlier merriment had now reached a crescendo – no amusement this memorable day could surpass it.

And then that old slyboots (The Devil himself) came out to play and he whispered a little sin into the heart of the crowd. For suddenly they let loose the reins behind Bazeen. Ah, the heathens – to do such a thing! Quicker than quicksilver the shocked Bazeen was catapulted through the intervening space between himself and Beauty. The frightened mare twisted herself and the reins and her master round the nearest telegraph-pole till it became an entangled mess of complex knots, almost strangling poor Bazeen and his gasping lungs. There followed a roar of mock approval and handclapping from the gaping onlookers. Ah, ye ghosts of Beauty's parents – how well did ye come back to reward poor Bazeen for the times he repeatedly loaded yeer animal backs with the heavy baskets of turf, marching ye out to the bog and back to the shed the livelong day! Was there none of the townies here to show a bit of pity for the wild man and his plight?

Out stepped Rambling Jack (his finest hour) in a noble effort to soothe the startled Beauty. He could see she was like a newborn calf with a river of sweat running down her flanks. With what patience did he untangle the man and the beast from the post. He lit a Woodbine fag and handed it into the shaking fingers of the bedraggled Bazeen: 'Thank God for the invention of the telegraph-pole,' gasped Bazeen when he finally came to his senses. 'I thought I'd be killed. Were it not for the pole entrapping us, both meeself and Beauty would have travelled clean out of the town and as far as Dublin and the moon'

The Huge Big Cup

Some people laugh sooner. Some people laugh later. A little later on in the day the houses re-echoed to the shouts of Bazeen. He was shining like the noonday sun. 'By the powers of heaven (they said) – who is this wild man (can it be Bazeen?) sweeping triumphantly round the corner of Jinnet Street with a rolling cloud of dust behind him. Bazeen was riding his cavalier mare in a new and unaccustomed way, kneeling his two knees on her back? 'Why – it's that old devil, Bazeen (sighed the crowd) – yes, the one and only wild man.' Ah, the triumph! Our hero was carrying The Huge Big Cup and it twinkling with medallions of silvery light and not one but three coloured ribbons dangling down from it (the red and the green and the blue). Fair play to you, Wild Man! Fair play to you, Beauty! Glorious the radiance of yeer eyes!

What a change can take place in such a short space of time. Bazeen was now the crowds own darling (especially among the women). There was an honest-to-goodness tear in the eyes of many and the appearance of Bazeen was no longer thought angry or comical. He was back to his radiant self – the man we saw regularly in Rookery Rally when he came down among us for his monthly messages. Indeed he had the noble look of the honourable Lord Plus-Fours himself. It was Bazeen's finest day – the day when he came into his own – when himself and Beauty walked away with The Huge Big Cup. And it went down in history. Enough said.

His Special Talent

One way or another neither the derision nor the applause of the townies meant a fig to Bazeen; there was nothing he needed from any of them. During the summer season, apart from The Show Fair and his prizes at the horseshowing, he could count on another singular way of earning his keep in front of the town's celebrities. He had an act, which was even more profitable to his back pocket than the money the town's Misty-Man earned in his races against the lame hare along the wire-netted stretch of The Callow Field. Bazeen's act was a good bit more hazardous than lads sliding the length of the greasy pole to catch the fletch of bacon before falling into the water. Indeed – it was not to be surpassed till many years later when one or two simpletons would dare take themselves up in the rusty buckets-of-aeroplanes for a quick spin round Tipperary.

Inside The Gateway

Inside the gateway of The Showground the visitors would gather to witness Bazeen and the barrel he had fetched from behind his half-door; it was like the one kept in everyone's Welcoming Room for the dead pig's salted pieces. Wherever you went (be it the Daffy-Duck Circus or The Kindy-Wells Regatta) the famed Bazeen took this barrel along with him. He filled it with wattlesticks three feet-long, all neatly paired and painted by his own fair hand in the red-lead paint of the horse's carts. On a fine sunny day it was sure to put everyone in the best of humour.

With a large crowd, eagerly anxious to witness the suicidal spectacle ('Cripes, byze,' said Tom Tatters, ' it isn't every day you get the chance to see a man killed') the brave Bazeen marched to the spot where he had set up his marker (it had been the same every year for the past ten years) twenty yards inside Jimmy's Gate at the northern entry to The Showground. This was a sensible arrangement since Doctor Glasses and the little yellow-faced ambulance-man might have to come out at a moment's notice and put a few quick stitches in Bazeen's sorry head – or else bandage him up like an ancient Egyptian mummy before pronouncing him altogether dead during the proceedings of the barrel and the wattlesticks.

He Stripped Down To The Waist

It was summer and the sun was beating down relentlessly. Bazeen stripped down to the waist. Who would have thought there was so much stockiness in a little man we thought hadn't a muscle on him? He lined up the sticks in a circle some twelve paces away from the barrel. He then began twisting himself down into the barrel: 'Roll up! Roll up!' he roared, inviting us all to let fly our sticks at him and offering a pound-note to any man who could knock out his brains – what he called his *hunger money*, though some of us called it his *danger money* as he was no longer so young or subtle-limbed that he could promise himself not to get hurt. It was a fair enough challenge. Who could resist the offer to knock the head out of his impudent skull?

Finally he was hidden inside in his barrel. For a minute there was pure silence round the ground. Then we heard the rumbling sound of Bazeen's echoing voice ('God made the sky for the crows – he made the barrel for meeself') coming up from inside the hollow barrel. We gasped at the sight of him. His antics were followed by a few scandalous farts (if he could rustle them up). Their echoes made us laugh our sides off. Then like some charmed snake Bazeen appeared – rising up mesmerisingly – slower and slower – from his hidey-hole in the barrel: 'Will ye look at the cocky smirk of the little ape,' laughed the women good-naturedly. We had seen it all before. It'd soon be time for their men to pelt their wattlesticks at Bazeen's head. You could never hit the wily devil. If only one of their fathers (sighed the children) could hit him on the nose and give him the finest of headaches next morning. If only we could see him stretched out dead before the end of the day (the rest of us thought), it'd be good enough for the old heathen.

He Weaved And Stretched Like A Snake

Bazeen rose up from the barrel a few more times – stretching out his unsteady arms and bending his skinny elbows. He weaved his head from side to side, his popping eyes widely scanning the crowd – behind and in front of him – to see which of the pelters was likely to get an accurate pelt into the side or back of his head. You'd die at the sight of him – his eyes glittering earnestly – grimacing like a monkey – poking out his tongue at the rest of us poor scholars and making lewd gestures with his thumb and forefinger.

And now the fun began. Bazeen opened wide his mouth. It was studded with broken and rotten teeth. We could scarcely hold back our merry tears of laughter. In a commanding voice and with his hands held aloft and he brandishing his fists at the sky – he started blistering the air with thunderous curses. These he rained them down in an unprintable list of vile obscenities on our pedigrees, defiling the ears of our women and goading our men to pelt at him and try and kill him: 'Coom on, ye basthards! Ye feckin whoors, tell me this – what were yeer mothers doing in under the bedsheets to have produced such manly specimens as yeerselves?

No-one had yet picked up a stick. They knew they were about to get a few better curses from the filthy tongue of the little jay-actor before long.

In language that only he could produce he proceeded to give them what they were looking for – complimenting the comely shapes and stature of the men's growing sisters and daughters – their innocent virtues – their virginal stature, which had unfortunately been recently lost (he claimed) through the delightful lusts of himself. He had had (he vowed) the personal satisfaction of ravishing most of them and he intended to finish the job before the summer was out.

'Why – the filthy little fecker!'

That was enough for every man in sight. Much to Bazeen's delight the men took off their coats and spat on their fists as if they were about to chop wood. The pelting of the wattles began to rain down like fair hell on his barrel. As soon as they heard the sound of the murderous wattles rapping off of the sides of Bazeen's barrel, the crowds left off whatever else they were doing at the other end of the field and gathered round the gateway. Bazeen continued to stand his ground though the fierce noise of the wattles must have punctured his two ears as he ducked and weaved away from each pelt. By this time we were in spasms of pure delight and an absolute lust to half-kill the rascal was all round the ground.

'Ye could give a day pelting yeer wattles at the little short-arse,' said Tenderfoot, 'but ye'd never kill the whoor.' Nobody was listening to him.

'Let me at the little fecker,' was heard again and again.

'May the Devil burn blisters on his arse,' said others.

'Pon-mee-sowl, byze – Il'll knock the thundering shite out of his britches,' said a good few more, the spits continuing to fly out of their mouths.

But after each lungful of air the wily Bazeen sucked himself down again quicker than a fox and hid himself at the bottom of the barrel. We waited and waited (would he ever rise up again?) and the children wondered if someone had already killed the poor man outright. And as we kept our eyes fixed on the barrel we offered up our prayers to the skies: 'Dear God-in-Heaven, if you or The Blessed Virgin would send us (just this once) an accurate pelter to knock Bazeen's arse sideways and put a stem of sense into his eejity old head!' And some of us shook our heads and wondered was it worth the poor fellow's life to get the heap of coins and notes that we'd be throwing into his barrel when the show was over? In the meantime, however, Bazeen's two sides were bursting from the merriment of it all.

Tenderfoot

Tenderfoot was a man known for his astute turn of mind. He was now sucking on his pipe and pondering the course of events – pondering it very well. At last he came up with a wonderfully roguish idea. He called his daughter to his side and gave her a fatherly nudge. Then he whispered laughingly into her ear. She was Noolah – an agile sixteen year-old from up the country and with dimples on her. You only had to look at her to see that she was at an age when her ripeness was just ready for any apple-picker amongst our men. She was full of vitality – with the freshness of a lump of rhubarb on her and blithe and comely in all her limbs. Enough said

She now proved herself the little hussy-one and not one bit shy. She shook her delicate curls at her father, feigning a bit of childish embarrassment and she began furtively fidgeting with the hem of her flouncy dress. Of course Tenderfoot knew only too well what the result of his infernal plan was going to be. He hadn't the slightest doubt that it might fail him.

Rambling Jack was standing not far from Tenderfoot and his daughter: 'What on earth are the saucy little madam and her father up to this time?' said he to himself. 'What are they planning for the great Bazeen? I wonder. Hymmph.'

Noolah Lifted Her Skirt

When Bazeen next raised his head from out of the barrel, Noolah lifted the hem of her skirt (just the corner of it) – ever so slowly. When she was sure she had Bazeen's full attention the little teaser started murdering him with her upturned eyes. She started to lift the hem a little bit more and a little bit more – her impudent father giving her the wink and the nod.

The next time Bazeen rose up from the barrel she showed him just that little bit of the delicate elastic round her lavender knickers, giving him a taster of it. She began stroking the inside of her soft white thigh with her delicate fingers

You poor open-mouthed eejit, Balzeen! What on earth got into you? For once in his life he had turned himself into an ass looking at a juicy thistle. In his moment of anguish he found his eyes gawping at Noolah's legs – gawping at the white thighs of her – gawping at the lovely knickers of her. His distraction was utter and complete for at that precise moment he had lost his heart to the wonder of this fiercesome young beauty and for the first time ever he remembered . . . absolutely nothing!

Oblivion!

There was not even a squeal of protest out of him. He never felt the pelt of Tenderfoot's mighty wattle as it sailed towards his impudent skull. Its accuracy left the poor man stretched out for dead, gazing lifelessly up at the sky. Would we ever forget it? For no man before had ever hit the invincible head of Bazeen. The startled crowds elsewhere, who'd been watching the little piggy races and the pelting of the sledge, rushed straightaway over to the barrel to see if the great entertainer was alive or dead.

His arms were dangling crookedly out over the edge of the barrel. His glazed eyes were fixed on the sky. His face was transfigured with blood as though a weasel had been attacking him. He was now a mere shadow of his cocksure self and a match for a graveyard ghost. Some of the women blessed themselves. Some of them knelt down and said a silent prayer for him. Others were only too glad to fire fistfuls of money into his barrel. Tenderfoot showed a bit of remorse and sent for the priest to come and save Bazeen's soul. He was sure the great entertainer was dead, having been hit by at least a dozen other wattles before he finally collapsed. We were all full of commiseration for Bazeen. In doublequick time a few stout lads lifted his tortured body into the air and carried him out Jimmy's Gate. The children all followed out the gateway behind them. It was not often that they saw a man dead. Rambling Jack and Tenderfoot then took over and carefully laid Bazeen and his barrelful of wattles into the ditch to wait for The Roaring Town's ambulance-driver to come speeding to the scene and mend the poor man's head (if at all possible) or carry his misfortunate corpse into The Mortuary. The news of Bazeen's disaster would spread far and wide throughout Rookery Rally and up as far as Currywhibble and the rest of north Tipperary. And in the meantime the brass band kept playing and filling our ears with *Way down upon The Swanny River* – to give us a bit of good cheer after this very sad event.

'You Couldn't Kill The Whoor'

However, you couldn't kill the likes of him. A tearful Bazeen would live to tell the tale of it and his cuts and bruises would recover before we knew it. For a few hours later (with half a dozen brandies stuffed down his belly as a solace for his misery) he had fire again in his eyes and was as right as rain: 'To hell with the basthards (said he to himself).' For by this time he had gathered in enough money from his barrel-antics to keep him in strong drink for the rest of the year. And (said he) nobody but himself would ever know the depths of his lustful dreams in his bedroom that same night: they'd be full of a summer day's frolicking and fun – full of the teasing and tussling he'd be doing in the tender arms of that fair young hussy-one, Noolah, and her fleshy lavender knickers.

His Fishing-days

Apart from his outing with Beauty to The Roaring Town Show-Fair and his entertainment with the barrel and wattles a good deal of his time was taken up with his jar of maggots from the dungheap and his fishing lines. All households had one good hazel-rod; he had half-a-dozen of them. He spent most of the day fishing scrupulously till evening greyed over him and the night came on. This would be just after the heavy rains came across The Mighty Mountain and when the waters were troubling themselves in Growl River – a time when the brown trout crept up from their slumbers, urged on by the changes in the rush of water and the excursions of little evening midges.

If you were brave enough to trudge your way across the heather of Bog Boundless and look for his rusty-roofed residence and his seven sharp-toothed dogs, you'd find his six rods strapped to the bushes – spaced out evenly along both banks of Growl River and left bending there throughout the night. By morning's light he was sure to have six of the best trout for his breakfast. These (if we were to believe him and his unbelievable lies) he ate half-raw and gave a good heap of the leftover fish to his adoring dogs. He suggested (the wag that he was) that we should do the same as himself – eat our few mackerels half-raw when we brought them back from town after selling our pigs.

Himself And His Wild Birds

In addition to his head-shattering work inside the barrel and his skill with his six fishing-rods he had a special relationship with wild birds. It was a gift in him. Each morning he had his ears cocked for the sound of birds outside his window. Roused by the sunshine of the early morning light, he heard them fluttering and twittering in the branches before he could ever see them. He loved their songs and was never as happy (it was a ritual for him) as when he was walking through the woods and watching the sky and listening to their many birdsongs. These were the times when he felt most keenly the presence of his forefathers' ghosts around him. He sat in the long grass for many afternoons trying to catch the meaning of the little birds' talk. And soon he found that his own soul was at one with them and that he had the gift of imitating many birds' whistles – their mannerisms of headshaking and feather-fluffing. He loved the times when the birds were teaching their fledglings to take to the wing – flying away from them to the nearby branches and teasing them to follow on. For a finish he was able to understand the feeble younger crows and their eight squawky *caws*, which meant that they were in need of food and protection. He could understand how the three *caws* from the mother crow to her young ones meant 'take good care, my little children!'

However – though he had the measure of each of his birds, his favourite was the pretty jaybird, whose mimicry was famous amongst us all. He brought home a young jay (no more than a fledgling) and held it in his fist and began to stroke its feathers and with kindly words to train it to mimic a farmer's voice when urging the horses to plough: 'Coom oop! Coom oop! Blasht you, coom oop!'

He then cured a wild cuirlew's wing but it was unable to fly thereafter. Each day it fluttered round the house and played on his shoulder. He decided to build it a wicker cage, which he hung on the wall next to The Sacred Heart picture. For a finish he had a way of trapping several other birds inside a number of these hazel-wand cages – birds of every variety that filled The Welcoming Room and kept him company day and night. The din inside the half-door was incredible (worst than the wattles hammering on his barrel) and they shared his sleeping quarters next to his settlebed on the floor beside the turf-fire. Oh, the glory of it all! He loved the birds. The birds loved him.

His Revenge On Tenderfoot

Some time later the enlightened Bazeen and his well-practiced young jaybird took themselves off to Tenderfoot's Seventh Field for a morning's outing and an act of sweet revenge. He crept carefully through the briars outside the ditch. He removed the bed-sheet that covered the jaybird's cage and whispered *'coom oop! coom oop, blasht you!'* into the little bird's ear. The two of them had been practicing this saying for hours on end – ever since the day of his disaster in the barrel. Whereupon his noble jaybird gave out the same order (*'coom oop! coom oop, blasht you!')* to the two startled horses of Tenderfoot, the unbounded rogue who had almost split Bazeen's head in two with the pelt of his wattles.

Tenderfoot's surprised horses started off at a tidy gallop, unmercifully twisting the poor man's face and body in the distorted reins as they hurried on across the flinty stones, dragging his body along the ground behind them. You'd think that the midday horse-bee had gotten in under the horses' smelly tails in search of the sweet ammonia scent that lay around their arses. It was a merry little scene and Bazeen ('How do you like your plough-horses, Tenderfoot?') had a stitch in his sides from the fits of laughter he took when he heard the curses of Tenderfoot ('Ye feckin' little shitty-arse, ye won't have an inch of flesh on yeer hide when I get hold of ye.') raining down on him and his kinfolk back three generations. Bazeen ran back home – thoroughly satisfied with the work of his coached jaybird against Tenderfoot and his impudent daughter, Noolah. His revenge had been utter and complete.

His Whiskey-making Still

Even if they didn't own one, most houses in Rookery Rally had the use of the still and the wire copper worm, which let out the precious potheen in delicate and delicious droplets of rawgut whiskey. The result was guaranteed to strike a man's eyes like a sword for it would deliver him the gift of Absolute Unconsciousness, dropping him into a sleep that would last till noon the next day. Oh, the beauty of it! The women of course were sick to the gills of their husbands swallowing jarfuls of this unwanted medicine: 'Blasht the potheen medicine!' they cried. They hated the smell of the drink and what it did to their men. It would have been the better of two evils if the men had remained below in Curl n Stripes' drinking-shop with their fists wrapped round a glass or two of The Black Doctor.

When summer was over and when boredom was likely to rule, Bazeen had prepared a still in his outhouse by the river. He soon found himself a market for making this unearthly medicine. Men in their crowds stayed away from Curl 'n' Stripes' drinking-shop and began to pay Bazeen regular visits – in spite of his seven savage dogs. They came as far as the banks of Growl River, their eyes glistening. They called across the waters to him. This was especially true at the time of The Harvest Dance and when The Hunting-of-The-Wran masquerade was approaching. They took buckets of his potheen away with them to celebrate properly these grand occasions and weren't happy till they had given it their heart and soul and had squeezed out the last drop of it from the buckets.

And just as the little woodland creatures store their nuts and relics for the hard days and then go and hibernate into a prolonged sleep, so too did these heroes store their jars of potheen in remote fields where their women couldn't get the raw smell of it. And when the days of all the seasonal merriment was over, these sound men followed up their bouts of drinking with snores that would have woken the dead in the graveyard in Abbey Acres – snores (said Dowager) that'd make a fine Cork orchestra throughout the length and breadth of Rookery Rally.

Where Are Ye Off To?

All this was the devil's nuisance for the women: 'Where are ye off to?' they'd say.

'To see the black doctor,' was the lying reply.

But when the women turned back to the fire to see to their burner of spuds and cabbages, the men had beaten a hasty scuttle up the hills to Bazeen's shack and to get a taste of the unmerciful medicine, which he had prepared as a royal treat for them from his still. Before the year was out it seemed as though he had charmed half of the men in the two parishes of Mureeny and Copperstone Hollow with his famed potheen.

All Were Caught In His Snares

It could be said that men and birds alike had been caught in Bazeen's captivating snares. For by this time the birds that he'd enticed into his hazel cages were as tame as himself. And whenever he wished to free one or two of them (his cabin becoming overcrowded and he not having the means to feed them all) it was not unusual for him to take a little bird in his fist and, stroking its beak, set it free from the front window with a prayer on its wings. But the loveable little creature (so well did all the birds warm to Bazeen) would come back in through the back window all over again. Clearly there was no way he was able to persuade any of his birds to leave him for good. He was like a kiss on their little souls and with no glass to his windows he was unable to prevent them coming back to him. What a performance! By this time he had realized that not only had he charmed the birds but that these little creatures had completely charmed himself – a marriage made by the saints above!

His Two Fiddles

Hanging on Bazeen's back wall were the two red fiddles of his father (Old Bazeen). The former gentleman had made fiddles out of the three traditional types of wood – fiddles sealed together uniquely from his homemade recipe for the tarry pitch that sealed the woods and gave them their sound. This (alas) and other family recipes Old Bazeen had taken to his grave with him.

As a small child Bazeen remembered his father sitting in a big tin bath on Saturday evenings and washing himself for Mass in front of the blazing fire and rasping away at the fiddle there in the bath for all he was worth. At the same time he kept one eye on the frying-pan where he (Young Bazeen) was learning to fry up a plateful of sausages for the two of them.

Although he wasn't able to follow in his father's footsteps in the making of these delicate fiddles, the music had forevermore throbbed in Bazeen's head and he could play both his fiddles with a haunting charm that'd make beautiful pictures rise up inside your head. Indeed that was why the birds came into Bazeen's hazel-wand cages in the first place – that is why they stayed with him till they died of old age. They simply loved to hear his fiddle-playing.

The Daily Fiddle

Each day our wild man spent a little while visiting his horses and his cattle on The Black Banks. He talked to them – the same way he talked to his birds. He examined the cattle for the various maggots and insects that could afflict them. He looked at his horses' teeth. Then he came home. If the day was warm and calm he sat on his chair outside his half-door beside the river. He played his lovely slow airs. Then he played his polkas, jigs and reels. He played them on one of his red fiddles the one day and played them on the other fiddle the next day; that was to give each of them a rest and not wear them out. On these afternoons the birds came out from the heat of the fireside. They cocked their heads sideways with a disbelieving look. There was no way their own sweet bird songs could compete with Bazeen and his fiddles: 'Will ye look at Bazeen?' they seemed to say as they perched themselves on the ditch beside him like a bunch of awestruck schoolchildren and listened to him: 'Curses on ye, birds!' cried Bazeen – seeing how they were depriving him of that little bit of peace he needed to get away from them all, birds and men alike.

At Weddings And Wakes

Whenever a wedding or wake came on, the crowds rushed out to the edge of the river and (aware of the savagery of his dogs) they respectfully called across to him: 'Coom to the wedding, Bazeen! Be sure to bring yeer fiddles with ye,' they begged.

At other times they cried 'Coom to the Dance of the Harvest!'

Sometimes it was 'Coom with us to The Wran Byze Dance at Din-Din-Dinny-the-Stammerer's!'

Bazeen was in pure delight. He didn't need to be asked twice. He got the razor-strop and shaved himself as quickly as he could. This was something he rarely otherwise did, preferring to let his beard hang down like a poet's. Then he ran down into the river and washed the dirt off of his face. This time it was no journey into The Roaring Town with his finest mare to meet the swanks and the townies. He was going to meet the *real* people – his own honest-to-goodness Mountainy Men.

Warning his birds to be good and to mind the house whilst he was gone, he followed his heart and dashed out across Growl River. Compelled as his eyes had been in gawping at the thighs of young Noolah, he found he couldn't stop himself from running to meet the people with his fiddles – such a lover was he of the music and the dancestepping and all the fine singing. For, though he had the daily company of his horses and his birds – his cattle and his dogs – all that was nothing in comparison with his yearning for the company of our red-faced men and their women at a noble-fine dance. The whole of Rookery Rally knew that whenever a dance came round he was ready without a push to leap from his chair, wave behind him his household birds and his dogs and come tearing out the Bog Boundless lanes, his fiddles under his arms. What his beloved animals and their sad faces made out of all this was nobody's concern but his own. He was off to spend four or five glorious days carousing at the dance and drinking down jars of his own medicinal concoction (the rawgut potheen) and merrily drowning himself in a gallon of The Black Doctor.

Of course his birds were as anxious as hell whilst he was away and from the moment that the first solitary star appeared in the sky they kept a lookout for him far into the night. They had seen it all before and they knew that when he returned to Growl River he'd be barely able to stagger across the stepping-stones. His dogs too were always fretful for him to return and they'd go out searching for him. By the time he reached the yard they had set up a woeful din that matched the birds' racket. Hearing his unsteady footsteps at the stream, they scurried back into the house and perched themselves excitedly on top of the table to greet their wanderer's return. It was as though he'd never left them, so happy were they.

His Hatred Of The Tans

Though Bazeen had a heart full of natural feelings for all his animals, he had a heart full of sorrow for his fellowmen and women. Old Bazeen had told him tales when they were lying next to each other in the bed and he still very young – tales of ancient wars and the screams of little children when the foreigners came in their midst during the middle of the night and put their blazing torches to the thatch of their cabins and smashed the walls down to the ground. And for the rest of his life Young Bazeen would hear the screams of these little ones as the flames surrounded them. And later in life he had seen at firsthand the superior forces of The Tan soldiers (in number and weaponry at least) during the merciless days of The Troubles – had seen how those jailbait Tans had followed our brave rebels out across Growl River – out across Bog Boundles – in an effort to track the rebels down and shoot the legs off of them. He had seen the dying youth outside his own door, crying like a child for his own mother, with a bullet lodged in his chest. He had seen the arrival of the bloodthirsty Tans and their cruel drunken laughter as he was lying there in his blood. From that day forth Bazeen had a well-versed hatred for all foreigners – a hatred that went well beyond the comprehension of the church-loving people down in Rookery Rally.

In the springtime when the hearts are young and the lambs are frisking round the fields our wild man forgot his animals for a while and took to drilling the youth in the hills round The Mighty Mountain. Glued to their shoulders they brought their hurley-sticks for guns. Under his instruction thry marched back and forth, back and forth:

'Attention!'

'Quick march!'

'Left wheel!'

'Turn!'

'Point and fire!'

"Ye'll be fighting men yet, mee brave little scarecrows,' he told them and he followed up these manouevres with a rallying call:

'Who do ye think ye are firing at?'

'The Tans!' roared back the children.

'Whose throats will ye cut open?'

'The Tans'!' roared the children and you could count the number of imaginary foreign soldiers that the children then killed.

But The Troubles (he knew) were not over yet – not until his young lads had grown a few inches and made a final rush at The Tans. Below in Curl 'n' Stripes drinking-shop, however, the drinkers found it difficult to take him seriously: 'There's little harm in him,' they said. But some years later Bazeen would be remembered with a jot of cynicism (if not embarrassment) when many of our sons and daughters were earning their grateful crust-of-bread across in John Bull.

When Winter Came On

When winter hurried in, everybody shut the front door. They stayed close to their fireside, swallowing bowls of broth to keep out the chill. Food was scarce during those dark days and (sad to say) some of Bazeen's favourite little birds died from the freezing cold. He then ached with a terrible sorrow: 'After all (said he to himself) birds are birds and they have their hearts and minds – have their feelings and worries – have their sicknesses inside in them like the rest of us'.

With the sun's irridiscent rays gone from his life and the drizzle constantly dribbling on the windowpane and the snow lying heavily round his door he found himself lying low in bed under the blankets, distressed and gaunt-looking. He felt lost and alone with not even a dance to distract him from his inmost thoughts – especially during the dismal nights with nothing to contemplate but the howl of the winds.

These were the times when he had to shake himself out of his droolery.

He'd walk a mile or two along the banks of Growl River. No matter how he tried he found his mind becoming addled and agitated. He wondered was this the result of his recent bouts of heavy drinking at The Wran-Byze Dance? The mornings were black as pitch. He took to talking to himself. There were three voices inside in his head and none of them were the voices of his birds – not even of his little jaybird. First to come out of his mouth was the voice of his mother: 'Why are ye not tending to yeer birds, my son?'

Then the voice of his father (Old Bazeen) came out of his mouth: 'Why are ye not getting yeer horses ready for The Show-Fair, Bazeen?'

Then out came his own guilty voice: 'Mother-o-god – what's the matter with me? Why am I not tending to my fishing rods?'

He Prepared For The High Road

It was reported in Rookery Rally that Bazeen's fishing-rods were empty of fish for the first time in living memory – that his horses were bawling for him – that his birds had given up their singing and were suddenly silent. Then we heard that Bazeen was seen setting fire to his ass-and-car. For sure and certain we knew what this meant: that, like other men before him, he was making his sad preparations to take to the high road that leads to the land of John Bull across The Herring Pond.

We knew what we had to do. The house of Tenderfoot was laid open. It wasn't the well-loved house of Din-Din-Dinny-the-Stammerer. However, it was the nearest and most decent and orderly-looking one we could find at short notice. The entire population of Rookery Rally had a hand in the preparations for such a grand occasion. It'd be better than a wake. There'd be full and plenty for us to wipe the grease from our mouths – what with the sliced pigmeat and skinned rabbits and the sandwiches stacked high like bricks and the women constantly helping to prepare the food inside in the back kitchen – with the frying pan forever busy with the black puddings and sausages: 'Ah, mee insides are pure delighted,' would be the cry from us all. Yes – there'd be many a tight girdle and belt that'd have to be uncramped before the first hour was out.

The Good-luck Barrel

The House-Dance for Bazeen was like none that went before it, as we listened to the sound of the hoibnail boots and the swish of the women's skirts and the shrieks of a happy crowd of hooligans (our own good selves!). His famed barrel was placed in the corner of the room. We pelted our small trinklets and heirlooms into it in order to keep Bazeen company on his long journey and to bring him luck in his new world. By midnight the barrel was well and truly full – what with the salted hams and the shiny money that we had earned from our rabbiting.

Bazeen had shaved and cleaned himself up a good bit (including his poet's beard). He was placed in the seat of honour underneath the Sacred Heart picture – as was fitting. And just as Our Lord protected our homes night and day we now prayed that the Good-God-in-heaven would carry on protecting Bazeen on his travels into the unknown lands.

He Was As Happy As A King

On this glorious occasion Bazeen once more felt the hair rising on his head. He was as happy as any king on earth, seeing the mighty send-off and merriment being given in his honour. And though the famed belts to his head by Tenderfoot's previous wattles had been unable to draw a tear from his eyes, it was impossible now for him to resist the warmth and affection of all his neighbours and his tears were soon hopping off of his jaw and washing the floor as the dance progressed.

His own two fiddles had been kept firmly in the press cupboard for Bazeen was the man-of-the-hour and couldn't be allowed to raise a drop of sweat. Instead, half a dozen other fiddlers had been brought in. Musicianers from far and near (like our very own Gus Gilton and Bill-the-Bee's-Knee and The Jugpussers) brought in their melodions and their knuckle-spoons and paper 'n' combs. And as the dance wore on The Welcoming Room of Tenderfoot became overpowering with the heat from the fire. Parading ourselves out into Tenderfoot's yard, we placed several chairs on top of the henhouse roof. Then we pelted onto the roof (you'd think it'd fall down) a dozen tin-whistlers and gob-musicianers ('Glory to ye, byze!) as well as the shy paper'n'comb Scissors Sisters for the half-set tunes of their ancestors. The fierce din of the musicianers' hobnail boots on the galavanize tin-sheeting was heard (it was afterwards said) beyond in the next county – Clare. Bazeen's birds and dogs had followed down the hill after their master. What they thought of it all, no words could possibly describe.

Nippy, The Dancing-master

For this grand event the high-lepping Nippy with his dancing pomps and kilt was marshalled in from beyond Crown River. They paraded him across the yard in a wheelbarrow. We knew that a master of the stepping-feet was second in importance only to Bishop High-Hat himself. The women had never seen a man wearing a kilt until now: 'Would ye believe it – a man in a dress!' said The Weeping Mollys.

So inquisitive were they as to what kind of knickers he was wearing that a certain bold hussy (Nancy from Mureeny, I believe) crept up behind him whilst he was distracted by forcing a ham-and-sausage sandwich into his mouth. She slyly lifted the back of his kilt to get a little peep beneath it. With a wink from the rest of the women she gave his screaming testicles a mighty hard squeeze. Nippy gave a seven-foot leap into the air and amidst the laughter and the cheers we agreed that one thing was certain – the famed dancing-master wasn't a woman after all!

Next Morning

Next morning the pale sun hid behind a pattern of frothy clouds. But though our heads were sore (for we had gone to bed just as the red sun was coming up over Growl River) a great crowd of us went out and gathered on The Creamery Road to see Bazeen go off. It was as though he was going to the moon. He had put on his best brown suit and had polished his black boots and emptied his piss-pot for the last time. He had said goodbye to all his animals and left them in the care of Rambling Jack.

With baited breath we waited for the sound of the wheels of his rattletrap, the one he'd borrowed from Jack-the-Herd. We heard him coming round the bend of The Valley of The Pig and he sitting high and grand. He was now on his way – going off to meet The Unknown World and with the wind of god-speed following behind him as he came round Sheep's Cross. Wasn't he the fortunate man and he scurrying away and leaving the rest of us poor scholars here behind him like sheep? It wouldn't be long before he had the smell of the salty sea on him.

He waved his ashplant high in the air – to the left, to the right, – to all of us. He had the important airs of Bishop High-Hat and his crosier staff. We took a last view of him and it seemed as though he was about to bless us all. It brought a smile to our jaws. For a moment there was a hush. Then he stopped in the middle of the road as if he had forgotten something: 'Goodbye my friends – I bid ye all a fond goodbye,' he said, wiping a tear from his eyes: 'I am leaving The Ould Dart forever.' And we all heaved a sigh. For this was a phrase we had used ('Welcome back to The Ould Dart') on the very rare occasions when we chanced to meet a returning emigrant in years gone by: 'Take a good look at me for the last time – and keep me in yeer minds,' he cried.

There seemed to be a little bit of melancholy and hurt in him. There seemed an anger too. It was like a tragedy from an old Greek book. He kept on bowing as the ass moved him along the downward slope. He kept a serious eye on the well-roped barrel and its rich contents. The rest of us wet our handkerchiefs copiously with our genuine tears for him and some of us averted our eyes – what with the heartbreak we felt for him, knowing that the dreamy echoes of him would soon to be left behind and he himself would be gone forever. No more would he tred the fields or breathe in the heady smell of a morning's dung. No more would he take his mares or his barrel into town. We roared out to him to remember – when he got beyond The Herring Pond and arrived in John Bull – the long list of names we had given him the night before – a list, which the combined brains of Dang-the-skin-of-it, Father Sensibly and Doctor Glasses could never have remembered between them.

That Evening

The early evening brought in a small quiet period of dusk – a time when the little birds everywhere were pouring out their eloquence to end the day.

It was a time of satisfaction and inner peacefulness enveloping every little farm when the work had been done and the milking finished. The daylight would soon be growing harsh and the surrounding hills pale. And though the moon was not yet visible it'd be dark before we knew it.

We found ourselves sitting by our fires – musing poetically about the weather in the harbour and the nature of the storm-tossed sea waves and the reflection of the moon on the waters and what Bazeen might be thinking to himself and he all alone, poor fellow. In between our sighs we laughed as we pondered what sort of welcome our old friend would get outside the king's palace once he came to produce his famed wattles and pig-barrel.

Later On

Later on when the moon was creeping towards us from over beyond Corcoran's Well and the first few solitary stars were appearing, there came a strange feeling over us. The sound that met our ears at this late hour of the night was the unearthly rattling of a horse-and-cart's wheels. Who or what could it be coming up the hill-slopes at this ungodly hour of the night? There was a hush and we listened. Was it a ghostly creamery cart from out of The Past? Was it an angel? Was it Saint Joseph and his ass? It wasn't our day for selling our cattle or for buying our salt. Whatever it was, it'd soon be here and we were left scratching our heads.

The next thing we knew was that a mighty crowd, their lanterns splashing pools of light ahead of them, had risen freshly out of their beds and were flooding up along The Open Road. In the midst of them was Bazeen. Some people were crying. Some were laughing. Still others were cursing him into the four corners of hell for having taken their precious good-luck tokens, their heirlooms and silver coins at The House-Dance and for not going on to reach the far-distant shore.

All the farmers along the road had now lined their flagstones. It was hard to hear what was going on – what with the uproarious noise of the crowd coming up the hillside. Bazeen (it seemed) had gotten as far as Yawn, some six miles from Growl River. He had another six miles to travel before reaching The Roaring Town itself. He made a misfortunate mistake and gave a last look back at the hills. From where he was standing high in the cart he could see the long black shadows of the pinetrees in Lisnagorna beginning to push out the daylight. Beneath the trees he could see the peculiarly-shaped field – that huge triangular field that we called The 'A' Field for it had a ditch strung halfways across its middle.

It was that one indescribable moment in Bazeen's life. The sight of The 'A' Field haunted him. Suddenly (he later told us) an unspeakable ache rose up inside his chest and a fierce pain stabbed him in under his heart. He had never experienced such a pain before. He could almost hear the ghost of Old Bazeen calling him to come back home forgodsake to where he belonged. He knew that his heart was about to burst inside in him from the unbearable loneliness he felt for his home – for his dogs – for the birds and horses he was quitting. He felt a great shame inside in him. He could stand it no more. He got down from his horse. He began to bawl like a cow does when they take her calf away from her after birth. He bawled for his mother. He bawled for his father. He bawled for his horses and his birds. He bawled for his cattle and his dogs and the fishing rods that he'd left hanging forlornly by his bed behind him.

'Ye thunderin' eejit, Bazeen. Why didn't ye take the cattle-boat?' said some.

'Blasht ye, what sort of a holy show is this to be making in front of the entire population of Ireland?' said others.

'It's nothing short of a sin,' said Tenderfoot. 'No man has ever before been so soft-hearted as not to take the entire package.' And the whole road yelled their agreement.

'I couldn't! I couldn't! I couldn't!' Bazeen kept bawling.

And then came the words that were to become famous forevermore amongst us: *'I got seasick below in Yawn!'*

It was then that the whole of Rookery Rally laughed their sides asunder – to think that Bazeen, some hundred miles from the sea and The Sweet Cove of Cork had gotten seasick in Yawn (of all places) – six bleddy miles from Rookery Rally's doorstep.

In the coming months it'd become the saying that beat all other sayings: 'Did ye hear how Bazeen got the seasickness below in Yawn?' Even Father Sensibly would pride himself in telling the tale of it. At breakfast he would split his sides laughing as he recounted across his silver teapot the *Yawn seasickness* of Bazeen to the heavy-fisted missioner, a man who had just arrived to give us the brimstone that would take us into hell if we didn't obey his commands and give him our few pennies for the coffers of the Church. And even that old sour-face-of-a-missioner had to laugh his heart out at the thought of Bazeen's premeditated seasickness.

He Returned To His Wildlife

With the insults of everyone ringing in his ears Bazeen counted himself lucky indeed to get himself free from the throng without receiving a few handy taps of our fists to his jaw. Finally he turned his horse-and-cart away from the whole pack of us and headed back up the trail that led onto the fields of The Wilderness and out over the ford at Growl River. By this time both himself and his poor horse were worn to a thread from all the excitement.

Leaping Into The Stormy Waters

As tired as he was, he fairly leapt down from his rattletrap when he saw his old shack-of-a-homestead. Bless the bit – if he didn't throw off every stitch of his clothing (the green unwashed shirt and all) and leap deliriously into the stormy waters of the astonished river as naked as the day he was born. He stood up and, rampant with joy, let out an almighty roar from the depths of his soul. It was a triumphant roar, which must have terrified the very spirits of the river themselves.

Without a stitch on his back he ran up the yard to the door of his cabin. He gave his wild call. His birds woke from their long sleep and began their twittering. Those that had returned to the wild woods began to come back to him – by one, by two, by three. His horses raised their bellies from the grass and ran back to greet him. His dogs ran back to him bewilderedly and licked the jaws clean off of his face. The Night Fairies swept down out of the misty shadows and wrapped themselves round them all. Balzeen knelt down on the slabbed floor of his little cabin and his tears of joy hopped in bucketfuls off of the flagstones. He hit his chest several belts of contrition and he thanked his Blessed Maker for all the gifts that heaven had bestowed on him.

FIVE

How White Snow taught us all a powerful lesson in the end.

Colours

In plain and simple terms we all knew our colours. There were the deep sepia shadows of night and the rosy tints of replenishing daybreak and the pink and lavender of the sunset finally warming the clouds. Each winter there was the sharp white of the new snow on the surrounding hills and protecting forest of Lisnagorna and then another kind of whiteness (smoky and pale) when the snow vanished, leaving the roads and lanes as clean as white paper. There was the rimy greyness of frost on the windowpanes in those early January mornings when the leaves of the holly-bushes were lined with silver and there were other times when the furze-bushes were spangled with maytime gold. Of course we all had the red of the fuchsia bushes round our pighouses and the bronze of our hens, not to mention our multicoloured cockerels. Little children spent ages playing with pink, biege, mauve and lavender stones from River Laughter. They drew pictures of their mother and father – and, if they were clever, they drew multicoloured sheep and cattle too on the flagstones across their yard stream. Even our neighbours had colours written into their names: there was Red Mick, Red Buckles and Red Scissors, all with the red in their names because of the unusually bright colour of their hair and faces. Then if we saw anyone with hair that was blacker than our own or if we saw that a man's jaw (no matter how often he shaved) was as black as a burnt saucepan then we knew that he was either Black Paddy or a cousin of his. Or it could also be the Roaring Town nurse with the soot-drop shaped into her jaw (what the townies called a beauty-spot) and who went by the name of Black Bess. And next to the schoolhouse there was yet another colour – the yellow of the quarry, which stood our for miles around us – The Yellowstone Quarry where Big Red in his fourteenth year had filled the wheelbarrow with rocks and in his maddened rage over the mistress's insult to his mother had returned through the school gates and destroyed every blessed window in sight. Enough said about colours.

One Fresh Spring Evening

One fresh Spring day – early in the evening – when the murmuring of awakening life was seen everywhere and our little cabbage shoots were dancing in the breeze, a new woman with an oak-pale face and an aquiline nose and a long swanlike neck and pallid green eyes stepped down unsteadily among us. She was straddled behind Taedspaddy on his mare and was marked with that shivering bit of shyness, which you'd expect from a total stranger. She came from the secret haunts of Hurricane Hill, which sloped away beyond our own Mighty Mountain – the mountain we saw every day for miles and miles above anything else. To be exact – she was from that solitary spot a mile or two passed Bazeen's Black Banks where the two rivers (Glown and Clashing) rose up and met before unrolling in a rambling ribbon towards the city of Limerick.

We stopped to stare at her. Who could it be? She was not an old woman by any means and yet (something we had never seen before) her hair was almost as white as snow. Though none of us knew it, she hadn't been born that way. Indeed her hair had lost its natural colour a decade earlier, a few days after her Confirmation. Prior to that it had been a most beautiful colour – a mixture of chestnut, auburn and resin and of such an unusual colour that her mountainy neighbours believed nobody in the whole of Ireland could possibly have had such a rare colour to it. In spite of its changed colour the day we first laid eyes on her, it still had its thick curly tresses all over it, falling round her face and neck. We didn't know how to describe this hair of hers. It wasn't as grey as Free 'n' Easy's mare. It wasn't quite as white as the fur of Old Sam's albino ferret. It was an intermingling shade of these two colours and we hadn't yet discovered a word in our language to put a name to it. So – because of this unfortunate whiteness in her hair (and she being so very young) we decided to give her the name of White Snow the minute she landed.

The Welcome She Got

Of course it wasn't long before the mean and niggardly amongst us went on likening the new arrival to an old grey badger. Those with a better pedigree, however, said that this woman was a white swan among those dull old ducks. Others with a somewhat poetical turn of mind said her skin reminded them of the milk in the buckets – of a white porcelain delicacy and not like the radish rosiness of the rest of the women.

Anyway – her whole appearance charmed our gentler men (and there were a few of these softhearts still around the hillslopes) completely out of their wits. Her fingers were long and stately like Bishop High-Hat's and she had a Madonna-like face with not a wrinkle on it. She'd remind you of one of our Lisnagorna pinetrees for she was taller than the tallest man in the parish (Jack Log), who had been given the laughable name of *The Walking Hayshed* from the time he left school, for she was over six feet in her stocking vamps.

And another thing which we saw a day or two later – she walked with that well-known long mountainy step, stretching her knees in a sort of bowing curtsy and throwing her heels and toes way out in front of her in a curling motion before they came back down to the ground. Her head (in rhythm with her feet) nodded gently like a breezy sunflower as she skimmed over the grass behind her cows, her arms folded across her waist. And when men were chasing after their own stray cows they'd stop to listen to her. They could hear her strangely-accented voice as she encouraged her cows to move on towards the cowshed and the way she rolled her consonants like a bit of bread in her mouth, drawing out her vowels like a slurp of water, the sound coming from deep in her throat like a tinkling bell. And whatever one or two of our cranky old men and their wives thought of this strange newcomer, the children could listen to her for hours on end.

Some Were Heading For The Train

Over the previous years a good number of our young men and women had put on a brave face and dressed up in their finest clothes before heading for the train that'd take them to the cattle-boat on the Dublin coast. From there it was a matter of journeying across the rough waves and getting as sick as a dog before reaching the Welsh coast and speeding on down to The Great City we called Pandemonium. Others were heading down to the coast of Cork and casting their eyes west to The Land of The Silver Dollar. And a few more were making their way to the far side of the moon – embarking on a half-a-year's journey to Van Diemen's Land.

The day that they left we all cried buckets of tears, knowing that we were unlikely to ever see their face again – as though they were dead and laid out in the grave. There was one thing we knew for sure: after the train took them out of our sight for good, you'd never hear us saying a bad word against them – never hear us making a sly or sneering remark such as 'there goes another old *blow-out*, leaving us behind here in the lurch.' And though it was known the world over that we had words for everything else, we had never dreamed up such a name as a *blow-out* for anybody. However – when a newcomer came into our midst from the far side of the mountains or from any place else outside our own world it was an entirely different matter. We'd spend a long time looking them up and down – and then up and down again. And after that (it's sad to say) there were a number of us who were immediately ready to label the newcomer nothing other than an old *blow-in* and make her feel thoroughly unwelcomed. This of course was due largely through backward ignorance (and there was a good deal of that among us – nor were we pure angels at times) or else through sheer jealousy – especially if it was felt that the new arrival had virtuous qualities or tangible riches greater than their own – or (let's speak the truth) through a downright lack of Christian charity.

With White Snow's arrival it was a chance for these old heathens to overlook her natural grace and charm and to imagine themselves a step or two above her – to look down their snotty noses and turn their backs away from her the minute she arrived in Rookery Rally. Wasn't it a handy thing for these old articles to find thmselves sitting on top of the haystack looking down on not just the mountainy men and the tinkers but on an old *blow-in* as well? For when such a *blow-in* arrived it was as though these sad creatures had found a bit of horsedung inadvertently picked up on their boots when bringing back turf from Bog Boundless. Led by The Weeping Mollys, who were forever the leaders when it came to imaginative lying and story-making, they would pipe up with their latest song:

'Aha! – here comes another old *blow-in'*.

'Aha! – will ye look at what the storm clouds have blown in today!'

You'd be in tears to hear the wretched lies that came pouring out of their mouths. Such-and-such an old *blow-in* couldn't read: such-and-such an old *blow-in* couldn't write her name: such-and-such an old *blow-in* was accompanied by a thousand fleas. And when the old gossips found that they had a right good hold of their listeners' ears they threw all caution to the wind and reminded them how when they were eating their meat a number of previous *blow-ins* had been known to scratch their backs inside their shirts with the blade of their knife so as to squash a few of their latest fleas. Oh, such cruelty. Weren't these old harridans the most miserably scholars we ever had in our midst? Would hell itself be able to welcome them through its portals? Of course by now even the most soulless among us had turned on our heel and walked away from them, shaking our heads and shrugging our shoulders in pure disgust at the likes of them.

How She Got The White Hair

On the day she arrived none of us knew how a woman like White Snow could have such white hair – and at such an early age. It was something of a miracle. It was not until Red Scissors found himself down south in Tipperary Town buying a new clydesdale mare that the news came back to us – the way in which White Snow had gotten the whiteness into her hair. He had met up with a distant cousin of his (Napper-the-Lamb) who was also down there on a quest for a plough-horse. Napper lived beyond The Mighty Mountain and was able to give Red Scissors a vivid account of the whole story so that he could bring back the unfortunate tale of the disappearance of the lovely auburn colour and the arrival of the whiteness in our newcomer's hair.

A Bright Shiny Afternoon

It had been a bright shiny afternoon with the sun's fingers pointing everywhere and gilding the entire world when White-Snow (then a child of thirteen-years-of-age) went off travelling with her father, Dinjo. They were always together and as close as two sides of a dinner-plate, for her mother had died of her wounds during childbirth. Dinjo (amongst other things) was a woodcutter. He and his daughter took themselves and their horse-and-cart to cut the annual tree for their wintertime fuel – just like they had done the year before. Their local gentry-man (Lord Forget-me-not, a distant cousin of Lady Posh-Frock) allowed them the gift of this once-a-year access to his broad estates. He knew well what he was doing for it was a handy way for him to clear some of his diseased trees as well as the branches knocked down in the storms and to thin out any other unneeded bits of his timber crop.

The hearts of father and daughter were as light as a feather blown down the yard as they headed across the fields, the sun warming them by the minute. But all that was soon to change. Over the years Dinjo had grown accustomed to the angle and direction of his axe-cuts and the way in which the tree would be leaning. This time, however, when the axe-cutting was satisfactorily completed and he was sawing into the trunk like fair hell and not keeping an eye on the top branches, the tree seemed to have a mind of its own. Were some strange evil spirits lurking in this particular tree? For without warning it came crashing headlong down on top of Dinjo, falling straight across his chest and almost burying his body into the ground with the dent that it made. Oh, the sight of poor Dinjo, thus bespattered with his own life-blood!

'Father-father-father!'

The young girl's heart leapt into her throat and straight out of her body. She threw herself across her father and buried her tears in his blood. Apart from the rambling spirits of the woodland there was no-one else close by. In the cruel unearthly silence she gazed at the poor misfortunate Dinjo – the father whom she adored next to Jesus himself. He was not yet quite dead, his glazed eyes rolling round in his head as he tried to utter a few dying words up to her whilst she ('this shitty-arsed tree!') tried helplessly to lift the fatal tree. Would she ever forget his sad eyes – eyes showing that he was still aware of her presence – still able to recognise her. However, the poor man could no longer call out her name. Oh, that he could (if only for a second) get back the gift of speech! There was so much he would have wanted to say to her: 'I'm dying, child – go get me the priest! Go tell him come quick and hear my last confession so I can enter the gates of heaven.' He couldn't even give her his last fatherly blessing. He couldn't tell her of his everlasting love for her and it was breaking the heart in both their chests.

Her Loneliness

In the days following the grisly death of Dinjo and after all the solemn obsequies of his funeral and burial had been ceremoniously accomplished, White Snow found herself in a bewildered state of loneliness. It was as though a sort of twilight had come over her. There were times when she felt dizzy and couldn't catch her breath. She was constantly looking up at the clouds as though searching for a sign – as if wishing to fly away over Hurricane Hill and join her father and mother in The Beyond. But with neither of them left to cheer her, the sunlight was completely gone out of her life. She had only the odd neighbour to come in and light the fire for her or help her look after the house and make sure she had a bit of dinner inside her. There was no-one to sit by the fire opposite her and while away the evening and burn the candle down in the long lonely night.

In the next few weeks the young Clare curate (Father Honesty) came repeatedly up the mountain trail, approaching the bereft young girl's half-door gingerly as you'd expect. The sight of her tear-stained face troubled him greatly. Would she ever get back her soft smile? Along with him he brought the sweet music of his melodion and gently played his haunting airs into her ears in the hope that the melodies would bring gladness back to her heart. But on these first visits (and for many more to come) the sad-faced child was unable to utter so much as a word back to him. The sight of that tree (more accurately, the sight of her dead father underneath its trunk) would haunt her till the day she died. It was a miracle (the neighbours said) that the poor girl hadn't given up the ghost alongside her father from the shock and dismay at the sight of him – a sight no thirteen-year-old child was ever meant to look upon.

The Change In Her

That was when the neighbours hit their chests in sorrow for her – such a change did they behold before the year was finished. Not one of the older men and women could recall an instance like it having ever happened before. Like a slow-moving cloud across the mountainside the misfortunate child's hair started to turn (and as if by magic) from its lustrous auburn colour to a mixture of its future grey-and-whiteness and they made the sign-of-the-cross and prayed that it wouldn't stay that way for the rest of her life. It was too much to bear. Hadn't they always stopped in their tracks to admire and marvel at the unusual colour of it – rarer (they felt) than the autumn leaves and outmatching even the beautiful colour of Lord Forget-me-not's ponies.

Their eyes would fill with tears when they recalled the deep love between a father and his daughter and how Dinjo had always been so proud of his daughter's lovely auburn hair. They would shake their heads sadly as they remembered the way he used to sit her on the chair in the yard – the way he would gently comb out her tresses in long sweeps through his fingers – the way he would patiently plait them into a single twisty rope right down to her waist. And they shut their eyes and tried to forget.

She Stepped Down From The Horse-and-cart

The day after she stepped down from her horse-and-cart White Snow began to realise what was in the heads of a number of the old gossips and what lay in store for her once she got herself settled in. There'd be no turf fire for her to visit – no half-door to cross over – not even the idle chattering at her flagstones. She might as well have gone into a nunnery – so quiet and lonesome would her days be were it not for her handsome new husband – Taedspaddy. He had told her what to expect from the likes of some of the hard-hearted ones in our midst.

She soon saw how even Sunday Mass was to have little or no effect on many of the grim-looking faces – even when they were wearing their knees raw and running their clackety rosary-beads through their fingers and thinking holy thoughts and a supposedly whiter-than-white love for their fellowmen. Surely the hearts of these old crones would soften to her when they were looking up at the statues of the saints and listening to the fine words of Father Sensibly and gazing bemusedly at one another like we all did at funerals when looking down into the brown pit and thinking of the shortness of life? But, whatever some of the more warm-hearted among us felt, not for a minute did these women attempt to give White Snow the little handshake or the little drop of welcome! Damn the bit – when all was said and done wasn't she nothing but an old *blow-in* and not one of us? Ah, there's nothing like the proud coldness of the human heart!

Her Previous Cottage

Had they known it, there was another side to this picture. Were you to put our old gossips up on their well-worn broomsticks and whisk them over The Mighty Mountain they'd have found that their most recent *blow-in* was far from the impoverished ugly duckling of their storybooks with a disease to her name. For unlike our own thatched cabins White Snow had lived in a small cottage made of red bricks and with red tiles for a roof and buckets of quicklime whitewash on the outside walls and a stream chuckling its way through her yard. Before too long she'd show these white swans of ours that she was the handsomest swan of them all.

The Exception Was Blue-eyed Jack

The exception to all this backbiting was Blue-eyed Jack. He knew what it was like to feel pain in his heart, having sacrificed his own chance of making a successful life for himself in Van Dieman's Land at the other end of the map. On the untimely day when his father (Handsome Johnnie) finally died – leaving Dowager forlorn and in bits – spitting up the last of his liver, the big man did the noble thing (as any honest son should do) and chose not to travel over the seas but to swear his undying allegiance to his mother so as to look after his several younger brothers and sisters and save the little farm from collapse and ruin. In everybody's eyes he was seen as an angel from heaven – taking up the mantle and ploughshare of his beloved father.

Before White Snow's arrival he had never forgotten his young sweetheart, the girl he had met at the Gibbet's Hill Platform Dance a year before his father's death. Damn it – if Handsome Johnnie hadn't died so unexpectedly, Blue-eyed Jack and his pretty Lilia would have found themselves trotting up the altar steps and into the Copperstone Hollow Church – would have found themselves getting sprinkled with the holywater and getting themselves blessed by the marriage sacrament of Holy Mother Church and its everlasting graces. He'd have had a family of his own abroad in Van Dieman's Land – a family to bring up and in turn get himself spoiled to death by them in his old age.

Following his father's death, however, he had given back the ticket for the wild boat-trip over the seas. In his new role as Man-of-The-House the boat-ticket was a useless bit of paper in his hands. And Lilia? Taking with her the whole of his heart on board ship she sped from his life for good and spent the rest of her days in that far-flung land – a lifetime away from her truelove, Jack. Sadly – it was the last we'd ever hear tell of her. Enough said.

Fates Are Not Always Cruel

However The Fates are not always cruel. And once more Blue-eyed Jack was seen to put out the good side of his nature (as once he did with Imagine) and stand side-by-side with White Snow at a time when few others appeared to give a damn about her. What a shock it was for him when first he laid eyes on her at Mass. His knees almost gave way at the comeliness of this lofty mountainy woman with her soft pale skin – a woman who'd bring a new pain to his lovesick spirits. He, who had never cast a sideways glance at a woman since committing himself everlastingly to his mother, found his schoolboy heart fluttering around in his chest and making its feathery way out towards White Snow. And then, when she opened her mouth to speak to him – when he heard the charm in her voice – he lost his head completely. But it was all in vain: White Snow was the wife of another man – the wife of Taedspaddy.

The Tanks To The Creamery

Every third week the farmers took it in turn in a sensible agreement with their two neighbours to get out the horse-and-cart, put on their best cap and scamper off to the creamery with all three tanks – theirs and their neighbours. It meant that when it was the turn of Blue-eyed Jack to take his high-stepping mare (Moll) to the creamery he would fill his cart with Fatty-Matty's tank and then with Taedspaddy's tank.

Shortly after White Snow's arrival it was Blue-eyed Jack's turn to face The Creamery Road. The minute he reached Taedspaddy's gate he found that it wasn't only the cart with the three tanks that he had filled: he had also filled his eyes all over again (just as the first time he'd seen her at Mass) with the pure look of White Snow. Who could have resisted her? He was at first tongue-tied and he blushed shyly, not knowing what on earth he was going to do with himself. From the rest of that week – indeed from that day onwards – he found himself stopping his horse-and-cart for far longer than he ought to in White Snow's yard, spending his time annoying her with the inventive wit of his lying tales and yarns while Taedspaddy was preoccupied elsewhere either out in the pighouse or in the haggart. Before he left her gate he'd have her in a gale of laugher and maybe (he sometimes felt) her heart reached out innocently to him – just that little bit – in spite of her wedlock bans?

Other Farmers

Each morning other farmers would be passing White Snow's gate on the same road to the creamery: 'Ah-ha – is this where our newly-installed *blow-in* lives?' they'd mutter to themselves. They knew, of course, what a fine-looking woman she was – as fine as ever they'd clapped eyes on for none of them had yet lost their eyesight. They could see that her graceful nature and her stylish dress contrasted markedly with their own wives. And yet – her virtues didn't have the power to soften their hearts and as they passed by the blackguards would rise up in the cart and sing that rude old song:

'She's down from the mountains, her stockings are white and I'd like to be tying her garters tonight.'

Well yes – that was what they'd like to be doing with her (at least in their thoughts), the confused and shy fellows that most of them were. What was it about White Snow that drew their eye to her? Unlike their wives she was as neat and clean as a pin and had the look of a tidy schoolmistress about her. Ever mindful of how a young mare's coat would glisten if attended to by the currycomb, she'd go behind the hayshed when dusk came on (something none of us knew) and strip to the waist to wash. Only the men did that on a Saturday night when preparing for the following day's Holy Mass. She would lash herself half-to-death with the icy rainwater from the tar-barrel, thereby keeping herself as clean as a royal queen. And if you peered from behind her into the looking-glass you'd have mistaken her for a walking nun with a fresh and beautiful face on her.

Her Green-Check Suit

She wasn't many days amongst us before she was seen kitted out with a green check suit for her Sunday outing to Copperstone Hollow Church. You'd think she was Lady Elegance – the style and twinkle of her – she wore a golden brooch (her mother's) in her Sunday coat and she had gloves to back it up and a pair of lace-up boots that no shop in The Roaring Town had seen the likes of. And, if anything, her stockings were indeed as white as the mean and dirty old song intended them to be. But the green-check suit was just for a Sunday and on weekdays she'd be dressed out in her working-clothes – a light three-quarter-length skirt covering the tops of her wellingtons when she sailed over the fields to bring back the cows for milking. To this she had added a dash of pink and a dash of blue to offset her day-to-day clothes. Such touches matched the merriment shining from her lovely blue eyes. Presumably it was this (her apparel and her friendly appearance) that caused Jealousy to sow itself in the hearts of a good few men and their women – but especially in the women, causing them to raise their voices high: 'Wouldn't you like to take the rifle and shoot the likes of her?' Oh, the heathens!

A Few Unwashed Articles

It wasn't any wonder that a few of the sniggery men on their way to the creamery found themselves put out at the sight of her. What had these hairy old articles ever done that they could boast about? Some of them had never slept with any woman other than their mother – and then only to keep the warmth in her body in the icy damp bed during the dark days of our winters.

Day in and day out they dressed in the same dark and drab colours. One or two of them even wore the same dirty shirt both day and night – never changing it – even sleeping in it. Most of them shaved but once a week in preparation for Sunday Mass – hence the hairy jaws of them for the rest of the week. They had a mouthful of half-broken teeth, stained from their pipe-tobacco and made sparing use of the soot on the hob to wash their mouths clean. Wouldn't the likes of this new woman irritate the hell out of them all! What else could she expect?

Some of the women (wearing a tam or a pixy on their heads) were often as drab as their men. A scarf on a market-day was a step up for them. By the time they reached fifty many men and women were as shrivelled as an old turnip – and not just from the sun that poured down on their heads. Few if any of them got down to the river in summer to strip off their clothes and give themselves a good scrubbing in their naked skins. Indeed washing was as foreign to some of them as the man in the moon – unless they sprinkled a few spatters of water on their cheeks in the privacy of their bedroom before heading out the door to town and the shops. As a result of this contrast between themselves and White Snow it was as natural as the rain that they'd start entertaining one another with the same old questions:

'Blasht it – why on earth did White Snow have to come down here and live among us here on the slopes?'

'Why did she come down and marry that old fairyman, Taedspaddy – of all people?'

'Why didn't Taedspaddy go and marry one of our own daughters, blasht him? Were our women not good enough for his hairy old puss?' On and on their tongues wagged. It'd sicken your stomach.

Taedspaddy's Great Need

Let's step back a bit. Taedspaddy had already been the wrong side of forty (beginning to turn fleshy-looking, but not fat – just solid-looking) when he went and brought White Snow down here to Rookery Rally. And therein lay the tale – though none of us knew it till later on. The woman-of-his-heart (namely his saintly mother), whom he had always idolised, was dead and buried a year previously, the father having drowned in the river a good while back. The night before his mother passed away she held Taedspaddy's hands in her dying grip so as to give him her solemn Mother's Blessing. And just before she closed her eyes for the last time her wish was for him to put on his best suit and go in search of a good woman to come in the door and take her place.

From then on Taedspaddy became increasingly anxious to go get himself a wife from whom to breed some children – children that would sit with him round the fire in the evenings and call him *daddy* and prop up the latter half of his life. But like all aging batchelors he was a shy boy at heart and puzzled as to how to go about fulfilling his mother's wishes. With the saintly woman gone, he was like a lost sheep with no-one left to direct him as before and could see that the days ahead of him were going to be the saddest time in his life. We had seen it all before: pure lonesomeness would soon start to haunt him and waste away the heart in his chest.

In the middle of his restless nights he'd listen and he'd listen for the ghostly footsteps of his mother coming in along the yard – till one night he thought he heard the mystical murmurings of her voice. It was like a call from the wild, whispering impatiently into his ear: 'Taedspaddy! Taedspaddy! What's keeping you? Time is not on your side – go forth, my child! Go get yourself a young woman and bring her back here with you before it's too late.' This caused the poor man to twist and turn and to sweat in the bed. As the nights wore on, his mother seemed to prod him even more – shrieking this deafening order into his ear – often following him round the field in the middle of the day whilst he was bent at his work.

A Blinding Flash Of Knowledge

Then finally in a blinding flash of light the knowledge came to him and with the reins and the bridle he went off looking for his mare (Slippaway). Mindful of his mother's dying wishes, he washed and shaved himself meticulously. He dressed himself in his one and only good clothes – the blue suit with the faint red lines running through it. He put on his Sunday boots and combed his black curls with his dead mother's brilliantine. Then with a wing and a prayer he leapt into the saddle and headed straight up through the pinetrees of Lisnagorna and out along the slopes of The Hills-of-The-Past and passed The Beige Sandpits.

By now the sun was burning away the mists of early day and his heart felt as light as a bladder. With the sun gilding his face he travelled on from there and out across the purple heather on the far reaches of Bog Boundless, determined to attack The Mighty Mountain itself and the rocky ford at Clashing River – the river known to the children as The River Sticks (the one in their storybooks). And soon he could hear its waves brawling angrily where it came zig-zagging its way across the remote valleys that surround our world before discoursing itself into Growl River and then into The Mighty Shannon River near Limerick.

He Had Never Forget That Wild Spot

To the day he died he would never forget that wild spot and the sunlit day ten years earlier and long before White Snow had given him her hand and come to join him in the marriage-bed. It was the day when a lovely young girl had come on the scene and saved him from drowning in a deep treacherous boghole – the day when he was standing on the turf-pitch alongside his own father's brother (The Gog).

They had been working like blazes – and airing and dressing the final stages of their turf – and had at last planked up the last bit of it, leaving it tidy (black turf and a good bit better than the brown). It was a grand and glorious sight to be looking at and they had time to soak in the tranquillity of the day. They had an awful thirst and hunger in their bellies. So The Gog sent Taedspaddy to the spring-well in the lower gully to fill up the kettle for their afternoon tea. Minutes passed and he started thinking that Taedspaddy (blasht him!) was an awfully long time gone. Was he ever coming back with the spring-water so that they could unwrap the sandwiches and boil the mug of tea over the bit of kindled heather?

It was then that this noble-looking young girl (the one some of us were infamously calling the old *blow-in* from the top of the mountains) came riding by like Jesus on her ass (Scallywags). It was a year before the tragic death of Dinjo. She was twelve-years-of-age at the time and had come in search of her father's stray cattle. Down through the gully she came – all the time sidling her ass carefully round the danger-spots. And then – in front of her she saw the boghole waters churning themselves and sobbing with an unusual sound. A gusty wind seemed to be forcing her to hurry on. It was as though some unknown and hidden force was driving herself and her ass towards the edge of the boghole.

Saints-above-us! – she was in the nick of time to prevent disaster. For there in the treacle-dark waters she found what seemed like the remains of poor Taedspaddy floating aimlessly round. A lump came up in her throat. All she could see were the two bits of his struggling arms and head sticking up from the mire where he'd slipped and tumbled in. She realized (it had happened to others before) that he was about to sink down to his final resting-place amongst the fairies of that place – unseen and disregarded by the rest of mankind. It was as if she'd been given a kick in the ribs as she jumped down from Scallywags and tied him to a nearby bush.

It must have been some sort of miracle (she thought) – some plan in the mind of God or in one of the heavenly angels that had guided her to this very boghole and at this precise moment – now to become the saviour of this poor man's life. The ass wasn't slow either in acknowledging what had happened (for asses too have brains). He could see that he and his mistress were about to become part of some deeply dark drama and that his help would be required the very next minute.

The young girl led Scallywags to the edge of the boghole. She directed his eyes to the legs of the man and ('You're the best little ass in all Ireland') she whispered those well-known ass-whispers into his clever ear. Leaning out over the bank she tied the reins round Taedspaddy's knees and heels, all the time crying out desperately: 'You are far too young to die, poor man

– far too young!' She and Scallywags fiercely toiled and struggled – pulling and dragging as never before at the frantic reins round Taedspaddy's legs. And under her breath she let out a string of damning curses against the bogland fairies (those filthy feckers) and their fiendish cruelty in trying to drag away a young man from his place on God's earth. She thought her lungs were going to burst asunder from all her efforts. But no untamed lion could have applied itself more energetically than she. With the last gasps of her strength she managed to haul Taedspaddy's heels (bit by agonising bit) out from the mire and the grip of Death until he was safely landed on the bank. The sight of him lying there, stiff with the cold – with no more than a kick left in his body and at the very doors of death – sickened the stomach in her. She hadn't a second to lose. She opened his mouth and began breathing the life back into him with mouthful after mouthful of her own breath, all the time pummelling on his chest until she finally saw him shudder and open his eyes.

Hearing her cries, the demented Gog came running through the heather, his heart in his mouth when he saw what was happening. Together they stripped the shivering Taedspaddy to his skin and laid him flat on his back. They hung his wet clothes on the furze bushes to dry in the wind. To see him there – so frightened – and he whimpering like a small child – ah me! They brought the kettle of freezing spring-water and time and time again pelted it into Taedspaddy's face to revive him. They washed away the mud from off his body. By this time The Gog had uttered to the skies every childhood prayer he had learnt at his mother's knee. And all the time he kept looking at this strange unknown girl and asking himself whether she was a real child or a ghostly fairy child or whether she had come down from the skies like the Angel Gabriel. It was indeed a small miracle: how else had she appeared on the scene so suddenly when there wasn't another soul around them in all the wide world?

The Strangeness Of That Memorable Day

The strangeness of that memorable day – the almost-drowned Taedspaddy and the lovely young girl appearing just in time – was like some intense scene from out of a fairytale storybook. Now that Taedspaddy had come back to his senses, the tea and the sandwiches were long forgotten and the kettle (gone for good) was lying at the bottom of the boghole where the poor man might well have ended his days. Instead – he saw the face of the pretty young girl kneeling over him and rubbing the warmth back into his two legs, his chest and his hands. A feeling of intense warmth and gratitude swelled round inside in him. The silent tears rolled down his jaw and joy swam up to the surface and into his helpless eyes. It passed into the girl's eyes and then came back again into him.

He Puffed Out His Cheeks

That was ten years ago. It was now the month of April. The air was soft and the sky was clear. He puffed out his cheeks and drank in the cool breezes that were up around Clashing River. He was indeed a noble sight, seated on Slippaway. He plunged speedily onwards passed the ford in the river. All the time he kept mumbling shyly to himself: 'I have coom for you, I have coom for you.' He didn't know what else his shy tongue-tied mouth would say when he reached the young woman's yard and (again thinking of his mother's words) he tried to summon up all the courage that his heart could muster.

His guardian angel was with him. She steadfastly led him on – and he all the while humming silently and the smoke dribbling aimlessly from his pipe – up through the shaggy woods behind the mountain and out across the heather. He was tired and he was weary. He steered his mare determinedly on till he came to the narrow path that skirted the pine plantations on the slopes of Hurricane Hill. And then he was there.

He drove Slippaway down the yellow lane and into White Snow's yard and entered the half-door, the shafts of sunlight streaming in behind him and silhouetting him. He felt as excited as a springtime calf and took off his cap with the usual polite *God save all here* on his lips. Then he bowed towards White Snow, unaware that both her father and mother were dead. His eyes had room for nought but the woman before him – the same woman who had once had a head of hair more colourful than the woodland chestnuts – a head of hair that was now as white as the driven snow. He was struck dumb at the sight of this former child for she had blossomed into a beautiful, tall and stately woman.

He reached out his arms towards his former saviour – the girl that had smiled down on him at the side of the boghole: 'I have coom for you, I have coom for you,' was all that the poor wooden man could stutter in the silence of her Welcoming Room. Renowned as the rest of us were for our inability to keep out tongues quiet for a single minute, this was one day in Taedspaddy's life when long speeches and finely-chosen words had sailed away with the wind. His aching heart could say no more.

She Knew He'd Come

And then The Fates that rule the clouds smiled warmly down. 'You are welcome, kind sir,' she greeted him. She always knew that he would come for her. Time and again her dreams had shown her this man's sad face that sunlit day in her childhood when she drove her ass to the edge of the boghole – the way the hand of God had directed her through the gully – the fierce struggle and rescue: – the bewildered face of the drowning man – his grateful eyes looking up at her – the joy she felt in saving his life.

She took Taedpaddy's hands in hers and shook them warmly. It was like a dream: one minute she had been busying herself with the cabbages and spuds in the two skillet pots at the side of the fire: the next minute she was packing a few bits of her best clothing into her father's old suitcase, leaving the remnants of her old grey life forever behind her and the allurement of the new life mapped out in front of her.

She closed her front door for the last time. With a happy heart she scrambled up behind Taedspaddy onto Slippaway's back and the two of them went sailing merrily (if not quite at a gallop) across the wild lands that would lead them the long trek to Clashing River and eventually to Rookery Rally. In that precious moment there was no mansion of any lord or lady that Taedspaddy would have wished to call his own – so high, so happy were his undaunted spirits.

Seated On Top Of The Mare

His new love looked at The Mighty Mountain in the distance. There were no words exchanged between the man and the woman. Soon they saw the valleys below – a beautiful sight. The thoughts that rapidly flowed through their minds had more urgency in them than the dashing waters of Clashing River itself – till at length the two of them came parading round the bend at Sheep's Cross by way of The Valley of The Pig. Their proud heads were raised high and the orange sunset blinked behind them and the ghostly shadows of early evening ached around them.

You should have seen the awestruck faces of everyone on seeing this latest *blow-in* – this strange-looking woman and she seated behind Taedspaddy and she following her sound man (obedient to his call) into an unknown future here in Rookery Rally and they jogging along on the high-stepping mare and she looking so stately, tall and pretty. And one and all we gasped at the sight of them. Was the likes of it ever known? We could scarcely raise a cough. We could scarcely blink an eye. Of course Taedspaddy was only too well aware of our uneasiness on seeing White Snow and he cursed the soul of any man or woman that'd dare say a single word against his beloved young wife-to-be – his lovely woman from beyond the mountains.

After The Whirlwind

After the whirlwind of their reunion the lives of the happy twosome were seen to change with a gathering speed. With White Snow at his side Taedspaddy developed a dramatic new lease of life. Not since his mother's death had he appreciated the goodly smell of the brown earth and the green grass. But now he could hear again the morning songs of the blackbirds and the larks. He acquired a jaunty spring to his everyday step and his limbs itched to be working. It was as though a rosebud had burst open in his chest – as though all those untapped energies lying asleep in him were once more pouring back out of him – as though the smiling spirit of his mother was rushing down from the clouds and back into his heart. And he raised his eyes in thanks to her in her new home beyond the clouds.

Her Hard-working Zeal

Like her husband White Snow was up before the cockerel had blinked an eye. She set about her daily tasks with a will and a driving force and was soon saturated with sweat. Armed with her bucket and her distemper-brush she helped Taedspaddy whitewash the inside and outside walls of their little thatched nest – the pighouse and henhouse too. She went back across Bog Boundless and brought home a dozen of her hens across Clashing River. She added to her store a number of ducks and geese. Round the edge of the yard she planted several flowers and loved the smell of them and she swept and cleaned the yard each day. Before the year ended she sold her bit of land back home without a moment of regret along with the cottage and its red-tiled roof. Everything was a pleasure to her.

Rafferty's Farm

With the new money the happy couple bought a parcel of land on the flat tillage fields – a stone's throw away from Travellers' Rest. It came as a great shock to hear that the two of them were now the owners of Rafferty's small farm right on our doorstep. Hands of disbelief were thrown up in the air everywhere. For some of us this wouldn't do at all. Until now (when we thought he hadn't a penny to his name) Taedspaddy was a fine and manly fellow – a good friend to chat with and pass away a few idle hours of the day. Now that he had a brand new wife and a brand new farm, he was no longer a friend in the eyes of some and they began to turn away from him Before the year was out Jealousy and Envy had raised their ugly heads into something of a roar and from then on Taedspaddy became a figure of fun for a number of his neighbours to despise:

'White Snow must have brought down foggins of silver along with her,' was all the talk now.

'How could that old article (Taedspaddy) have anything more than a shilling or two to rub together in his arse-pocket?'

'How could the likes of him have bought a farm like Rafferty's?'

But other more generous spirits (and there were still a good few among us, thank God) would give the likes of these old misery-guts the cold elbow: 'Ah – 'tis the mountainy women that have the piles of fine money from the sale of their horses and dry cattle. Fair play to the woman from the mountains!

When To Work And When Not To Work

Our women were an example to our men when it came to work and they spent hours on end up near the window with their needle poised by the flickering light of the candle and they darning a huge pile of socks or turning a collar on a shirt while they listened to the evening birds and the odd cow bawling from across the fields. Of course they weren't farmers like their men. To give them their due the men were known to be the most powerful farmworkers whenever the mood was on them. At those times each man seemed like ten men and as soon as Spring was here, you'd see them spreading the manure across the fields: you'd see them leaping around like lambs and slicing the fields with the plough or levelling the earth with the roller and the harrow before sowing their oats and barley: you'd see them whetting the scythe when the hot days of summer were melting close and see them cutting back the briars from the haggart as late as the dusk of evening: Why – they were like thrashing machines.

But all that could vary from season to season. In the ghostly months of winter when there was only a grey sky and many of the little field and woodland creatures were hiding themselves under the ground or in the ditches, our men paid heed to as little work as possible – apart from a few hours foddering and fencing. On those dreary days they'd be upto all sorts of devilment so as to avoid doing work of any kind. You'd find them sitting almost on top of the fire and trying to create a new reel or jig on the tin-whistle: you'd find them (if the weather permitted) tying their legs upside-down on the branches of a tree in their effort to prepare themselves for next year's Daffy-Duck Circus: you'd find them walking the top of the five-barred gates like the circus tightrope walkers and the far-more-dangerous twenty-foot bridge-rail high above River Laughter – all in readiness for the summertime Show-Fair inside in the town. All they seemed to want was a bit of distraction from the real business of fieldwork.

White Snow Was Different

But White Snow was not a woman that blew hot and cold with the seasonal changes. It wasn't in her nature to spend her hours putting on the tomfoolery like the men in their efforts to while away the lazy, harsh days of winter. Whatever the weather – as long as there were hours of daylight to keep her working – she toiled away without pausing for breath and kept looking for ways to improve her new farm's appearance.

We hadn't seen anything like this since the days of Slipperslapper's cousin, Matty. Our newcomer had the strength of a strapping young mare and was proving to be a powerful addition to the life of Taedspaddy. She knew what was in the back of some of our minds and kept trying desperately to show that she was a fitting neighbour for us to rub shoulders with. Weren't we the pack of fools that we couldn't see the sterling qualities in her?

Ever Since Her Childhood

Up till now a woman's place had always been in the house or around the yard or the cowshed with an odd bout of thinning out the rows of turnips when that type of work was needed. To see the way White Snow worked was a new one – not only on her neighbours but also on Taedspaddy – a way of working taught to her from her earliest days of childhood – bred into her from her ancestors and like everyone else she could never escape from her breed. From the time her father died (and she still only thirteen-years-of-age) she had taken herself off to spend her days slaving for the nearby farmers: up at sunrise: working till sunset before going back to sleep. They marvelled at the strength of her for (despite her many jobs) she never seemed to grow tired: pulping the mangols at the crack of dawn: preparing bran-mash for the geese and the ducks: killing and plucking the hens: feeding the cattle: training the cantankerous ass and pulling at his winkers: tending to the bull when he fell short of the longed-for spot in his coupling with a taller cow.

Still a child, she was watched over by the daily visits of her kindly mountainy neighbours and managed to keep herself alive and well with the money she was earning. The Guards and her priest (Father Honesty), seeing how well she was coping (though living on her own and being so young), had turned a blind eye to her situation and had simply ordered the neighbours to keep a look-out so that she didn't entirely kill herself from all her tireless work.

How Well She Had Settled

A year after coming to stay among us White Snow was well and truly settled into the new farm that Rafferty had sold them. Each morning before the lark was barely throating out its first morning song she drove Taedspaddy out from his dreamy bed – even in foul weather when few other souls would have the heart to stir abroad. She herself was also up and ready to begin her day's work – shovelling out the dung from the cowshed with her spade and piling repeated loads of it high on the Sink-Pool from her wheelbarrow.

We Began To Feel Uneasy

Life can change suddenly and as though an inexplicable force or some sort of brilliant light had burst forth from the clouds, one or two seeds of Shame and Self-Doubt started creeping mysteriously into the irreligious souls in our midst. We began to bow down our heads – began to feel strangely uneasy in ourselves. Our previous sniggering coughs up our sleeves began to turn upside-down on themselves. It was as though the powers of heaven itself were slowly unfolding – opening up in front of our eyes and finally getting a hold of us all. We began asking ourselves were we doing something wrong in turning our hearts away from White Snow for it was clear by now that she was a match for any of us in her efforts to face up to life.

There was more: we could see she was overstretching herself and working herself to the bone. There was a noticeable change in her – and in Taedspaddy too – from the blistering attack the two of them went on making at their daily work – as though they were vying with one another to see who could do the most work in a day. We saw that there wasn't a pick of fat left on either of them. Indeed (we said) Taedspaddy had become as thin as a brush-handle. As for White Snow (who was already on the slim side) – she was getting thinner by the day. This left us scratching our heads in search of the reason behind their fiercely competitive attack on the work: it was beyond our understanding. One thing was certain: we knew that in the long run it wouldn't do White Snow any good whatever to go on working the land as though she was a big strong man.

Following This Bout Of Soul-searching

Following this unexpected bout of soul-searching the new season of Spring came round, bringing rapid changes in our midst. And like the new fruitful seeds coming up each day out of the ground an increasing number of us began casting our eyes on her with a growing admiration and getting up on our hind legs and showing bursts of goodwill towards her. At bedtime we'd say the odd little prayer for her well-being in the hope that God would help her put a bit of weight back on her body like the rest of our women, who were all big-chested ladies and as heavy as an ox. We included Taedspaddy too in our prayers – a handsome and inspired man in our eyes once more – a man that had found a woman who could plough the fields like a horse.

Of course there were still one or two less charitable ones (those Weeping Mollys). They never gave up their trade and were shocked to see these changing attitudes in some of their previous friends and tried to hold back the softer hearts among us from these new bouts of Christian Charity. Seemingly The Devil was still alive and well and able to give these old harridans a nudge or two. And (oh, the heathens!) they started inquiring whether White Snow was indeed a woman at all or was she . . . perhaps . . . maybe . . . you never could tell . . . a man merely dressed up in the guise of a woman. For to see White Snow working abroad in the fields (they said) couldn't even the dumbest eejit recognise that no woman ever born had worked as hard as she was doing – steaming away like a young mule – that it would take a strapping man in his youth and prime to keep pace with her. Of course these poor scholars (the rest of us could see it) had once more been blind to the truth: White Snow was simply a better worker than the rest of our women put together. Enough said.

The Children Could See It

Unlike those evil-minded old gossips, our children were possessed of pure Innocence and shared none of their miserable feelings towards any new arrival. They wouldn't even have known whether a *blow-in* was a bit of air in a pig's bladder or inside a German airship or what on earth it might have looked like, were they asked by their schoolmaster. On the way home from Dang-the-skin-of-it's schoolhouse they'd regularly stop at Taedspaddy's gate. They'd admire White Snow's new garden with her beds of rhubarb, lettuce, cabbages and onions. Never willing to disown the arrival of the children, Taedspaddy and White Snow would give them the odd few carrots to chew on: if the carrots were good for the brains of an ass then they were also good for the children.

Taedspaddy loved to see them skipping across the field on their way to meet him. When he gazed at their shiny faces and they soaking up the sunshine he was reminded that he had once almost missed the chance of extending his own childhood – that day long ago when he fell into that miserable boghole. Whenever he took the haycart to the far meadows for a load of hay, he was sure ('Lep up, blasht ye! Lep up, can't ye!') to let half-a-dozen of them ride behind him on the wooden boards as the horse led them out over the giddy headland, the iron-bound wheels of the cart rattling along. And then, amidst the smell of the new-mown hay in their nostrils he would entertain them in that modulating voice of his with his songs and earlier school-day rhymes and the double whistle which only a few of us could master (and then only if we had the singular gap between our front teeth). The tobacco-pipe was forever cocked in the corner of his lower lip and he sucking on it. The children loved to breathe in the delicious smoke belching back from it like honey.

When they hopped down from the haycart they spent the next hour playfully vexing him and rolling round all over his hay like a mad crowd of puppies. Then with fleet feet they ran away home (The Exuberant Fairies behind them), chanting back at him and wickedly calling him names in the hope that he'd chase after them and try to catch them and give them a good tickling:

'Taedspaddy's an Irish Paddy!'

'Taedspaddy's a skinny laddie!

The noise of them – the valley would ring out with their cries and their body-shaking laughter.

All She Wanted Was To Make Her Mark

At this stage nobody had ever come close enough (except Blue-eyed Jack) to know what White Snow was truly like. Had they simply given her the time of day, they'd have realised that all she had ever wanted was to make her mark in our world – that it was her daily prayer. She had this compelling force urging her on and our earlier lack of respect for her had helped drive her on all the more. She was the type of woman always planning ahead. In the quiet of the evenings she'd sit down with Taedspaddy and she'd tell him her wishes – making plans to bring in a new press cupboard for the back wall of her Welcoming Room – a new elm table to replace the deal one – together with six new chairs. In time she lined the three front windows with green boxes and filled them with geraniums. She told her man that if her purse allowed it she'd turn one of the bedrooms into a parlour for one or two visitors to come and have tea now and then – once the day came when they had forgiven her for being just an old *blow-in*.

Whereas We Wanted To Jog Along

Of course the rest of us were not into such detailed planning. For years on end we had jogged along very nicely – content to be singing the same old song as one another. No-one wanted to be seen stepping higher in the world than his neighbour. That sort of thing wouldn't do at all. If any of us had a notion of White Snow's plans and what was in her mind, we'd have been up in arms immediately and accusing her of being the high and mighty one – living beyond her means:

'Wasn't Taedspaddy's little cabin good enough for the likes of her (some would have said)?

'Wasn't it always good enough for him before she came down and threw her hat into the ring' (others would have reminded us)?

It didn't matter – for things were different from now on and it wasn't long before White Snow was to show us a clean pair of heels. She took the horse-and-cart to The Town-of-The-Monks where she purchased a number of iron gates for her yard and fields. And then she introduced herself to Lord Plus-Fours and purchased from him a number of poplar-trees with which she and Taedspaddy lined the ditches so as to put a stop to the prevailing Kerry winds that threatened their chimney.

The Forestry And The Wagging Tongues

She was beginning to realise she'd need a deal of fresh money to gain further improvements. She encouraged Taedspaddy to find work in The Lisnagorna Forestry. Mindful of bygone days when her beloved father had taught her about planting the young spruce-trees and had shown her the particular details of thinning out the shoots and how to direct the roots against those old Kerry winds, she passed on Dinjo's skills to Taedspaddy. Indeed she proved to be the perfect tree-scholar as she directed her sound man into the arms of forestry work and he soon took up his new role as a Plantation-Man.

The Wagging Tongues Returned

Just when many of us had softened our hard hearts – just when we thought that White Snow had earned her place in Rookery Rally – as soon as Taedspaddy started driving his horse-and-cart up to the forest the wagging tongues got busier than ever:

'Wasn't the new farm good enough for herself and Taedspaddy?'

'How could a *blow-in* be anything other than a greedy wretch?'

And they summed up their contempt with 'what made the two of them think themselves so different from the rest of us small farmers?'

Clearly (they said) White Snow was treating Taedspaddy like a footstool – purely for her own ends – that she was making him as snooty as herself – too big for his boots – that he no longer knew his proper place alongside the rest of us farmers.

We had to close our ears to this rash of new words. Blasht their hides – would they ever give their tongues a minute's rest or our ears a minute's peace? To tell the truth – there wasn't a word in our language for praising a woman with White Snow's driving ambition – a woman who wanted to better herself and be respected in her own lifetime.

By now she had a far different air to things but she kept this to herself. It was the other small farmers (she told herself) and not herself, who were too grand and stuck-up in themselves as to be seen going out looking for some extra forestry work in support of their farms:

'What – *meeeeeh* (they'd say) – to go out looking for work in The Forestry.'

'What – *meeeeeh!* Do ye think I'm that poor a wretch as to go begging for more work?'

'Can't ye see I'm a step above all that?'

'Can't ye see I'm a farmer for godsake!'

It was a step down and not a step up for them to be seen as a pathetic road-worker or a miserable ditch-mender or a greedy little forestry-worker. And in her bedroom at night White Snow would smile to herself and then she'd shake her head and sigh: 'Fair play to you, Taedspaddy! – it's not *you* that has become the high 'n' mighty one – it's not *you* that has the airs and graces about your station. You jumped at the chance of earning a new bit of money in a regular job.' It was true for her. And though Taedspaddy was uncertain at first and almost frightened at the depths of White Snow's energy and ambition, he let her drive him out the door each day with a dash of holywater on his nose and take the horse-and-cart up into the forest.

She Worked Harder Than Ever

Whilst Taedspaddy laboured in the forest, looking after the growing shrubs and clearing the briars away from the riverbanks, White Snow was forced to do twice her own work on the farm and undertake all the difficulties that this work placed on her shoulders. Of course the big money soon came rolling in and the manager in The Market Cross Bank began to smile sweetly on the two of them and he brought them in for tea and chocolate cake. And then with the soft tears in White Snow's eyes the babies came into their lives in steady measure – until there were six smiling faces adorning their Welcoming Room. These were the happiest days in the lives of Taedspaddy and White Snow. Tired though he was, the big man (the old softie) got down on his knees in the evening and played with his children for hours on end. Indeed he was something of a child himself in the way he teased them, cajoling them and petting them. And they adored him. The serious business (as always) was left to the woman-of-the-house. And White Snow, like a cat with her kittens, scrubbed the children's cheeks and necks till they were red-raw and made sure that they cleaned their teeth with the soot from the hob. Then she knelt in the middle of them and they said their long list of prayers, ending with the prayer 'And God bless me!'

The Sad Fates

The happy couple would have liked to keep pace with the rest of us and have half-a-dozen more children to their name. And they might yet have had them, if Destiny had given them half a chance. But those secret and troublesome fairies (The Sad Fates – the enemies of all that is good) were always seething and miserably ill-at-ease for they had been born without a heart to their bodies and they couldn't leave Taedspaddy and White Snow alone. In their cavern on top of the mountains they never seemed to sleep. By now they were already dressing themselves up for a cruel day's destruction on Taedspaddy's farm.

It Was Just Another Morning

It was just another morning like all other mornings. Taedspaddy was away in the forest. To the surprise of us all he had already earned a sum large enough to buy eight additional acres adjacent to his farm in Travellers' Rest.

On seeing the way White Snow was killing herself doing her husband's work as well as her own, the women shook their heads: 'It isn't right. It isn't right. Can't ye see it isn't right?' Isn't Taedspaddy the mean old devil that he has to go out and grab for more and more money? Hasn't he enough of it? Wasn't he always a bleddy mean man (they reminded us) – sleeping at the foot of the bed across his mother's ailing feet rather than light a good turf fire in the bedroom to keep the life in her.'

May God forgive them the cruelty of their tongues. Taedspaddy had loved his mother beyond their wildest dreams. And unknownst to any of them, when she was at death's door and there was no chance of her ever regaining her strength, he had nursed her and had turned her wet sheets for her – had wept over her as no man before or since had ever done. And then he had buried her quietly below in Abbey Acres Graveyard without wake or interference from any of them.

The Afternoon Came On

The afternoon came on. Bunches of dark clouds came rolling lugubriously down the hillsides from behind Corcoran's Well. White Snow never saw the threatening nature of those dark clouds, so busy was she at her work. She was beyond in The Seventh Field, hoping to bring in the thirty-six trams of hay like the previous year. This time, however, she was working on her own. She threw the metal chains over the base of each tram – again and again – her back and shoulders soaked in sweat and the insects clinging to her. This was the way with her – throwing the chains round the base of the tram rather than spending half the day firing the hay into the horse-and-cart. She yoked the tram's chains onto the horse. With her whip she drove her hard-pulling horse and the chained tram down the hill and into the hayshed rather than wait for the horse to lumber down the fields with his heavy load of hay slowing him down. It was a new one on all of us.

It was dusk. Theose mysterious cold dews were falling fast, replacing the earlier breezes. White Snow had drawn into the haggart twenty-five of the thirty-six trams of her hay. She had worked at wind-speed. No man in Rookery Rally (let alone a woman) had ever matched this staggering load of work. In the following days when news of it reached us, our brains were so addled that we were left wondering where on earth this woman from the mountains had gotten so much strength. Some of the more imaginative among us said that as soon as they were born in those faraway places, the women were put in beneath the cow that was chained to the half-door for this very purpose – that such a sound nurturing at birth was the source of their Samson-like strength. But the twenty-fifth tram was to prove the last tram that White Snow would ever throw her chains around. She had (even for her) overworked every muscle in her body: 'After all,' (said a tearful and heartbroken Blue-eyed Jack a day or two later), 'she hadn't the mechanics of an alarm clock inside in her, had she?'

White Snow stood in the yard, her work for the day done. She took off her working wellingtons. She put her head into the bucket of cold water to cool her head and wipe away the sweat from her face. All of a sudden she felt something like a fierce sledgehammer hitting her a blow in her chest. She must have known it was her heart. She staggered across the yard where she fell down in front of the half-door, never to rise up again. She lay there – like a small bird with a broken wing that had fallen out of it nest, helplessly awaiting its fate, its heart still pumping furiously. She couldn't move a muscle and, knowing that her hour of death was close at hand, she lost consciousness.

As Happy As A Field Of Thrushes

In the meantime Taedspaddy was returning with the six children from the other side of the wood. They were as happy as a fieldful of thrushes, singing their summertime songs as the horse carried them behind him in the cart. As soon as they entered the yard they saw the sad state of their mother at the half-door. They set up such an almighty din that the birds in the trees round the haggart almost died of fright and fled. Between them they carried White Snow into The Welcoming Room and from there they lifted her onto the bed – the children all the time ('mother, mother, dearest mother!') dancing around their dying mother and bawling at her to get up out of the bed and come back and join them.

He Sent For The Priest

Though he knew that his dear wife hadn't a single sin on her soul, Taedspaddy sent for Father Sensibly to come and give her his blessing and final Absolution. And though Doctor Glasses came in along with the priest, there was nothing that he could do for her in spite of all his ministering. White Snow had had an almighty stroke and she was dead within the week, her soul soaring off beyond the clouds on its final journey to meet her Maker.

The Depths Of His Grief

It was impossible to feel the depths of Taedspaddy's grief – the fierce heaviness of the pains in his chest. The sunshine had gone out of him. His previous joys – listening to the little birds singing in the laurels and to the howling winds knocking at his windows during a stormy night when he was safely locked in the warm arms of White Snow – were gone from him in a flash.

A day or two later he dressed himself in his spotless wedding-suit and he placed her coffin on his horse-and-cart. He would take her with Slippaway and the cart on the sad journey back across the mountains to be buried in a final resting-place alongside her mother and grandfather. With the children in tow, he crossed Clashing River. It was a long and painful journey, the tension in them unbearable, and there wasn't one word said between any of them till they reached the graveyard. Taedspaddy asked his children to hand him down the pick and shovel. With his tears hopping down from his eyes, he opened up the grave. They all knelt down silently and prayed the rosary over her coffin. Little did the good man know but it wouldn't be too long before his own soul would be sucked up into the skies to come and join her.

A Year To The Day

A year to the day Taedspaddy was coming home from The Roaring Town with a few bags of messages and six cream buns for his children. The good mare was clip-clopping her way along The Creamery Road towards the yard. The children ran out excitedly to meet their father. He had been spoiling them more and more since the death of their mother. They knew he'd be bringing them home a gramophone record or two (he loved the music at night around the blazing turf-fire) and big bags of their favourite peggy's-leg sweets. They raced one another up the lane towards the lace of the horse-and-cart. They looked up at their father. He was as still as a church statue. He was stone cold dead. He had (we all agreed) died of a broken heart. According to Doctor Glasses, he had been dead all the way home from The Roaring Town. The faithful mare had delivered her last rites for him.

The Following Evening

The following evening the praises of White Snow, the praises of Taedspaddy, reached a new dimension below in the church in Copperstone Hollow. We could see that Father Sensibly was not his usual cheery self. He had a face on him like a thunderclap as he looked down on us and gave us such a lambasting lash from his tongue for the cruel ways in which a number of us had given White Snow the cold shoulder. But by now he was wasting his breath. Not a day too soon the sun had finally discovered itself and was jabbing its porcupine rays into our sinful souls. Even the most niggardly of us didn't need to be listening to his sermonising to make us hang down out heads in shame for the way we had behaved. Our sincere, if belated, rosary-beads clack-clacked against our knees as we offered up our fervent prayers for the souls of Taedspaddy and White Snow.

Love and Romance

The words Love and Romance were foreign words amongst us in our part of the world – although we had our own words for being warm-hearted and loving to one another. But everyone agreed that this was the end of a beautiful love story, a match made above in heaven between Taedspaddy and White Snow from the day they'd met at the boghole. And if the angels have wings in heaven there never had been two happier souls than the two of them. It was the end of the life of a *blow-in*. It was the end also of our own lives of small-mindedness. It was the end of our jealousies over a new arrival coming in amongst us from beyond the mountains.

The Following Day

The following day was the day of Taedspaddy's funeral. For the first time ever Rookery Rally was silent and there wasn't even an echo of man, woman or child left behind on either road or field. Throwing away our previous unkindness and hiding from our recent guilt – and in order for some of us to gain a penitential remission for our sins – we all traipsed up the long winding road towards Bog Boundless. A faint breeze stirred up around us as though our ancestors had arrived in our midst and were egging us ever onwards. We crawled our way out passed the top of The Mighty Mountain, on towards Clashing River and to Hurricane Hill where our men insisted on making use of the few pick-axes and shovels that they'd brought along with them. They reopened White Snow's grave and with bell, book and candle they lowered Taedspaddy down next to his beloved wife.

We Gained Forgiveness

In this way we gained the good Lord's forgiveness. Taedspaddy's uncle (The Gog) came down and started a new life at the ripe old age of seventy – himself and the six heart-broken children in harmony. And from that day onwards there wasn't a *blow-in* who wasn't given a fighting chance to win glory in life's race amongst us – there wasn't a *blow-in* who wasn't made to feel as welcome as the flowers in May – with a far fairer treatment than that given to the once lovely grey-and-white haired, sweet-natured horse-of-a-woman who was known as White-Snow. May the Lord be good to herself and to Taedspaddy in their home in The Beyond above the Tipperary skies.

SIX

How I'll-Daze-Ye and his cudgel spent a day in the town faction-fighting.

'Twas In The Stamp Of Him

The man couldn't avoid being what he was. And if Big Red was famed for being our one and only true giant, I'll-Daze-ye (a modest-sized man of five-and-a-half feet in height from toe to head) was our greatest champion when it came to the use of a fighting man's fists. To state his pedigree (as one would with a bull) his mother was Tarry Nan from out near The Black Banks. His father was The Holy Terror from the Valley of The Black Cattle. His grandfather had been known as The Hard Hands, a great bit-of-a-fighter in his own right. And that fellow's father (The Great Bear) was said to have learnt his fighting skills abroad in The Crimea before destroying single-handed a dozen Hussians during The Battle of Inkerman. May God rest the entire pack of them after the hardships that they each saw in this life and may He give them a soft bed above in heaven. Like I'll-Daze-Ye himself, they were all good fighting men – but above all, good people in their time. Enough said.

The Malignities

It was Saturday evening and Holy Mass was the next day. It was time for the once-weekly shave with the cut-throat razor and for the washing of a man's upper body. I'll-Daze-Ye was abroad near the flagstones, his shirt stripped open down to the waist. He was the only one in Rookery Rally who had a pump in his yard and he was giving himself the full flow of the achingly cold water.

The Malignities had the right of way through his yard. And though the three of them were the well-fed and manly fellows and each over six feet in height, they couldn't but envy the size and strength of I'll-Daze-Ye when they saw his bare body for they had to admit that they themselves were each a small shade less powerful than himself in the width of their chests and the muscles in their upper arms. I'll-Daze-Ye's physique was as trim as a cat's and there wasn't a pick of fat on him. The Malignities knew that he had the reputation of having the strength of half-a-dozen fists on him and at least the brains of two prizefighters in the use of his knuckles. He also had (though they didn't know it at the time) his father's wise motto: strike first: ask questions afterwards.

The Scurrilous Remarks

I'll-Daze-Ye was drying himself with the rough towel when these fine fellows made a vile and scurrilous remark about big-chested men like himself – how it was a well-known fact that such men were found to be very small in other more intimate parts of their bodies. Ah, them and their wicked tongues. I'll-Daze-Ye didn't take their uncalled-for scurrilities too well – especially as it was on his own doorstep that this insult was given him. The row started up in earnest and got hot and heavy. The finish of it was that The Malignities ungraciously tipped over the milk from I'll-Daze-Ye's two creamery tanks and spilt it all over his yard. Then they and their merry laughter went gallivanting out through the gap of the haggart-field. The likes of this (the spilling of the milk) was never known before and such scandalous behaviour was bound to burn the anger in our fighting man and prompt him to make use of his mighty knuckles on their impudent skulls – big men though they thought themselves to be and safe in their numbers (three against one small man like himself – however broad his chest.)

No Milk Left

It was a sorry situation. There'd be no milk to take to the creamery – no skimmed milk later for the feeding of his calves – no cream from the milk to bring home to his wife (The Saintly Woman) to shake into butter in her sweet-gallon tin. The poor man was fit to be tied and he thought his chest would burst asunder from the anger rising up in him. But (rest assured) he was a man of inborn cuteness and of sound self-discipline. He held tough for a short while and took his time shaving himself, leaving just a few cat-hairs here and there, which were always visible beneath his eyes as a sort of trademark. He took the soapy water and he groomed his wavy hair with it so that it stood up straight in a handsomely-curved quiff. He looked at himself in the broken bit of looking-glass and he stroked his jaw. His hair looked more remarkable than ever, giving a further twist to the unusual silver sheen in it, which (alone among our men) had been its colour since his twentieth year. He smiled to himself as he inspected his fine set of knuckles and he blew on them and polished them. Said he to himself, 'I'll eat the three of those Malignities alive, so help me God. I'll redden their faces. I'll rattle their teeth for them. With mee flailing fists I'll make three horizontal sportsmen out of them as soon as I reach their yard – them and their playful antics – wait and see if I don't.'

He loved a good fight – loved the very challenge of it. However, had the ghost of his great-grandfather stepped out of his grave, he would have shaken his wise old head sadly. For the thought of I'll-Daze-Ye's fierce desire to beat and chastise the lives of The Malignities would have sickened his stomach. Mighty prizefighters such as The Great Bear had been the very shy men of old when it came to showing the drinking-shops and the rest of the countryside the size of their knuckles. Of course I'll-Daze-Ye would have argued with his great-grandfather: 'Surely ye'd agree – a family's milk is a delicate matter – as precious as a family's snares or rabbit-traps.' He was going to put a finish to this evening's fun and games. He could see The Malignities stretched out before him in a forlorn heap – the blood from their noses and lips flowing along the yard like his own spilt milk. God would forgive him for the anger that was about to galvanise his fighting fists and help him beat the impudent scoundrels to within an inch of Purgatory's gates.

He Put On His Best Boots

He put on his best boots. He didn't even have time to shine them with the dab of butter. He put on a clean white shirt. He looked a fine specimen of a man. Then he headed for the haggart gap, his wife (The Saintly Woman) all the time clinging to his back and dragging at his coat in an attempt to prevent him from going to fight the three huge men and getting himself half-killed by them. I'll-Daze-Ye gently cast her aside. He hopped out over the ditch and in a roaring thunderstorm hurtled his hobnail boots up the field, tearing towards The Valley of The Pig to introduce his fists to the three Malignity gentlemen.

He Stood On The Malignities' Flagstones

His boots rang on The Malignities' flagstones, echoed by The Wilful Fairies. He was bent on giving them the most thorny introduction to his fists – a welcome they had least expected from him – a welcome they were unlikely to forget. He invited the three mighty warriors to step outside their half-door and get the benefit of his knuckles: 'Coom on out, ye basthards! Coom on out to hell – till I nail ye to the yard!' he yelled, the sparks flying from him. His blistering voice would have frightened a priest out of his boots and you'd hear him like a bull below in Abbey Acres. He threw off his coat and rolled up his sleeves. He spat on his fists and wiped the spittle from his chin. 'Upon mee soul, I'll make a Devil's eyesight out of the three of ye – I'll paste yeer two eyes into one – ye'll see if I don't before I leave yeer yard!' Then he did a few cartwheels round the yard and danced the finest of jig-steps over to their half-door, all the time promising to daze the three Malignities out of their senses. They had to laugh and hold their sides at the notion of him. If he was anything at all, I'll-Daze-Ye was always true to the name he bore for he had proved more than once that he was able to daze even the mightiest of Rookery Rally's brawlers. But to the three Malignities (with their superiority in numbers) to fight against I'll-Daze-Ye seemed a safe enough action to be taking. Jeering all over again, they took off their coats and swaggered across the yard to fight. They were the essence of contentment as they surrounded I'll-Daze-Ye – their fists held high and menacingly in front of his face – the face they felt sure they'd be pounding to smithereens in a moment's time.

But the laughter soon left their eyes and you'd pay good money to see what happened next: I'll-Daze-Ye (the vitality of him) met them like a thrashing-machine whirling before a field of corn. He proceeded to paste their faces and clout the skin clean off of each of them till their ears were almost put out throught their jaw, their blood bespangling the chicken-dung in the yard and terrifying the ducks, hens and geese. He threw the three of them, senseless and glassy-eyed, up onto the ass-and-car and not a twitch out of them: 'Lie there and rue the day ye crossed me, ye gob-shites,' he said. Then he turned on his heel and hopped back out the way he'd come in. It would be a while before The Malignities knew which day of the week it was. Peace and quietness once more filled his soul. The villains would keep themselves quiet for a good while now. He had taken the squeak clean out of their boots.

Small Matters Could Start A Row

In Rookery Rally little things had always started the row. It needn't be those age-old arguments about boundary fences or boundary streams. Nor was it always about the odd stray bull braking loose from a man's field and trying to engender his neighbour's cows with his precious seed. Nor was it about the stealing of impudent glances at another man's saintly woman. It was often a much smaller thing – like the annoyances at Holy Mass when we were all on our scratched knees and praying like fair hell, saying one decade of the rosary after another for our departed ancestors or making a silent offering to The Blessed Virgin or to our Heavenly Maker to save us from perils and unexpected woes and guard our cattle from falling into drains. Suddenly you'd hear an almighty yell, followed by a savage oath from someone at the back of the church as a misfortunate wretch felt the jaw cut off of him from a well-aimed bit of turf with its hard edge.

Donie Baloney

The irreligious Donie Baloney (a young man who liked nothing better than eating black-puddings raw) attended Mass regularly like the rest of us, not wanting to receive a mortal sin on his soul. But (God help him) the restless fellow was more often than not bored out of his mind by the constant jaw-

jawing and Latin sing-songing of Father Abstemious, the eighty-year-old in-between priest (before the arrival of the new priest). To amuse himself he liked nothing better than to fill his pockets with half-a-dozen handy-sized sods of turf (just the rough corners of them) before setting out for church. Halfway through Mass, as we looked over our shoulders, what did we see? Donie Baloney (a squint in his eye and he twirling a lump of turf) slipping out from some shadowy corner at the back of the church and steadying the aim of his right fist in our direction before deciding which one of us to kill with the first pelt of one of his sharp bits of turf. Across the back of the church skimmed his turf-bit like a flat stone on the waters of River Laughter. Kneeling with one knee on our caps (as we always did), we quickly sought refuge and hid our ears behind our coat-collars. Some of us dived for cover to the ground so as to avoid a broken jaw in the face of the oncoming missile. Our rosary-beads became twisted round our fists. It was then you'd hear the row rising up and the sermon of the saintly priest being interrupted: 'Sweet suffering Jaysuz, if I ketch the little fecker who has damaged mee jaw I'll knock the shite out of his britches! Let me at him!'

And Other Prime Byze

Donie Baloney was not the only devil working at the back of the church. Of course the saintly women were all up in the front pews, sanctimoniously hitting their chests with belts of their fists and looking up adoringly at the statue of The Sacred Heart and the thorns around it and kissing the feet of the statue of Saint Francis opposite Jesus. This was something more than foreign for our men to be doing – kissing the toes of the man-statue of Francis when they had their own wives at home to slobber over if the need ever occurred to them?

But what happened next was a pure sin. A man would find himself about to celebrate the anniversary of his mother's death by going to communion when some almighty eejit would stealthily tie the fellow's bootlaces together in an unbreakable knot. When the time came for the Holy Communion bell to be rung and for the good man to get up off of his knees and march down the aisle to the starched altarcloth, he'd no sooner get to his feet than (bless the bit) he'd fall helplessly our on top of his nose. Once again the sudden bursts of impious cursing ('wait'll I ketch the whoor!') filled the holy church. What the children made out of all this, heaven alone knows. Was no-one able to live here in peace? Was nothing sacred in Rookery Rally? Ah, religion indeed!

Children Themselves Could Start The Row

Outrages were often even simpler than these. Children themselves were well able to start the row. September was the time for the apple-trees to be swollen with goodness. A bright soft day came on with a promise of later heat when a band of children (I'll-Daze-Ye's six chicks among them) chose to rob the orchard of Curl 'n' Stripes rather than go down and rob the orchard of some poor old woman without a penny to her name. They knew from their parents that the cash-box in Curl 'n' Stripes' drinking-shop was full to the brim with shiny coins and that the old miser was loath to share any of them with the likes of us.

Curl 'n' Stripes, however, was lying in wait for the little robbers when they were coming back over his wire-fence and crossing his yard, their skirts and jerseys full-laden with apples stolen from his precious trees. This time he was not going to be beaten: he'd knock the happiness off of their faces (said he to himself). From the upstairs window at the gable-end of his house (ah, the inventor of roguery) he emptied his rage by means of the double-contents of his pisspot straight down on the children's shitty heads. It was an indignity never heard tell of in all the annals of our history.

A child's revenge can often be sweet. The rage they felt was unspeakable and their language unprintable (feck! feck! and feck again!) in any fairytale book. They weren't big enough to attack Curl 'n' Stripes himself. Instead – they began kicking his two innocent dogs round and round the yard till the poor souls were both half-dead. Not satisfied with this, they wheeled the old miser's horse-and-cart out along the laurel laneway and fired it into the middle of the dyke. Could children in their turn be so cruel and heartless here in a Christian establishment like Rookery Rally? The answer was clear.

A few days later (and their rage still bubbling up inside them) they saw poor harmless Simon-not-so-simple bringing home on his horse-and-cart the heavy sacks of flour from the mill to bake his monthly supply of bread for him and his mother. To his surprise they sprang out on him – repeatedly jumping up and down on the back shafts of his cart till they spilled his flour all over The Creamery Road. It was clear that their anger against Curl 'n' Stripes had spilled out all over the young ragamuffins and there would soon have to be a heavy price to pay for their crime.

A Family Dispute

The argument over the stolen apples in his orchard and the subsequent attack on the children with his shitty pisspot now rose into an all-out family dispute between I'll-Daze-Ye's people and The Malignities, who were related by marriage to Curl 'n' Stripes and more or less his blood-brothers. Even though the art of faction-fighting was almost a part of ancient history elsewhere, both families began to prepare in earnest for the oncoming fray: The Malignities and their own crowd against I'll-Daze-Yer and his kinsmen (The Out-and-Outers), who had arrived here some years ago from Cork. There would be a dozen men collected on either side.

The Knowledge Of Woods

Essential preparations would be made and their cudgels inspected and repaired from previous fights. A sound knowledge of wood was always thought advisable in any household – be it the whitethorn for lighting our fires or the imported hickory (as hard as the handle of a shovel) for the wheels of our pony-and-trap or the flexible ash for our hurley-sticks (the olden-day elm no longer being considered good enough even for our children to hurl with). The whitethorn saw to it that our fires glowed from morning till night: the hickory saw to it that our wheels would last for a hundred years: the ash (though less hard than the elm) would still be useful enough when connecting with another man's hurley-stick on the top of his skull.

An Answer To Prayer

If a man were to trust in his God there was always a tidy answer to his prayers when his sole ambition was to smash a few arms and legs and chastise another man or that man's brother or indeed his entire family, be they from our own flock or from those we called The Black Protestants. In previous years there were a variety of weapons at hand depending on the ardency required and the seriousness of the aggrieved dispute: the rusty billhook: the spade-handle: the flail: the scythe: the bayonet: even the odd rock. And before the day ended, very pretty fighting it had always been for the townie women to crowd the upper windows of Jinnet Street and behold.

The Fierce Cudgel

But the fierce cudgel had finally become the best weapon for these present little wars and it was a handy thing to have tucked under the jacket. Whilst other men were using cudgels made from oak or crabtree and with a naturally-formed lump at the end of it, I'll-Daze-Ye preferred the wood of the blackthorn – a cudgel he called his loaded butt. It had a hole bored into its root and it was filled with molten lead – an idea handed down to him from his father and grandfather.

Wasn't Our Blacksmith The Mighty Man?

Wasn't our blacksmith (Hammer-the-Smith) the mighty man? We knew that he drank the iron-shoe waters every day ('good for the blood') and that he was able to come to a man's rescue and make a weapon like I'll-Daze-Ye's loaded butt with as much lead in it as he could melt down. The hurley-maker (Tom-the-Bee) then wrapped a few hoops round the boss of it. I'll-Daze-Ye measured the strength of his cudgel, twisting it round and round his shoulders and smiling that little smile of his, for he knew that his weapon was unbeatable – that he'd be as safe as houses when armed with it and ready for any faction-fighting that had to be done against The Malignities or the orchard's owner, Curl 'n Stripes and his pisspot.

Confidence

Like I'll-Daze-Ye the rest of us had every confidence in Hammer-the-Smith and we placed him almost alongside the priest who absolved us from our sins at Easter-time. The man was gifted. His bellows and anvil were never silent. He could shod your cartwheels and fix up your plough. From the rim of a cartwheel he could make a Celtic cross as your grave-marker if you were unlucky enough to lose your life from the belt of a cudgel during a faction-fight. And so well did he use his rasp and pincers on the shoes of our horse or ass (as well as the knife for pairing their hooves) that they were no longer tripping over their feet but were seen dancing a fine jig-step next morning on even the slippiest of our roads.

His White Shirt

Though his smithy was filled with sizzling smoke and grime Hammer always wore a white shirt beneath his apron and went home at nightfall without a stain or a smudge on it. This was a mystery to us all. Even those old gossips (The Weeping Mollys) couldn't fathom it out and gave half-the-day talking at the wellhole about his fastidiousness. To put it simply – for a big rough-fisted man like him our smith was neatness, cleanliness and tidiness all rolled into one. His wife boasted that she never had to pick a sock up off the floor after him before he stepped into bed to join her. She knew (but she wouldn't tell you) that alone among us he wore a pair of inner white drawers and that, rather than give them to her, he'd first remove the little pissy stains with a stealthy washing of his own before giving them to her for the Monday washing. In later years (when he was dying) the last thing that he did was to call for a bowl of hot water and lay his feeble hands in it so as to get the imaginary bits of grime washed away from him.

Smith and Bonesetter Like His Father

Hammer was the only man who could repair your loaded butt and at the same time fix you up more than decently with metal splints and plates in your arms or your knees or head, having been given the unuaual blessing of the powers of bonesetter as well as smith. Fair play to him! Indeed the smith's own father had been known by everyone as our homemade body-physician and went by the name of Bonesetter (never having been given any other name for he had never been christened). It was he that could mend an animal's bones and fix them up even better than The Bearded Vet. With his mixture of laurel-leaf paste and oils he could cure the body-burns of a frail woman like Gentility when she fell into the fire: he could cure a broken thigh-bone with a heated politice of cowdung and cream: he could put a fistful of goose-grease round a man's aching muscles till the pain was gone: he could use the milk of the redshank to cure a man's warts: he could use cups of flour and herbs to free them from blood-poisoning – just like his own grandfather (The Cow Doctor). And if that wasn't enough – he could reach his hand inside a man's jaw and pull out a tooth or a bit of loosely-growing bone before the fellow knew he had done it and without him feeling even one shnig of pain. And it was said that though his jowls were beardy and as rough as sandpaper Bonesetter's fingers and hands were as smooth as a little child's. Even The Weeping Mollys had to admit that God must have come down and lodged in his hands since he was able to turn old Gentility into a racing greyhound within a week of her seeing him. And (they said) if the Pope in The Holy City was a man to be sainted then Bonesetter should have been given a holy ring round his own head. Enough said.

In Recent Times

Recently there'd been the odd occasion when I'll-Daze-Ye had to go up to Hammer-the-Smith and get his cudgel repaired – so fiercely had he damaged it from rapping it against his enemies' ribs in the brutal faction-fighting that had raged the length of Jinnet Street. As a result of the children's raid on Curl 'n' Stripes' orchard and the consequent punishment with the pisspot, he'd again be needing his weapon for a beautiful day's carousing and might even be needing the bone-setting skills of Hammer-the-Smith to tend to his wounds or breakages – unless he came home with a broken backbone and found himself entirely dead.

Doctor Glasses Was Aggrieved

Praise for our blacksmith wasn't universal and what grieved one man in particular (our own Doctor Glasses) was the fact that, in spite of his own personal wisdom and book-knowledge (not to mention his professional leather bag and his sleek, velvet moustache and all his years of training below in Cork) our men preferred to test the bone-setting hands of their blacksmith after a day's faction-fighting rather than run to the doctor's surgery. Although they feared the wrath and rebukes of Doctor Glasses for their devilish love of these wild sporting battles, in reality the reason for attending the smith was the fact that his fee was a good bit cheaper than the doctor's. Of course they knew that Hammer-the-Smith was a man born of the same clay as themselves and not an old blow-in from Cork. They also knew that their beloved blacksmith (not having the great education of Doctor Glasses) would not be inclined to speak words of rebuke to them but would measure his praise of them by the bravery they'd shown in the most recent battle and the consequential seriousness of their injuries and loss of blood.

The Youthful Days Of I'll-Daze-Ye

I'll-Daze-Ye hadn't always been the mighty scrapper that he became in later life. In idle moments as he sat by the fire opposite his wife (The Saintly Woman) he shuddered to think of the helpless weakling he used to be when he was a small child. Those were the days when he hadn't yet been given the friendly name of I'll-Daze-Ye but was known as Sammy (after his mother's father). He remembered the regular drubbings he received from the fists of the other schoolchildren – especially from those massive giants,

The Malignities – each of them already as huge as a plough-horse. From the day he first entered the schoolhouse they started calling him their little popinjay. Thereafter they continued to tease and harass him on his way to and from school. This was a terrible predicament to be in. It saddened his poor mother to see how delicate and underdeveloped her child's body was for he was almost half-a-foot smaller than the rest of the boys.

The Shepher Boy

Added to this he was forever plagued with an ache in his ear (the imagined cause of Sammy's lack of growth). There seemed to be no cure for him and even Lord Elegance's own helmsman (Doctor Fingertips) couldn't get the better of it. However – this time round The Weeping Mollys proved good and they brought back the news that there was a shepherd boy out near Clashing River, who had the very cure for healing these pains in the ear.

The shepherd boy rode his horse down the hill, armed with his mysterious medicine bottle. The yellow liquid was as bitter as a lemon and was hard for Sammy to swallow. The youth gave him three or four eggcups of the mixture – a concoction of dandelions, eggwhite and a few of his own hand-me-down secrets. Whatever it was – it worked a royal treat and in no time at all Sammy was free of the cruel pain in his ear. Moreover – the weakness in his body was soon seen to depart from him and his growth shot up remarkably. Before the summer was over he was jumping round like a lark and hopping around the fields the same as the other children (thank God).

Before His Confirmation

Finally Sammy was twelve and making his Confirmation when he'd become a stout-hearted soldier of Christ. However, the mighty fists that were to manifest themselves in later years with the strength of a mule's hooves were nowhere yet to be seen. In spite of his newly increased growth he still had the appearances of a gentle lad – a lad that was expected to stay that way in later life. He couldn't help having his father's handsome face and a pair of startling green eyes belonging to his mother and the delicate jaws of a pretty girl.

Seasons Can Change

Throughout the rest of his schooldays he continued to avoid The Malignities like the plague. But seasons can change unexpectedly and a day was to come round which would prove the truth of this – dramatically. He was halfway home from school when The Malignity children caught up with him in the field that ran along the banks of River Laughter: 'Aha! – mee little goose-of-a-man,' they cried as they surrounded him. They swore they'd cut off his two ears – if not worse. Sammy was trapped like a fieldmouse crouching in a stubbled field. They stripped him of his clothes in front of the giggling girls and threw him into the icy waters of River Laughter. It was a miracle that the heavens didn't fall down on top of these cruel heathens for so great a sin.

The despoiling of his body, however, was to prove not the end of Sammy's world. Wonder of wonders – it was at this precise moment in his life that (almost like the good Saint Paul) an almighty and indescribable gift came down from heaven and filled his spirit. And what was this gift? It was the gift of Rage – a rage that would stand him in good faith when the right time came.

A Few Years Later

A few years after Sammy had left school he was walking home from The Roaring Town. It was a bright evening with a little breeze rustling its way across the fields. The Malignities followed him out along the road and caught up with him near Yawn (Bazeen's historic turnabout landmark). By now Sammy and themselves were just about fully-grown. He himself was a good five-and-a-half feet tall and had a fine curly head of hair on him like a wild cauliflower. What's more – he had filled out considerably across his backbone and chest.

His sour-faced enemies reached him, expecting to see the tears trickling down his jaws as he staggered to the side of the road. He shoved his back up against the stony ditch to prepare for his inevitable fate – or at least try to save himself from their thudding fists by putting up a bit of a fight lest they again strip him to the skin.

Ssneeringly his enemies informed him of his imminent death. Sammy knew he wasn't fleet-footed enough to escape from them and that he was in for a bad beating. It was no use calling on the ghosts of his ancestors to come down from the skies and give him the strength he needed. The misfortunate lad leaned in submission against the ditch and awaited his inevitable fate.

But there comes a moment in life when everything inexplicably changes. For suddenly he looked up to the clouds as once he had done at school when trying to find the answer to a difficult sum or catechism question. Desperately he called on Almighty God to come down and rescue him – if only this once in his life.

For many months thereafter Sammy told his story around the drinking-shops of Abbey Cross and beyond:

'I called on mee Heavenly Maker to come down from the skies and rescue me from the brutal fists of The Malignities.'

'The good God-in-Heaven came down to me in the blink of an eye when I needed him most.'

'I saw a flash of light pouring down on top of mee head and heard him whispering in mee ear.'

'He told me reach behind me with mee fingers along the stony ditch-wall.'

'Lads, would ye believe this? I found that God had given me the present of a mighty big rock from on top of the ditch – behind mee right shoulder.'

'I shouted at the three Malignities: 'Run, let ye, run for yeer lives, ye mushrooms! – I'll daze ye! I'll daze ye! – ye pack of shitty-arsed basthards!'

'Had I a reins I'd have hanged all three of them there and then.'

'Ye should have seen the startled look on their faces as I struck out at them!'

'Giving thanks to mee Blessed Saviour, with all the powers in mee body I belted that mighty big rock straight up into their heads, putting the blood pumping out of their faces and I left them there – dazed and for dead – the beautiful imprint of the rock warming their foreheads and leaving its print on their sad faces.'

The rest of us knew that this story of I'll-Daze-Ye was perfectly true. We remembered how The Malignities had walked into Curl 'n' Stripes' drinking-shop a few minutes later and were welcomed with,' 'I see ye have been warmed and reddened with a rock' (for the news had already gone on ahead of them). And from that day forth we saw the purple marks on the hooligans' foreheads from the belts of the famous God-given rock and saw the nonchalant Sammy walking the roads unchallenged, his hands in his pockets. Gone forever was the timid lad of old – gone the weak and undergrown child with the diseased ear and the piss-in-the-bed look on his face. In his place stood I'll-Daze-Ye, the man-of-the-hour – the man who had fought The Malignities with a big rock. Before too long (just like with Big Red) he was to become a living legend in our midst – his sad and lonesome boyhood a memory forgotten by us all.

The Malignities Were In Dread Of Him

So – from then on – the mighty Malignities were no longer guffawing at him and were half-in-dread of this erstwhile goose-of-a-man. Whenever they saw him coming their way it was like a dismal cloud passing over a harvest-field and they kept to the far side of the ditch, never knowing when the inspiration of the Heavenly Maker (who had once placed a rock in the young man's fist) might again come down out of the clouds and give I'll-Daze-Ye another big rock with which to tear the skin off of their heads.

And After Chastising Those Vagrants

Ane now – a week to the day after he had chastised those vagrants for spilling his family's milk – I'll-Daze-Ye woke up early, wiping the sleep from his eyes as the first streaks of light crept into the sky and whitened his window. Beating the blackbirds and the cockerels in his hurry to be out in the morning mist, he staggered to the enamel bucket for his first drink of spring-water. He took his bicycle-pump and blew up the tyres of his twenty-eight inch bicycle-wheels. He hopped the tyres off of the floor to test their readiness. He took down his loaded butt from the shelf beside the hob and gave it a swish and a whirl. Without a backward look at The Saintly Woman he marched out the half-door along with his eldest son, the eight year-old Patsy.

How manfully did young Patsy wear his new corduroy britches, his cap cocked to the side. How bravely did he carry his father's loaded butt. It was heavy enough to sink an ass. Swelling with pride, father and son went out along Simon-not-so-simple's Lane: 'Let two-men-of-us go forth and make our mark this blessed day among the rowdy townies,' roared I'll-Daze-Ye. And in honour of I'll-Daze-Ye the leprechauns put a stop to their singing and dancing in the haunts of Fort Dangerous. With Patsy perched on the bike's handlebars the great man pointed the way towards The Roaring Town and the rowdy business that would now be in hand.

They Entered The Town

It ws mid-morning and already gone were the morning cobwebs and mists from the steely grasses inside the ditches. The glorious sun was well up in the sky and spreading its warm tentacles down onto the handlebars of the bike. I'll-Daze-Ye cycled his twenty-eight inch wheeler downhill by The Sheep Field and on into the town and along Bacon Street. It was a great shock for young Patsy – to hear the jingling sounds of several bike-bells and the clatter of horses' hooves and harness – to see the jostling crowds of people, more numereous than crows in a cornfield, and the women and girls in their dotted pink-and-blue dresses and the men in their fine brown suits and their well-hung caps (back-to-front or with the peak opened here and there). And then for him to see the several mud-splashed shop-windows and the large castle walls and the graphite-coloured church that seemed to touch the clouds.

Finally they came to The Widda-Widda-Woman's drinking-shop where I'll-Daze-Ye gave the bike to the ostler in the yard. He went in to meet up with his close relations (The Out-and-Outers). They were handy lads to have about you when it came to a faction-fight like today's main event.

Up Along Jinnet Street

To prepare their bodies and boost the strength in their arms they were anxious to get themselves a good feed of ham and mutton – with cabbage, turnip and eggs thrown in as well as a mug of strong tea that'd put the sweat hopping off of them before battle commenced. They marched up Jinnet Street and plunged into Meg Mires' shop. Meg was the daughter of another distant relation on the mother's side. She had a seven-year-old son (Gallop) and a second son (recently named Rarity), who was sitting in the corner playing with a few marbles. These two children were the joy of her life – 'the two apples of mee eyes' said she.

Meg Was A Tailoress

Meg was a tailoress. She made the black-and-white altar-clothes that the town's altarboys wore in church. She made dresses for young women too. Each evening saw Gallop seated beside his mother's dressmaking-table where she was busy with her huge scissors whilst fitting out these young charmers with their wedding-dresses or (maybe) their smart suits for their going-away journey to Wolverhampton, Sydney or Baltimore. She knelt the women on top of her table – all the better to cut the hemline of their dresses. As they stripped off down to their calico chemises Gallop saw more women's exposed flesh than Doctor Glasses did in a month of Sundays. At times Meg made the growing Gallop put on some of the dresses she was making. This was to give her a better idea of the way the dresses would look when they were finally finished. Her young son found that he liked dressing up in these colourful outfits and he became the devil's own for parading himself in women's clothes in and out the lanes and stable-yards at the back of the town.

Gallop And Patsy

On a day such as this (the proposed battle) Gallop and Patsy were sure to be sent a good distance away from the battleground – for their own protection. They took their hurleysticks off with them so as to while away the afternoon hurling rotten apples and mangols down the back lane in mimicry of the famed hurlers of days gone by. In the meantime Meg was whaling the third and fourth plateful of fine food into I'll-Daze-Ye and The Out-and-Outers.

Meg Mires

Sad to say – it wasn't only with platefuls of rich food that Meg was generous. Eight years earlier when she was just a slip-of-a-girl she had lost the one and only handbag she'd ever owned – stolen from her (she complained) at the Institute Winter Dance. You should have seen the fuss and the hullabaloo she made. Oh how she bawled. She gave the rest of the night trying to find her miserable handbag. What would her mother say when she got back home? You'd think she had gold and silver coins in it.

The hour was getting late. It wasn't safe to be walking home all alone. However – a kindly young man (one of the ticket-sellers from the dancehall) came to her rescue: 'It was just what she'd always been looking for – a man and not a bleddy handbag,' said her scornful mother a month later. She wasn't the only one who saw through Meg's scheming: other jealous townie women said that Meg had lost her handbag deliberately – that she and her feigned bout of mischievous tears had been bent all along on capturing the soft heart of the soppy young ticket-seller, whom she was anxious (they said) to snuggle up to for an hour or two's blandishments in the hidden corners of the graveyard.

The heavenly young charmer paraded Meg down the dark avenues till the two of them came to Lovers' Setback, which led to the quietness of the graveyard. The echoing patter of his boots matched the clip of Meg's high heels. It was not for nothing that this district got its romantic name. The fever soon took hold of them and the earth went round and round on them and for a honeyed hour they found themselves preoccupied in the dark corners (the jostling and the tussling) where love-makers had for years past taken their delicate and clumsy delights.

Very soon Meg found that she had acquired a taste for this fumbling and jostling – found that young men were always longing for a woman with a fine big chest like her own – one that was like a pair of bladders with a gap for a blackbird's nest or a man's foolish head to lodge down into. And thanks to the repeated acts of the vanishing handbag Meg found herself a few more manly specimens to escort her home from the dancehall during these winter Sunday nights.

Of course it wasn't just the handbag that she lost. Having carelessly lost her virginity, she got herself a fine baby boy (Gallop) – the boy who later loved wearing women's clothes. Not knowing the father of the child (it could have been any one of her three most recent suitors) she at first called him Gallop and then added Micky and for good measure also threw in Dan. The three names stood the little fellow in good stead: it was Gallop-Micky-Dan at his christening: it was Gallop-Micky-Dan when he entered the school gate.

You'd think that Meg would have learnt her lesson after the sudden appearance of this baby boy. Not a bit of it. A few years later her mother was coming home from Mass on a Sunday morning. Meg was still slumbering peacefully in the nest after her latest bout of lovemaking. Her mother lifted the latch of the front door. What a jolt she got when a terrified and bare-arsed man (dressed only in his shift and holding onto his trousers for dear life) came flying out passed her jaw, knocking her onto the broad of her back and into the horse-dung in the lane.

A Miracle Happened

Four more months came and went. Meg (a dumpy lady at the best of times and still only twenty) showed no sign of the results of her carousals. Yet when the next five months passed by, a miracle happened and out popped Rarity – a second child in Gallop's wake and again born out of wedlock. By this time Father Charitable and The Guard had had enough of Meg's sinful debauchery. They came strutting down the lane to do their duty and remove the two new infants to the safety of the nuns' orphanage.

And then came the downpour of tears from poor Meg, roaring and bawling like a stuck pig. However – good fortune was about to come round the corner in the shape of I'll-Daze-Ye, who'd been drinking merrily in Goosey-Goosey-Gander's Hotel nearby. When Father Charitable and

The Guard reached Meg's door and were in the act of rolling up their sleeves to lay hands on the two small infants, whom should they meet but I'll-Daze-ye and his fighting fists. The priest (for all his unearthly powers of cursing his enemies into hell) was a smart enough man and on this occasion able to see good sense. He grabbed The Guard by the wrist and bid a hasty farewell to I'll-Daze-Ye before retiring fleet-footed down the lane.

The Faction-fighting

It was always the same routine. As soon as the faction-fight began The Guards suddenly became very wise men and retreated (a bit like Father Charitable) to the far side of the town. What use would they be in curbing such savage men when their fighting metal had risen to such an uncontrollable height? By the time these law-and-order boys had gone to the nearest town for reinforcements and the necessary refreshments, the faction-fighters would have ended their battle and long gone back to their homesteads to bathe their wounds at the wash-tub and see to the repair of their cudgels in preparation for the next big war. Indeed some of them would already be getting themselves carried up to Hammer-the-Smith's forge to get their heads fixed before the daylight faded.

The Townie Women

It was a shame (said the townie women) for all the hilarity and hysteria of faction-fighting to be coming to an end all over Ireland. What on earth was wrong with our men (they said)? Were their bodies getting worn out from all the cudgeling over the years? Behind all their moaning and groaning they were still happy enough since there was this one last gasp of it (thank God) here in The Roaring Town where our men still had a bit of strength in them for the odd battle or two. Otherwise (said the townie women) there'd be no excitement left for anyone to celebrate up and down Jinnet Street – except looking at the tinker-women drunkenly brawling on the evening of a market-day.

Of course these same townie women wouldn't dream of letting their own men run out into the street and catch hold of a cudgel: it was enough to see the farming yokels belting the heads off of one another. They pretended to have forgotten a thing or two – that there had been one or two deaths from recent blows to the skull. This was sufficient cause for the farmer's wives and the priests to throw their hands in the air and demand that all faction-fighting be stamped out for once and for all throughout the length of Tipperary. On this memorable day, however, no-one was prepared to step in and forbid a fine afternoon's entertainment. The recent excuse of I'll-Daze-Ye's spilt milk – coupled with the destruction of the children with the contents of Curl 'n' Stripes' pisspot – was a just and righteous cause for a good old-fashioned bout of faction-fighting (said the men) – not to be missed. It was a chance to test the strength of their cudgel for neither side knew if they'd ever be let loose to use them hereafter.

They Set Out For The Fight

After he'd finished his fine feed of Meg's meat I'll-Daze-Ye tapped his belly below his belt and put on his cap. With his cousins (The Out-and-Outers) he headed down the lane towards Jinnet Street. They were followed by a lively bunch of townie children. I'll-Daze-Ye looked at his pocket-watch. At this time of day the streets would be less crowded. It was a good time for the use of a man's cudgel – three o'clock and The Lord's own magical hour.

Since ten in the morning there had been a good deal of heavy drinking (the raw gut potheen and The Black Doctor). The Malignities and their opponents could be seen sitting side-by-side on the barrel-planks inside in The Widda-Widda-Woman's drinking-shop, exchanging pleasantries and wiping their wet lips. They seemed to be drinking friendly enough. But for the past hour the calm and laughter had died down until it was replaced with more words than a priest's sermon as challenges and counter-challenges were offered by the opposing groups. It was now time for the coats and ties to be thrown off. It was time for the cudgel and the fray.

They Were Awfully In Earnest

The two camps stepped outside earnestly and twirled their cudgels and wattles aloft. Danger lurked behind each man's eyes and you could tell that they were about to murder one another. They began to shout and scream and to send wolf-like yahoos to the heavens – enough to raise the dead from the graves in Abbey Acres five miles away.

Their recent complaints against each other seemed modest indeed for they had far more hateful memories going back beyond the cradle. They proceeded to curse each other's families with unprintable oaths – back to the fourth and fifth generation. They prayed to their God-in-heaven to give strength and vigour to their cudgels – give strength to their boots and to their fists. Their prayers ('hell and damnation to ye!') were more imaginative than a first rate poet's and any fair damsel who had been foolish enough to be driving her ass-and-car along Jinnet Street was now sent off scattering and screaming at a tidy speed – with a belt of a cudgel on her ass's old arse to save her pretty little head from the imminent battle. This gave the creature a set of legs that would do a racehorse credit.

The Gobful Of Spit

The confrontation and the joy of the cudgel was about to begin as the warring factions positioned themselves – The Out-and-Outers at the south of Jinnet Street and The Malignities at the north. I'll-Daze-Ye and the eldest of The Malignities approached the middle of the street. They gave each other the customary gobful of spit on each other's boots. They pulled down each other's caps over one another's eyes. Then the caps were snatched off and pelted high in the air. This insult to one another's caps was the signal for the fight to commence. I'll-Daze-Ye had blessed his boots well with holywater that morning. He had also blessed his cudgel and fists with lashings of the same. And with the first kick he almost destroyed the testicles of his enemy. The true beauty of a battle then portrayed itself.

Where Were The Women And Children?

Where were the fighting men's women? Where were their children? Some of them were waiting nervously at the edge of the town. All were desperately praying. They stood there silently – helplessly waiting for the return of their men after the battle. They were sick and tired of this faction-fighting. Though usually tyrannized by their husbands, they were now every bit as angry as them. But their anger was a different kind of anger – not the cudgel sort of anger but an anger of the spoken words that could hop off of a women' s vicious tongue and cut a man better than a sword – so that a brute of a faction-fighter might be seen crying and bawling after his wife's verbal assault when he got home. For the moment, however, a woman's harsh words had to give way. For with the insult to each other's caps it was time for the men's fists, boots and cudgels to take over the street and for both sides to beat the living daylights out of one another's heads. The roars were so loud that you'd think the shop walls would fall down into the street.

The Fine Gentlewomen

Unlike the countrywomen, the fine young gentlewomen of the town were burning for the fight to start and to hear the sound of wattles and cudgels filling the street. They lined the upper windows along the length of Jinnet Street. Their cheeks aflame, some of them were helping themselves to the odd little thimbleful of port and brandy: 'Ah-ha, mee byze – will ye look at the handsome men and their muscles and their cudgels!' they sighed. Their thoughts ran wild – pining their little hearts out and screeching infamies and insults to encourage the warriors on both sets of men:

'Will ye look at Mikey. Will he go home with the same head and brains this evening?' they agonized as they craned their necks down onto the street with a sadness that was soon taken up mockingly by others:

'Aye faith – and will Patsy still have his two fine testicles inside in his trousers?' they cackled, splitting their unladylike sides with laughter.

Like The Rush Of A River

For a second or two there was a hush and a quietness. If ever the hair stood up on a fighting man like a cat's before conflict it was at this very moment – so tremendous was the fearsome energy in the hearts of the fighters as the war began. With the blood buzzing like a swarm of bees in their ears the warriors rushed wildly forward in a mass of cudgels and wattlesticks. Without a thought for their safety they hit out randomly at one another's ribs, arms and legs. Such was the noise. Such was the joy of the battle. You'd think a haystack was on fire: 'Success to yeer cudgels,' cried the townie women and 'Shove into yer man and grind the basthard's bones into the ground,' they roared and they prayed to The Blessed Virgin to aid the men's cudgeling in the breaking of limbs.

In the meantime the blanched-faced countrywomen set up a great wailing at the edge of the town in case their men were getting killed on them. And between all the knuckling of heads and the cracking of sticks on elbow and kneecap you'd think the end of the world had truly arrived. Furiously gnashing his teeth and all the time cursing ('Coom here, ye scarecrow till I nail ye to the street') each man now guarded his face, chest and inner thighs . . . waiting for a chance to do the utmost damage . . . leaping to the left and then to the right and fixing his eyes on the man in front of him. It was the same as a rushing river that couldn't make up its mind which way to flow as now one side was driven back to The Market Square and now the other side was forced to retreat to The Railway Bridge above the trains from Limerick.

And soon they were all in a ball of sweat, no man holding back. And as the war waged on, injured compatriots (their faces the colour of the rainbow) were nursed back to consciousness on the side of the road. The Widda-Widda-Woman was as busy as a gnat as she ran out dangerously from her drinking-shop and into the street with a jug of whiskey and ladled it into the staggering men with their livid bruises. After that she pelted them back into the front of the battle for another good leathering of the cudgel or a chance to go and crack a poll or two or break a few bones.

The Evening Sun

But, like the daylight itself, the warriors at last grew tired from looking for yet another head to purchase and break open with their cudgels. The clattering of their boots and cudgels finally came to an end, the fire of the battle having gone out of their bellies. The evening sun in its ball of redness began to go down beyond the Lisnagorna woods and The Mighty Mountain. The last men left standing amongst the fighters shook hands somewhat confusedly, almost sadly.

And after doing the cockerel on it abroad in the street-battle, they now picked their way silently across the roadway. Arm-in-arm they went in to attack The Drink in The Widda-Widda-Woman's drinking-shop where they sat once more on the barrel planks, the broad flow of their voices soon blazing up to the rafters. They began to quench their thirst ('droothy work indeed, mee byze'), whipping The Black Doctor and the fiery rawgut whiskey down their throats – so strong, it'd burn a hole in the wall. Their heads were soon muzzy from all the fine drinking they were doing. Both sides grew happier by the second and, so friendly were they to one another as they drank each other's health that you'd think they were brothers, good humour taking over from their previous angry rage. And apart from a few broken teeth and damaged ribs no-one had gotten himself severely injured or killed in the battle. 'Thanks be to God,' said the women who had braved it in from the edge of town in order to follow their men as far as the drinking-shop door. It had been a grand fight and both sides came out of it equally balanced, complimenting one another with poetic little pleasantries for their bravery and for their fighting prowess. One thing was sure – they knew that their family honour had remained in tact:

'No, blasht ye, it was yeer fine fists that did the trick on mee cousin Mikey.'

'No, be-cripes, it was yeer two boots that were the tidier in sending the fatal blow to Paddy's danglers and got him taken away from the street.'

For the following hour or two you'd hear the same old song again and again out of them.

At Seven O'clock

It was seven o'clock and getting late. The drinking had been good but the merriment in the drinking-shop was beginning to die down and the place would soon be empty and spider-quiet. The sun had gone behind the rooftops as the daylight was milked out of the sky. Dark silhouettes began to creep in and the clouds in the west were already purple and pink.

By this time I'll-Daze-Ye (pale and jaded) was like a sleepwalker as he stumbled out the shop-door. He staggered off to fetch Patsy from Meg Mire's lane. He put his tired young son up on the handlebars of his bike. Still warm from the battle, he took off his own short coat and wrapped it round Patsy to keep him warm in the damp cold of the evening. He gave him a handful of Missy Pink-Frock's best tomatoes to suck on when they'd be facing the new stars and the mournful hills. He cycled out by The Sheep Field. He looked back to see the houses of the town being swallowed up in the mellow light. Then he looked forward towards the shoulders of the misty hills beckoning him home to his family. The wobbly bike and its frail lamplight crawled towards Rookery Rally, a faint breeze stabbing its way behind them. The only sound (apart from his puffing and panting) was the lonely sound of the last bird still awake.

Home At Last

The two of them crossed the flagstones and the younger children ran out excitedly into the yard: 'Father-father-father!' they yelled, jumping all over I'll-Daze-Ye like young puppies. Great was their relief for to see that their father had not been killed. I'll-Daze-ye went in and sat near the crackling logs on the fire – almost on top of the flames, warming his hands and thighs. He lit a cigarette for himself. The yellow lamplight shone on his face across the flagged floor and made dark waves on the walls. His wife (The Saintly Woman) looked tenderly at him. She knew only too well that if she gave out to him with a lash of her tongue for endangering his life and the livelihood of his family, his humour might turn sour in a second and he might lay into her and give her a few tidy taps on the seat of her skirts. For men in Rookery Rally were an odd mixture. They didn't trouble the women too much in the bedroom. There was no *coom-into-mee-arms, mee charmer* about them – even though their songs were full of such nonsense. Few were the stolen kisses in Rookery Rally following our fears of tuberculosis sweeping the land. No and no again – kissing your good woman on her wet lips with your own spitty kisses was almost as foul as using a dockleaf on your gable-end after easing yourself abroad in the haggart. This would leave visitors from across the sea scratching their heads; for it was an absolute wonder how any of us came to be born in Rookery Rally. And in the present case it was something that happened mysteriously between I'll-Daze-Ye and his good woman in the stealth of the night beneath the dark sheets when only the fox was out and the rest of the ghostly house couldn't spy on the pair of them.

He Was In A Splendid Mood

That evening I'll-Daze-Ye was in a splendid mood – back home in his little clot of gold and as happy as a king in a palace. He sang song after song for his children. He sang *Little Nell*. He sang *The Black Sheep*. He sang *The Jacket so Blue*. He sang songs he'd learnt when he was a ploughboy in Travellers' Rest – songs from the lips of the men who had come to plough from The Land-beyond-the-water. He got down the concertina from the bacon box and the children danced step-for-step across the floor with the same vigour that had been seen in their father this bloodstained afternoon. The big man finally knelt down and carried each of the children around The Welcoming Room on his back, swinging this way and that way so as to topple them off. He was like a young horse as he skinned the knees out of his britches. Then he carried the youngest of them up the ladder on the broad of his back to the loft and laid him gently in the settlebed. He lifted the others up into the air so that they stood trembling on his shoulders like the Daffy-Duck Circus acrobats. They screamed till they wet their knickers: 'Can ye see The Big City?' he said. Again and again, with each of them, he repeated this performance. The Saintly Woman smiled and she laughed to herself over her long sock-darning needle as she listened to the wind whistling through the trees outside. It was good to see her husband home with the rage against The Malignities driven clean out of his body. Yes (she thought) – I'll-Daze-Ye was just like a little child betimes, a balm to her mind.

The two older girls were soon asleep in the second four-poster bed in their mother and father's bedroom behind the hob. Their two brothers were asleep in the settlebed on the floor of The Welcoming Room. In their beds in the loft the two little ones were already dreaming of the fairies in their storybooks. The pale moon shone down on them so that the mist and the dew on the bushes and the yard were covered in white gauze.

I'll-Daze-Ye enterd the bedroom and stripped off his britches. He got in under the soft-wadded quilt and rested his head on the musty pillow. He crept close up beside The Saintly Woman in the four-poster bed. It was placed next to the henhouse wall where he could keep an alert ear out for the visiting weasel, the fox or the rat. He also kept a cute little ear alert for the two girls sleeping nearby in case they would wake and hear him breathing. Then when all was quiet and hushed he dangled his arms round his wife's neck and he lifted her innocent chemise and he placed his warm belly and thighs close to her own, enveloping her.

Finally as the day died away, he fell into the black caverns of a vast sleep with his wife's achingly-longing arms around his bruised and exhausted limbs. A few stars dimly appeared. One or two bats went off deftly hunting along the length of River Laughter. It had been a giant-of-a-day. It had been a diamond-of-a-day – a beautiful faction-fighting day to be forever remembered and cherished.

SEVEN

How Deelyah said goodbye to the rest of us shortly before the new baby (Sally) brought joy back into the heart of Dowager.

Deelyah

Little Deelyah – may her name last as long as there are fishes in River Laughter and bees buzzing about each year in the children's secret haunt below in Old Sam's grove. It was a year or two before the Eucharistic Congress of '32. Handsome Johnnie had been dead for over four months. The poor man had died on a Tuesday afternoon in February – in the very same room where Deelyah (his frail eight-year-old daughter) was now about to give up the ghost on Dowager, her broken-hearted mother, and the rest of her brothers and sisters. It was February again and one of the coldest months ever known when one of our many great floods came tearing down The Open Road, almost destroying the wooden bridge that lay across River Laughter.

Dowager, As Silent As A Monk

Dowager was as silent as a monk these days. You only had to look at her to see that she was dreaming her life away. She kept on bringing back that day four months back when Handsome Johnnie found himself clinging on to the last vestiges of his life in his battle with Sergeant Death. The children (old and young alike) hadn't been able to understand the huge depths of their mother's sorrow or share it and sympathise with her. The passing women would put their heads in the half-door and were dumbfounded when they saw the younger ones playing with their jackstones in The Welcoming Room, seemingly indifferently to all the commotion going on in The Big Cave Room at the back of the hob – seeing the older ones building a patient house of cards on the front table or arguing with each other over which priest gave the best sermon or spent the shortest time on the altar at Sunday Mass.

The three oldest brothers (Blue-eyed Jack, Lofty Larry and Warbling Will) were out in The Bluebutton Field, hurling unripe mangols until they and their hurley-sticks were nearly senseless. They had turned their britches inside-out with the white showing – to look as if they were wearing real hurling-togs. The older sisters (Darkie and Little Nell) were sitting quietly on the upturned ass-and-car, quietly playing their card games of *Old Maid* and *Beggar-Mee-Neighbour* and humming to themselves like bees buzzing happily in a lilac bush. The farmers and their ass-and-cars and their two creamery tanks were busily wending their way down The Open Road as usual on their way to Copperstone Hollow. From time to time (like the women) they'd stop to view the scene, the news of which had transported itself throughout the length and breadth of Rookery Rally – how Handsome Johnnie was about to meet his death at such a ridiculously young age (forty-nine), coughing up the last bits of his liver and the children (little lost souls) wearing themselves to a thread with their playfulness and games all around the yard and the stream and the fields:

'Ah, the poor young children,' sighed Moll-the-man. 'Bless them – they don't know a thing what's happening!'

'And their father in the bed and about to die on them,' nodded the sympathetic Cackles as she rushed passed Dowager's yard-stream flagstones and hurried off to Old Sam's spring-well for the buckets of water.

'Will ye look at the crathurs – it's unnatural,' shouted By-Jiggery as he gave his ass the ash-plant across his scabby old back to hurry him away from so sad a scene.

To tell the truth – most of the neighbours on The Open Road had the good grace to keep well back from Dowager's half-door, knowing that she was full to the gills with her tears: they didn't want to cause her any added pain by coming in and crying their hearts out alongside her during these sad times. Of course none of the children realised (how could they?) the serious consequences of a future life without their father. After all, they had never seen their father die on them until now!

Her Lovely Man

When Dowager, dressed in her robes of black widowhood, laid her lovely man down in the clay it all became too much for her. She had no-one to turn to and she went out to the ash-pit where she secretly cried bucketfuls. It was then that her children woke up to the reality of what had happened. Each day they began to see a steely coldness creeping over their mother's heart – even though she was expecting the last and final gift that Handsome Johnnie had left her – another child the following August. More often than not they saw their mother on her knees, praying that the ghost of her lovely man would continue to stand by her – would continue to give her the strength she so badly needed in these days of her dark sorrow – and she having thirteen children now to bring up on her own and educate in the Christian Duties of Life.

A Frail Puny Bundle

Among her children was Deelyah. She was a frail puny bundle if ever there was one – no bigger than a turkey or a guinea hen. She spent most of the day sleeping inside in the black pool of shadow that was her crib. Dowager prayed that Handsome Johnnie's loving ghost-spirit would rise up out of his Abbey Acres grave to bring comfort to Deelyah and enliven the cockles of her heart.

In answer to her devout prayers the ghost of Handsome Johnnie came in across the fields near the cowshed each night and he stood over Dowager: 'Biddy! Biddy! Please forgive my poor sad soul for all mee sins against you and the children?' (Biddy was his intimate name for Dowager, she having been christened Bedelia).

'What sins, I ask you?' sighed Dowager back to his ghost.

To tell the truth, the few debts that Handsome Johnnie had left behind him had long been paid off by Dowager at the three drinking-shops in

Abbey Cross, Copperstone Hollow and The Roaring Town. This was due in no small measure to the weekly shillings she was receiving of late from Blue-eyed Jack and Little Nell in their newly-adopted services to Lord and Lady Elegance below in The Big House. Praise to the lords and their ladies for keeping the wolf from the door!

To be fair – the only over-indulgences of Handsome Johnnie's pockets during his short lifetime had been on Fair Days when he'd sell a few of his two-and-a-half-year-old bullocks and go treating his townie sisters to whiskey after whiskey, whiling away the night singing them his little-known songs such as *'The Black Sheep'* and *'Come With Me Over The Mountains'* – until the very rafters shook around him and the little birds had long gone to roost in their nests.

How Did It All Begin?

How did the illness that was to kill her strike Deelyah? The summer after her father's death the hay was being harvested everywhere. The new stallion (Blackie) that Blue-eyed Jack had brought back from Tipperary Town was working in The Seventh Field. If you were standing below at The Kill (half-a-mile away) you'd hear the laughter of the little girl re-echoing across Corcoran's Well. That summer's day seemed to be a carefree part of heaven as each tram-of-hay was being winched up along the haycart. Higher and higher the screeching chains winched up the final tram. Deelyah was humming merrily, a straw stuck between her top teeth. She was lying back against the front of the tram, waiting for it to bounce down onto the cart's shafts and force her to laugh and giggle all over again.

The Changing Clouds, The Merry Sun

This dreamy little girl's thoughts (the changing clouds and the merry sun) were pure poetry and she was no longer holding onto the tram and its binding sugans as tightly as she should have been. Suddenly the haycart slammed heavily down – onto the cart-shafts and the rattling chains on Blackie's back. Losing her footing, Deelyah found herself unexpectedly in a frightening new world – embroiled with the horse's tackling, its tail and hooves. Together the two of them (the horse and its hind legs and the child and her spindly knees) began struggling in a twisting mass beneath the cart-of-hay. And to this day no one knows if the cracking of Deelyah's skull against the horse's alarmed hooves was the cause of her present impending death.

Dowager Had Begged For A Girl-child

Of her numerous brothers and sisters, Catherine had died three days after she was born and (being the firstborn of the girls) had left Dowager crying in the arms of Handsome Johnnie and begging him to give her another little girl-child to take her place.

Dowager would one day lose count of all her children but after the first three boys a girl-child was indeed born in the shape of Darkie. And then came another girl-child (Little Nell) and then yet another girl-child. When this third infant girl reached the crib she was given the name of Deelyah after her our mother (Bedelia), who for reasons too complicated to mention had come to be known by all of Rookery Rally as plain and simple Dowager – the same as the name given to the sad old lady, Queen Victoria.

Free As The Birds In The Sky

Like all other children in Rookery Rally, Deelyah had been as free as the birds in the sky. She had had a reasonably charmed but uneventful life until that horrendous accident with the haycart and Blackie. After rescuing her from underneath the horse's feet, Blue-eyed Jack and his demented mother gently brought her into The Welcoming Room. The two of them opened out the settle-bed onto the floor with the help of the other children. They surrounded the unconscious child with kind whispers and the warmth of their loving hearts.

Doctor Glasses

It was a sad Thursday afternoon when Doctor Glasses and his green tweed suit came running into Dowager's cabin. He laid his leather bag on the front table near the St Brigid's cross. For the next half-hour he was all alertness and action. Later we saw him standing at the half-door, tucking away his spectacles and gazing down somewhat mournfully at an imaginary drake that seemed to be occupying his mind at the half-door.

At last, facing Dowager, he spoke with a doctor's grave finality: 'Dowager, my good friend, you will never need to unbutton your purse or give me another shilling for my services; for in all my days' travelling I've never met such an unhappy case as this.'

He paused and for a minute seemed stuck for words: 'The truth of the matter is this: Deelyah has been stricken down with the dreaded bone disease. It has reached her marrow. There's no use mincing my words: God is going to take this little girl away – going to take her back to the angels from where she came.' And with that, himself and his watery eyes slumped awkwardly out midst the hens and ducks and vanished across the yard-stream.

Within A Few Weeks

Within a few weeks the wasting bone disease began to set into Deelyah. And a few days later this unfortunate news spread across the length and the breadth of Rookery Rally. Men on their creamery carts talked about it on The Creamery Road. Herald-the-Post on his letter-rounds cycled the news of it into a dozen more houses, scarce giving himself time to take off his bicycle clips. The holy priest himself (Father Sensibly) was met at the foot of the stairs before he had time to fasten on his starched priest-collar or eat his bread soldiers and boiled duck-eggs.

She Was Dying

Everyone knew it: Deelyah, an eight-year-old little girl, was dying. There was a gloom in every Welcoming Room as the aching took a hold of men, women and children. In our small community the news of Deelyah seemed to blot out the sun from our farmyards – seemed to quell the laughter from the rest of Dowager's children and they called a halt to their games of skittles on the flagstones.

Poor Dowager – for this to happen after only recently losing her lovely man. Each day she lifted the little girl's wasting limbs from the crib and tenderly whispered her own childhood prayers into her ears. Then she took her out to the blazing fire where the flames growled in the fireplace under the hob. She sat her on her knees and dressed her – all the while crooning those musical rhymes and rhythms into her childish soul. She could feel Deelyah's young heart throbbing breathlessly against her own heart as though they were one and the same person.

Outside In The Yard

Round about ten the windows of The Welcoming Room were bright and the red geraniums were shining in from their home in the green window boxes. A few fat flies shot in and out of the dust-laden bars of light. Dowager took Deelyah outside the half-door and sat with her on the stone steps. By now the sun was blazing down merrily on the cobbled yard and the stream's flagstones. The farmyard fowl were scattered about colourfully and Deelyah was glad to be out here in the pleasant air after the hot turf-fire inside in The Welcoming Room. She could smell the summertime flowers, especially the rambling roses and the sweet williams in her mother's small privet-hedged garden. The flowers on Simon-not-so-Simple's ditch were a flame of reds, yellows and blues. Their fragrance, scented with lavender, was a joy to her. She could listen to the cheerful tinkling of the yard-stream – fragile as an egg and scintillating as a feather – as its brown waters swelled and flowed musically over the stones.

The cat (Henchaser) slept blissfully on the bit of straw on top of the empty ass-and-car. The new family of ducklings followed their mothers awkwardly down the yard and took over the stream. Out underneath the haggart singletree went the baby goslings, still waddling unsteadily. They paraded down the haggart through the wheel ruts and dockleaves. Underneath the horse-and-cart stood the hens, waiting for Dowager's skillet of bran-mash and spuds, turning their heads with sudden jerks – this way and that. The gander stretched out his long neck whenever he saw the sow coming near him from her home in the pig-house. He turned and flapped his wings, frightening the bold cockerel poised on top of the upturned horse's cart and watching the fray. A minute later the cockerel flew down and strutted self-importantly across the yard winkingly defying the gander, now that Dowager was here. When he was among them the hens pecked and groomed under each wing to attract his attention. They ruffled their feathers and shook them out invitingly. All this Deelyah could see and hear – more intensely than ever these last days.

Warbling Will

Warbling Will was next in age to Blue-eyed Jack and Lofty Larry – born three years after The Year of The Big Wind. He was the most enthusiastic child imaginable when it came to the natural order of the world around him. To oblige his dying sister he went off looking for wild bird's nests and eggs. One evening just after milking-time he brought home an abandoned nest. Patiently he pointed out the style of its making to his little sister.

Next evening he cavalierly rushed in the door and showed Deelyah a young rabbit that had lost its mother. He intended to make a pet of it for her and build her a wooden hatch and a netted lane so that the little creature would have freedom to run round in. Alas – how frantic were the screams of the little girl when she saw the tiny rabbit – so much so that she nearly fell in the fire from the rocking she made on her stool. Her mother understood. With a wisdom far beyond her years Deelyah had increasingly become aware that her own life was going to be short – that she wouldn't be left to look after this tiny creature for too many months of its life – of her own life. And another thing – she feared (and Dowager seemed to sense this too) that when the little creature became a fully-grown rabbit her brothers would kill it and (heavens forbid) eat it on a plate – or (maybe) throw it out to the dog.

A week went by. And then – the same Warbling Will returned with a crane that he'd found dead below in The Bog Wood. The children gathered round him, their curiosity mingling itself with their excitement at such an unusual sight. They begged him to cut open the lovely bird's belly and satisfy them as to the number of small fishes a crane could hold inside itself. Snip-snip-snip went the scissors of Warbling Will. Once more Deelyah took up the harmony and her eyes shook the place with water as she beheld the sad relic of what was once a noble bird – to see it here on the front table when once it flew so majestically above them all – to see the many small fishes that were inside its belly – was too much for the dying child.

Not Many Months Left

There weren't many months left in Deelyah's fast-spinning life. She no longer had the strength to sit outside the half-door and view all the colours and all the creatures in her small world. However – from her threepenny-stool at the side of the fire (the stool that her father had made for her shortly before he died) she was still able to listen to the raucous crows and the chirpy little robins. She could hear the gabbling ducks and the geese. She could hear the grunting sow. She could hear the cackling hens celebrating the fact that they had laid yet another egg abroad in the nettles in the haggart. Through the open window she could breathe in the brightness of the sunshine on yet another glorious day.

The creamery-tanks and the cartwheels came clattering down The Open Road. Voices beyond the stream's flagstones were sometimes muffled. And barking dogs (she could hear) were being called for their bran mash. The ass (Lazybones) in Cheerful Nan's Thistle Field was being cursed yet again. Cows and horses were coming into their sheds, mooing and braying in subdued tunes. And their neighbour (Cackles) was leaning out her half-door, calling on her children to take the buckets to the well and fetch water for the skillet of spuds and the washing of clothes.

Her Brothers And Sisters

Deelyah's brothers and sisters sat silently at the half-door where only a few days ago she herself had sat. They gazed dreamily at the farmyard scene before their eyes. From the first day they could walk a step all of them had yearned to be out in the summer airs and breezes. And now – they (and not Deelyah) had the good fortune to be able to watch the ducks tumbling about in the stream – to watch the old sow attacking the gander unsuccessfully and they laughed good-naturedly to themselves. And on her stool by the fire Deelyah caught hold of their laughter and found herself laughing too. Her mother was watching it all. In her wise head she began to wonder what on earth it must be like – to be inside the head and the heart of her little daughter – knowing that Death was near and that she was about to die: 'Until we're able to milk bullocks,' she would say to the rest of her children, 'we'll never see another child like Deelyah and that's a solid fact.'

Her Reflections

It was true for Dowager. In spite of her spindly legs and arms, which could do little or nothing, Deelyah's soul shone through her earthly flesh more and more clearly as the days loomed onwards and she stepped towards her inevitable end. Her skin (unlike her brothers and sisters) was now a satiny white (almost yellow) and her eyes had become a doll-like china-blue in their new delicacy.

She had all the time in the world to reflect. She too wished for the happiness that comes from the world outside the half-door. But instead – inside in her head, inside in her heart – during recent days there had grown a heaviness in the knowledge that her life was to be cut short – that the outside world was to be hers no more. No more to go to the spring well. No more to go to the cowshed and get her eyes squirted with cow's milk by that rascally big brother of hers (Blue-eyed Jack).

Desperate For Her Happiness

Her brothers and sisters became desperate for her happiness. What could they do? They hit on a plan. As soon as they came home from school they ran out past the yard-stream onto the road. From there they reported back their news – shouting at the top of their voices to Deelyah as she sat on her stool, listening for their voices:

'Cheerful Nan's bull has escaped again. He's running across the heights towards Old Sam's hayshed to get himself a feed of oats.'

'Uncle Bohorlody is doing his famous trick. He is hanging down by his two heels from the branch over the stream. He's like an old bat.'

'Shy Dennis has just gone by. Will you look at the antics of him – tearing down the bumpy road, his two knees on the saddle of his bike and his hair plastered back on his poll with the soapy water from the pan.'

Such an amount of news did they pour back into her ears – bringing a lift to her heart as she stroked the fur of the cat beside the fire. Again Dowager sighed and her thoughts strayed from the spuds she was boiling in the skillet-pot. How good it was to see and hear the laughter of the rest of her rosy-cheeked brood. But (alas) – how it contrasted with the frailty and pain of Deelyah and her rickety spine.

And when it was time for her to sleep, her brothers and sisters vied with each other as to who would sit with their little sister under the oil lamp beneath the tapestry stretching across the hob. With their mother's permission they brought down the bacon-box that housed their schoolbooks and prizes. They showed Deelyah their copybooks. They taught her the simpler words. They taught her to shape her own name with her weak fingers. When she had the slightest thirst on her they ran to the bucket to get her the mug of spring-well water behind the door where the axe was kept: 'It's better for you than stout-porther,' laughed Dowager.

Some of them went one better: they ran to the jug of foaming milk and they watched Deelyah drink it fast as it made a white moustache over her lip. And then they all laughed until their sides hurt.

Making Her Little Crib

The day had come to an end and they knelt and said their prayers. Then they took it in turn to help Dowager make up Deelyah's tiny crib. In turn they carried her weightless body into the crib and tucked her in snugly, tenderly. With Deelyah soundly asleep, Dowager returned to the fire. Her heart by now lay firmly in her boots. She was like a dark cloud crossing Growl River abroad in Bog Boundless. The pain in her ribs was too much for her.

The Last Few Weeks

It was the last few weeks of Deelyah's life. Once more she said her morning prayers with her mother. She prayed that the blessed saints would come and one day take everyone from Rookery Rally to heaven to live happily with her forever. She prayed that meanwhile her brothers and sisters would not go ravenous with hunger (now that their father was no longer with them and able to help with the land) but would have loads of cabbages, spuds, eggs and milk to devour for the rest of their lives.

Each new day saw another little change coming over her. She spent the morning sitting patiently underneath the oil lamp. The black metal tongs was too heavy for her fingers but with the wire silver tongs she took to drawing pictures on the black-velvet soot of the hob. She drew her mother. She drew her dead father. She drew her brothers and her sisters. She drew The Holy Family (Mary, Jesus and Joseph). Humming cheerfully to herself, she was the image of good cheer. She kept the light of Dowager's heart somehow aglow – in spite of these sad times.

Tiny Timmy

These mornings when her brothers and sisters who were of school-age set out for Dang-the-skin-of-it's schoolhouse, she felt an increased loneliness coming over her. She missed all their lively activity. She missed their fun and laughter. She missed their tears too. But close beside her she had her delicate brother (Tiny Timmy) who had not yet been allowed to walk the long three miles to school. Two years older than Deelyah, he was the skinniest little fellow you ever laid eyes on and everyone thought he had worms in his belly and that they were soaking the strength out of him.

The Little Entertainer

It was left to this little chap to entertain his dying sister in these last few weeks of her life. As soon as Dowager was off down the yard feeding her hens and ducks or scuttling up The Open Road with half-a-dozen eggs for Moll-the-Man, he would stand on tiptoe on the back table and reach up to the top shelf of the press. He took down his mother's heavy tin of buttons – all assorted sizes and colours. Slowly and carefully (so as to keep the amusement going) he laid them out across the floor, making a large patient square of them followed by an increasingly smaller and smaller set of squares inside the outer pattern. The colours made beautiful and imaginative shapes. Himself and Deelyah spent several hours playfully arranging the colours of these buttons. After that he took the gramophone needles and wound up the old gramophone. He put on Deelyah's favourite record (*My Old Home Town* – the one with a crack in it). He marched across the floor from the dresser to the half-door – Blue-eyed Jack's hurleystick strapped stoutly on his shoulder. Deelyah watched him strutting back to the fireplace and off into The Big Cave Room where he gave as long as half-a-minute shouting out his orders ('*quick march! attention! about turn!*') and marching round the broken-down piano that Lady Brindleton had given Dowager as a thankyou present for her earlier services years ago (inside the lid was kept the icing sugar and her flour).

He wasn't finished: he took the pack of playingcards from the side of the baconbox. He knelt on the chair beside the Thomas Hood framed poem (the one which said *The little house says stay, the little road says go*). As if there was nothing else he'd rather be doing, he gave half the morning building a house of cards for his little sister. Soon he was able to build a double-storey of cards. Then (not entirely by accident) his clumsy elbow hit his new card-house. He jumped down from the chair, theatrically bemoaning its sudden destruction. Once more he attempted to build his card-house – showing his frustration by threatening the cards with mischief if they dared fall down on him again. And as they repeatedly fell down on him Dowager (from where she was feeding her hens) could hear the shrieks of Deelyah's delighted laughter echoing out the half-door.

The Old Pair

Dowager and Deelyah's grown-up brother (Blue-eyed Jack) had become known as *The Old Pair* now that Handsome Johnnie was lying in the grave. Not knowing the entire story, some children even thought that they were man and wife since there were but twenty-three years between them and just as many years between Blue-eyed Jack and the new baby yet to be born.

Each day the two of them were abroad at the morning milking before Blue-eyed Jack set off to rise up a brood of pheasants for Lord Elegance. On these occasions it became Tiny Timmy's ritual to lift Deelyah tenderly from her crib. Already she was feeling pains in her shins and spine from the spreading bone-disease. As young as he was, her delicate brother was able to dress her carefully and gently. Then he sat her down on her stool. He gave her Dowager's rosary-beads to hang round her neck. Deelyah would start saying her prayers, her eyes lifted up to where she imagined Handsome Johnnie was sitting in heaven.

When Tiny Jimmy saw she was tired from praying he sprang out onto the floor, performing a new set of cartwheels. Then (the devil that was in him) he stood on top of his head and sang her favourite song (*The Green Bushes*). After that he climbed onto the front table and tried to jump up as far as he could towards the black thatch – to see if he could catch a bit of straw for her. Then he leaped out into the air as far as he could – to see how far from the dresser was his jump. And again Deelyah squealed with pleasure.

When she fell from her stool he became frantic with grief and he gave the floor and the stool a mighty good thrashing for trying to harm his little sister. And then Deelyah wiped her eyes and started laughing all over again. A minute later, when Tiny Timmy fell over the selfsame stool and was sent hopping off of the hob, she saw him roaring in pain:

'And now (she thought) I can never take my bold stool to heaven with me.'

She Knew It Would Be Soon

When Tiny Timmy had to leave her and go and fetch the buckets of water from the well, Deelyah returned to her beads, asking God to help her get into heaven. She knew it would be soon. She fidgeted with her mother's Saint Brigid's cross on her lap. She thought of poor sad Jesus with his feet and hands nailed into the wood and the spear drawing water and blood from his side. She thought of the floggings he had suffered and the purple cloak torn from his back, bringing the skin with it. She thought of the crown of thorns sticking into his head. What would a silly little thorn in his foot out in the fields have ever been to Jesus? 'Faith 'n if I was Jesus, I wouldn't let the soldiers do them bad things to me,' she said, shaking her angry little head.

Death Is Near

Increasingly she felt Death's presence – not yet knowing if it were a friend or foe. She wanted to be in heaven beside Jesus – and soon. She gazed into the fire – into its blazing redness. What must hell be like? She thought she saw agonising souls locked in the flames. She heard the twigs sizzling and hissing as though each of them was screeching in pain and she thought of her favourite prayerbook – the one with shiny drawings of the saints and of Archangel Michael winning the battle against the devil and his fallen angels. She imagined them too crying in pain as they took the long road down to hell.

After that she began praying her long list of prayers: *The Our Father – The Hail Mary – The Glory be to the Father – Into thy hands, O Lord, I commend my spirit – O angel of God, my guardian dear – O Sacred Heart of Jesus – Jesus, Mary and Joseph, I give you my heart and my soul – I Confess – I Believe – Hail Holy Queen – The Act of Contrition.* And then she was finished and fell asleep with a smile of contentment on her lips.

Father Charmingly

A month after the momentous visit of Doctor Glasses and his predictions a new face came on the scene: it was Father Charmingly, the newly-ordained curate from Clare. Our women (and on this oaccasion our men too) tripped over one another, leaping out over stiles and ditches in order to kneel at his feet and get his blessing. We all had it drummed into us that a blessing from a newly-ordained priest had more than special powers in it and that it would bring us good fortune.

Father Charmingly was informed of the sanctity that shone out daily from Deelyah's innermost soul. He hurried up the hill and stood on the flagstones in whispered conversation with Dowager: 'Make sure ye call me, (he said) when the time of the child's death is near – any time of the day or night, it doesn't matter. A saint like little Deelyah is a rare sight for any of us to behold. We must all gather in and bear witness when her soul takes its final departure and gets carried up to heaven.'

A Bad Friday

The next Friday was not a good one. Blue-eyed Jack returned home, tired and weary from ploughing for Lord Elegance. As always – he took his small wages out of his trouser-pocket and handed the money to Dowager. Like all men, he never kept money for himself. All that was ever in his jacket was his penknife for the squid of tobacco, the tobacco-square itself and his dead father's pipe and the box-of-matches to light it. His mother always insisted that he kept back an extra sixpence for himself. He had been in the habit of giving these weekly sixpences to Deelyah to store in her bib – a little present for her to keep and treasure. These shiny sixpences were a small fortune, gradually gaining dust in her tiny fists when she took them out to count with Tiny Timmy. By now she had a large pile of coins for which she had neither want nor need. For what did silver of any shape mean to Deelyah?

He Tiptoed Into His Mother's Room

This evening, believing that Deelyah was nodding off from the heat of the blazing fire, Blue-eyed Jack tiptoed into his mother's room. In the drawer amongst her mothballs she kept a bag of boiled sweets (the humbugs). When he thought no-one could see him he took a sweet from the bag. It was just the one. But Deelyah saw his thieving hands (ah, the rascal, to be doing such a thing) craftily at work. She let a plaintive little screech out of her. She knew that her lovely Blue-eyed Jack, whom she adored even more than Tiny Timmy (if not quite as much as Jesus), would have to go down into hell for all eternity – that she would never meet with him in heaven. She was inconsolable and in her unbearable sadness she offered a score of prayers up to Jesus, asking him to pardon Blue-eyed Jack on her behalf and not to disown him altogether. For she believed that a single bad deed would be enough to make her unworthy of heaven – that it would deprive her of everlasting happiness. No-one had ever seen her committing a single wrongful act against man, woman or child. In these last days of her life she reminded her brothers and sisters what God would do to the bad people – how the angels would soon be coming for her and (if she was good) would carry her off to an even better crib somewhere in The Beyond. This caused them to rush out the door and burst into a fit of tears behind the pighouse.

She Couldn't Get Up Off Of Her Stool

The last few days of June arrived. She couldn't get up off of her stool. All she could do was imagine the sunshiny yard and her brothers and sisters and their childish happiness. Another day and another hour came. 'Would the priest ever get here?' thought Dowager to herself.

Her Meaningless Confession

Father Charmingly stepped in across the flagstones: 'God save all here!' he whispered and he bowed. Silently he raised the latch of The Big Cave

Room door. His stooping shoulders leaned in over Deelyah's crib and everybody left the room. The bright-as-noonday sunshine no longer shone from her eyes. She'd been lying there almost lifeless the last day or two. Father Charmingly took out his missal. He kissed his stoll and put it round his neck. It was his duty to bring Deelyah the sanctifying grace from the Last Sacramental Rites and to hear her small Confession. Dowager stood behind the partition, her eyes red with weeping. Confession? What on earth had this little girl to confess to? Everybody knew that she was as innocent as a lamb and had been since the day she was born: 'It's a pure mockery,' said the young priest when he returned to Dowager for he had to acknowledge that the child hadn't a single stain on her soul: 'It's she that should be hearing my Confession.'

A Tender Moment

There came a tender moment when the curate stood in the middle of the bedroom floor. He had been told of her agonies over Blue-eyed Jack – the sweet he had stolen and the gates of hell awaiting him. He stood in the centre of the floor. He brought down the Sacred Heart picture from the wall and placed it on a chair. He made Blue-eyed Jack kneel solemnly down before it. Then he made him confess his sin of theft – made him confess it loud and clear and not whisperingly (as in the church confession-box) so that his brothers and sisters (Deelyah especially) should all hear it. Blue-eyed Jack dutifully confessed his sin and promised he'd never again steal from his mother's drawer. Father Charmingly was satisfied. He gave Blue-eyed Jack his Words-of-Absolution and blessed him with the sign of the cross: 'I absolve you from your sin, my child. God has forgiven you. Go and sin no more.' And for Deelyah the heavens opened up and the sun shone down and banished the depression from her face. Weak as she was she smiled faintly up at Blue-eyed Jack from the depths of her blankets. She began making her wistful humming noises. She was as happy as a queen.

The Last Week

As the final week of her life drew near Deelyah was seen rapidly losing the last bit of flesh left on her. She seemed to grow more and more mystical in the affronting face of her pain. Her prayers took on a new meaning. She wanted ('please, dear Heavenly Father!') to be taken from this earth if not this day then tomorrow and be carried up to the blessed saints in heaven. Father Charmingly came often now. He'd bring with him his father's squeeze-box and would softly play her those haunting airs which seemed to raise her spirits during the morning hours when her brothers and sisters were mostly away.

The Last Days

The last days were here. Dowager and Blue-eyed Jack carried the meagre little girl and her crib into the small room at the far end of the house where Dowager herself slept. This was for privacy's sake and for Deelyah to be close to her mother during the long remaining nights. They cleared out the laurel leaves and the hive of honeybees from the empty fire grate and lit a fire in it. The holy picture of The Sacred Heart and the big blue picture of Our Blessed Lady were cleaned and dusted. The dozen candles for a happy death were not yet lit but were ready with the box-of-matches in the drawer. When lit, they would light up all the dark corners of Deelyah's fading world and banish those haunting spirits that came in the night in the shape of boodeemen to bring evil to the dying child. Hour after hour Dowager and Blue-eyed Jack spent praying beside the crib, their long shadows stretching out across the back wall. Spiderweb stillness filled them and the entire room.

Her Brothers And Sisters

On returning from school the other children played silently on the stone floor next to Deelyah's crib. Tiny Timmy was heartbroken in his grief for his dear sister. She was now on the borders that separate Life from Death. Dowager could feel the little girls's struggles and she tried to share her pain. Deelyah smiled back brightly but her thoughts were far away by this time. Something extraordinarily good was going to happen to her – coming from another world that none had seen.

Her Death

Her death came in without drumroll or fanfare. She could hear unusually sweet music – unlike any other music she had ever heard before. It was coming from above the clouds out beyond The Mighty Mountain. She mumbled how she could hear the laughing voices of bygone children calling to here. All that her brothers and sisters could hear was the loud ticking of the grandfather-clock by the dresser – ticking away Deelyah's last few breaths. All were kneeling in prayer on the floor.

Dowager was fussing like mad and trying to avoid letting flow the tears that were blinding her eyes. She lit the dozen happy-death candles so that the bedroom was a white blaze of church-like glory. By this time a crowd of neighbours had already gathered in the yard, their rosary-beads busily twisting in their fists. Even the hens and the geese were quiet. The yard-stream itself seemed to be hushed into silence in honour of Deelyah. Wasting away to nothing (thought Dowager to herself) – mere skin and bones in the middle of the quilt – her frail little neck shaking giddily – the little blue veins on her extended fingers – you could count them one by one.

There followed a last plaintive look from Deelyah's eyes. She tried to speak: 'Mother! Mother!' she whispered. 'Come and take me! Come and take me! Oh, mother, please come and take me!'

'I am here! I am here, my child,' said Dowager softly. 'Of course I'll take you.'

Blue-eyed Jack, his heart bursting inside his chest, was slouched tearfully behind his mother. He glanced back over his shoulder at the picture on the wall – the portrait of The Blessed Virgin in her blue-jay robes – the portrait of *The Mother* with the child, Jesus, in her arms . . . smiling calmly . . . gently . . . down into the crib. He realised that his little sister was being blessed with a wonderful vision of the next world at this moment of her untimely death:

'Mother! Mother!' again the child cried. And her eyes were full of starry joy and an ecstasy unknown to anyone in Rookery Rally. It was like a dart out of the skies:

'I am here! I am here, child,' said Dowager.

'Mother,' said Blue-eyed Jack (almost reproachfully) gently tapping his mother on the shoulder: 'Deelyah isn't talking to you – she isn't talking to any of us – she is calling on her Heavenly Mother Mary behind us in the picture – she is talking to our Saviour's mother.'

As if she understood the intervention of Blue-eyed Jack the child extended her matchstick-like arms towards the picture . . . her eyes steadily transfixed on the eyes and face of her heavenly mother, Mary. And then (in spite of her weakness) she sat up fiercely in her crib and she shouted out in a huge voice full of all the hope and tenderness she possessed: 'Mother! Mother! I am coming. Please take me. I am coming now. I am coming home'.

Below In Abbey Acres

Deelyah was buried below in Abbey Acres Graveyard next to her sister (Catherine) who had died (many years before) a few days after being born. On holy days Deelyah's brothers and sisters would traipse down to the graveyard to tidy up her grave. They picked wildflowers on the way, be it honeysuckle or foxgloves. They placed them reverently on their little sister's grave in a colourful pattern as once amused her when Tiny Timmy set out his mother's tin of coloured buttons. And then they knelt down and prayed to Deelyah above in heaven – the little Saint from Rookery Rally.

Before July Was Over

Before July was over, a cry filled the slopes of The Valley of The Pig as Dowager struggled to give birth to her fifteenth child. Only the day before she had been hoeing among her turnips and carrying home the two-stone bag of spuds on her stooped back. Cheerful Nan and Cackles heard her cries and hurried down to her Welcoming Room. They brought with them some grains of tea, some sodabread and some jam. They brought a few more candles and a candlestick holder to light up the belabouring skirts and belly of their good friend. They took off their scarves that were tucked under their chins and they unwrapped the potato-sacking from their backs that they'd brought with them to keep out the rain. Cheerful Nan smiled and nodded to Cackles: 'Praise be – there'll be another soul in Dowager's family this blessed night.'

'Yes,' thought Cackles. 'Deelyah has only just left (lying low in the graveyard) and now – a new baby is taking her place here tonight.' They filled the kettle with hot water to clean down the expectant mother and her newborn child when it arrived. They had done it many times before. It was going to be a lengthy night.

Long After The Birth

Long after the birth they returned along the dark road just as the pink dawn was rising. They were worn to a thread as they stopped and looked hopefully up at the departing moon that was now an old lemon. Cackles took her leave of Cheerful Nan and went off towards The Valley of The Pig. Cheerful Nans lifted up her skirts to ease herself beside the ash-pit in her back car-way.

'Yes (said she to herself) – Deelyah is dead and Dowager's heart is breaking for the loss of her little saint. But Sally has been born (thank God) and Dowager will be glad all over again.' She tidied up her skirts and the smell of spearmint came into her nostrils from her little haggart. Her yard-stream chuckled over the stones. She was full of rich feelings.

Next Evening Came In Achingly

The following evening came closing in. The last ribbons of sunlight were leaving the sky behind Fort Dangerous and the Danes' Hill. The yard-stream gurgled with a greater intensity than usual down near the rusty kettle and the little waterfall. Blue-eyed Jack and his dead father's ash-plant led his little flock of six sheep back across the haggart gap. He went along the winding path at the side of The Bluebutton Field and hurried on towards River Laughter as though to slake his thirst.

There on the dewy bank he hid his face amongst the ferns and rushes. In the semi-darkness where no one could see him he began to howl like a stray dog over the loss of his beloved Deelyah. The very fairies that dwelt on that riverbank stopped their evening dances to look upon him as he mourned in secret for his little sister.

Dowager put away the happy-death candles. They'd not be flickering on the mantle-shelf for many a year to come (she hoped). There was darkness in her soul in spite of the tiny baby girl lying beside her. Deelyah was no longer with her in the house: 'I must be busy,' she said with a tearful shake of her head. Her clicketty-clacketty boots echoed away from the room as she left behind her the scenes of her daughter's death-crib.

Each Night Was The Same

The next few days passed quickly. Each night was the same. The hens were fed and watered and were counted and shushed back into the henhouse. The nights seemed strangely deserted. Out of respect the rabbiters and pitch 'n toss boys stopped their storytelling on the singletree in Old Sam's grove. The road-menders put away their shovels quietly and quenched their Woodbine fags and didn't come in the yard but left the good woman to her own thoughts.

It was time for bed. In the silence of her room a little dusky breeze blew up, pretending to be a whirlwind. Dowager was lying in her bed, turning and twisting nervously, trying to find a comfortable position. The air in the room was breathless. She felt the ache of Deelyah's loss like a stabbing pain underneath her heart. She heard a goose in Ducks 'n' Drakes' farmyard down near the bridge. It was caught in a fox's snapping jaws. She finally fell asleep and in her sleep she continued to dream away her sadness. A full moon peeped in the window of the room. The drowsing newborn baby snuggled up closely to her sleeping mother's breast. The two of them lay there warmly in the bed with its five fat blankets wrapped around them.

What was that? Dowager turned in her half-sleep. Was it a flickering of the moonlight trying to climb in through the back window? Was it the ass (The Lightning Whoor) trying to draw her attention as he'd often done by bawling her awake with his *eey-yaws* in the early mornings? No. It was something else – something here in her simple thatched cabin – something beyond the poor woman's understanding. She felt an inner Peace as never before – a feeling that was once in the heart of her daughter at the time of her death.

And then a noble radiance surrounded the bed. In spite of her semi-conscious protests the coverlets were gently pulled back from her shivering grasp. She pressed her baby instinctively to her heart. Surely (could it be?) it was not one of the fairies coming to take this child away from her so as to keep Deelyah company in the skies above us?

The smiling face of the ghostly shade of Deelyah crept in through the windowpane and leant across the bed. Her angel face gazed down at her baby sister – the child not yet born when she herself had been carried away to her new life in The Beyond – allowed back into her previous world for a moment in time to glimpse at her newborn sister. Her ghost smiled an indescribable smile that no painter-in-oils could produce. Not once did she look at her mother. Then she put the coverlets back tidily, almost fussily, around Dowager and the newborn Sally. Then – armed with a secret not to be shared – she vanished away and went out past the cowshed.

Dowager turned in her half-sleep. She pulled the coverlets in around her ears. She pressed the baby's warm lips close to her breast. It was now nearly dawn. The dying moon, still round and yellowy, was giving up its ghost to the skies.

EIGHT

How a small child from The Wilderness grew into the heart and the soul of us all.

Her Early Days

If ever there was a woman who lived her life more colourful than the rest of us it was Kate – Kate Solitary. She was born out passed Growl River and her dwellingplace was three miles north of Mureeny and a stonethrow from the Mighty Mountain itself. The area was known as The Last Outpost. We all knew her birthplace well – that is, we knew it from the outside for we passed it on our way to save the turf abroad in Bog Boundless. We passed it again towards the end of summer when we were on our way to Growl River's huge sally-hole for the annual full-washing with the bars of carbolic soap. The little cabin's haggart was verged around with tall pinetrees that protected Kate and her father (Joe) from the hearty winds that swept through the topmost branches. They (the pinetrees) shot out spears of blue shadow and yet let in shafts of the sun's flowing gold. At times the pineneedles made a deep carpet in the yard with sweet smells perfuming the air.

Each day seemed to be full of calm and spiderweb stillness – apart from the swallows that flew down from the treetops and played in the haggart dews, upsetting the hens foraging on the dungheap. The cabin itself was a ramshackle affair, with the thatch wellworn and a bit green and a few bits of rusty galavanize sheeting patching it up here and there. But inside was a different tale for it was a beautiful place, filled with a love that would outshine even the bishop's palace over in Clare.

Kate was a child with one green eye and one blue eye. She was the only daughter of Joe Solitary and his young wife, Lizzie-from-the-south. Lizzie's story was short for the poor girl died when giving birth to Kate. But, rather than give his little daughter up to the outstretched arms of the grasping nuns, Joe decided that he'd bring her up all by himself, come hell or high water. As you'd expect, the two of them were closer than two sides of a sheet and it would be a sad day if anything were ever to come between them.

Unlike what you might expect, Kate wasn't always on her own or even a bit lonely. She went to the schoolhouse in Feathery Edge with the rest of the children and for the whole of each summer she had the company of her cousins, Ned and Trisha from The Roaring Town. Their mother was Joe's sister and she sent them out to get what she called a lungful of fresh mountainy air.

A Father And His Worries

Joe was forever anxious and fussing over his lovely daughter. You'd think that one of the eagles was going to swoop down and carry her off to its nest in the clefts of The Mighty Mountain! Throughout those hot summer days when the flowers were thick on the heather and the white clouds hid themselves behind the mountains he took Kate, Ned and Trisha with him across the length of the fields when he went rabbiting or fishing. Best of all – he showed them the singular place where they could make their way down through the ferns to a little sandy bank – a secret place where they could sit and catch the sun – or paddle their toes in the river and wade in a few harmless feet of water no higher than their knees.

This was a quiet stretch of Growl River and hidden in the shadows of the misty hills – a place where the foxes and badgers came down to drink alongside the horses and cattle. It was a safe enough spot for Joe knew that the men had blocked off an inaccessible sally-hole further up river so that they'd have enough of a depth in it to enjoy a day's bare-arsed entertainment for themselves. He had seen them carrying the big branches from the bushes (like beavers, they were) and topping them off with the purple heather. And with the river half-blocked and just a mere trickling stream getting through he knew he'd found the grandest place imaginable for the children to have fun and laughter and a good day's splashing about. The calmness of the river was the very place to roam freely (thought Joe to himself) and he went off home puffing his pipe of tobacco merrily.

Fantasy and Enchantment

The three innocent children slipped down the bank and touched the chill of the river. Slash! Splash! Splash! They were as happy as the frivolous butterflies – enjoying their horseplay in the river – watching the wagtails skimming from rock to rock and bobbing their tails up and down after dipping down for a drink. They tried to catch the glistening trout in their fingers (a devil-of-a-job) and they failed time and time again. Then they laughed at their own stupidity.

Ned and Trisha were indeed the clumsy dancers. The underwater reedbed tickled their legs as it brushed against them. The delicate soles of their feet tippy-toed mincingly over the jagged pebbles of the riverbed. For, like all children from inside the sheltering town they were used to wearing shoes on their soft feet every day of the week. The contrast between themselves and the redoubtable Kate could be clearly seen when they saw her running all over the riverbed like a jaunty young stag. For her feet were as hard as a lump of leather since she never worn a shoe except on Sundays for Mass.

The Dangers Of The Great River

Although news always travelled faster than lightning amongst us, neither Joe Solitary nor any of the three children had heard of the great river-escape four years previously down here in Rookery Rally. It was the day that Little Nell and Peggy's-Leg almost drowned in a similar quiet stretch of our own River Laughter. It happened down by the deserted mill – the mill which had once welcomed over sixty men and their sacks of flour after the harvest. Every time we thought of this near-disaster we made the sign of the cross on our chests. For that was the day when the men put on their clothes after washing and said goodbye to the river and the sally-hole for the rest of the year. They unblocked their dam and unwittingly let free a raging torrent of water down towards the lazy bend of the river and the two unsuspecting little girls.

WHOOOOOSH!

The peaceful Fairyland of Little Nell and Peggy's-Leg was suddenly shattered when they found themselves swirling round and round and tumbling fifty yards downstream towards the dark shadows of the waterfall at Lady Posh-Frock's Bridge – a sure and certain ending to their young lives. But a sorrowful tale can sometimes turn into a happy one. A miracle was suddenly thrown to them from the skies when they found they were saved from the hands of death by the appearance of a guardian angel – none other than our own Red Scissors. Running like the wind, he leapt in over the wall and caught the two exhausted children in his arms like you would a stray goose.

But Four Years Later

And now – four years later we were once more to witness children revelling in a quiet stretch of a seemingly harmless river and with the laughter of Kate and her townie cousins ringing out loud all over the heather. All of a sudden a hissing avalanche of water came hurtling down towards them from the men's loosened dam further upstream. The bogland fairies from all over The Wilderness heard the terrifying screams of the three children destroying the tranquillity of the birds as Growl River's waters gathered speed before churning the children's legs round and round, dragging them along like bits of flotsam towards God-only-knows-where.

Were they to be washed away forever off of the earth – three innocent children, who had come out for an innocent day's paddling and recreation? They didn't know whether they were alive or dead – whether they were in heaven or hell. Meanwhile Joe Solitary sat at home by the fire, smoking his pipe as contented as any man in Ireland.

The mighty river thrashed the three bodies over and back across its width. One moment their heads were above the waters – the next moment they were dragged down to meet the startled trout. They would soon be heading for an early grave somewhere out in the middle of The Great

Ocean. Certainly this would have been the finish of it all had not God in his goodness looked down from the clouds and put out his hands to them. Jack-the-Herd was out and riding his piebald horse. He was searching for a few stray cattle. The children's screams frightened the horse. The horse frightened Jack. He ran down to the river and saw the torrents of water and the drowning children. Having heard the children's screams, the men had left the sally-hole and were racing like hell through the heather. Their previous fun and hilarity from their day's bathing was completely ruined as they witnessed the scene – to think that three young innocents were drowning before their time was up – after they themselves had been the cause of it by unblocking the dam and letting loose the water's full force.

But, like the near disaster four years previously this little story was not to have an unhappy ending. Overcome with alarm for the lives of the children and not caring how much their shirt and trousers got drenched, Matt-with-the-Machinery and Spare-Ribs showed untold bravery and leapt mindlessly into the torrent. From somewhere deep inside their hearts they found the strength of two wild horses. For a moment there was silence across the heather. No-one knew whether the outcome would be life or death – until finally the two heroic men broke the fierce spirit of the river demons and brought the three children (corpse-like and trembling) safely out onto the bank. Praise-be-the-day! They had saved three young lives and God smiled down on them from above. The rest of the men were so out of their mind with worry from looking at the warfare between Man and Growl River that they completely forgot to clap their hands.

At Feathery-Edge

Once her cousins had returned to town – as soon as Kate was washed and dressed by Joe (her boots well-polished) she went scurrying with her bottle of milk and her satchel of books each day to the schoolhouse in Feathery-Edge. She was always in a dreadful hurry to avoid a birching when she reached the school. It was the only one within miles and was situated on the borders of The Wilderness and scarcely deserved the name of an educational establishment. It had a rusty tin roof like most of her father's roof back home. It was sheltered by a number of overarching trees which gave it protection from those banshee winds that wailed across the heather and gave the area around Growl River its threatening name. With the trees waving their chequered branches close to the sides of the windows the children were warm and snug throughout the winter but in the summertime (though they were still warm from the sun pouring its rays in through the windows) they were continually itching themselves from the presence of a thousand midges and moths swarming in among them from these now-unfriendly trees.

Comfort Inside

Admittedly there was some sort of comfort inside. The priest from Clare (Father Simply) had painted the four walls a bright cream colour. The fireplace in the centre of the hob was always full of resinous logs and blazing sods-of-turf, brought in by Kate and her schoolfriends from wherever they could steal them on their way to their lessons. This fireplace area was painted a brilliant red like the altarboys' cassocks. Even the cement lines in between the red bricks had been painted – a delicate white, giving the room a grand finish to it. Father Simply must have fancied himself as a bit of an artist.

However, the fire in the fireplace was the only other joy seen in the place. For each morning the children had to greet Dropsy with his big smoky glasses and the pen behind his ear and he dressed in his greenfrock coat. With him was his wife (Hairy-Chin) with her venomous nose and the candle of snot on the end of it and the trace of a black moustache over her lip. The two sets of cold eyes stormed in from the doorway in a great hurry and stretched their yellow hands out towards the blazing fire, which the bigger boys had lit in anticipation of the important couple's arrival.

Dropsy

Dropsy cast a cowlike eye around the room before throwing the copybooks across the desks at the children for the handwriting to begin. He handed out the slates for the sums. Keeping his coat on him and his scarf wrapped firmly round his shoulders (for a strong wind was rattling the windows) this charming fellow then gave the children the usual few scurrilous sentences to copy from the blackboard – that is if he had the time or inclination to write them down. Or else, standing in front of the glowing fire and parting his coat-tails so that his rear-end got a good toasting, he introduced the tedious subject of Dictation. Whereupon he spent several minutes amusing himself – observing the children and their scratchy pens trying to write down the mysterious doggerel he was spouting at them. Kate and her school-friends were transfixed like rabbits and kept their eyes down low. If only they had wings to escape! Each morning they were well-used to writing something to the detriment of their neighbours – any piece of salacious gossip that Dropsy could drum up.

The Dictation

Dropsy rolled out his words from his soft wet lips: 'Old Gleegaw put a crease in his pants last Wednesday,' he began. There was a merry twinkle in his eye. The children knew what was coming next for Old Gleegaw was the father of Matty Hoppity (a child with a damaged leg since birth). The poor child and his reddened face was sitting at the back of the classroom and wishing he could find a short route down through the earth and into Australia. The children (Matty included) wrote down the words, shaping their copperplate letters carefully with their scratchy pens:

'Old Gleegaw walked all the way to The Clare Bridge,' shouted Dropsy. The sound of the forty pens dipping into their full inkwells broke the echoing silence:

'He took his cow there to sell her,' went on the wise old master. Another pause and the eyes of the expectant children looked up in wonder at Dropsy:

'When he got to The Clare Bridge, Old Gleegaw was unable to sell his cow.' Dropsy gave a little cough and then a smile. A minute passed before the children saw their master giving a hearty guffaw:

'Old Gleegaw was awfully cold from standing on the bridge the livelong day. He had to walk back home again with his cow.'

There came a groan from poor young Matty: 'He had no money in his pockets.' By now Matty was in tears.

'He was very sad indeed,' said the great tragedian that Dropsy had become. The eighth sentences were completed and the children put down their pens. They looked back at the tear-stained face of Matty Hoppity and their hearts went out to him. Like Matty's father, they felt very sad when they thought of the miserable day the poor man had had – standing there in the market-place – and his inefficiency in trying to sell his cow – and the way he had travelled all that way to The Clare Bridge without a bite to eat – only to come home again empty-handed. Sometimes Life wasn't worth living (they felt). And so ended the lesson as Dropsy finally ordered the copybooks to be collected in and handed up to him. The children (no fools) couldn't help noticing the little smirk from the self-satisfied schoolmaster and one or two of them whispered how they'd dance on his coffin when the day came for him to die.

They knew what would happen. When it came to the end of the school year and the copybooks were all completed, Dropsy would take these masterpieces down to the drinking-shop of Lapping-Guinness. This royal occasion was a good excuse for him to load his belly with a few handy pints of The Black Doctor. The woman-of-the-house would tear out the pages from each copybook, delicately wrapping her wrist round each page and turning them into scooped-out paper cones. During the long summer days she filled the cones with peggy's-leg sweets, which the children bought with the few coppers the passing poachers gave them. The rock hardness in these sweets would rot a dragon's teeth from out of its mouth. By the time the summer holidays were over everybody for miles round Growl River had read the children's fine copperplate writing and had absorbed the contents of the *Dropsy Dictations* from inside the cones. Then (the shame to think of it) the likes of poor Matty Hoppity and many others became the laughing-stock of The Wilderness.

A Bout Of Theatricals

With the finish of the early morning Dictation the day continued on its merry way. Dropsy could talk so fast. He should have been a politician.

With his red-and-white pointer he prodded the map that was thrown up on the wall. The children were in for a bout of theatricals as they saw him marching up and down – introducing them to the rivers, capes and bays that lay around the world and bidding them re-echo his *repeat-after-me*. Occasionally he cracked his pointer on a lad's desk to make sure the young devil was still alive and well.

He Stole Out The Back Door

As soon as he'd satisfied himself that all the little heads of his pupils were down on their desks and were busy scribbling out the *Times Tables* on their slates, he stole out the back door and set off at a tremendous gallop on his horse (Whirlwind) to the drinking-shop of Lapping-Guinness. He spent half the morning leaning in across the counter and telling the landlord how he badly needed a few drinks – how misfortunate he was to be the master of so many foolish children. Back at the school he had left his dry old wife (Hairy-Chin) and her fierce sally-switch to chastise any child that might dare look up from their copybooks or slates. To see her was to fear her.

Whilst he was warming his belly with The Black Doctor, Hairy-Chin was contented enough to bring forth her own few eccentricities – warming her cold gable-end at the banked-up roaring fire, which was flaring halfways up the chimney. Close beside her and behind the blackboard (where the children couldn't get a look at them) she kept a dozen bottles of The Black Doctor. She wasn't half as clever as she thought she was – as if the children didn't know what she was up to. The heat from the fire didn't do the gassy mixture in the bottles a bit of good and they began to expand. The serious reflections of the children on their Tables were often punctuated by the explosion of the popping corks and the curses of Hairy-Chin ('these feckin bottles') as she ran to lap up the frothy flow of the heavenly medicine flooding over the bottle-lips ('Get on with yeer slates and yeer copies') before it got away from her and spilt around the classroom. Meanwhile the children prayed that the bottles of booze would make a knot in her stomach and give her the sick.

A Polite Little Stroll

At times – her cheeks all red and radish-looking (for she'd taken a drop too much) – she got up off her stool and made a polite little meander round the room, touring in and out between the desks (as though she was Florence Nightingale) to inspect the studious work of her little treasures and their bent heads. Glitter-eyed from the drink and with her arms stretched out in front of her (so as not to fall), she'd pause and teeter on her heel. Though she was only four-and-a-half-feet high she was well able to administer the odd little cuff with her knuckles round the bigger boys' heads or give them a good clatter to their jaws – just in case they might be thinking of making a run for the door's freedom or otherwise stepping out of line during the master's necessitous constitutional at Lepping-Guinness's drinking-shop. After this bit of entertainment our charming little mistress came and sat herself back down behind the blackboard to commence swigging into the drink till her eyes ran rolling round her head.

The Rhythm Of Exploding Corks

If the fire didn't shake the quiet of the room with the exploding bottle-corks, Hairy-Chin had time to set up her own handy rhythm of corks popping as she quietly unscrewed them from the bottles and poured the delicious medicine down her throat. By the end of the morning she had consumed a good few bottles – hard labour indeed for any woman to have to drink so much of it. And for the rest of the day both herself and Dropsy would find themselves swaying round the room as drunk as a rat that had fallen into the harvesters' bucket of booze. These then were the so-called lessons (dismal enough to turn any child into a pure fool) that Kate and many another child came to shudder over when they thought of them in later years.

On Sunny Summer Afternoons

On sunny afternoons, when the school day was over and the sky was a hazy blue, Kate's father brought out the ass (Tomboy) from the shed. The two of them then went off on the ass's back across The Wilderness to spend a few hours tending the grave of the little girl's tragic mother (Lizzie). The older women in Rookery Rally still recalled the day she died – and how Joe and his tearfulness had taken her in the horse-and-cart to the other side of the mountain. After inspecting their handiwork of removing the odd blade of grass from Lizzie's grave, Joe and Kate knelt on the grass and offered up their decades of the rosary for the repose of her soul. If she were not inside heaven's gates as a result of all their prayers, then none of us would ever get within an inch of it. Before leaving the grave they placed a few sad bunches of wildflowers below her headstone. They waved their hands back at her and they bid her farewell ('till we meet again'). Then themselves and Tomboy went off home.

Her Youthful Days

On reaching her adolescent years Kate, along with her devoted father, left The Wilderness. They took the long road that led down amongst us here on the slopes. Like many before them they had been badgered (they said) into taking the fine load of money offered to them by The Gadfly Men from The Forestry. Although they had been as happy as songthrushes in their little cabin they knew it was best to come and live in the healthier and less breezy tillage lands that lay between Rookery Rally and The Roaring Town.

Off To The Dance

By this time Kate was no longer a child but closer to twenty. The thought of her running around in her bare feet was a thing of the past. There was now something of the magic in her – with her long slender legs like a crane's – legs that were made for dancing. And then there was her head of jetty-black hair as long as an eagle's feathers – reaching down her back and parted in the middle (what we called the Sunday way). To set her on towards womanhood her father had bought her a violet velvet dress. On summer evenings she would dress herself up in this one good dress of hers.

She managed to get hold of a few bangles to compliment her dress and off she would trot to The Platform Dance-in-The-Fields, a dab of scented lavender behind her ears (the little devil). She and her clean good looks would while away a pleasant few hours with the other young men and women. And soon she learnt how to do the fancy set-dance steps and the polka-sets on the wooden boards beneath the light of the stars.

When winter came on and the darkness prevented the musicianers and steppers from going into the fields to dance she took herself off to The Roaring Town where she danced the modern quicksteps, the waltzes (she loved the slow ones) and the foxtrots inside in The Evening Institute. These wintertime adventures gave Kate a wider education (she felt) than dancing her evenings away in the fields among the simple country lads with the smell of cowdung on them. The Institute's dancehall was larger and far more formal with its dazzling lights and the smell of polish on its floor and benches. Here was a bright new world for someone like Kate who'd come down from the mountains. Suddenly she had the good fortune to rub shoulders with the far cleverer lads from the fancy houses with their trimmed hedges and railings inside in the town. These townie lads with their smart wit and their fancy togs had the edge over us poor scholars back here in the hills.

Kate Was In Her Glory

Kate was in her glory. There was nowhere on earth like the dancehall for the assemblage of feverish young hearts. She began to put on a little powder to her jaw and a small dab of warpaint on her lips. Every Saturday night was like a starry Christmas for her with all the excitement it presented. The young men sat in a row at one end of the hall, their eyes cast down and pretending that they were feeling a bit shy (the women loved a shy man and couldn't wait to get their hands on him). The women, some with their legs crossed high and brazenly, sat in another neat row at the far side of the hall, tapping their painted nails on their bangles to the strains of the music. The more adventurous hussies from the lower regions of the town seemed that bit restless and gave the younger boys (the truly shy ones) a little glimpse of their white thighs. Ah, the little heathens! And where now was their mother's yardbrush to be seen hopping off of their legs?

There were one or two rakish country fellows, who loved acting the part of the wild man. They knew how snotty-nosed some of these townie girls were. These lads were dressed up in their best suits or in their sports jackets with the white shirt-collar out over the coat collar. But to enliven the merriment of the proceedings some of the rascals had purposefully left their socks at home. They sat down nonchalantly and made no attempt at shyness. They garishly lifted their trouser-legs to expose their hairy shins opposite the women. This was followed up with bouts of sniggering and laughter at both ends of the hall. You can picture the embarrassment of the younger innocent girls at this downright rude behaviour. The nuns in their recent convent days had been right to warn them against such rogues and what they might get up to later on in the evening. The little innocents would rather make a run for the door than let these wicked men get their lustful hands wrapped round their waists.

She Was Thinking To Herself

As the weeks went by Kate began to see all the advantages resulting from having a man's strong arm round her and having his chest against her own chest and his warm breath panting down on her neck as they went racing through the newest quicksteps. Added to this there were the little gasps in her lungs from the fierce twists and the sharp turns of the foxtrot. The devils that these men were – she couldn't get enough of it.

And Then The Gale Blew In

And then, on her third visit to the dancehall, a strange thing happened: from the minute she entered the dancehall she realised that the same brown-haired young man ('what is it with this fellah with the pink face?') kept asking her to step out with him onto the floor. He was indeed a dasher-of-a-man – him and his big green eyes. And for a while she felt that she was marooned in space with him as the dance ebbed and flowed up and down the length of the hall. Wasn't she the lucky lady to be receiving such attention from the likes of him!

That Name – The Gale

And as the first hour came to an end he gave her his name: The Gale. Kate was more than puzzled. This was a mighty strange name for a man to be having: it wasn't like Jack-the-Herd or Bill-the-Bear. And though she herself had spent her entire childhood in a very windy spot, she now wondered if this man had grown up in an even more remote and windy outpost than her own. She could picture him and his bike getting blown all over the hills as he attempted to cycle down to town to try his hand at these fancy dancesteps and give a woman a twirl or two round the floor.

The Gale? No – he'd never ventured into any windy parts of the country such as The Wilderness. Indeed he had never set foot outside the town. If she'd looked more closely she could see that he was a gentleman with fine features – snow-white teeth (unlike our own) and clipped fingernails. After each dance he gave her a little bow and led her back to her place amongst the women. And then he told her that he wasn't The Gale at all: his name was The Gael and amid a fit of good-humoured laughter he spelled it out for her with his four fingers: G-A-E-L.

Closer And Closer Together

As the night proceeded and their intense eyes locked closer and closer together, Kate began to understand how he had come to have such a curious name for he loved nothing better than to glorify the native Gaelic language with his tongue: in fact he used the speech of what he called the foreign settlers very sparingly, if ever at all. If Kate was to make his further acquaintance (she thought to herself) she had better get a move on and swallow a dictionary-load of Gaelic words in the next couple of weeks.

Rappity

The Gael was a bit on the nervy side and he began to talk to her as fast as a flowing river. His father (he told her) was Rappity and he had come up from the Gaelic-speaking regions of Waterford. After that he had married into a small farm out near The Mighty Shannon River where a fresh-faced spinster (Holy Mary) was the last soul left – living on a small piece of land. She had been what was called *a fine catch* with her nine fields of land and they all in good heart and working order.

Indeed old Rappity had shown himself to be a most patient man. For on the two previous occasions that he'd made the trip into Tipperary to get himself the land and a hardy bit-of-a-woman not in too bad a shape and with thigh-like arms on her – a woman with an aged father – a woman looking for a man to help her cultivate the land in the old man's place – he'd gone home empty handed. Of course the land would always count first for a man on a mission (we all knew that).

On those previous occasions nothing had gone right. Before stepping down from his mare the first time and getting as far as the house to shake the hand of the prospective maiden's father he proved himself no fool and (his first task) had climbed in over the ditch to go *walk the land*. Any man who wished to marry would do that very same thing – go *walk the land*. But he saw that the land was too boggy and he went back home with his boots and socks soaking wet. On his next visit he didn't even step over the ditch for he saw that the fields were full of rushes and he speedily pedalled back south. On his third visit, however, he was well-satisfied with the land and went on to meet the woman-of-the-house where he found (joy of joys) that she too had a good bit of merit in her. So he married her – married The Gael's mother and stayed in Tipperary thereafter.

Within a year of the wedding their only son (the mother being nearer to fifty than forty at the time of the match) arrived in the shape of The Gael – the present foxtrot specialist. Rappity's joy was finally complete. He had the land. He had a fine stout woman. He had a son. Unfortunately his wife died in the process (God be good to her).

The Courtship

By the time Kate was introducing herself to the liveliness of The Evening Institute, The Gael was a teacher of the native language inside in the town's

High School each evening. In some ways he was as determined as his father and anxious to get things done in something of a hurry. That meant that his courtship of Kate went on for a very short time (only a year) unlike those long-winded shake-hands that often lasted up to ten years before a hairy old fellow whipped up enough courage to remove his togs and hop into bed beside a young damsel. And another thing – gentleman that he was, The Gael and his sensitive soul never laid a hand on Kate's leg or in those places where his hands (rest assured) might have yearned to go wandering – nor would he do so until Father Goodfellow had blessed the two of them with the sacramental graces of the marriage-bed. Our shy couple's courtship was to remain a tale of innocence and modesty throughout the time they went stepping out together. They'd meet by the river – he, skimming stones across the ripples or casually bringing down hazelnuts for her. There might have been the odd fretful kiss when they were hiding beneath the willowtrees but there was never so much as a glimpse of a garter or petticoat between them before Kate would run breathlessly home to her father.

No Feasting And Carousing

After obtaining Raffity's blessing they got married in a quiet sort of way – no feasting and carousing for this careful man and his even more careful pockets of jingling coins – just a few cream cakes and a pot of tea inside in the parlour of Goosey-Goosey-Gander's Hotel.

It was a day they'd always remember – Kate's captivated father (Joe) all the time sighing – his hands clasped in wonder of the occasion – and their new priest blessing them and praying over them. It was a moment when Time was caught sleeping – to see Kate with the bit of lipstick on her mouth and The Gael with the brilliantine covering his curly locks. The wedding joy seeped thenceforth into their souls and it stayed there. In the coming days The Gael serenaded his young wife all over the town and she too lionized him to all and sundry. Shy though she was, she didn't mind the young townie-fellows gawping at her or wondering what the two of them might be getting up to in the middle of night.

They Were At Peace

Later that summer they went off in the pony-and-trap to spend a day with Rappity. They hummed merrily to the mare as the wheels sang them speedily on towards the old man's door. Woe and alas – it was a sad sight indeed to see the shape the poor man had turned into. He was stuck to the stool next to the fire, the potato-sack wrapped round his shoulders to comfort his limbs with the heat out of the blazing logs. In the short space of time since they'd seen him at their wedding his ailing lungs had turned into a pair of worn-out old bellows thanks to all the fine pipesmoking he'd enjoyed over the years. He had the utmost difficulty in catching his breath – let alone welcoming Kate when she arrived in the door and came across the floor to shake hands with him.

The Shop In Town

From now on – Kate and The Gael were seen as a comely and energetic pair. They pooled their resources (Kate selling a cow or two on her father's new farm) and a year after their marriage set up a shop a stonethrow from The Market Square. They put a sign over the door – *The Haberdashery Shop*. From the first day they opened it to customers you'd see your face shining in the windowglass – so neat and clean were they.

Inside they assembled a mixture of goods and articles – a motley of smells such as cheese and tobacco – and the leather of shoes, wellingtons and handbags on pegs on the wall. The green shelves were filled with scythes and horses' harness and chains hanging on hooks and with nails and gate-bolts. On the rafters were hung hams and sausages. You'd have to move a bit skilfully round the sawdust floor, it being filled with kegs of flour and boxes of soap and candles and there were baskets of vegetables and apples and pears.

The passing children often came in to have a look at the fruit-jars and stone jugs full of sugarsticks (twelve for a penny). For the older folk there were threads and twine. And there were pastilles, ointments and bandages for a man's toothache and a five-gallon can of oil to keep everyone warm in the winter. In the far corner – on The Gael's counter – there was a shiny scales and next to it a yellow ledger for him to keep an ink-score of the money. And all the time ('Yes I have this! Yes I have that!') he kept padding round the shop in his slippers and squinting excitedly when he made a creditable sale. As for Kate, she had everything labelled neatly in a fine copperplate style of handwriting – even though she always said that old Hairy-Chin had taught her nothing whatever above in The Wilderness.

When the country lads back home heard about Kate and the shop they were left scratching their heads: they had misinterpreted the name of her new-fangled shop as *The Have-a-Dash-at-Ye* shop and were half-expecting Kate to be selling a parcel-load of greyhounds that would dash out the door after them when next they found themselves in town.

We Were Left Open-mouthed

By now we were all left open-mouthed at Kate's advancement in life. To think that within so short a time she had made the four steps that would take the rest of us three generations to reach: with her father she had hopped down from the mountains to the tillage lands of Rookery Rally: she had then left him and hopped into the sophistications of The Roaring Town: she had hopped into bed with a more than sophisticated gentleman: she had hopped in over the counter and become the proprietor of the haberdashery shop. She was a lady in a devil of a hurry. And some put it down to the fact that in her earlier childhood she had almost departed from this world in an even bigger hurry than now so as to reach the gates of The Kingdom – the day she almost got swept to her death at the hands of The Growl River fairies.

She Became A Heathen

After her marital whirlwind Kate astonished us even more: she became a heathen. She stopped going to Mass – a thing unheard of (except for Red Scissors) in all our known history. The gossipy Weeping Mollys spread the news that Kate had taken up not with the religion of the foreign settlers but with a group calling themselves The Quakers. We were unsure of the name and wondered if these strange people were quaking in their boots or expecting the world to end in some sort of devastating earthquake. This fifth step in Kate's re-education beggared all our beliefs. It was the last straw and left us flat on our backs in wonder at her. Such a great distance had she travelled in a single lifetime. What on earth would her father (Joe) think of her now?

Pink-cheeked Happiness And Quakers

Happier by the day from this new spiritual awakening, the loving twosome took to the roads in greater style than ever. It was as plain as the writing on a slate to see the pink-cheeked happiness written all over their smiling faces. That's when we began to put our fingers to our lips – began to wonder what it was like to become a Quaker. Indeed one or two of the more adventurous lads (those young devils who had forgotten to bring their socks to The Evening Institute Dance) thought it was high time for themselves to have a change in their religious duties. May God strike them down dead.

Thanks to The Weeping Mollys we soon learnt that our two new Quaker friends believed that their earthly bodies were not something to call their own but merely lent to them by God – that we were all part of a much larger plan which God was holding in his hands – that we were all going to come back to earth one fine day inside the shell of another body. We weren't sure if this was true or not.

Perish the thought. And yet – we ourselves already half-believed this to be a fact of life. For many of us found the ghosts of our dead forebears forever whispering in our ears – as if they were inside in our heads and warming themselves inside in our hearts and breathing the air all around us – whether we were at the milking or at the thrashing or abroad in Bog Boundless. And some of us felt that these ghostly spirits had control over our every movement. We were frightened to death of them and we threw the holywater with earnestness round ourselves whenever we walked out the door.

The Spanking New Bikes

In spite of our fears for their souls we could see that the winking pair were as close as both sides of a dinnerplate – could see how they lifted up their heads in pride. They bought two spanking new racing-bikes the likes of which we'd never seen before. No matter how bad-looking the weather was they'd cycle away on their merry jaunts over valleys and hills as soon as they got someone to give them a day or two free from the shop. It's then that you'd hear the strangest of tales about them:

'Lasy Saturday I met Kate and the Gael beyond in Clare.'

'Last Sunday I met Kate and The Gael beyond in Limerick.'

When Micky O'Keefe (the famous wrestler) was showing off his skills against Cool Clancy below in Kerry, Kate and The Gael were seen cycling south in a dreadful hurry. Little dreamers that the two of them had always been, poets they now were to become. For after their long-distant journey they returned breathlessly and said that they would never forget the shape or the colour of every passing cloud – of every flowery bush – of every tuneful bird. In minute detail they recounted the adventures of their once-in-a-lifetime outing. It was as though they had momentarily left this world for none of us had ever been so far away from home – only a few of us having ridden our horses into Clare in search of a wife. Could we ever forget the tales they brought back and the Kerry pictures the two of them were able to paint for us – pictures that were stamped on our minds and would last us forever.

The Step-dancing

The Gael was getting livelier by the minute. Whereas other men, who had of late found themselves coupled in the marriage-bed, would spend most of the time tumbling and tussling with their new wife in the darkness of the bedroom, The Gael took on a new role – he took to the step-dancing in earnest. You'd catch him leaping all round the place. Quicker than a wink he had learnt the jig and the hornpipe and had bought a wind-up gramophone for himself.

Poor Old Rappity

It was a raw grey Sunday when The Gael was given the news that poor Rappity (and the potato-sack wrapped round his back to keep in the warmth) was finally on the verge of death. He was the colour of soap and was stooped nearer than ever towards the fire with the heart quaking in him. The Gael knew that his father loved the music and that his dying wish would be to see his son stepping the new jiggy dance-steps, a sight he'd never seen before. The old man called for him to come ('like the good man you are') and dance his new steps for him. Then he got ready his pipe and his jug of whiskey.

For once in her life Kate found herself in second place to her sound man. However – The Gael (teacher that he was) had taught her a few fanciful steps of her own and these she was able to offer poor Rappity with the aid of the two records that they'd brought with them. Like all our country-women she was a bit on the shy side and insisted that the dying man turn the peak of his cap down over his eyes so as to get only a little squint at her feet and not her entire body. That was the way with our shy women – be it the dancing or the singing: none of them liked to be looked at.

The dying Rappity dutifully turned down the peak of his cap. Kate insisted that he turn his face in towards the firelight, confident that it would be only the squint of her feet and not her whole self that he'd be gawping at. But (dying though he was) he was still an old schemer and he raised the side of the cap's peak just an inch from his eyebrow. He'd be damned if he didn't get more than a glimpse of Kate and her fiery dance-stepping. There was a new air to Kate as she leapt round the floor like a stag and she was aware of nothing other than the steps in her head. As for Rappity – it was the happiest day of his life, mesmerised as he was by the pure savagery in her. Indeed such was the power of Kate and The Gael's dance-steps that it kept Rappity's soul safe and sound for the next week and he would take to his grave the memory of the fine dancing of our two lively cyclists. And another thing – he even caught a bit of their Quakerishness for himself and this too he would take with him on his long last journey to The Beyond.

Rappity's Ghost Called Upon The Gael

And so – two weeks later Rappity (the astute man who'd once come to inspect the lands of the Gaels' future mother) passed away from us. But (would you credit it) his dead spirit couldn't get a bit of peace and he returned a few nights later and began whispering to his son to come and inspect the road that would lead father and son to The Beyond and the gates that welcomed all godly souls to the kingdom prepared for them. And so – within a short month The Gael met his death. It was most unexpected for he had been such an active man – what with his regular use of the bike and the stepping of his jigs and hornpipes. On a Sunday morning Kate found him propped up dead in the bed with a half-drunk cup of tea in his hand – the victim of a broken vein in his head from all the learning ('twas said). She went down to Abbey Acres Graveyard to bury him the following Tuesday. Like their wedding, it proved to be but a small and private affair – herself and her priest (Father Goodfellow). Amen to it all (she said) and she wept silently.

The Gael's Hat

The hat that The Gael had always worn (with the red cock-feather stuck in the side of the hatband) was lying on top of the coffin. It was covered in black grease from his constant wearing of it. Father Goodfellow passed this memento onto Kate at the far side of the grave in the hope that she'd accept it as a symbol of her beloved Gael and the kindness that he'd always shown her since their first twist of the foxtrot at The Evening Institute Dance. There was a pause – a solemn one. Then Father Goodfellow nudged Kate and urged her to throw the hat into the grave after he had blessed it with a dash of holywater. There stood Kate – bewildered and wiping the salty tears from her eyes with the aid of the hat's brim. She was about to throw the hat into the grave when she gave a last look down at the coffin and had a little thought.

It Was Just A Little Thought

Like many things it was just a little thought that had suddenly come into her head. No (blasht it!) – she would not destroy the hat and bury it under the clay. To the astonishment of Father Goodfellow she arranged The Gael's hat carefully on her head. A woman wearing a man's hat – was such a thing ever heard tell of before? Then she rode her bike out from the graveyard with the hat cocked sideways on her head – the way The Gael had always worn it and to keep his departed spirit within her. From that day till the day she died she always wore the greasy hat of The Gael. 'She sleeps in it,' said one or two of the smiling go-byze (the rogues).

A Shop Full Of Tomfoolery

Sadly, without the attendance of her sound man, Kate's haberdashery shop began to turn into nothing short of a mockery. Her merchandise, once so carefully chosen, (the scythes and the plough-handles) soon lost their appeal and she began to sell all sorts of tomfooleries: there was a wide selection of tobacco pipes, both red and white – as though anyone in their right mind would be seen buying them or smoking them: there were footballs in the window – as though any of our hurling youth would dream of kicking a football when they didn't even know what a football looked like: there were cricket bats and balls too. The same sad fate met these articles and no-one came into the shop to buy them: no-one would be seen dead playing with these godforsaken articles. Poor sad Kate!

The Plateful Of Sandwiches

All wasn't lost and Kate was still able to make a shilling. She had always been a good-natured wretch and now she would get you a plateful of sandwiches if you needed them once you'd sold your cow on a Fair-Day. With a touch of her previous liveliness she'd make a dash out the back door and down the lane to Meg Mires before returning with the ham for the sandwiches, wiping it clean on her blackened apron if it fell to the ground on the way back; for Kate had of late donned the careless apparel of dirtiness. But (Quaker that she was) she gave enough of her doorstep sandwiches to fill a man's gizzard for a week-and-a-half – so much so that no matter what time of the evening a fellow returned to Rookery Rally he'd feel as hearty and well-fed as two stout pigs.

The Little Nipper

Although he had given us a great shock by dying at such a young age, The Gael had had the good sense to leave behind him a very special gift for his precious Kate – a frail rat-of-a-boy known as The Little Nipper. And in the next few years as this tiny speck grew in wisdom and strength we were astonished to see that he was no longer the weakling of his babyhood. Like a former ugly duckling he began to grow into a real iron man. And so – from his early adolescence onwards he went by the charming name of The Little Iron Man. Once he left school he found himself turning into a somewhat stray dog – walking in his own ways just like his parents, who had formerly disowned the rest of us and become Quakers. And another thing – he developed his own personal religious habits and much to Kate's surprise he asked to re-enter the folds of Holy Mother Church and be baptised and confirmed by Father Goodfellow.

The Music Was In Him

The interests of The Little Iron Man soon strayed even further away from the wild vagaries of Kate. He took to piano-music with a vengeance, scale after scale rising in magnificence to the top trebles and played with a delicacy unheard of before. In a short time a real volley of it could be heard echoing out the front window. It was not, however, the music of our own well-known jigs and polkas that he was playing but the classical arias and the ancient motets of the church. Very soon Father Goodfellow noted The Little Iron Man's unaccountable talent and invited him to come and practise on the great big organ in The Roaring Town Church (The Holy Innocents).

Just as Kate had astonished us with the rapidity of her former changes so did her son's musical advancement begin to fill us with one surprise after another. His mother was as proud of him as any mother hen when she saw him taking to his organ-practise with such an unheard-of bravado. By the time our own lads had reached the age of sixteen and were learning to dig their lips into their first pint of The Black Doctor The Little Iron Man had made himself the official organist in the church. The music was coming out through his two ears ('twas said). Fair play to him!

The Drop Of German Blood

Some of the women (was it The Weeping Molly?) spread the rumour that he had more than a drop of German blood running through his veins. Where it came from they didn't know. This was enough to make us stop in our tracks and wonder if it could be true. And there and then we began to malign him; for no-one other than a cracked German could play such an old rigmarole type of music as The Little Iron Man was playing. A young man who could love such quare-sounding music must surely be stone-mad. And madness was something we knew about, only too well: the madness from loneliness: the madness from religion: the madness from music. And the poor Little Iron Man (we said) had caught the last one of these.

Jinnet Street

At hurling-matches and Fair-Days the crowds roared up along Jinnet Street. When they reached The Haberdashery Shop (it getting dirtier and shabbier by the day) they stopped and listened. There was a change in the air. By now some of them were getting used to this strange but beautiful foreign music pouring out from the open window as The Little Iron Man rehearsed his tunes for the following Sunday's Mass. Some of them had stopped being so narrow-minded as to love only our jigs and polkas and they were beginning to take a shine to this new German style of organ-playing – were beginning to hum the little fellow's tunes in their heads – were even beginning to hum them to their startled cows when they were milking them abroad in the cowshed. The rumour soon got round that the new fandangled music was filling their buckets with twice as much milk as before. Fair play to you again and again, Little Iron Man! You put power into a man's milking.

Kate's Sad Spirits

Life wasn't always full of roses and sunshine. And it was soon noticed that Kate was growing a kind of soft in the head, for she found herself feeling the coldness and the stillness of the place. Her innate good humour started to desert her. A causticity replaced the soft side of her nature. Oh, how she was missing her lovely man! Was there no way she could mend her broken heart? In spite of listening to the musical outpouring from her gifted son we could see her pining away, the gossamer thread of her love – a love that had always bound herself and her sound man together – was everlastingly broken. When The Little Iron Man was firing away at his music above in the church-loft there was nothing left for her to do for her daily amusement. Increasingly she became anxious to join The Gael in his new home in The Beyond. We had seen how two ducks would fly high in the sky above the hunter's gun – had heard the roar of the rifleshot and the way a poor drake would tumble down to his sad death. We had seen how his sobbing mate would fly around and around in delirious circles as though begging the huntsman to end her unwanted life with his gun. We had seen how, in answer to her wishes, the hunter's gun would shoot her down to lie in death's embrace, chest-to-chest beside her drake. That's the way it was with Kate at this stage of her life. Her spirit (without The Gael) was as broken and bereft as that poor duck's. Her cycle-rides became a thing of the past. Alone and lonely stood The Gael's shining bike, gathering rust alongside hers in the corner behind the back door.

The Brown Suitcase

On Sunday afternoons she'd sit with her son inside in the upper room. She'd look out at the passing crowds on their way up Bacon Street to the pageantry of the hurling-match. Nobody spared her the time-of-day.

Nobody came into the shop to buy one of her strange cricket-bats or join her in a cosy little chat. There must be something she could do to gain their attention. In desperation she took from under the bed the brown suitcase, which was one of the hiding-places where The Gael had carefully horded his money. She leaned out the window and waved her wrists at the passers-by. There was no-one waving back at her as they raced off towards the entrance to the match.

She'd put a stop to their wanderings this very minute. She took a fistful of poundnotes from the suitcase. What good was The Gael's money to her anymore? She threw showers of the greenbacks down on the street. The startled crowd came running back under her window with flames out of them. It didn't need the gossip of The Weeping Molly to tell the rest of us that something fierce was astir for the news of Kate's lavishness had spread like a cow's fart and was followed by a gale of hilarious laughter. Indeed so great was the commotion that it closed the gates of the hurling-ground altogether. This was better than any circus and people gathered in increased numbers ('Kate! Kate! throw us down a few more poundnotes, will ye!') as though they'd been captured by the sudden arrival of Bishop High-Hat himself:

'Will ye look at that pack of simpletons,' said Kate to her son. For a finish she tipped the entire contents of the suitcase out the window and onto the street: 'Here,' she roared. 'take it to hell! May it do ye eejits a fat lot of good!'

The spellbound crowd stumbled around the road. Such good fortune was not seen every day of the week as they tried to catch the falling confetti of the pound-notes. Like crumbs (thought Kate) before chickens in her father's yard. She was going back for more money under the bed when The Little Iron Man came to the rescue – in the nick of time. If anyone could stop her losing her mind, it was this son of hers.

The End Of The Little Iron Man

But as if her drama hadn't been enough till now Kate was to get herself another surprise. She took a long hard look at the pale face of her son one morning and the rose on her own cheeks quickly vanished. Then it hit her like a rock to the head: the Little Iron Man had turned yellower than a quince. His bones had started to wither and shrink inwards on themselves. It was another Job-like dart straight into her heart. For it was the wish of the Man-in-the-sky that The Little Iron Man should meet up with Sergeant Death and there was nothing that Kate could do to stop it.

Had she looked a bit more closely in recent days instead of all the time pondering over the death of The Gael, she'd have seen that all the studious musicianship had been wearing her young son away, drying him out and exhausting his fine limbs into an old lemon. The energy of his music – the fanatical pace at which he was compelled to go at it night, noon and morning – as though he had been the town's answer to Mozart – had put an extraordinary and unfair burden on his adolescent brain. Didn't Kate realise that he wasn't a pure machine – that he couldn't go on pounding the keys like that forever?

Tall and robust as he had grown in recent years, his fleshless arms were no match for the galloping consumption that she spotted in the red spots on his alabaster cheeks. The cruel disease stole in overnight through the open window – crept inside the shell of The Little Iron Man's frail body as stealthily as a rat after the oats. As Rambling Jack said: 'Such a rare talent was never meant to be shared for long with the rest of us mere mortals'.

Unlike the sudden death and quick burial of The Gael, the prolonged coughing and spluttering of The Little Iron Man went on for days on end. Kate's previous grief was nothing compared to the heartache she now felt. Each day, as soon as twilight came, she lay her body down beside her lovely son in the hope that she too might catch his illness – that God in his goodness might see fit to take herself as well as her hurt lamb to the grave when the moment came for him to die.

And when he died a few nights later, Kate found herself unable to let go of him, all the time gazing down at his sad long face. She propped him up in the bed and kept him there for the next five days, giving out the excuse that he was too sick to get to the church and play his organ. And all the time she continued to speak to him in words of quavering affection – taking him up his hot jar to place around his icy feet – vigorously rubbing them as though there was still a chance to bring him back to life.

Father Goodfellow was no fool and guessed at the truth. In the dead of night himself and The Guards came stealthily in the back door when Kate was sound asleep. Between them they took The Little Iron Man's corpse to The Chapel-of-Rest. Before Kate came to her senses and realised the impact of her son's death the little musician was buried alongside The Gael and Rappity in the heart of The Abbey Acres Graveyard. God rest his soul. And for the next two weeks the good priest kept the lid of the church-organ firmly shut.

A Crucial Time

Now was a crucial time in Kate's life. With no one left to talk to her, she could either sink or swim. But somehow or other the sun was still stirring with its sunlight and the leaves were still on the trees and the flowers were still budding and the small birds were still singing their songs. So – remembering the mighty battle she had once waged against Growl River and its demons when she was a child, she ran upstairs and foraged around her. Under the floorboards she found a second hidden treasure of poundnotes, which The Gael had thoughtfully stored away for the rainy day and their happy old age together. With these she made one last push to come back to her senses. Fair play to you, Kate! It was as though God was giving her another chance – that he had thought fit to restore her to her former sanity.

The Motorcar

She went out the week after The Little Iron Man's burial and bought herself a motorcar – what we started calling *the ould contraption* when we saw it coughing and spluttering round the town. It was one of only five motorcars we were ever to see in our lives. Of course she was getting on in years and within a month it became every bit as dirty as herself – as though she had taken to trucking in pigs and hens with it. She was a strange sight with the greasy hat of The Gael pitched on the side of her head.

There was still a bit of life left in her and before we knew it she had turned herself into a hackney-car driver. For a while she outpaced the two undertakers, who used their cars for the hackney-car trade above at The

Railway Station, making it her business to be there ahead of them. You'd hear the tyres of her old rattletrap stuttering their way onto the station platform even before the train rounded the bend from Limerick.

Whereupon – not even giving the startled passengers time to draw breath or get down the steps from the train – she made a grab for their suitcases and led them out to her car. She threw their cases into the car in front of them and sailed off out the gravel drive before the undertakers had a chance to come in the gate and (you'd think later) prepare the new arrivals for their impending burial! For while she was driving her weary passengers out to the countryside she made sure to keep them wide awake by constantly turning round to chat to them and taking her hands from off the steering-wheel. By the time they arrived at their destination the poor wretches were terrified to death. They quickly threw their money at her and sometimes they also threw the sick from their stomachs out onto the floor before making good their escape, thereby making her dirty old car even dirtier with their fresh vomit.

Her Other Selected Victims

She became known for stuffing the shiny coins of her selected victims down into a dirty blackened rag that was tied to a string round her neck. The rag was stuffed deep inside Kate's dirty blouse and it'd take a brave man to put his hand down between her withered old breasts and look for the change that was lying warm and snug in that dirty bit of rag. What a difference the years had made! Where on earth had her self-pride gone to from the days above in The Wilderness? Where on earth had all her neat housewifery gone to that had been implanted in her long ago by her kindly father, Joe Solitary?

Herself And Father Goodfellow

Still wearing her husband's greasy hat, Kate permitted herself a new purchase and got herself a pair of men's hobnail boots, which were soon to be heard stamping themselves all over the town. All she needed (we said) was a pair of six-guns round her belt to ensure that we paid her the respect she felt she deserved.

From time to time Father Goodfellow met her in Jinnet Street. And though she was not of his flock (still being a Quaker) he always gave her his priestly blessing. He was the one true friend Kate had to her name and on these precious occasions the two of them called back to memory the fine music of their protegy (The Little Iron Man). Kate became a daily joy to the saintly man for he recognised her unusually honest turn of speech and even enjoyed the coarseness of her outrageous language when it raised its head.

He recalled the day when our two great hurling teams (Tipperary and Cork) were whaling the hides off of each other inside the town's hurling-ground – how she had enraged the good bishop after he had thrown in the hurling-ball to commence the match – how to everyone's surprise she'd started running hysterically up and down the sideline encouraging on our own hurlers:

'Sit down, you bleddy old fool!' roared the bishop.

'Go kiss mee arse!' shouted Kate, not one bit frightened of his holiness. And then she showed him the colours of her drawers, causing us to spit our sides laughing. The bishop found himself laughing too and we heaved a sigh of relief. What pure insolence must have been engendered into Kate after the death of The Gael and The Little Iron Man is anyone's guess.

And when the match was finished she stood alongside the saintly Father Goodfellow in the middle of Jinnet Street and you'd hear her over-excited voice echoing halfway down the street: 'God be with you, Father,' she rasped, 'how good it us to see you – and you shining like a diamond.'

'It's decent you're looking yourself, Kate,' said he in that little syrupy voice of his.

There then came out of her mouth the words we were never likely to forget for the rest of our lives: 'Hold on a minute, Father – I'm bursting to piss!'

Such irreverent talk was never heard tell of before – to treat the ears of a holy man in such a disgraceful way. But that was nothing to what followed next as Kate politely pulled out the front of her skirts with her pinched fingers as though drinking a cup of tea. It was clear to the good-humoured priest that she was wearing no drawers. Then she proceeded to engage him loftily on the course of the recent war and the shortages of sugar and tea. Without the blink of her rascally eye she began to trickle her steamy poolie down the length of the dusty gutter. Memorable day! It'd take a fine artist to draw the astonished faces of The Weeping Mollys and the rest of the open-mouthed gossips to see the rogue that was encased in Kate and now let loose. It had always been there, of course – trying to burst out from her inner soul. It was The Devil himself that was surely calling on her to give the likes of us a savage jolt.

Hymph!' Said Dowager

'Hymph!' said Dowager, as she dropped her knitting-needles, 'is it Kate Kiss-mee-Arse and her exploits that ye are talking about?' as she got up from the table. She suddenly recalled the recent floods that had flowed across The Road-to-The-Hollows and how Kate found herself and her car on one side of the ford's increasing waters and Father Goodfellow and his car on the other side. Taking off her boots, Kate paddled into the middle of the ford somewhat warily so as to test the depth. By the time she reached the middle of the stream the water was well above her knees. With a mischievous gleam in her eye the rascally woman raised her skirts high up along her old thighs. Then she spoke the words that the wily priest knew would come pouring out of her outrageous mouth: 'Father – there you are . . . standing on that side of the stream and yer hands in yer pockets. Here's me . . . stuck in the middle of the stream and there's nobody else between us.'

Abruptly she pulled her skirts right over her chin and gave him a filthy grin: 'Father, take one good look at me now . . . would ye ever remove yeer hands from yeer pockets . . . would ye ever take a chance?' She held onto her skirts for a split second. Father Goodfellow was in no doubt of her meaning for she wasn't asking him to chance wading into the river alongside her. The humorist that he himself had always been, he split his sides laughing till he got a pure pain from it.

For the next week or two the presbyteries of north Tipperary were full of the amorous advances made by the daring Kate on her young Confessor. You might have expected that sort of lewd behaviour from one of the tinkers after a feed of strong drink (said the women) but not from one of our own kind. What had the world come to? The rest of us couldn't help laughing with the merriment of it all – Kate and the piss from her bladder that had newly christened Jinnet Street – Kate and her mocking efforts to enchant her holy man into her drawers on The Road-to-The-Hollows. It filled Rookery Rally with laughter (possibly The Weeping Mollys too?) – a laughter beyond description.

Other Scarcities

Though the recent world war had rolled away and gone, these were still dark days for some of us. Apart from all the fine food we were having – apart from our trips to the henhouse, the pighouse, the tillage headlands, the rivers and rabbit-warrens above in The Hills-of-The-Past – there were a few souls less fortunate than us in one particular aspect – *petrol* . . . or rather the lack of it. This made Doctor Glasses wear a permanent frown on his face when he was out on his visiting rounds. The Bearded Vet was another casualty that rarely gave us anything but a scowl. And lest we forget – both Kate and her good friend (Father Goodfellow) were in dire need of any petrol they could get their hands on – the priest especially.

One morning he finished his prayers and then he had an inspired little thought. He had always admired the way Kate was able to pick herself up when the hazards of life seemed to be giving others a kick in the teeth – the way she and The Gael had been able to hoard up all that money secretly in the brown suitcase, most of which she had carelessly thrown to the four winds – the way she drove at speed each day to The Railway Station, ensuring she was always there before the first of the other two hackney-cars.

There wasn't a tint of petrol left in his spare can and he was going to have the utmost difficulty driving his motorcar round the parish so that he could visit the sick and pray over them. The old women were already growing desperate for him to come and hear their confession. Of course they had no real sin on their soul. Nevertheless they depended on his monthly visits and for him to give them his priestly Absolution and administer a Penance to free them from their imaginary guilt. Besides (as we all knew) these old dears were always sure to fill his pocket with a few crisp poundnotes ('say a Mass for us, Father – be a good man, won't you?') and to give him a basket of their eggs. Damn the bit – how were they going to receive another of his visits – how were they going to get the blessed host on their tongues if he couldn't get his hands on a few cans of petrol? Poor Father Goodfellow! He was in a very bad situation . . . unless . . . unless . . .

It was then that this cute little thought came to him – his good friend, Kate. She must have a stash of petrol hidden away – possibly above at the railway engine-house. More out of curiosity than amusement he decided he'd go and give her a call.

As soon as he had his foot inside the door he lunged into her: 'Kate! Kate! My dearest friend, Kate! Think of your poor Saviour hanging up there on his cruel cross. Wouldn't he want you to help Holy Mother Church in these very hard times?'

The Devil was now hard at work in him: 'It would also be good for the Quaker soul in you if you found a gallon or two of petrol to give me'.

But Kate was no fool and knew how to respond to the cheek and impudence of him – coming here to steal away her last few drops of petrol: 'Blasht you, Father. Take a long look at me. Do ye think I'm the Man from Galilee?'

And then she uttered the words, which he (the good-humoured rascal) knew that he'd hear pouring out of her filthy gob the moment he arrived in the door:

'Do ye think I can work miracles like Jesus himself? Do ye think I can piss petrol for you, Father?'

Scarcely able to keep back the roaring chuckles that were bubbling up in his throat, the saintly fellow went back to his presbytery with an empty petrol-can. Once again he had had the delighted privilege of hearing the outrageous Kate and the coarse language of her wicked answer – an answer he'd remember till his dying day. This merry exchange was also to brighten up our day and went the rounds of Rookery Rally. But imagine his surprise when the saintly man opened his garage door a week later and found . . . three green drums of petrol staring up at him and almost smiling at him. Ah, Kate!

Hitting The Whiskey

Now that Kate was beginning to age, it seemed that a whirlpool had finally overwhelmed her. It would take a brave man to enter her dirty motorcar. She was increasingly forgetting her Quakerish ways and was seen hitting the whiskey-bottle in earnest – indeed drenching herself in it (some would say). She kept a half-bottle of it inside the folds of her dress next to the dirty rag with the money. Her *golden licker* she called it. On a Fair-Day if you were too drunk to redeem your ass-and-car, she'd offer you a mouthful of her fiery whiskey whilst driving you home. She was like a madhouse maniac, driving at tremendous speed round every bend and twist of the road – bouncing the car off the ditches and cursing the bushes whenever they placed themselves in her way (as though they were an ass). Were you in the passenger seat you didn't have to wait till nightfall before getting yourself the finest of nightmares. But (what with her past cycling) Kate knew every bush and every flower on her way.

The Ould Buzz

There had to come a downfall and it came in the form of *The Ould Buzz*. That's what we called the new and dazzling bus that arrived among us from Limerick City. It was a neat little item – plush on the inside with bits of red carpeting. The seats were also red and they were comfy and would keep your gable-end warm as you went on towards town. We were forever clambering into it.

Besides – the fares of The Ould Buzz were half the price of Kate's. Not to be defeated, she got up even earlier than usual and took to stationing her old contraption at various staging-posts along the route half-an-hour before the arrival of the new bus. For a while customers continued to come to her, amused at the dirt of her and her foul language (it had its own charm). But each day they were getting fewer and fewer in number. The Ould Buzz was the tonic of the hour (they'd tell you). The gossipy women particularly enjoyed the company of one another when they piled together onto its comfy seats. And so – like all good things the livelihood of Kate was finally coming to an end. The car was deserted. The shop fell apart. Both the car and the shop turned to rack and ruin – like Kate herself. She sold them both.

The Nuns In Kilkenny

For a finish Kate turned into a shadow of herself with the look of a withered old turnip on her. She recognized her situation: it was time for her to travel on. Thoroughly bemused and with a sigh of regret she looked back towards the Hills-of-The-Past and The Wilderness and at Growl River that once almost drowned her. It was to be the last time she'd look in that direction. Like Soolah Patricia before her, she steered her ass towards the nuns in Kilkenny – herself and the poor tired creature arriving just as the sun's bands of coppery rust were starting to make creases in the sky and the day's cloudships were heading our way from the east.

She handed her last few poundnotes into the nuns' grasping fists. She had brought with her the few possessions left to her by The Gael – the wind-up gramophone and the boxes of gold and silver needles. She had brought with her The Little Iron Man's religious records to while away the evenings in her new abode. From then on she was the life and soul of the old people's otherwise dreary afternoons. She quickly learnt how to make use of the gloomy hospice and its nursing sisters and to push her soul into the arms of heaven – she learnt how to change her wilful ways and to bury deep in the past her colourful use of coarse language. The wild and wicked woman of former days (ah, the little old schemer) replaced those previous ways of hers with the manners of a coy and mild-mannered old lady. She learnt to charm the nuns and to make use of the chamberpot rather than direct her piss down along the yard. In more ways than one she became the nun's favourite – the Tipperary blow-in that they always referred to as The Lady of Shalott!

NINE

How Balaraggin went out in the moonlight to meet his mother.

The Eucharistic Congress

During the year of The Eucharistic Congress (it was in 1932, I believe) some of the children (like Warbling Will and his little brother, Gabby) were seen on the long summer evenings making their annual pilgrimage up to the deserted cabin of Balaraggin. They went there to see the sad bloodstains on the green door. Some invisible strangers (the women, probably) had managed to get up there before them in an attempt to whitewash off the cruel bloodstains and the shame of it all with their scrub-brushes. But the redness of Balaraggin's blood had forced its way out through the whitewash again and had established its place there for once and for all: it was as though the pale ghost of Balaraggin was still at large in his Welcoming Room to remind everyone that this bloody monument to his name ought never to be effaced.

Men Could Talk The Legs Off Of An Ass

It was hard to understand our men. The women spent these long evenings writing their eight-page missives to their children far over the seas. The men (what was wrong with them?) never picked up the pen. However – they made up for this by talking the legs off of any ass that might care to listen to them. You couldn't stop them unless they were attending Holy Mass on Sundays and were forced for once in their lives to shut their gobs and listen to the smart talk of the holy priest (in this case, Father

Sensibly). The rest of the week you'd hear them gabbling on and on – not only in the drinking-shops but also idling away the daylight hours on the lace of their ass-and-car. Whenever they got a chance, children would sit around them, taking in their tales and their lies for half-the-day till the cows came ambling in to be milked and the crows had filed back to Old Sam's rookery. But try to bring up the subject of Balaraggin and what once happened to him, it was as if our men had lost their memory. They suddenly turned white in the face and stopped their chattering. If they could have hidden themselves under a thistle they would have done so. That's how coy they became if the children mentioned Balaraggin's cruel death and they began to fish anxiously in their pockets for a match to light their pipe or to start up a conversation with their ass as though the children weren't there at all!

The Children Pricked Up Their Ears

But the more they tried to hide these events from the young scholars, the more the children pricked up their ears and poked their noses everywhere till they finally had a fairly good version of Balaraggin's life established in their heads. They knew that his story would have to be brought out in the open and given an airing some day or other and as they sat on their logs in Old Sam's orchard and puffed out clouds of smoke from their stolen fag-butts, they made up their minds that if none of the grown-ups were prepared to tell it, then it was left to themselves to present this tale.

Danny-sez-I

Danny-sez-I (the son of Old Dyke) was an early riser – even before the first lark had wiped the sleep from its eyes. If you were up at that hour of the day you'd see him sitting on the lace of his ass-and-car and talking away to his patient ass (Blue-Shoes) as he brought home a load of ferns for the stable. If you jogged along behind him for a little while, you'd find out where Balaraggin had once lived – you only had to follow Danny's ass-and-car along those ancient weed-entangled lanes till they turned into impassable and overgrown tracts, put there to bar the way from the rest of the world.

You couldn't mistake Danny-sez-I. He had a different cap for each of the seven days of the week. He had a necktie for Sundays only. He called this holy day The Day of The Necktie. Of all The Mountainy Men he was clearly the most gentlemanly in appearance. He was the only man to shave his pink face not just on Saturday night but on every day of the week and his jaw was as shiny as a pig's bladder. And another thing – he was always dressed in a fine grey suit as though he were off to a wedding – though he himself had never married since (he said) no woman was ready to give her nose up to the smell of his cowshed.

But that was all the praise that could be given to him for he was a bit on the lonely side and a bit on the sour side these days and he would not be your best choice for a companion. The truth was that he missed enormously his friends from the past and the scores of hillside children who were once packed into so many thatched cabins that you couldn't count them all. That was before some of them took courage in both their hands and hit the open road, which took them over the seas to where the streets of Baltimore (they said) had gold in the stones. The few men and women who were left behind on the hills suffered from a type of lonely melancholy that was similar to Danny's and it was often accompanied by an overdose of their rosary-beads and other religious endeavours.

The Grassy Lanes

If you bade goodbye to Danny's ass-and-car and took your wandering footsteps out through the far side of The Valley of The Pig and a little to the west of the pine-muffled Lisnagorna woods, you'd come to a further maze of grassy lanes behind The Valley of The Black Cattle. And on one particularly summer's day the children were seen stepping out along these grassy lanes after looking back and giving a final wave to Danny-sez-I and his ass-and-car and, of course, to his ass (Blue-Shoes). A minute later they stopped at Balaraggin's spring-well for a taste of the deliciously cold water before going on and stepping into his deserted yard with the final remains of his ruined cabin left standing in the middle of it.

The Virgin Birth

And now for the man himself: Balaraggin was the one and only son of Sally. He was such a little rat-bag of a baby that she could think of nothing else to call him only Balaraggin. She was forty-five and would have you know that she had never so much as kissed a man on his whiskery lips. At the time of his birth it seemed to her and to others amongst the women as though she was having *A Virgin Birth*. Maybe future pilgrimages would be made to her door? Maybe The Roaring Town folk would come out in their hundreds and scrape their knees round her spring-well and ask her for a blessing or two. Sally's mother (Lena) knew better – in fact she knew the whole truth. And though this daughter of hers was just a few months short of forty-five Lena was sorely tempted when she heard of the imminent delivery of this baby (this special virginal birth), to give Sally a few belts of her broken chair-leg across her skinny pagan arse.

The Rabbiters

How had this birth happened? This is how: just when the sun was rising Sally would be visited by half a dozen rabbiters on their way back from their nightly lamplighting for rabbits over in The Valley of The Pig. Tired but proud, they were on their way home to The Roaring Town to spend the rest of the day in bed. That's when they passed by Sally's back window (it was her bedroom), swinging their rhythmical bikes and they full-to-the-gills with floppy rabbits and their necks broken. From time to time Sally looked out shyly at them from behind the geranium box. She marvelled at the huge pile of dead rabbits hanging down from the handlebars of these clever rabbiters' bikes and she was a jumble of emotions as she started counting them.

At first, for the price of a shy little kiss or two, the sly townie rascals gave her one or two small rabbits for the pot. Bit by bit the summer was growing hotter – very hot – and the evenings lurched heavily onwards that bit longer. Folk found themselves melting with sweat and it was often hard to catch their breath. It was then that the rabbiters on their way up into the evening hills began to tease poor innocent Sally – to give her the odd little wink or a bit of the glad eye and to praise her comely face and the curves of her plump body. And in time (the brazen heathens) they were asking her to raise her skirts so that they could get a little peep at her knickers. Gradually they began to introduce her to new and unheard of refinements so that she followed them out into the dusky fields and into the forest of Lisnagorna where she learnt about those earth-shaking bodily pleasures – so much so that it frightened the life out of her as the woodland fairies heard her crying in terror and cackling with fits of laughter at one and the same time. As a result of her playful battles with these townie wildcats she mysteriously found herself nine months later gazing down at her one and only offspring, Balaraggin, this little rag-bag of a child.

When The Old Pair Died

A few years later when the old pair (Lena and Be-Chrysht) died there was only Sally and Balaraggin left to talk to one another across the firelight. But as the years sped by, Balaraggin got itchy feet and he found other ways of passing the time. Shortly after leaving the schoolhouse of Dang-the-skin-of-it and after pelting the customary rock in through the school windows as a final statement of contempt for the misery he'd endured in that place, he became (once he was able to hold a pint-glass in his fist) the best customer in every drinking-shop this side of The Roaring Town. He was forever taking his thudding boots down the lane in the long-tailed evenings and handing in over the counter his hard-earned money from his night-time rabbiting with his terrier, ferrets and nets.

Sitting On The Barrel-planks

Most evenings this dreamy adolescent would sit on the barrel-planks in Curl 'n' Stripes' drinking-shop and turn himself roundabout to roast his shins in front of the crackling fire – a lovely pint of The Black Doctor wetting his whiskers and they scarcely yet grown. On the barrel-plank across from him sat Reilly-the-Cripple and his mouth organ. And beside him was Cleverly-the-Cattle-Drover, his belly jutting out through his galluses. On the counter in front of him lay another six pints of booze in a ceremonious line, poured out for him by the eagerly grasping hands of Curl 'n' Stripes.

A few hours later when the three drinkers had well and truly supped and sipped the last of their beer they hunched up their shoulders and hung down their miserable heads and stared silently into the blazing fire, its glaring light streaking their faces. By this time they were too tired to raise their spirits and offer Curl 'n' Stripes even a yarn or two – too tired to join in the forty-five hand wheel being played in the far corner by the serious-minded cardplayers puffing on their pipes, their hats pulled down guardedly over their eyes and they all anxious to win the pound-of-tea prize. To tell the truth Balaraggin during these early adolescent years loved his corner by the drinking-shop's fire even more than he loved his mother's blazing hearthstone at home and he'd stay there till the fire flickered and died.

Time Moved Along

But time moved along. Balaraggin passed out of this troublesome stage of his life and grew into a fully-fledged man with one or two little warts on his jaws, remininscent of that heathen, Cromwell. Because his hideaway was so far back behind The Hills-of-The-Past Father Sensibly forbade him to walk the six miles every Sunday down to hear Mass: fortnightly attendance would do. As for Sally and her recent pains and aches from the rain and wind, she was excused from the church altogether:

'God will spare you from hell, my child,' said the kindly priest.

He Took The Short-cut

On these precious fortnightly visits to hear Mass Balaraggin kept himself back from the lanes and took the shortcut, walking across the fields, his best leather boots buttered well and they laced across his shoulders. In his bare feet he made his speedy way amidst the cows and sheep and caught the dew of the morning grasses between his frozen toes, knowing it to be a cure for any bunions or corns that might trouble him. A mile or two into his journey the fog of steam worked its way out from his sweaty forehead and could be seen as far as The Creamery Road. It looked as though he had dipped his face into a barrel of rainwater.

In the meantime the roar of Father Laudable's new motorcar could be heard as it sped the three miles from Ballinahoola Crossroads to Copperstone Hollow. He was the parish's young curate fresh in from Clare. Unlike Balaraggin's hour-long journey and with the priestly riches to own this spanking car he found it a small hop from his front door to the altar-rails of the church.

Somewhere in between the two distances that he and Balaraggin had to travel, there were a number of men making their own journey to Mass – a few miles at most and only half as far as Balaraggin's mammoth search for God. Of course others could hold their chins up high, being the proud owners of bikes. Weren't they the lucky rascals (you'd think) since they could snugly fit on their crossbar the flowery dress of a comely damsel later in the evening before throwing their bike in over the ditch for an evening's dancing at The Platform-Dance-in-the-fields. The older folk (the majority of folk) came to Mass on their ass-and-car or even the horse-and-cart, should the family be big in number. If anyone was the cousin of a priest or (better still) a bishop, he could lay hold of a pony-and-trap and then he was indeed the swank of all swanks! Amen to that.

Moving Like A Well-orchestrated Jinnet

By the time Balaraggin neared Abbey Acres and the road that led to Mass he was in a tearing hurry with the speed of a well-orchestrated jinnet and with the worry of death stamped on his face. Would he be early for Mass or would he be late? Would he be in church before the bell rang – before the priest stepped out on the altar? Would he have time for a moment or two's reflection and to say his first decade of the rosary? Maybe he'd be the last one in the church door, meeting the rest of the sniggerers as the saintly priest wound up his sermon or began washing up the Communion vessels? He was full of self-doubt.

His Grandfather's Watch

This question of what time of day it was and the possibility of being early or late was always a puzzle for Balaraggin. He was damned if he could fathom which way the sun was heading across the hills. Of course he had his grandfather's watch in his waistcoat-pocket and was always taking it out and gallantly swinging it round on its chain like a pendulum and showing it off to anyone he met on the way. However, it was no longer in working order. Poor scholar that he was, he couldn't (though nobody knew this) tell you what time it was – or how the two hands of this blessed watch worked, – not even if you offered him a bag of silver shillings.

He Hopped Out Over The Fence

He hopped out over the fence and stepped out onto the road amongst his fellow-walkers. He stood there a moment and fumbled in his waistcoa-pockett, letting them know that he was the owner of such a magnificent watch. He took out the watch. His fingers caressed its chain. He looked at it thoughtfully. He put it up against his ear to see was it ticking the proper time. He gave it a few studied and bemused squints as though he were a weasel mesmerising a rabbit. Then, as though speaking to a child, he solemnly spoke to it: 'My dear friend-of-a-watch, tell me this and tell me no more – what time – the true time, mind you – do you say it is this morning?'

It was a beautiful little scene and fortunate indeed were those who were witnessing this handsome comedy. One or two rascally go-byze gathered in close round Balaraggin and peered over his shoulder to get a good look at the watch. Somewhat maliciously (wouldn't you know it) they began to question him as to the accuracy of this famed timepiece: 'Balaraggin! Balaraggin! Make your watch tell us the true time. Coom on, blasht you! Stop fooling us – don't keep it all to yourself!'

In amazement Balaraggin gave another squint at his watch and held it up close to his ear – scientifically – to see if it was ticking correctly. Then he jumped in the air in absolute horror: 'Cripes, byze, would ye ever think it was so late? We'll be late for Mass if we don't hurry on.'

Like a rabbit with a shamrock in its buttonhole he took to his heels and went speeding off to Mass, leaving a few roars of ribaldry behind him – he himself believing he'd convinced everyone by this bit of cunning roguery that he understood the complexities of the watch's hour and minute hands. With the hasty re-pocketing of his watch he had managed (or so he felt) to fool the watch's admirers and keep them guessing as to whether he could or could not tell the real time – just when they were hoping to see him put out of step by the slyness of their artful questioning.

As a result – his star ascended high in the sky – at least for a moment. A clever one was that Balaraggin, knowing that few if any of us knew anything about the hands on the face of a watch. Was there ever anything so wonderful as a gift from a grandfather's dying hands? And all this in the days when the only watch known to the rest of mankind was the rise and the fall of the blessed sun.

With The Speed Of A Whippet

With the sped of a whippet (in case he'd be late) Balaraggin was a mile from Copperstone Hollow and the church. He was coming up to the haunted house at The Blue Gates where the man with two farms and a pretty wife (and an even prettier daughter) lived. He was almost at Busy-Bee's when Father Laudable's little motorcar came screeching to a halt behind him:

'Hop up! Hop up, my child.'

The good-humoured curate, realising how far Balaraggin had been walking and the way the fog of steam was lifting out of his head, beckoned his gloved hand in the direction of our wild man. But the man from the mountains almost jumped in over the ditch, so frightened was he from the sudden roar of the motorcar. He was a reformed man these days (halfway to sobriety) thanks to his mother's constant tongue-lashing over his nightly feasts of The Black Doctor and he could now see a chance to make an honest man of himself. He would have doffed his cap charmingly to the curate had he been wearing one:

'No, no, no! yer lordship,' said he with a deprecating wave of his hand, 'I'd only turn yeer little bandbox over!'

There was some truth in this for Balaraggin was as broad in his shoulders and girth as Hammer-the-Smith and I'll-Daze-Ye. Father Laudable's car resembled the size of a mere matchbox in comparison. For a second the incredulous curate felt he'd been struck by a thunderbolt and had to get his breath back – so shocked was he at Balaraggin's refusal (was the damned fellow mad?) to accept a lift from him.

Never before had anyone refused the offer of a carry – especially in a new car. He was inclined at first to think that the mountainy man had offered an insult to his priestly collar and his beautiful machine. But being no fool, he quickly came back to his senses. Anyone could see that Balaraggin was no haughty cockerel – could see the honesty written all over the wild man's face. That's when the holy man almost burst his sides laughing at Balaraggin's cavalier grace – what was clearly the strangest and most unusual expression of politeness he'd ever heard – a refusal to accept a lift simply because the fellow might damage the car's springs with his hefty weight. Balaraggin's mother, Sally, would have been proud of her son and the stately way in which he'd answered the curate's invitation.

Later that morning after a fine hearty breakfast the same Father Laudable could be seen hopping round the dining-room with his fists stuck through his galluses and good-naturedly mimicking Balaraggin before the merry eyes of Father Sensibly: 'God knows, your lordship, I'd only turn your little bandbox over!' he cried – ringing his hands – his eyes turned towards the ceiling and quoting the remarkable innocence of Balaraggin. Himself and the parish priest almost fell in the fire from laughing – it was as good as The Daffy-Duck Circus. The Weeping Mollys and their skills for gossip soon spread the news of this polite interchange between the curate and Balaraggin and it kept every tongue busy for the next fortnight.

Then Came The Mission

Then came the Church Mission to put the final capstone on the good work being done by Sally to get Balaraggin off of the accursed drink for once and for all. The firebrand-of-a-missioner was Canon Oratory from Clare. He must surely have come down from the moon, so remarkable a priest was he. And as a result of his fine sermonising Balaraggin rapidly turned his back on the drink altogether. None of us would ever have recognised the young rascal that had once stoned the schoolhouse windows and drank The Mighty Shannon River dry. It was as though a light wind had spun him round and had blown into his soul, caressing and soothing his wild spirit. Like St Paul he threw off his former snake's skin and took on the new mantle of loving kindness, which his mother with her novenas, litanies and rosaries had been praying for throughout the past few years.

A dogged determination filled Balaraggin's new thoughts. Not only was he ready to walk the long six miles across the fields to Mass but was seen to parade his generosity before the rest of us in more practical ways. It was as though the goodness that had been lying asleep inside him had come speeding out like a gush of air from a pig's bladder. He started to deny himself his previous pleasures – started almost to take on the hairy shirt of Saint Francis. Not only had he left Curl 'n' Stripes' drinking-shop in the lurch but he gave up his heavy feasting on pig's fat meat and Sally's eggs and spuds. Instead – he made himself half-a-dozen hazel rods and each morning (long before anyone had left their nest) he headed out to Growl River where he fished in earnest, tempting the trout with the juiciest of maggots from his mother's dungheap. His life became a diet of fish: fish for the breakfast: fish for the lunchtime dinner: fish for the evening supper. On days when he was misfortunate enough not to catch a single trout, his plate was left empty on the dresser.

Those Blasted Weeping Mollys

Then, as people started to wonder at him and to paint rosy pictures of his reformed saintliness, there came a rumour from those old malignerers, The Weeping Mollys and their everlasting antipathy to all that is good: 'Did ye know that Balaraggin eats six or seven trout at the one sitting and leaves none in the river for the rest of us to catch – that he has taken most of the salmon out of Clashing River?' Ah-ha! Wasn't Malevolence a fine thing? But (the devil blasht them) it was all a pack of the old gossips' ongoing lies. For, though the rod was forever in his fists, Balaraggin continued to deny himself and kept only the smallest plateful of fish for his table and gave the rest to others – especially to the old folk.

He Turned To Downright Neighbourliness

These were the years when to be a fine punch-of-a-man and to have a fat belly or paunch was the height of fashion. It showed how well-fed a man was and (therefore) the number of silver coins he had in his pocket. Clearly it could not be said that Balaraggin had a paunch to his belly. In through his shirt you could see each of his ribs sticking out. Indeed if you looked close enough you could count them one by one for he had become as thin as the handle of a yardbrush in the weeks after The Mission. His self-denial was soon seen to turn into out-and-out neighbourliness. He had so many fish on his daily rods that he didn't know what to do with them all. He was seen taking fish into several houses down the different lanes. Dowager and Moll-the-Man were brought a fine salmon or two. Even Lady Demurely was treated to the finest of Growl River's foot-long trout. Added to his delight in sharing his new wealth of fishes was the equally fine pleasure that many of us received from Balaraggin's own back-pocket. If he sold a dozen fish at one of the drinking-shops he was sure to count out the money in shillings and pence and put it on Sally's windowsill for them both to consider. They had little use for it and Balaraggin gave most of it to those with greater need than himself.

Christmas Parcels

When the parcels came at Christmas from his two cousins in the Land of The Silver Dollar he couldn't wait to share his good fortune. He went running to the nearest houses with the bit of boiling beef bought in exchange for his foreign cousins' gifts or with whatever else he was able to purchase with his new wealth. And this sudden change to his life (it was felt) was all due to Canon Oratory and the wonderful gifts of his tongue. Wasn't The Missioner a mighty man to have captured the heart and soul of Balaraggin to such a degree?

Good-luck-sharing Was Common

By now you'd think Balaraggin had turned himself into a walking saint. Good-neighbourliness, however, was not a prerogative given to him alone but was common to the entire community of Rookery Rally. Farmers and their wives often ran breathlessly to the nearest cabin whenever good luck came their way so as to share out what they'd newly got hold of. But Balaraggin was seen to go a step further than the rest. Wherever there was a dangerous sickness or where death itself had danced in the doorway, he with his warm heart made himself foremost to come striding in behind it. He it was that helped in the digging of the overnight grave. He it was that helped in the tearful burying the day after The Wake. He it was that helped and comforted the widow and her orphan children once the body was lying in the cold grave. His charity was the more remarkable in that he had walked such a long way from his cabin door above in the mountains.

Brains Versus Goodness

People began asking themselves what had brains to do with a man's goodness for they knew that Balaraggin had spent only the odd few days of his childhood at the schoolhouse. As he himself said, 'I met the scholars coming home most days, since mee mother needed me a good deal more than mee head-and-brains needed that old schoolhouse'. Indeed when Father Laudable was polishing his motorcar shortly after the little bandbox encounter he began to have a little thought: Balaraggin (he felt) was possibly the most unschooled man in the whole of Rookery Rally. But (the same curate added) what the good man's head lacked in learning, his heart made up for in the abundance of his love for his fellowmen. Father Laudable had the right air to it: he knew that this nobleness in Balaraggin's soul came not from the school desk – not from the ashplant lashing of the schoolmaster's stick – not from any holy priest's confession-box. What then? Whereas much had indeed to do with the ministries of Canon Orarory's Mission, the most prestigious praise of all (he felt) should be heaped on Balaraggin's saintly mother (Sally). Like The Magdalene in The Good Book she had long made up for her earlier sins-of-the-flesh with those wild rabbiters and had made several visits to far-off holy wells. She had performed countless novenas in front of the side-chapel altar at weekday Masses. Sally (said Father Laudable – and Father Sensibly added his voice) was a pure saint if ever there was one: 'She must have powerful influence with Jesus,' they said, – 'to have been able to turn the degenerate Balaraggin round from his selfish nights in the drinking-shops.' Ah, the wisdom of a priest. Enough said

The Gravedigger

But the road to heaven isn't always smooth and there came a twist to the fate of Balaraggin. He had become the leading gravedigger in the graveyard in Abbey Acres – often going out in the middle of a cold night, his teeth chattering and he up to his backside in water if the rains had been heavy. In the hard rocky corners he dug his spade where no other man could dig. In the wintertime when the frosty ground forbade even the sturdiest of men from lifting a spade he again dug his spade. He dug away the fierce anger in his heart which nobody knew he felt – an anger against those who had spurned and condemned his dear mother for her earlier sins with the rabbiters abroad in the forest of Lisnagorna.

Children (sometimes as many as fifteen to a family) were being born as fast as men (aided and encouraged by the powers of drinking The Black Doctor) could give them to their women. However – the dreaded pneumonia from hillside wettings and the untimely tuberculosis that came rotting away some of our lungs were the two arch-villains seen wiping away wave after wave of us. And so – Balaraggin was kept as busy as a gnat, digging up to fifty graves a year. His digging was coupled by the many fervent rosaries Sally offered to her God for all the poor dead souls as she knelt before the turf fire each night. Her knees must have been red-raw from praying for them all.

The Devil Cursed Balaraggin

Yet the Devil's rage was always at work. He cursed the piety of Balaraggin and came calling on his soul one windy wet evening. It was the day his old schoolmaster (Blistery-Mouth) was summoned to die and be buried – a day that Balaraggin would be anxious to forget when next Easter came round and he'd be forced to take his yearly chance and tell his sins to his priest inside the confession-box.

Blistery-Mouth had been an awful oddity – with the cork forever in his spitty mouth and the needle stuck in it so as to keep the magnetism (he said) inside in his body. Apart from that – he had been a devil-of-a-schoolmaster and had belted poor Balaraggin across his skull so often that he'd knocked out all the brains inside in the poor lad's head. And for what? For no better reason than that he (old Blistery-Mouth) had had a head full of drink on him each and every morning.

And so – after the mourners were let loose from the side of the grave and had gone across to Merrymouth's drinking-shop to drown their sorrows, Balaraggin seized the moment he had secretly wished for all his adult life. Before emptying the earth down in Blistery-Mouth's grave, he blessed the departed schoolmaster with a shower of his hot piss, sprinkling it ceremoniously on the lid of the coffin: 'Isn't hatred a beautiful thing?' said the Devil inside in the head of Balaraggin. Then he leapt down into the grave and danced the finest of jigs on top of the cursed schoolmaster's coffin. He danced the rage right out of his body and lodged it squarely into the coffin where it had always belonged.

That Other Church

On the spot where now looms the beautifully-sculpted Catholic Church there once stood a black gloomy monstrosity called The Protestant Church. The houses all round it were small. The church was huge. It dominated the entire village. Although there were but a few Protestant gentry entering their Sunday pews, this huge empty church saw to it that we lowly ones from the mountains and hill-slopes still had to remember our place – and that was in our tiny wooden church hidden behind their stately Protestant Church.

Some years after the time of Balaraggin the clergy decided to banish forever the notion of subservience, which that big church had always symbolised. And so they set out to build a fitting Catholic Church to replace the miserable little wooden one. With what relish did our men step down from the hills and give their coppers for the building of this fine new edifice. They headed to the centre of the village. They picked up their fighting crowbars to ferret out stones to take home for their new cowsheds. Now it was their turn to use their crowbars in a way similar to the baillifs of past absentee landlords who had callously smashed down our forefathers' cabins – days when The baillifs had burned the thatch round our poor people's ears before forcing them out on the road to die or stagger to the poorhouse door. Men now raced like hares to see who would be first to reach the Protestant Church and smash it into bits. Some scaled its walls like dragons and fought with each other to drive their blissful crowbars in through the Protestant Church's windows. And again The Devil laughed.

Us And The Protestants

In the days of Balaraggin to be seen marrying a Protestant was a thing unheard of. If anyone gave so much as a favourable glance at one of those whom we labelled *black Protestants*, the neighbours would put the curse of the evil eye on that family – back to the third and fourth generation. Ah, the heathens that we were! Had we lost hold of our senses? Hadn't everyone been only too glad to take the Saxon shilling from the gentry – either as a ploughboy or maidservant?

Dowager (a model of later rectitude) was once a ten year-old child working for Lady Demurely's mother (Lady Elegance). One unforgettable morning found her taking the cake from the good lady's oven when she had the misfortune to burn her fingers: 'Why,' she painfully shrieked, 'this cake's hot enough to burn a Protestant in hell.' Vainly she tried to shake the burns from her hands.

Behind her at that very moment stood the gentle form of Lady Elegance:

'Why, Bedelia my child,' she chided (using Dowager's christening name), 'are there no Catholics in hell?'

What mortification came upon the tearful child! She couldn't apologise enough for her cruel jibe – having just repeated in her childish way the thoughts of her forebears. She wished the ground would open up and swallow her. It was, however, the moment when she realised (child though she was) that there were surely a good number of Catholics in hell – that she herself was well on the road to joining them in its fires if she ever again bore such wicked thoughts against any of her Protestant employers or their kinsmen across the sea.

A Man Among Pygmies

There is a turning point in any man's fortunes and Balaraggin's moment finally came when he was to prove himself a man among pygmies. Not one of us had ever dared enter a Protestant church and we wouldn't for many years to come – not until that miserable day came to knock the Protestant church and leave it in smithereens. But Balaraggin was always a strange fellow and he refused to join in others' fears and hatred. He knew that God wouldn't condemn him if he entered the foreign church and he made this known to all the cowardly souls he came across. Not for a minute did he believe it to be the home of the heathens and a shrine to Impiety or some estranged God. As a result his neighbours quickly forgot his hitherto works of Christian charity and began whispering their malice and poison against him.

Lady Posh-Frock

How did it all begin? The news had spread that Lady Posh-Frock (after choking on a wishbone) had given up the ghost in the middle of a February night when the landscape everywhere was streaked with snow. Being one of the few foreign settlers left here and also a Protestant she had no-one to dig her grave for her. And besides – the ground was as hard as a shovel. It was indeed a very sad case and there was a profound silence among us.

That's when Balaraggin put up his hand and stepped forward to do the honest thing. The very next night he made whatever religious preparations were needed for Lady Posh-Frock's burial and the washing of her corpse for her final journey across the fields and into The Protestant Church. It was the middle of a dark night and the moon and stars were hidden in the mist. Balaraggin fetched the wheelbarrow from Lady Elegance's shed and he lifted Lady Posh-Frock onto it. He was not alone, however. Three handy-sized men, armed with several pints of The Black Doctor, bravely helped him load up the poor soul's coffin onto the wheelbarrow. When they got near The Protestant Church they proved to be the brave little fellows and they helped carry the coffin from the wheelbarrow and onto their shoulders and up to the very front doors. Suddenly, however, as they were laying the old lady's coffin reverently on the church steps, a haunting fear came over their manly hearts. They were afraid they'd now be struck down by lightning and they repeatedly blessed themselves. In the following weeks they related how they saw a black serpent crossing over the moon and how the hair had stood up on their heads – how there was an eerie silence all round the foreigners' church. They said they saw the eyes of God looking scornfully down on them. They said they saw Jesus weeping (the liars). The hush and the expectations of God's wrath (as though they were back in Eden) made them think the gates of hell were opening up beneath their feet (they said). That's when they took to their heels in scattered flight, tripping over each other as they leapt out across the ditch – as though The Devil was trying to catch a hold of their heels. In short they turned into frightened little bunny-rabbits with the sparks flying out of their britches.

Balaraggin had to hold his sides from the pain of his laughter at the spectacle of their heels disappearing from view. He turned back towards the Protestant Church and took off his cap. With the help of the wheelbarrow he pushed Lady Posh-Frock's coffin quietly down the aisle and loaded the dead woman up onto the wooden trestles. Then he knelt down reverently in the Protestant Church (was there ever so great a sin?) and said a silent prayer for the repose of her soul – that she might find an everlasting home for herself in The Beyond. A day later he went to bury her decently behind the church wall. Not a shilling payment did he take from the good woman's brother (Lord Elegance).

Black Poison Came Seeping In

The Weeping Mollys spread the news about Balaraggin's journey into the foreign settlers' church. This was the moment when the black poison came seeping into the hearts of others. The neighbours (aided by the same old Weeping Mollys) spread their hatred of Balaraggin far and wide. Wasn't it all too clear that The Devil had risen up from hell and gotten a hold of their former hero's two heels and then gotten a hold of his soul too. They could see that one day soon (some of them were already praying for it) the filthy blackguard would be rushed down into the fiery pit of hell. Each night a number of them prayed that before the year had finished, some sort of misfortune would be heaped on the head of Balaraggin for having the impudence to go inside the heathen's church.

In The Harshness Of Winter

In the harsh wintertime it was not surprising that a single son would occupy his mother's bed (he at one end and she at the other) and that they'd keep each other's cold bodies warm and spare the need for going out in stormy weather for a bag of logs. It was at times such as this that the souls of Sally and Balaraggin were as close as two sides of a windowglass. Sally (no matter what others might now be saying) had the utmost faith in the actions of Balaraggin. She had turned his soul towards heaven and was the inspiration for all his acts of kindness (as in the case of Lady Posh-Frock). By now he had captured the soft spot in her heart. A son and a mother: a love from her eye into his eye and a love from his eye back into her eye. Enough said.

Sally Was Alone In Bog Boundless

But, sad to say, this love story was soon to come to an end for the sky was not always virginal blue and even the beautiful sun was able to forego her brilliance amongst us. There came a grey and dismal day when Sally found herself alone at her work abroad in Bog Boundless. She loved nothing better than to be out in the bog's fresh air, her nose sniffing at the breeze and she plunging her spade into the soft boggy earth. The lonely wilderness lay around her as far as the eye could see. There was nothing to listen to but the mournful song of the cuirlew.

She was working like blazes and had built up a fine sweat on her forehead whilst planking up the last of her turf from the dried-out footings. Before she knew it an unbelievable tiredness came into her bones and she fell into a deep sleep. The song of the weary day continued its way into the silent evening. The customary damp dews came down from The Mighty Mountain. Sally was soon covered in the evening mists. Miserable, cold and lonesome, she awoke to see nothing but the eeriness and the ghostliness of it all. Like many before her time she began to be very much afraid. She knew those old stories – how the wilderness fairies came alive at these indescribable times of the day (when the light was neither daytime nor night-time) how these same fairies in the days of old had removed from this earth the souls of good women, taking them with them out beyond the rowan trees. Dark dirty clouds continued to waft round her. She felt these same spirits straddling her. She heard their voices calling her unto the other world: 'Sally! Sally! Sally!' She walked off into the darkness of the bog.

Next Morning

Next morning, when no-one had heard from her, a great crowd gave the entire day searching for her. The demented Balaraggin led the pack:

'Mother-mother-dearest mother!' he kept calling.

'Sally-Sally-Sally!' the crowds kept bawling.

By this time the hearts of the neighbours had turned upside-down and some feared the worst. All the old backbiters (such is human nature) had forgotten their bitterness against Balaraggin and were full of anxiety for him. They began to mutter to each other:

'Didn't we always know she was too good for this world?'

'The wilderness fairies must have taken her.'

They heard the shaky voice of Pat-the-Hat calling from the boghole where Taedspaddy had been within an inch of getting himself drowned after going for the kettle of water for the tea and sandwiches. His uncle (The Gog) and White Snow had found his flailing arms sticking up frantically out of the boghole, the kettle close by. Almost rupturing their guts, they had pulled his bruised body out with the ass in the nick of time.

The giddy crowd now rushed across the heather to where Pat-the-Hat was standing, his father's hat reverently in his closed fists. Balaraggin was the first to get there. All he saw were the two sad wellingtons of Sally sticking up out of Taedspaddy's boghole. A giant sob rattled round in his throat. Men came running up with a reins the way they'd often done so as to drag out a belly-deep horse.

It was too late! Sally was gone – snatched down by Sergeant Death into the peaceful purity of the fairyland kingdom, to appear again as a fairy-child in years to come.

Sadness Like A Knife

Next day a fierce woe took hold of Balaraggin's soul. It left him trembling and sobbing like an ass in the rain. The day's light was nothing but a knife in his chest and he passed his hand over his eyes. He was dull-eyed with fatigue – as though he'd been wrestling with The Devil all night, not knowing which of them had won the battle. There was no more warmth in his bed. There were no mother's arms to comfort him. He lay there in a feverish torpor with but brief snatches of sleep. He was entirely alone – himself and his sad thoughts – himself and the empty fire-grate – himself and the mice in the rafters. The house-ghosts and spirits of his ancestors that had once been so friendly to himself and Sally now seemed oppressive.

In the night-time when there was no-one to spy on him he went out and began collecting wildflowers. With these he covered the floor around his mother's bed. He took The Sacred Heart picture off of the wall and placed it in the centre of the flowers. He gathered together his mother's few possessions and placed them in a drawer in the chest. He knew she'd be coming back for them. He spent the following night talking foolishly to her, a strange smile on his lips. The talk was friendly and good-humoured, almost a laugh:

'Mother, do you remember when we took the white calf out into the field for the first time?'

'Do you remember how he frightened all the cows with his newfound freedom and how they ran headlong down into the river?'

The talk of the deranged man went on and on:

'Mother, do you remember when the gander turned on the sow and pecked his two eyes asunder and he ran into the Welcoming Room and buried his head in the sack of flour?'

He imagined he saw the poor dead soul lying in the bed beside him with the rosary-beads in her fist. But as he talked away to her ghost, no answer was given back to him.

In the middle of the dappled night (the day after Sally had been taken away to The Roaring Town in Black Bess's truck) he woke up and sat upright in the bed. Stock-still he listened and listened. He could hear the moaning of the wailing wind (as though it were a child). He could hear a few scattered raindrops. Then he heard the rattle of the phantom ass-and-car pulling in across the stream's flagstones and on across the moonlit cobblestones. He heard the mystical ass being tied at the singleree. He heard the clink of the ass's chains. His mother had come back. He felt a great fear as he listened to the well-known click of Sally's boots and felt the spectre of her crossing the yard towards him.

She paused at the front door. She stood there a long time. He held his breath. His ears on edge, he heard the latch of the door lifting. He heard the door creaking. Sally entered The Welcoming Room. It was pitch black. Balraggin was in a river of sweat. He could hear a pinprick. His mother's boots scraped back and forth around the floor. She began to jerk open the drawers in the tall press. She began to fling out saucepans and boot-polish, the boot-last and the river jug. She was looking not for her few priceless bits of finery, her rosary or her holy books but for her cardigan. All old women wanted their cardigan to keep them warm on the journey to The Beyond – the best one, their Sunday one. The poor man was in terror of his mother's ghost for he could smell the pungent scent of her – a warm pissy scent mixed up with mothballs. The ache was killing him. His heart was about to stop beating. Sally would be back the next night – he knew. She'd want the rest of her possessions to be loaded onto the ass-and-car so as to get her soul into heaven.

Next Morning

Next morning Balraggin got all the clothes and bits of trinkets that his mother might need for the journey. He placed them in a heap on the floor. When his mother would come back she'd have no hardship loading up her ass-and-car. Then, leaving the heap behind him, he ran out and closed the door. At full pelt he ran down the hill to Dowager's half-door. In a strange gibberish he told her that his mother and her ghost had come back – that he was too frightened to return to his cabin – that Dowager had to give him the loan of one of her seven sons to keep his body warm throughout the night – at least till after the funeral.

Dowager feared that madness was about to catch hold of him. Her son (Punch) was young at the time, barely six. He was a little on the paunchy side, hence his name. She sent him home with Balaraggin. That night when Punch got into the bed beside Balaraggin, the lonely man placed the head of the little child against his own chest so that they both could share in the warmth and drive away the loneliness. But Punch couldn't sleep. He heard the phantom ass-and-car coming across the yard-stream.

"What is it?' he cried.

In the bright moonlight he heard the chains and axle rattling round the yard.

'Who is it? Tell me, Balaraggin!' he cried again.

'Whisht! Keep quiet – 'tis mee mother,' said Balaraggin.

The child heard the door opening. He heard Sally's ghost loading up her ass-and-car with her possessions and setting off across the yard-stream. A mere child of six, he was terrified. He couldn't escape from the clutching arms of Balaraggin for the poor man was himself scared out of his wits and was holding Punch in a grip as tight as death. The two of them began to kick the matress asunder and the child pissed in the bed.

Next morning – and long before the cockerels had peeped out their heads or had started to crow – Punch broke all speed records in flying home to his startled mother and he never again returned to share the bed of Balaraggin or to help him keep off the loneliness that was turning the poor man into a pure deranged madman. Enough said.

The Funeral Arrangements

The priest's arrangements for the funeral were now in hand. On a cold and overcast evening with the wind whipping the trees Balaraggin went off towards High Straits to collect the black suit that was being made up for him for the funeral by The Two Little Tailoresses. He was crossing The Pool Field behind Old Sam's hayshed where the mottled branches of the sycamore tree overarch the pool. It was a place where young rabbits from the ruins of the old hedgeschool came out at dusk to skip round in silence. He tried to cross the field. He battled as hard as he could. But no matter how energetic his efforts he found himself unable to proceed on his journey. The Wilderness Fairies that had taken away his mother stood firmly in his track, preventing him from getting the made-up suit for the funeral. Unable to go forwards, he found humself slipping back along the damp grass. He felt the hands of an invisible force surrounding him, driving him to his knees as though wishing him not to go on and collect the funeral suit of clothes to honour his mother.

He returned home a puzzled man and took the bedroom candle and went to his bed. The neighbours told him the truth – that Sally had no need of him to wear a fine suit of funeral clothes so as to get her through Saint Peter's pearly gates – that Sally was now firmly established in The Beyond – that all she required of him was his pure heart and for him to say a decade or two of the rosary on his beads for the repose of the other souls in Purgatory and the good of his own soul.

Late For The Funeral

By the time the funeral came round, Balaraggin didn't know which way to turn. He rose up later than the morning cockerel and knew he was going to be late for The Funeral Mass. For such a great occasion he rode the bike he'd stolen like fair hell the ten miles to The Roaring Town. By the time he got there the rain was swooping down in devilish sweeps and he had visions of his mother lying there in that gloomy old coffin. The congregation had scarcely got in out of the rain and sat themselves down when they heard the jingle of Balarragin's bell as he rode his bike in along the churchyard. Had we all lost our senses? He rode it straight in through the church doorway and up the central aisle of the church to the very steps of the altar. In an astonished silence all watched this unheard-of blasphemy – a scene that now brought ruin to the entire sollemnity of the ceremony. All were left scratching their heads when, with slow and devotional reverence, the tragic Balaraggin circled his bike three times round his mother's coffin in the same way as a priest would do when blessing a coffin with holywater. Everyone could see that Balaraggin's spirit had entered a new and mad world – that nothing would ever mollify him. And they marvelled to see so great a sorrow in a son for his mother – to see how the manly heat in his soul had quailed and how the shivers of a sick child had taken its place.

Suddenly he hopped off of his bike. He took it out the church doorway and came back in to join the rest of the congregartion. They felt that the cycling round the coffin had been part of an historic and remarkable dream. Then in between the priest's glowing words in praise of Sally they heard Balaraggin mumbling heartbreakingly to himself – heard him babbling. He couldn't stop. A minute later his disgruntled voice (it was neither a laugh nor a sob) rang out all round the church statues in what was a bloodcurdling roar (almost a curse) cutting through the quietness of the holy place:

'Oh mother! Oh mother, Oh dearest mother! Why can't ye get up out of that old box and come home with me and stay with me like before?'

That Night

Was this how it was going to be for the rest of his life – now that his motherly *Angel of Comfort* (his sunlight) was gone from him – a misfortunate man doomed to spend eternity in a vain effort searching for his lost mother? Balaraggin could see that every day was going to be the same. He could bear it no longer. He longed for the freedom of death and he could hear its clock ticking away inside in him.

A Night Came

A night came when there was a frost that would cut off your nose and your ears. The loneliness of his cabin was choking him. He put on his thick coat and scalf. He crammed his pockets with boiled crabapples from the fire's heat to keep his hands and belly warm. Then, in an effort to escape from the company of Sally's oppressive ghost, he wandered blindly out the lane and headed towards the drinking-shop of Curl 'n' Stripes in search of Forgetfulness.

It was six long years since he had darkened the doors or sat on the barrel-planks – in the days when there was just himself and Reilly-the-Cripple and his mouth organ alongside Cleverly-the-Cattle-Drover. Somewhat guiltily he reached for his first pint of The Black Doctor: 'Could you not wait a little longer till I was well dead and buried?' complained Sally's whispering ghost in his ear.

He hunched himself down on the barrel-planks as of old, the crackling logs on the fire illuminating his sad face. He took a few furtive sips of his drink. He tried to hide the glass from view in under his coat as though he was some imaginary tinker running away with an egg. For a short while he seemed to derive a bit of solace as he looked into the bottom of his glass. Soon, however, it was glass after glass – the whiskey as well as The Black Doctor. And though he felt that these drinks were doing him a power of good they began to turn him from sad to morose – and finally to being badtempered with the rest of the world: 'Throw me out your twins and be quick about it,' he roared as he swallowed yet another pint of The Black Doctor, twinning it with a glass of the whiskey. Eying the bottles of raw-gut potheen on the top shelf, he added, 'And give me some of your top shelf, mee good man – top shelf is the drink for me!'

Soon his voice became papery thin and his eyes began to look fiercely tragic. Every man has a heart and reluctantly Curl 'n' Stripes poured Balaraggin yet another drink. Somehow it felt good for the shopkeeper to be filling the poor demented man's gizzard with strong drink – it'd help him stave off the ensuing madness which (if he wasn't careful) would carry Balaraggin off in a month or two to the sombre grave after his mother.

Midnight Came On

Midnight struck and Din-Din-Dinny-the-Stammerer was sent for. He carried the drunken Balaraggin out from the artificial light of the shop and helped him up onto his cart. He drove him home and put him into his damp bed – a bed in which there'd be no peace for his poor demented soul.

The ghost of Sally rose up out of the grave. She came and stood before Balaraggin. She called him out of his drunken sleep:

'Balaraggin! Balaraggin! Her ghost was utterly powerful in its calling.

His eyes blinded with forlorn tears, he sat up in the bed and an unmerciful impulse took hold of him. He was sick to death of wrestling with Sorrow. Sad and angry he crawled out on his unsteady hands and knees and followed the ghostly voice that beckoned him. Out the door and into the black night he staggered, answering Sally's call. He crossed the haggart singletree where the steely moon and the millions of sharp stars perched above his yard and blinked down on him. The ass and the seven cows from across the ditch looked on bemusedly.

A Long Look Back

Balaraggin stood a moment. He cast a confused look back at his life and felt the frozen universe whipping rapidly passed him. He took from his pocket the sharp cut-throat razor, which was always reserved for shaving himself for Sunday Mass. There under the cover of the lonesome sky he felt for the soft spot beneath the stubble of his chin. He knelt beside the hayreek and said his last farewell prayers, speaking silently into his mother's ears: 'Mother-Mother-Mother! I am coming . . . I am coming . . . can't you see that I am coming home to you, mother?' And there in the quiet of the secret night the black branches of the pinetrees gathered closely round him. And then laughing sardonically he cut his throat from ear to ear. Unbelievably he managed to stagger to his pighouse and spread the blood all over the cross-lats of the pighouse door. From there he swayed a little further and came to the green door of his cabin before floating away above the clouds to the Land of Sunshine in The Beyond where his mother (he knew) was waiting to greet him. The ruby red of his blood was a fitting match for the red of the geraniums in his window boxes – wedded together as closely as himself and his mother in death.

Next Morning

The Guards and Father Sensibly and Father Laudable came next morning. They took his body away before the foxes or carrion crows could get at it. Despite all of Balaraggin's previous charitable works, the fact that he had killed himself meant that on this saddest of all occasions Holy Mother Church didn't even give him The Last Sacramental Rites or bury him in Abbey Acres Graveyard and his bones would lie forever under a heap of rocks in God-knows-where.

A Child's Initiation

From that day onwards it became a sacred part of every Rookery Rally child's initiation into the realms of adolescent fascination and adventuring to be taken up to see the ruins of Balaraggin's cabin – to see where the demented man had cut his throat. On dark evenings and with the early moonlight guiding them it was a journey known only to runaway children and to see if they had finally become brave little men. The older children would lead the younger ones by their trembling hands – up along the green lanes before trudging on passed The Hills-of-The-Past. They'd put the blindfolds on the mouse-hearted little ones as soon as they got close enough to the edge of Balaraggin's haggart. The place was deserted. No cockerel had ever been heard crowing there since the death of the wild man. The little procession would tiptoe cautiously to the green bloodstained doors of Balaraggins' pighouse and cabin. The blindfolds were taken off and the bigger boys took over the ritual:

'Can ye hear the rattle of Sally's ass-and-car?'

'Can ye see Balaraggin's ghost behind the henhouse?'

'Can ye see the immense quantities of blood that the wild man shed? He must have had a barrel of it inside him.'

The list went on. The little ones saw the bloody streaks across the green door of the cabin. Rather than feel frightened or sad, they became as excited as a cow on heat. They had witnessed (though they didn't understand its depth till later in life) a terrible mystery – a manifestation – a revelation – of a truly tremendous love – the absolute love of a son for his mother. They had been privileged (though this too they didn't yet know) to see into the heart of Balaraggin, – into the blood of Balaraggin, whose grief and lonesomeness after Sally had drowned and left him was so utterly unbearable that he cut his throat from ear to ear. May God spare you, Balaraggin. You meant no harm.

TEN

How a young girl found and lost, then found and lost again the true love of her heart.

Black Neddy

Sadie was the only daughter of Deed'n-be-Chrysht and Tickle-mee-Fancy. They lived on the lush green hills behind Hammer-the-Smith's forge. She was the apple of her mother's eye and her father called her his little sunbeam. Sadie was a lovely young girl of nineteen with cheeks as soft as a rose. She had a beautiful head of unusual sandy hair. It fell down in a shiny rope along the broad of her back. We were all the time admiring her, at which she'd blush up abruptly all through her young face and run away from us, leaving us all looking after her like a pack of asses without a bit of clover. Wouldn't you give your two good eyes to see a sight such as her?

When Tickle-mee-Fancy sent her down from The Valley of The Pig on the two-mile journey to warm the bed of Black Neddy on his farm, he had all that a man could possibly wish for. You should have seen the crafty smile on his hairy old jaw as he got ready to welcome the tearful young soul into his Welcoming Room. It seemed like only yesterday that she had been a child wearing her ankle-socks to The Platform Dance-in-the-fields. It was thirty years and more since Black Neddy had been able to run after a chicken, let alone chase around the bedroom after a fair young damsel like Sadie.

She Was As Hardy As A Snipe

She was as thin as a rake and as hardy as any snipe from the sound training that her father and mother had given her at both the milking of the cows and the bringing home of the turf. There wasn't a thing that she couldn't or wouldn't turn her hand to. And so (like her three sisters before her) she had become the object of her father's need to match her off with this old fellow and thereby secure her lifelong future and well-being. After all, what else could a young girl do these times?

The alternative was to get herself a vision-from-God and take herself off into some hidden convent – that is if the nuns would let her in the door. If your face didn't fit, there'd be no welcome in those places either. So if your heart wasn't truly set on a life of knee-breaking devotion to God, your next best option was always this one – to set up home with a tried and tested old farmer (in this case, Black Neddy) knowing that he had a few pounds in the bank and that he could buy you a new suit of clothes for Sunday Mass and a brooch and a black hat to go with it.

It was no use a damsel trying to get herself matched off with one of the younger men since their fathers never gave those fellows an inch of land till they themselves had one foot in the grave. Black Neddy's own father had died the previous year and he was now the inheritor of what was a fair-sized farm. Sadie, therefore, had to get her skates on quickly and go down and get hitched to this old obstacle before any other young madam got her thieving hands on him. 'He's a fine catch,' said Tickle-mee-Fancy. 'And he's only fifty-two,' said Deed'n-be-Chrysht. After all the sobbing and crying there wasn't a tear left in poor Sadie's red eyes and she shuddered throughout the sleepless nights when she thought of being cast off and latched into the arms of this hairy old yoke.

Choices Were Limited

But that's the way it was. For girls of Sadie's age, if the convent or the old farmer failed to ensnare them, they had the other stark choice: they could climb briskly on board the cattle-boat which took droves of them off to The Land of John Bull across The Herring Pond or (if they lived near Cork Harbour) they could seek out a ship to Van Dieman's Land like a great number of our Tipperary ancestors or maybe take the shorter route to The Land of The Silver Dollar across The Atlantic. You'd see the quayside crowded with waving handkerchiefs and crying relations, who had come down to see them off. Such a sad scene – the same as burying their departing children in the tomb, never to set eyes on them again. The boats were so heavy-laden that they almost sank like the Titanic – those on deck as sick as wild donkeys even before the good ship lurched out onto the waves – so much did they miss their beloved mothers. Indeed their hearts were often irreparably broken.

And that's not all – there was yet another choice for a girl (the last choice of all for someone like Sadie) and that was to get herself kicked out the door onto the roadside and go find herself in some questionable establishment inside in The Roaring Town. She couldn't be left at home (the lazy article) with one foot resting in the ashes and the other one propped up on the hob, could she? Even if she worked like a mule for the next thirty years, she would still have to be fed and watered by her parents – she couldn't be seen eating them out of house and home opposite the neighbours could she? That wouldn't do at all – they'd never live it down.

The Morning Of Departure

It was now June and the corn would be getting yellower by the day. The sky had been robbed of its charcoal and there was now a motleyed series of ribbed purple 'n' blue clouds as the sun started hitting the hill. It threw a bright bar across the ass-and-car whilst the flies danced round like rushing stars. This was the day of poor Sadie's departure – the saddest day in all her young life and she was trembling like a little bird that was lost. Deed'n-be-Chrysht tackled up the faithful ass to the jambs of the cart. Still idling in her bedroom, Sadie smoothed down her sandy ropes of hair and took the candle and gazed at herself in front of the looking-glass: 'Tomorrow I'll be different – forever different,' she told herself. There would be no bridal gown in white for her: no rich bouquets of flowers: no jewels in her ears: no rings on her fingers: no ribbons in her hair – just a black veil to cover her face and modesty.

She came out into the yard with her father's brown suitcase and her mother's hatbox. The ancient ass had seen it all before. Together with her father (a separate bedroom having been arranged for her, prior to the wedding) she was heading off for Black Neddy and The Road-to-The-Hollows.

The Sunny Day Led Them On

Off they went. The sunny day led them on. Sadie's heart was broken in two. Her mother's heart was damaged too. She hadn't had the courage to come out into the yard and wave her handkerchief over Sadie and give her the dash of holywater. She hadn't even peeped out over the windowsill geraniums to give her that last little smile but had sloped off to her bed and collapsed in a heap of grief. How sad the place would be without her daughter's light laughter. Between herself and Sadie they could have filled The Mighty Shannon River this day with the anguish of their tears:

'Wipe away your tears, my good woman,' said Deed'n-be-Chrysht to his daughter. There wasn't even the comfort of a kindly word, let alone a fatherly hug. It was unknown for men to be slobbering over their daughters with that sort of tomfoolery:

'It'll all be for the best in the end, you'll see.' We shall later recall how prophetic were his words.

One Last Look Down The Lane

Sadie took a dreary last look back down the lane at her old homestead where she had played as a child with the four kittens on the upturned ass-and-car. What must have been the thoughts going through her mind – piercing her young heart, puncturing her soul? She was young enough still to be wearing her best dress which she had worn to Sunday Mass when she was fourteen years of age. Until that very day she had slept with her mother's favourite doll beside her under the blankets. It would be a far different bed that now awaited her after her wedding took place and Father Sensibly had dealt with the officiating of the sacramental ceremonies in a fortnight's time.

The Stumbling Ass

As the two of them and their ass stumbled along towards Black Neddy's farm Sadie was as silent as the grave. Rather than talk to her father she preoccupied herself with listening to the buzzing of the bees in the honeysuckle and the foxglove, to the sudden hum of the horse-bees in the cattle-dung in the centre of the lane behind her. In the back of the cart her father had folded a blanket over the traditional dowry, the half-grandfather clock. At the last cattle Fair-Day he had placed a purseful of silver dollars (the gift from his sister in far-off Yonkers in The Land of The Silver Dollar) into the fist of Black Neddy.

They pulled up the ass ('Sight, blasht you!') at the flagstones of the old farmer. Sadie stepped down from the cart. It was one fatal step and she was very afraid. She was turning her back on the past and was about to spend the rest of her days with a man she had never before laid eyes on.

Black Neddy shuffled across the yard to meet her. He gazed at her with his drivelling gawk-eye. Ah, what a lovely sight – a young girl with all her own teeth on her and they all in a row (he thought). He hadn't a leg left on him strong enough to give a kick (she thought). She stepped across the yard towards him and her heart beat fast. Good God-in-heaven! Black Neddy was as wrinkled as a dead leaf and old enough to be her grandfather.

The Bedroom Department

In spite of her understanding of the bull and the business with the cow (how often had she helped a small bull to mount towards his joy!) she had no real knowledge of what was expected of her in the bedroom during the weeks that were to follow. She'd be fine in respects of the daily farm work alongside Black Neddy: feeding the hens and the geese: giving the calves their buckets of skimmed milk: milking the seven cows: collecting the eggs: chopping the logs with the axe for the fire: fetching the six buckets of water from the well, and so on. There was no more industrious soul than Sadie. She would wash and mend his shirts as her mother had taught her – as good as any wife in The Hills-of-The-Past. She'd ensure that he looked decent when he took out the pony-and-trap for Sunday Mass. His boots would be polished asunder and she'd put the dab of butter on his toecaps. But for the murky business of churning out a new little baby every year as any good wife worth her salt would do, Sadie was completely flummoxed. The bull – yes. The stallion – yes. The boar – yes. She had even taken

Uncle Danno's goat up the hill for his annual performances amongst the fortunate she-goats. But now it was her turn to be at the whim and the will of Black Neddy.

She Prayed To Saint Teresa

She was caught in a birdcage. She took out her rosary-beads the first night. She prayed as hard as Saint Teresa of The Little Flower – asking God to make Black Neddy treat her decently and not bring any shameful acts upon her. She would offer up her prayers each Sunday at Mass. She would make the nine first Friday visits to the church in Copperstone Hollow and receive Holy Communion at the rails. She would offer further prayers to Saint Jude the patron saint of all lost causes so that he would stand by her and not let her be disgraced.

Fears and uncertainties had visited her before, a common enough state of affairs for all our growing girls who were often plagued with the nerves. She recalled when she was fourteen years of age and had found herself (like the rest of the girls) bleeding in under her skirts. She thought that she was about to die from a burst pipe inside in her belly. She came to know what fear was then. She had fled like a young greyhound across the fields but had the good fortune to land in the arms of Father Sensibly as he was on his way out from Fat Nora's establishment with his basket of eggs.

At nineteen years of age, however, there were many secrets yet to be learned. She had tried to force all thoughts of the coming nuptials to the back of her mind. And to stomach the marrying-acts of Black Neddy she would have to close her eyes. But she promised herself that, as ordered by Holy Mother Church, she would give her new husband her heart if not her soul. And wouldn't that surely be enough for the old man?

The Days That Followed

In the days that followed the house of Black Neddy was cold. The fire-grate was a mean little spark with no trace of a log on it. The man himself was a mean old yoke. There was little true welcome in his Welcoming Room.

The bed in the black night was colder still. He himself had the smell of farmyard manure wafting round her. She kept her soft linen shift wrapped tightly round here chin. In the silent bedroom she hugged herself to sleep with only the crickets to serenade her. But thank The Virgin-in-Heaven! – she soon realised that the hairy old man was just as shy and ignorant as herself when it came to the removal of the secret night shirt and the business of rattling the bedsprings and injecting her with a child.

Her Father's Frown-lines

In a few months the frown lines on her father's forehead doubled. He began to see that there was no child being born from this union. What had his family done to deserve this? He was as embarrassed as hell in front of the other farmers. What on earth could be wrong with his daughter? Soon his embarrassment turned into something like rage. He couldn't set his foot inside the doors of Curl 'n' Stripes' drinking-shop. The men were forever making a laugh and a joke at the weak state of himself and his breed: 'The old breed is beginning to shrink away,' they sniggered. 'It's worn out like a cabbage-stump.'

It was true, he knew. What good was a daughter if she couldn't perform her nightly duties – if she couldn't deliver at least half-a-dozen sons and daughters in her first six years of marriage? One fine evening Deed'n-be-Chrysht called at the door of Father Sensibly. He gave the knocker a loud rap. Following their conversation Father Sensibly took his motorcar out along The Creamery Road to Black Neddy's half-door in order to carry out his priestly investigations. In his hip-pocket he was carrying (a useful introduction) a naggin of whiskey. In his overcoat he had another small bottle of potheen. A mixture of these two drinks would surely do the trick. He needed a drop or two of it himself so as to get up the courage to approach the subject of a man's use of his private equipment underneath his night-time shirt.

The Priest And Black Neddy

As for Black Neddy, not a drop of drink had ever passed his lips before this time (the mean old bugger). Father Sensibly soon put the life into him by pouring a few drops of it into his teacup – and then a few more drops until Black Neddy was getting a liking for it. And so the afternoon rolled along, merrier and merrier by the minute. The holy man advised Black Neddy as to the nature of a young maiden's charms, the feelings she might have in her young breasts and lower down (ahem!) elsewhere. He talked in detail about the need for bodily coercions and the detailed arrangements that now had to be acquired by Black Neddy when it came to the bedroom cosiness. The potheen and the whiskey worked their way rapidly all the way down through Black Neddy's burning throat and on into his gizzard, making his eyes look red and bloody-looking. But, alas, they never made their way down into the private regalia resting lamely between his thighs for him to perform his joys!

Sweet William

Isn't Time a wonderful healer, a wonderful bringer of good news? In the course of the summer, when the heat was almost oppressive and the meadows were the purest of colours, Sadie leapt into the arms of Hammer-the-Smith's youngest son, Sweet William, a lad of sixteen. She saw him lightly stepping down the steps after Sunday Mass. She had never noticed him this way before. From being a young boy he had suddenly turned into a handsome swan with an almost-demure look on his face and a bit of hairy fluff on his chin and the trace of a moustache on him. He displayed a flock of wavy ginger hair and a snow-white shirt. He was wearing a tweed sports jacket with the collar of the shirt out over the jacket. He seemed gentle and well-mannered with a smile on his lips and a sparkle in his boyish blue eyes. He was more than a dash amongst the young men – like a gift from out of heaven amongst the young ladies. And another thing – he was wearing his first new cap. He had put it on over his wavy locks at a rakish angle. And afterwards it was said: it wasn't so much that Sadie fell into his arms as that he fell into hers.

The Following Saturday

It happened on the following Saturday. Sweet William was riding the rickety old bike, which his farming employer had given him the use of so as to visit his ailing mother. Like all young men the lad was mad for speed. What a sight he was as he tore round the bend of the road near the gateway of Black Neddy's haggart. You could see how anxious he was to get to the bedside of his poor mother, whom he missed so much?

After Mass the very next day the news sped as fast as a jig-step. Some said that it was The Drink (the lad had never tasted it before now, they said), which had caused Sweet William's accident. He had fallen off his bike at the very bend of the road where Sadie had just been driving her cattle into the field. There she was – dallying in her yard, which was situated a bit underneath the side of the roadway. The little dreamer was admiring the sunset and hoping (the romantic little fool that she was) that one fine day a gate would open in her heart and that a Prince Charming like the one in her schoolday storybooks would come speeding along the highway – that he would rescue his Princess (her own good self) and whisk her away on his white stallion to some faraway Fairyland palace beyond the clouds. Oh how she had prayed that God would lighten her burden and let a young man land in her arms: 'Dear God-in-heaven, if only a handsome young man (please! please! please!) would fall in the door to me and speed me away from this hairy old man and his cold old arse in the midnight bed!'

Incredible as it seemed – her wish was granted quicker than she could ever have imagined. For, whilst she was standing there at the half-door she heard the tingaling-tingaling song of a bicycle bell and the rattling of the speeding wheels as Sweet William tore along on his runaway bike.

The next thing that happened was like a visitation from the Angel Gabriel himself. A vision of youthfulness appeared in front of her eyes as Sweet William was hurtled out over the handlebars of his bike. Into the air the young lad sailed and landed – in a pure heap of disfigurement with his several cuts and bruises and his sudden cries of boyish pain – into Sadie's two arms. And there he lay – senseless. The good God-in-heaven had indeed listened to her cries of anguish. A man had come down from the skies and (wonder of wonders) fallen straight into her arms! In future years as they sat across from each other at the evening fireside men and women would wonder what infernal magician had worked the magic upon Sadie and Sweet William so that they should have met in such a very strange manner.

She Tended And Nursed His Bruises

Sadie brought the damaged youngster in the half-door and she put him down on a blanket near the heat of the fire. For a short while everything was black night for him. But she tended and nursed his wounds with the delicacy of her fingers, which (in spite of the harshness of her daily work) were still soft and tender. When he awoke, she smiled down at him and Sweet William saw in that clandestine moment the charm of Sadie's features and that she had a pair of striking china-blue eyes, which were fast now glittering their dovelike charms into his previously-untroubled soul. For a minute it was as though he were struck dumb – as though a merry fire had lit up inside him and his young heart started to melt away on him. In simple terms – Sadie had struck a love that soon turned from merry to smouldering for she had firmly trapped him in her clutches and he'd be hers for now and forevermore.

The Bedroom Tingle And Jingle

That Saturday was a Fair-Day in town and Black Neddy had driven his cattle into The Market-Square. He'd be there all day with the drinking and carousing that always followed a sale. The time now came for some youthful lovemaking and in his absence the hungry young lovers withdrew to the bedroom and there they played out their enchantment like two turtledoves, throwing their steaming bodies into jostling and tussling till the room began to tingle and jingle with the sweaty tumbles of these two little savages. Their dizzy antics continued throughout the afternoon till they almost jumped out of their skins and were exhausted from it.

Following the activities that were Sadie's natural birthright a child was conceived in her and the birth of a son followed nine months later. Would you credit it! In the eyes of us all the fame of Black Neddy went soaring up to the moon:

'Why, the lecherous old bugger!' said some.

'What miracle cure did Father Sensibly bring up to Black Neddy's door in the motorcar that the magic of love should take such a hold of him? said others.

Father Sensibly stuck out his chest like a turkeycock. Whatever secrets he had imparted to Black Neddy it was now seen to have done the trick. At the next Saturday's Confessions where there were usually a dozen rows of sibilant women kneeling outside the confession-box (all anxious to fill the priest's ears with their own scarcely impure thoughts and those secret emotions which they were far too timid to pour into the ears of their own men) they were joined by a similar number of old men. All of these hairy old schemers had come shoving one another in through the church door, wanting to be the first in the queue and their hearts as light as a bit of paper. Once inside in The confession-box they hoped they'd get hold of the secret, which the holy man had in his powers to give them, so that they could acquire for themselves a bit of Black Neddy's brute joys. Yes, Father Sensibly (he who was the receiver of the parish's confessions and had enough knowledge of the bodily goings-on of the entire population to fill a book) was going to be the answer to the prayers of every man-jack of them.

In the weeks that followed, Rookery Rally proclaimed the fame of Black Neddy as never before. It even went into our rhymes and our songs and the children themselves sang it on the way to school: '*Fair play to you, Neddy, you gave her the blast – you gave her the old injection, at last*!' But only Sweet William and Sadie knew about the bedroom frolics that were the real source of Black Neddy having apparently fathered so fine a child.

As for Black Neddy himself he was now in a terrible fix. The rage, which he was forced to keep inside his chest, had no bounds. He knew that since the first day of his marriage he had never been able to raise so much as a cough in the marriage bed. And from that day onwards his mind was made up: if ever he found out the dirty little whoor, who had been giving Sadie her pleasures, he would cut off his danglers and stretch him out dead with a belt of his pickaxe handle.

The Loving Went On – And On

Days moved on into weeks and the weeks moved on into months and thence into years. The two young lovebirds met in secret trysts whenever and wherever they could: behind the haystack: in under the shelter of the woodland trees: along hidden riverbanks where only the spirits of nature could behold their hot bodies and their discarded heaps of clothes. But these sharp and irregular volleys of lovemaking were in no way enough to satisfy the youthful desires that they had for each other.

The Devil Entered The Scene

Sweet William could contain himself no longer. The Devil now came along on velvet feet and got a firm hold of the young lad's soul and then he came and took a grip of his fair damsel as well. In the coming days the two young lovers began to plot and scheme and to whisper unheard of thoughts into one another's ears – devilish thoughts. And such were the powers of their love for each other, even the fear of hell's flames couldn't stop the wickedness that eventually fixed itself inside in their wild heads. Sweet William was so urged on and inspired by the beauty of Sadie that the moral restraints taught him by the priests and at his mother's knee fell away from him like a pair of horse-chains.

A Starless Night

It was a starless night with no moon when the villainous Sweet William crept into Black Neddy's Welcoming Room. From there he tiptoed up to the bedroom door. At the last minute Sadie herself was not nearly as sure as her lover of the steps about to be taken and she (the little heathen who had goaded Sweet William on) stood in her shift outside the bedroom door, shivering far more from fear than from the midnight cold. She had never dreamed (she kept telling herself) that matters would have gone this far. And yet, as she listened to Sweet William sidling his way towards the side of Black Neddy's bed, she didn't lift a finger to hold back the wicked hand of her lover.

What were the thoughts inside the head of Sweet William? Had he no father of his own on this earth? Had he never heard tell of hell and heaven?

For a moment there was no sound in the room – only his intake of breath. He took the bolster in his fists. He placed it over the snoring face of Black Neddy. And in spite of the poor man's thrashing around on the matress, he held it pressed down tightly until he was sure he had choked the old man and there was no further quiver out of him. And then, when he was sure that Black Neddy was as dead as a fly, he crept out the creaking door of the bedroom. No-one had seen him come in. No-one saw him going out. No-one had witnessed the dark and deadly deed. No-one except the hundreds of ghostly ancestors of Black Neddy who forever had been his trusty companions in the days before Sadie had come to greet him. And without so much as a backward look at Sadie, Sweet William whispered his stealthy feet across the dark haggart (the trees gazing down sadly on him) to where he had stowed his bike. What on earth had he done? The angels looked out pitifully at him from behind every twig and leaf and, with The Hounds of Persecution running fast after him, he rode his terrified way home with a speed that outmatched even the wind.

The equally terrified Sadie, realising what Sweet William had finally plucked up courage to do, now found herself in a damp cold sweat and she took Black Neddy's greatcoat from the back of the door. He wouldn't need it anymore. Then she stirred up the tiny embers in the black grate with a few hawthorn twigs and a few small bits of turf till the blaze was yellow and red once more. Wrapped in the greatcoat she spent the rest of the night huddled near the fire, dreading what the outcome would be when next day's light came in. The coat would keep her warm and free from the cold of the night. But free from the stain of such wickedness she never again would be.

Not Even A Raised Eyebrow

Next day when she ran down the road and raised the alarm there wasn't so much as a raised eyebrow. Neither did Doctor Glasses have any questions to ask when he came to sign the death certificate the day after this sad event. Along with him came Father Sensibly to pray for Black Neddy's soul. They could see for themselves the sad state of the old man's yellow face and his grotesquely twisted mouth lying there in the bed. Doctor Glasses came out quietly into the yard to meet the crowd of old keening women, who had come to light the death-candles and to cry over Black Neddy and help prepare his corpse for burial. He told them that it was not only his old age that had beaten the aging farmer but (he tapped his nose and gave a discreet little cough) his unusually exertive practices in the bedroom that had proved too much for a delicate old man like him and he warned them to be sure and tell nobody.

By this time Father Sensibly was feeling as miserable as a tree without water. There was no need for him to speculate about the death for it was he himself and no-one else who had encouraged Black Neddy to put a bit of a spring in his legs in the nightly bedroom tumblings and jostlings. In spite of Doctor Glasses' instructions the whole of Rookery Rally (wouldn't you know it?) soon recognised the reason for Black Neddy's death and they raised a great big shout of approval. Indeed there wasn't a man that didn't envy the dead man the powers of his fierce lovemaking. Thanks to Father Sensibly's original visit they knew that the old fellow had died in utter ecstasy and gone up to heaven in a blaze of glory. The following day Sadie buried him in haste below in Abbey Acres Graveyard.

The Wedding

The following May, Sweet William and Sadie called out their marriage banns inside in The Copperstone Hollows church. Wouldn't you think that the little heathen would have kept to her honour and worn her black widow's weeds for the full duration of the customary twelve months? Free at last and anxious to bury the recent dark deed firmly in the past, the two of them were now in their absolute heaven. They couldn't get enough of the lovemaking and in the next few years children and more children followed. There was one, then two, then three and four:

'Doesn't the love-making flog all!' said the two cosy ones.

And Then – The Depression

But the fourth child proved a much more difficult and unreasonable birth than the others and Sadie found that something unexpected had crept inside her: she was suddenly the inheritor of her mother's failing – a natural depression, which was common enough in many of our women-folk after childbirth. This accursed depression (she thought) had been sent to her by none other than the dead spirit of Black Neddy – sent to her as the final punishment for her mortal sin of disfiguring her previous marriage-bed and helping Sweet William to cause his violent death.

It was good enough for her: her deranged state-of-mind would be as much her birthright as her bodily carousing and the gift of her lovely mane of sandy hair. She knew there'd be no lasting peace of mind for the likes of her. Night after night the great sin of Sweet William in suffocating Black Neddy haunted her and for the first time in her life she couldn't get a wink of sleep: she couldn't eat a morsel of food: she became as snappish as a wasp. It was her nerves, goddammit.

She knew that Sweet William, when the time came for him to die, would go straight down into the bowels of hell. She didn't want to join him there. She regretted the haste with which she had taken part in planning the suffocation of the old man, even though he'd been cold and useless in the bed since the first day she met him. But the next time she went into Father Sensibly's confession-box she hadn't the brazen audacity to tell him about the way she'd helped plan this wicked crime. He would never be able to forgive her. What on earth was she going to do with herself?

She Made Up Her Mind

Finally she made up her mind. And though she had her four young children to look after, she realised she couldn't stay looking at Sweet William for the rest of her days. 'The middle of the night is the stealthy time for killing old men,' she kept repeating to herself. 'The middle of the night is also the stealthy time for me to get mee few possessions together from the chest of drawers and take to the high road.'

She got up and dressed herself. She put on her stout brogues. With tears glittering in her eyes she touched the curly locks of her four children. She touched the wavy hair of Sweet William – just for a moment. Her fingers were impatient to be packing her trunk. She took the holywater from the font at the half-door and she blessed her children and her man. Quietly she closed the door behind her. She wept silently over the thought of her babies wrapped in peaceful slumber. She and her ass-and-car headed for the coast of Cork and the Kerry borders. It'd be a long journey that would take days if not weeks. Sweet William continued to sleep like a lamb in the bed.

Next Morning

Next morning the news of her departure came as a shock to us all. Hitherto there had been many children (older ones of course) who had given up on their parents – either leaving them to go into service in The Big House or to take the cattle-boat when the old folk were least expecting it and when they hadn't been given time to perform The Family Blessing on them. But we had never heard tell of a woman leaving her four small children behind her like this.

Dowager Put On Her Boots

Dowager knew what to do. She put on her boots and tackled up her ass-and-car underneath the ass (The Lightning Whoor). She drove across to The-Road-to-The-Hollows to comfort Sweet William in his desperate hour of need. On the way she kept asking herself had Sadie taken leave of her senses? Was the woman completely mad?

He Was In A Terrible State

When she entered The Welcoming Room how sad the place looked – laughter all gone. She saw that Sweet William was in a terrible state – a look on him like the grey graveyard. He would soon be facing the prospect of misery and ruin if he didn't bestir himself and tend the land. She ran over to the fireplace and took his hands in hers. There wasn't a bit of life left in him. Nor had he a word to say to her – as though he had completely lost his powers of speech. Dowager quickly summed up the situation: all alone and by himself the poor fellow would never be able to cope with the four children as well as the racking heartache in his chest. The youngest of these little mites was barely a day out of the cradle: the eldest of the four was not yet old enough to go stepping off to the schoolhouse of Dang-the-skin-of-it.

She washed and dressed the children. She stood with them in front of their young father. There followed a moment of pain and indecision. Sweet William – unable to fathom the miserable treatment that Sadie had handed out to himself and the little ones – managed to whisper how Sadie had packed her trunk and disappeared in the dead of night. He found it difficult to hold back his anger. His wife's hard heart might as well now take the children away from him too (he said). As much as he loved them, there was no way he could look after them and tend to Black Neddy's farm at one and the same time. It was hopeless. It was insane even to think of it.

She Gave Herself A Shake

There were tears in Dowager's eyes to see such heartbreak in a man so young. She had never experienced such sorrow before. She felt helpless and awkward, standing there frozen in the middle of the floor. She gave herself a shake. She had thrown her hat in the ring (she told herself) and it was too late to back off now. She ladled up the four children on her ass-and-car. The eldest one seemed to know what was happening and his eyes were heavy with tears as he looked back in the door at his father. With a broken heart Sweet William waved them goodbye from the half-door, not knowing if he'd be able to have them back and enjoy their company round the farm in happier days. And Dowager, unable to stand looking at his pain a minute longer, laid into her ass with a savage belt of her ashplant and drove the pitiable youngsters down the length of The Creamery Road.

An Uphill Battle

As soon as she entered her yard she realised what she had done and what an uphill battle was about to face her. Three of her older children were already working in service for Lord and Lady Demurely. And though two of her children had died young, she still had her ten other children sleeping higgledy-piggledy round the floor. She also had the three young cousins who came out from The Roaring Town each summer for fresh air and to help at the hay. They were strong and sturdy lads and (with her husband, Handsome Johnnie, dead these last few years) she was grateful for their help and support for she needed as many hands as possible to turn and tram the hay and help build the reek. The whole houseful of children would be company (she hoped) for the four little orphans and help them forget their mother's treachery.

It Was Hard To Keep Her Head Above Water

It was all that Dowager could do to keep her head above water with so many children hopping round The Welcoming Room like a family of mice. If a neighbour suddenly came in to borrow a grain of tea, they'd see blankets piled in heaps in every corner for there weren't enough beds for all the children to sleep in and they'd find them sleeping nose-to-tail all round the floor, in the settlebed and even under the beds.

Yes – the extra children from town were a blessing when it came to stacking up the piles of logs and turf or bringing in the buckets of spring-well water. But at dinnertime it was a different story when so many mouths to feed became the devil-of-a-curse. Poor Dowager saw them emptying the contents of the baking-burners again and again and for once in her life she had to shoo them away like chickens at the half-door. There were even times when so empty were their bellies that she was forced to send them into the grove for hazelnuts and berries. She told them to cut themselves fistfuls of young nettles and bring them back in the buckets. It was as bad as when she was a girl herself and had to go out and hunt alongside her brothers and sisters to catch blackbirds in nets and bring them back for the next day's dinner.

Enough Was Enough

The other women could see that Dowager and her stout heart was turning into that old nursery rhyme:

'There was an old woman who lived in a shoe – she had so many children she didn't know what to do.'

Enough was enough (they said). Dowager had the heart. Dowager had the will. But she needed their help. Cheerful Nan and Cackles (good neighbours as always) looked at one another and then they came to a decision:

'What need is there to go down to The Daffy-Duck Circus and look for one of their jugglers to come up here?'

And Moll-the-Man agreed with the pair of them:

'We have Dowager – our very own juggler – living here in our midst (said she) – and will ye look at the way she's trying to keep all the balls in the air at one and the same time – all by herself.'

The three women came in across the yard. Without so much as a by-your-leave they took three of the four small orphans away with them. Dowager kept back the oldest one (Patsy) for this tender child was the saddest of all and needed the most help, being old enough to miss his mother and father more than the rest of them put together. Dowager would now put all her energies into training the little fellow in his prayers and counting. She'd be sure to have him ready when the time came for him to go off to school with the rest of her children and shake hands with Dang-the-skin-of-it.

Training The Little Fellow

Her eldest son (Blue-eyed Jack) began training the little fellow along with his own younger brothers and sisters – showing the bemused child how to throw the sods of turf into the cart when the turf had to be saved in the bog. Over in The Seventh Field he playfully fired maggots at him whilst teaching him how to fill the potato-sack with the newly-dug spuds once they had shaken the dirt from them. He let him help carry home the sack of cabbages for Dowager to wash and clean away the slugs – let him carry the rabbit-traps and snares to The Bluebutton Field – let him carry the fishing-rod down to River Laughter on his shoulders.

Meanwhile . . .

Meanwhile Sadie was speeding away across the stormy ocean to begin a new life in The Land of The Silver Dollar. The journey was a living nightmare that no dreamer could ever have imagined. The rickety old boat was all the time pitching and tossing from side to side, forwards and backwards. and the waves kept coming up over the sides and threatening to toss the shrieking passengers overboard for the fishes to feast on. The engines cranked to absolute breaking-point – to be matched only by the sickening groans of bellies without a morsel of food inside in them.

Amongst the women Sadie counted herself fortunate to have survived the crossing in one piece. Other women and children were often too sick to have lasted long and were thrown into the sea and secretly buried in the dead of night. Several more managed to hang on to life but were afflicted with unimaginable diseases. As soon as they reached the new lands they were sent back home on the very next boat. Others shook hands with madness itself, certain households in Rookery Rally being inclined that way anyway from the overuse of religious trimmings or from loneliness and constant in-breeding. When at last they reached the landing-place (*The Island*) it was a sorry state of affairs to behold what remained of the passengers. Along with the others Sadie was unceremoniously stripped of her clothing and put in a long room where she was washed down with a hose and painted with a white distemper-brush and deloused.

She Stepped Out Wearily

Mindful of the stories brought home from The Land of The Silver Dollar – tales of the harsh exploitation of new Irish arrivals by a previous batch of Irish emigrants – she stepped out wearily and warily towards her cousins' establishment in Yonkers. She held on tightly to the clasp of her purse. In it she had the old Yankee dollars, which had been her father's marriage gift to Black Neddy at the time of their ill-fated marriage.

Her Cousins Had Died

On reaching Yonkers Sadie found that her aged cousins were sadly dead. Alone and weary, what was she supposed to do? One thing was sure – finding the companionship of a man was the furthest thought from her mind. But work (she realised) was plentiful in this new land of dreams and opportunity. She rolled up her sleeves and not only did she find herself work, but she held onto it.

For seven long years she scrimped and saved as the dedicated housekeeper to a little old priest. Father Tim was a saint-of-a-man if ever there was one. He had a heart full of gold and the virtue of nobility stamped all over his face. He became Sadie's very own guardian angel. He fed her well. He clothed her well. He cared for her guilty soul and she knew that her dark secret would be safe with him inside in his confession-box.

It seemed that God had finally forgiven her and given her a chance to make amends with her life. As the months flew by she found her saintly confessor a rare treat in contrast to one or two rakish priests she had previously laid eyes on back in Tipperary – priests seen living in splendour with fine fat fare and bottles of red wine at their table and a servant girl who (unlike herself) was seen on one or two occasions to avoid a priestly penitential threat by sharing with him her maidenhead in the ecclesiastical bedroom, thus learning a love of which no Church could ever have approved. Father Tim was a true man-of-the-cloth – an example to all, having managed to hold onto the echoes and teachings of his ancient mother back home in Ireland (a place he still called The Ould Dart). Indeed he was a match for Saint Peter at the gates.

The Surprise

Sadly, however, their peace and harmony came to an end when the angels came calling on Old Tim and closed his dead eyes. Next there followed a big surprise when Sadie learnt that she was the recipient of hundreds and hundreds of dollars, the dying priest's last wish for her. With so much money in her fist she'd be able to return to the land of her birth. It would not be an easy journey, for in spite of having made her peace with God for the way she had helped plan Black Neddy's death, she was unsure what sort of welcome she'd get when she reached Rookery Rally's doorstep – especially if her little children had learnt of her treachery in once abandoning them.

Good Fortune Arrives

However, before she'd even set foot on the boat in Baltimore good fortune was already on its way – bringing her the chance of an additional dose of happiness. One of the last of the big houses in Rookery Rally (Tangledyke Hall – the one below in Travellers' Rest) had run into a downward spiral of misfortune. Lord and Lady Elegance had both died in recent years and had been taken back across the sea to be buried in the family vault in The Welsh Hills. Some of us (especially the ploughmen and cooks) were sad to see the polite old couple's stay with us coming to an end: they had always treated us fair and square.

At the time when Sadie was getting herself ready and packing her trunk for the homeward journey the only one left in Tangledyke Hall was Augustus George: he was the youngest unmarried son. However – young though he was – the poor fellow was now lying on his last lonely sickbed and rapidly approaching the hour of his death. He had never been in the best of health and, saddened by the deaths of his parents, he would now follow them to the grave after surrendering to a terrible bout of pneumonia. Sadie was only halfways back across the ocean (on board a much sturdier steamship than the rickety old boat that had taken her out to Yonkers seven years earlier) when his body was taken across the sea to be buried alongside his parents in Wales.

Time – The Great Healer

When she set foot in The Roaring Town Station she found that Time had proved a great healer and that all her worries were unfounded. Hadn't she always known that her friends in Rookery Rally had hearts of gold – that they'd take her back into the folds of their aprons like any returning prodigal? All anger and sorrow from the day she left us was swept away and replaced with our bouts of child-like joy on seeing how she'd not forgotten us and had come back home to the fold. And in the very next week such was the welcome we gave her at the house-dance in her honour that not a string was left on any fiddle – not a sole was left on any hobnail boot.

She Had The Pick Of The Men

She found she had the pick of the men to choose from for Sweet William (the joy of her first warm bed and the killer of Black Neddy) was nowhere to be seen. He had died three years earlier – taken away unceremoniously by the wrathful hands of God and a smothering dose of consumption. Her babies were now well-established elsewhere and wouldn't have recognised her anyway – even if Dowager, Moll-the-Man, Cheerful Nan and Cackles had had the hearts to tell them of their mother's former deceit and abandonment of them.

She Was Still A Fine-looking Woman

Sadie was still a fine-looking woman in men's eyes – especially now that she had a good pull of money behind her. And so – she looked around for a man that would warm her bed anew. She remembered Leppalong Lacey, her childhood partner when she was fourteen and going to her very first Platform Dance-in-the-fields. She thought about how he had given her a taste of her first innocent kisses behind the racks of bikes on the ditch. She then surprised us all by up and marrying for a third time – a thing unheard of in the annals of our history.

This last time she was marrying not for the cold belly of an ailing farmer nor for the honeyed tingling with Sweet William in the lustful bedroom but for the chief talents that were Leppalong Lacey's – for riches galore. He was the owner of a hundred acres of fine grassland beyond The Sandpit and she herself had the full of her hands of Yanky dollars. Together they pooled their wealth and a month after returning from Father Sensibly's marriage-blessings they put it all to good use and went to Travellers' Rest where they bought Tangledyke Hall for themselves.

A Fine House

Life was startling in the changes that began to take place. Sadie gazed in wonder at the fine features of the house: the ruby be-curtained ballroom: the red and white roses that covered the entire side of the house: the orchard full of every sort of apple, plum and pear imaginable: the haggart-garden full of cobnut trees. This was indeed the style of living (she thought) unto which she was born. She began to put on the odd dab of perfume and a bit of paint and powder to her lips and jaws and generally to become the demure lady-of-the-manor.

Not so with Leppalong Lacey. For his new life was far-removed from the pigs and the goats and the several black cattle and horses that had given him his wealth and his pleasure in the first place. Poor Leppalong Lacey! He'd never be able to adjust himself to this grand style of living inside in such a fine big mansion. Rarely was he seen on this side of the hill, preferring instead the company of his black cattle and his shiny horses and the smoke rising up from his tobacco-pipe in that little shed which he had built for himself so as to escape from the unwelcoming refinements of The Big House.

But apart from their differing desires, the resplendent twosome still had their good times together. They often spent their evenings with a fine roast dinner set out on the table. They pulled out the card-table and invited Leppalong Lacey's hillsmen down for the game of forty-five-hand-wheel. They welcomed the lamp-lighting rabbiters on their way up into The Hills-of-The-Past and gave them a glass of hot whiskey to set them on their way with fluttering hearts.

Father Sensibly was also a regular visitor seen hanging his coat on the nail. He came for the odd drop of port that was thrown down his throat and for the odd few sovereigns, given to him by Leppalong Lacey and Sadie (especially Sadie) for the saving of their souls against too long a spell in Purgatory's flames. Over and above these particularities the two of them managed to hold onto their memories of earlier adolesecent days and the uncertain feelings of their clumsy youth. They found time to snuggle up close to each other in the goose-feathered bed and have the odd jostle or two beneath the sheets. As a result a child was born to them – a child who was meant for the Bishopric of Kikmaloosha two generations later. Father Tim would have been as pleased as punch.

The Furies Were Sailing In

Bad fortune and good fortune seemingly come round in their own good season. The Furies were already sailing their way in across The Mighty Mountain and before the year was out Sadie's dreams were once more filled with a consuming guilt for the death of her first husband (Black Neddy). For several nights in a row she was terrorised by dreams of Sweet William suffocating Black Neddy with the bolster. She had other sad dreams of him and his handsome wavy hair as he fell into her arms from off of his rattling bike outside her doorway. If only she had known then what was to follow! Suffocation had been the lot of old Black Neddy. Suffocation too had been the lot of Sweet William when the callous and vengeful consumption had carried him off – a just and righteous reward for his heinous sin.

A Final Punishment

Leppalong Lacey now gave her the gift of a second child. But after the birth of this child, Sadie (still a young woman) received a final punishment for her indirect part in killing Black Neddy under the bolster and the cruel abandonment of her four little ones in the days following his death. A dark depression again rose up in her after the birth of this child. At dusk she found herself wandering down to the tombs of Black Neddy and Sweet William and standing there silently for hours on end.

Days turned into weeks. She was full of inexhaustible urges and found herself getting up stealthily in the dead of night and walking round and round in the graveyard. Weeks turned into months. Early in the morning (even before the lark or the cockerel had dipped their heads in the dew) she took to wandering distractedly through the drizzling rain out across the fields in her nightshift. Her heart and her mind were caught in a web. She was entering a new world – a fairy place, but unsure whether it was a bad or a good place.

Strolling Through The Dew

The unkind gossips (those wretched Weeping Mollys) as usual painted an unreal picture of her and said that she was strolling through the dew of the early-morning fields without a stitch of clothes on her. Those idle men, who previously had been too late to make an early start at milking their cows, now leapt up smartly from their beds so as to catch a glimpse of Sadie honouring the new sunlight and worshipping the woodland fairies in her pelt. Poor Leppalong Lacey was the laughing stock of us all. The misfortunes of Sadie (both the true tales and those in the imagination of the gossips) were toasted below in Curl 'n' Stripes' drinking-shop – glass after glass after glass.

The Priest And The Guards

It was a cold and hungry morning and the frost was steaming up on every bush and dungheap. Father Sensibly and The Guards came into Leppalong Lacey's yard. They found him sitting on the upturned lace of his horse-and-cart. God only knows how long since dawn he had been sitting there. They took him by the hand, as you would a child, and brought him into the fire. With words of kindness and patting his knee they assured him that his wife was no longer in a fit state to remain by his side. With floods of tears in his eyes ('do with her what ye will') he pointed out across the haggart singletree to where Sadie had disappeared, taking her morning's ramble. It was to be her last stroll.

They Stepped Out Across The Field

Father Sensibly and The Guards stepped out along the fields in the wake of Sadie. Gently they tried to coax her back into the yard and to the awaiting van that would take her to The House for Nervous Disorders. Sadie was no fool. She was like a wild animal that tries to escape from the trap and the cage. She fought them as though they were the ringing devil. It took four strong men to run across the fields after the priest and The Guards and help pin her down by her arms and feet.

They took her away in the van. No more would she see The Big House in Travellers' Rest. No more would she see the green fields of Rookery Rally or the snow on the top of The Mighty Mountain. She arrived in The House for Nervous Disorders where she died a few months later in the arms of the nuns – their rosary-beads clacking over her – their shiny row of candles and their prayers for her happy death looming over her.

The Day Of The Funeral

On the day that Sadie came home to be buried we saw how Father Sensibly stood over her grave – himself and his bucket of holywater. He had heard Sadie's final confession. It was cool among the tombstones with just a little breeze through the trees. The young woman was at peace now. There was so much he could have said had the vows of his priesthood allowed him. He must have showered half-a-gallon of holywater down on top of poor Sadie. Then the first fistfuls of pebbles rattled their way down onto the lid of the coffin. Her three year-old year son (The Bishop-to-be) was restrained at the side of his mother's grave. He had seen her coffin being lowered into the pit. He ran across to the ditch. He saw the rosebush overhanging Delaney's Shed. He picked out a wild rose. He ran back and threw it into the grave on top of Sadie:

'Will ye look at the child!'

'For the love of sweet Jesus, look at him!' The crowd wept buckets at the sight of the child and the coffin of his mother.

In The Months That Followed

Time (as always) flew quickly by. Although the crows and their good-luck charms had left Abbey Acre a hundred years previously a strange thing happened a few weeks later: the grave of Sadie was surrounded at night-time by the pitiful screeching of the returning crows, seemingly mourning her death. They cried out their pitying cawing song as once they did on that early morning years ago when Sadie and her streaming tears had waved them goodbye as she passed down The Creamery Road on her way to Yonkers:

'Take good care, Sadie!' the crows seemed to say on that day. 'Take very good care!'

He Never Recovered

Leppalong Lacey never recovered after the death of his wife. It was as though the fire in his belly had been quinched. Nor did he ever remarry or lose his boyhood love of Sadie. He continued to half-heartedly farm his estate. But The Big House at Travellers' Rest became wild and the orchards were soon deserted.

Each morning, as the children welcomed in the new day's sunlight and took their feet off towards the schoolhouse, they saw Leppalong Lacey, a man rapidly and prematurely aging, sitting on the ditch outside the graveyard gate. Later in the day they again passed him on their way to the well for the buckets of spring-well water. By now his beard was growing down onto his chest like as though he were a poet or a writer of plays. It had turned white and creamy and yellow-stained from his smoking of pipe-tobacco. He never uttered a single word to the children. His very appearance frightened the lives out of the little ones and they gave him a wide berth. He filled their nightly dreams with nothing less than terror.

In the evenings, once all the children had said their prayers and were tucked up in bed, parents would sit across from each other at the fireside. Their thoughts were often about Sadie. They thought of Black Neddy and they thought of Sweet William too. But they never knew the truth. In spite of all his miserliness whilst he was here on earth Black Neddy had died and gone up to heaven – straight as a die to the home of the angels. He was a simple and innocent soul who knew nothing of the needs of a woman in the marriage-bed.

Of course Sweet William was dead too and (unless he had made his peace with his Heavenly Maker – and none of us knew whether he had or he hadn't) he was now on his way straight down to hell for the savage way he had ended Black Neddy's life. Sadie from Yonkers (poor thing) was dead too and none of us could tell you (not even the saintly Father Tim were he still alive in Yonkers) where she might have eventually ended her days – be it up in heaven or down in hell.

And another thing that none of us could ever truly discover was the depth of the pain that constantly remained inside the chest of Sadie's third husband, her childhood dancing-partner, Leppalong Lacey. With his sad face he was like an old dog with a blinding loyalty to its master – even to the point of death. He had been as true and loyal as any old sheepdog to his lovely Sadie from the very first day he'd set eyes on her – the time they had given one another their few shy kisses behind the ditch at The Platform Dance-in-the-fields. From that moment onwards he had found himself trapped and had henceforth loved her with a profundity that knew no bounds. It is true to say that his love for Sadie had been a love that would never die – a love that surpassed all time and place.

ELEVEN

How, and with what dire consequences, Rapper fell out with Bohorlody.

A Singular Shame

Throughout the summertime we were all up with the smoky grey of daybreak and our thoughts were preoccupied with saving the hay and the turf, with rewarding ourselves with the enjoyment of the Daffy-Duck Circus and The Show-Fair, with stamping our dancing boots on top of The Mighty Mountain or getting ourselves baptized like The Big Y'hoo in the arms of a roguish woman from the town. We had, for instance, little or no time for re-educating some of our dogs. And on occasions this proved to be a singular shame in the case of one or two of them whenever they stepped out of line.

Bohorlody

Bohorlody lived on the other side of the metal bridge. His family of six children (the young Hazelnuts) had the most beautiful hair imaginable – a mixed shade of yellow and orange and brown and red. But what was of more interest was the vocabulary that each of them had – even the youngest of them (Trixy). Whenever they managed to string a few words together it was always in the soft tone of their father's voice or that of their big brothers and not as other small children spoke. They had acquired such a tone-of-voice ever since their earliest cradle-days as a result of keeping their mouth shut tight and listening to the unusual voices of the elder Hazelnuts in the same way as a crow would listen to its mother. Their accent had a broken-glass throaty sound to it and was remarkable all over Rookery Rally – so much so that when Bohorlody brought home the news from the creamery that the Pope was dead, instead of getting down on their bended knees and lamenting the poor man's death, they gave the reply (forever to be remembered): 'Why wouldn't he be dead when he let the cattle stamp on him'. When news of this got out, a great deal of merry laughter ensued – even on so sad an occasion as the Pope's death. For the children had always sounded the word *pope* as *pawp* and had the very same sound for *pup*. But enough of that.

The Red-tiled House

Unlike our own thatched cabins Bohorlody had a neat little red-tiled house, much the same as White Snow's before she came in amongst us. And whenever he had a moment to spare he'd be dabbing it here and dabbing it there with his paintbrush. His father had been just the same – painting the outer walls of his cowshed in a cream colour and the foot of the walls in a black colour – and then dipping his horseshoes into red paint and stamping their imprints across the black paint.

Bohorlody's house lay on a steep slope and had a magnificent view of the winding curves of River Laughter as well as The Mighty Mountain standing out above our other lesser hills. Thank God for his very fine view for he had nothing else to please him other than his beloved batty pony (Rusty), having but three cows to his name whilst the rest of us had six or seven and a few calves as well. That didn't trouble him a bit for more than anyone else he was a man of the most sound and astute principles. It was unheard of him to go pestering The Guards when any domestic controversies (legal or otherwise) raised their ugly heads. If the rats were eating his eggs Bohorlody knew what to do: he'd supply them with the pink poison-paste and they'd be dead and gone in an instant. The matter had been resolved. If the foxes ate his chickens he went and set a trap for them outside The Bog Wood. They'd be dead and gone and he'd nail their tails to the henhouse door. If the old badger ran riot in The Bull Paddock, he took his spade from the shed and chastised the impudent fellow's snout for him. If Timmy Bellows allowed his bull to cross over the boundary fence and perform on his three cows, he simply invited Timmy and his fists out into the field. The two of them took off their waistcoats. There and then they proceeded to belt the living shite out of each other. The winner of the brawl was also the winner of the legal battle (at least for the time being) and a bloody nose either way was enough compensation for the pair of them.

This state of affairs was what Bohorlody called *going to law*. Of course within our own families we each had what was called The Family Law when a father bade the rest of his household to follow and obey the rules of his house and it was rare for anyone to sleep a night in The Roaring Town Jail. If Bohorlody was not at home to solve a dispute, his six children would sit glumly and stubbornly around in the yard and solemnly declare: 'Not a hand's tap of work will we do until father comes home: not a single bucket of water will we draw from the well: not one log will we cut or chop up for the fire. As soon as he gets in, we'll bring out the chairs into the yard and we'll get him to give us the law – yes, we'll go to law.' That (they knew) was the way of the world: – the judgment of their father would bring a just and proper solution to the immediate problem troubling them.

The Children And The Law

Of course it wasn't always possible to sit all day like poor scholars and wait for their father to come home and deliver the law: sometimes he might be a long way from home – buying an ass or a mule – and the children's own inborn wisdom and brains might handle the arguments and disputes perfectly well. They'd bring out their chairs as usual – or they'd fetched a few large logs to sit on from the grove. In imitation of their father and with their excellent eldest brother (Barbaha) leading them, they'd argue out their concerns fair and square and the big lad would deliver his verdict: it was their own singularly childish way of *going to law*.

They Waited For Bohorlody

On this particular occasion, however, the matter was far too serious an issue and not even the wisdom of Barbaha could fulfill the law the way the children would have wished. So they sat in a ring near the upturned ass-and-car and they waited for Bohorlody to come home and pass his sentence. It wouldn't be long now.

He Was At The Creamery

He was spending the morning at The Creamery in Copperstone Hollow with the horse-and-cart and the reins wrapped firmly round the tanks of milk. This happened one week in every three when (along with the big milk tanks of Easy-does-it and Red Buckles) he'd exchange his own tank of milk for the skimmed milk and a pound or two of butter. With only three cows to his name he had one of the smallest tanks on The Creamery Road and yet he managed to fill it to the brim. A wise man was Bohorlody. How much milk your tank got from your cows depended (said he) not just on how many cows a man owned but on a cow's good nature. The sweeter the words a man whispered into his cow's ear and the softer and more melodious the songs that he sang her, the better humour would she get into for giving him his daily milk. Ponder the thought.

His Neighbours (Red Buckles And Easy-does-it)

Red Buckles was always a red-faced jovial fellow without a care to his name; he seemed to sail through life. But that other poor chap (Easy-does-it) had been having more than a fair share of our sympathy in recent days. The previous fortnight he witnessed his finest cow (Bluebell) falling down in front of him into a deep drain. He was unable to get her out with the ass and the reins and with no-one nearby to help either himself or the cow he took a look into the poor creature's eyes. He saw that she was going to die a miserable death for her two legs were broken. He had to go back across the yard for the rifle. With the tears running down his face and saying a sincere Act of Contrition he gave Bluebell the last rites before delivering the final blast of the rifle into her forehead.

The week before that he had been down at a wedding in south Tipperary. He came home after a fine day's outing where he had swallowed a table-load of hams and chickens, mixed together with spoonfuls of jellies and puddings and other such nonsense (we won't mention the mixed drinks that the greedy devil poured down his throat). When he got home he lit himself a furze-bush fire to warm his toes and toast the thighs of his britches. He fell asleep and tumbled into the fire, the arse getting burnt on him. Oh Blessed Saviour – he'd been well and truly chastised after all his day's enjoyment and tomfoolery down in south Tipperary!

Next morning we heard that he had spilt one of his tanks of milk all over the yard, the simpleton! And (would you believe this) the next day he was in the same poor shape. His cows knew him well, his moods and his whims. In recent weeks one or two of them had grown sick to death of seeing him coming home late in the afternoon and drunk as a mule from Curl 'n' Stripes' drinking-shop. By the time he threw his bike on the ditch they were bent on chastising him. As soon as they saw him at the gate they staggered off down the field, looking back at him dragging his boots along after them. The devils then hid behind every little bush and tree they could find whilst he followed them further and further in across the fields with his milking-stool and empty buckets ('here, Betsy! here, Pixy, blasht you!') so as to milk them at the side of the ditch. What with chasing all round the field to milk his cows – what with tripping over his tanks and his buckets in the yard and losing his finest cow in a drain – Easy-does-it was the saddest man in all of Rookery Rally for a short while. Dowager and Moll-the-Man had him at the top of their list of prayers and had everyone else down on their skinned knees too – all praying for his return to better times, poor man. Fair play to the women!

Bohorlody Wasn't Home Yet

Bohorlody hadn't yet come home. The children were getting awfully fidgetty and making the odd little run out over the flagstones to listen for the horse's hooves and the cart's wheels and see was their father coming up the hill. At the same moment the big man and his pony was a mile from home – passing The Blue Gates where the haunted house stood. We knew that the ghost of a young rebel appeared there from time to time, ever since the morning when a gunshot from a young soldier had blown his face away during the war with The Tans and that his shade had come home to the spot where he'd spent his childhood days.

The Musical Procession

The rest of the farmers were forming a nice little musical procession behind and in front of Bohorlody: asses and their cars: horses and their carts. The jingle of the harnesses were making a steady rhythm in time with the clippa-cloppa beat of the asses' and horses' hooves on the silvery road and the occasional trumpeting farts from under their tails. The tackling and the glistening tanks were clanking and clinking to the well-known tune of The *Keel Row*.

At this hour of the morning the misty grey dew of the fields and hills had already turned green and amid the fluffy clouds the sun's fat face was well up in the sky, shedding its slanting rays onto the metal of the milk tanks and breaking up into hard slivers among the dappled trees along the banks of River Laughter.

Bohorlody counted twenty carts in all. The air was filled with gobfuls of their pipe-smoke. On the wayside he could see women feeding their ducks, geese and hens in the yard. He doffed his cap like a gentleman would do and they waved merrily back. What could be better? Other henhouses and cowsheds soon re-echoed to the cries of their own ducks, geese and hen – their asses and their pigs. The noise was enough to frighten the Devil himself and Bohorlody was as contented as a little bunny rabbit out in the morning dew. He was sixty-seven last March – a man in his prime. But (ask anyone) in his new corduroy britches and his hard white collar he had the step and the gymp of any of the young high-steppers going out to their first Platform Dance-in-the-fields – himself and his golden thoughts and he humming happily to himself as he drove Rusty along. The cart-boards were giving his voice a nice little tremor.

The Carts Behind Him

Behind him he could see the hooves of the little red mule of God-be-with-the-times belting along the road and he himself slapping the reins gently against the ass's back and filling the road with his singing – the latest homespun tales brought back to us by Toby-from-The-Hill from The Land of The Silver Dollar. But (ah and alas) a cart's distance ahead of him and about to disturb his beautiful reveries was Hannyways (bad cess to him) and his white jinnet (Raggity), the product of a skillful union between the jack-donkey of Ducks-and-Drakes and the draft-horse mare of Rambling Jack. He could see the dainty strides of Hannyways' little black-and-white terrier (Crack-Jaw) – a dog that had gotten his name thanks to a kick in the head from Raggity last May. Crack-Jaw was on his tippy-toes as usual – daintily strutting along between the wheels of Hannyway's ass-and-car in the rhythm of the ass's hooves and the rattling creamery-tanks and swanking his little backside like the front-pew women (the darlings of Father Sensibly) at Sunday Mass. Raggity was a mad old jinnet and had his legs loosely string-halted so that (like the usherettes in The Daffy-Duck Circus) he had a jerky high-knee step to him. This was because he had lately kicked the hell out of Hannyways' previous ass-and-car and the string-halt was the surest way to put a stop to the ridiculous antics of a rascal as bold as himself.

Hannyways

Hannyways was a raw-boned sort of fellow with a few red veins in his nose and a pair of glassy eyes from his love of the whiskey. He wasn't the most popular of men and everyone was sick to their stomachs from the political sermons he drew down whenever he met any of us who were simple enough to stop and listen to him. And on this bright summer's day (although Bohorlody was ambling along at a safe distance behind him) it wasn't enough to save his own skin – not one bit. He could see the old devil standing up between his tanks and getting himself worked up into an atrocious fit of fighting-talk about the state the country was in. This morning's sermon was going to be the death of everyone within spitting distance of him.

Three weeks ago the selfsame Hannyways had had the misfortune to be twisting his neck round and laying into Red Buckles in a terrifying argument about the virtues of that redoubtable politician (De Valera). Of course the rest of us knew that Michael Collins (De Valera's arch rival) was the next best thing to Jesus-on-the-cross and a national hero: even our women knew that as a fact and revered his gallantry.

The row and the ruction got so hot and heavy that Red Buckles stopped Sammy (his clydesdale stallion) and leapt down from thr cart. With a face as cold as adamantine he took off his jacket. Then he took off his waistcoat. It was time (he felt) to administer a firm bit of his own homespun diplomacy; he was determined to give Hannyways a smack of his fists up into his unruly gob in order to resolve this particular debate and satisfy the law:

'We're here at The Blue Gates, Hannyways (shouted Red Buckles). Let you and me step in over the gate and settle this matter once and for all. Coom on, blasht ye – spit on yeer fists and be a man – till I nail ye to the grass. Coom on, ye scarecrow – show me the metal of yeer knuckles as well as yeer miserable gob!'

Red Buckles then proceeded to give Hannyways a few tidy jabs to the jaw and into the belly and leave him with his legs cocked up in the air, a pure rake of himself. It was good enough for him (we all said) and he was left to crawl home, sulking like a bear with a sick head. The matter had been settled: the law had been delivered.

Three Weeks Later

But that was three weeks ago. And the same incautious old fool was here again and as bold as a cockerel – turning round in the cart and wrangling with the same old provocative attitude. This left Bohorlody in a bit of a fix and he couldn't hide his face anywhere:

'H-H-H-H-Hannyways,' roared the impudent fellow, looking back at Bohorlody. He always had this damned stammer on him (like Din-Din-Dinny-the-Stammerer) when he was excited about any sort of political subject. Indeed that was how the other men had come to christen him with the name of Hannyways:

'H-H-H-H-Hannyways,' said he again. The sight of him was enough to make Bohorlody sick – the old eejit's godforsaken nose pointing up towards the sky and the runny candle of snot hanging down from it. A few more H-H-H-H-Hannyways and the ears of the rest of the men finally caught their would-be politician in full flow as he prodded at the sky with his pipeful of spitty tobacco so as to emphasize his latest argument:

'Whatever the rest of ye poor scholars say about yeer brave little Michael Collins, didn't he hike himself over the sea to John Bull – didn't he do the traitor on the rest of us – didn't he sell the souls of us all to the rotten British – didn't he hand them on a plate six of our precious counties above in the north? Of course he did, the bleddy whoor!' And that's the way he went on and on.

You'd have to put your hands to your ears. What other hero was there on earth that could disguise himself as a spy and parade round the streets of The Big City on his bike, exchanging pleasantries with The Tans outside their very own barracks? Those young simpletons, who were supposed to be out looking for him and putting a gun to his forehead, didn't have a notion whom they were speaking to. Why, the man was a pure miracle-of-a-man – a patriot if ever there was one. That's what men and women alike would have said had they a chance to meet up with Hannyways this morning and educate his gob for him: that was the reason (they'd tell him) why their hero's picture was hanging almost sacredly on our walls alongside the bespectacled pope and The Blessed Virgin and The Sacred Heart: that was the reason why the first thing to greet you when you set foot in The Welcoming Room was the man himself (unless you were that thundering eejit, Hannyways). That's what they'd have told him. Enough said.

With the sun shining and it being a grand bit-of-a-day until then, the antics of Hannyways was too much for Bohorlody and he gave Hannyways an answer that he knew would boil the inside of his chest: 'And what is that prime upstart of yeers – De Valera? Tell me this – what is he only a half-breed Spanish basthard!'

At Bohorlody's cruel jibe we were beginning to enjoy the morning's bit of sport tremendously – especially the change that suddenly appeared on Hannyways' face; for the harsh words had almost knocked the pipe out of his impudent gob and he appeared to swoon in an utter faint on top of his horse-and-cart. Indeed for a minute or two Bohorlody thought it likely that the old goat was going to fall down out of the cart and hit his brazen head off of the road. Of course we knew that Bohorlody could be every bit as big a reprobate as Hannyways – that he was always looking for a good long-winded argument like this one – that, when it came to politics, the two of them were evenly matched with one another and a good bit more stubborn than the jinnet and the pony leading their carts.

Bohorlody Arrived Home

Bohorlody was about to step down from his horse-and-cart and let fly at Hanniways with his fists when he realized he'd already reached his own flagstones. By this time the jeery fellow had gone up past Cheerful Nan's and was still standing up defiantly in his horse-and-cart: 'That thundering eejit, Hannyways, (cried Bohorlody) – could somebody hand me a reins till I go and hang him – or at least a rock to put hopping off of his brazen skull the next time I see him?'

He unwound the reins from the creamery tanks and threw himself down from the lace of the cart. He tied the pony to the haggart singletree. He could still hear Hannyways singing like a morning cockerel on a dungheap. Before he set foot inside the haggart he said a silent little prayer to The Blessed Virgin – that the Devil might come along during the night – that he might snuggle up close beside Hannyways – that he might chastise his gobby tongue for him – that he might ask him to come and sit beside him in the burning corner of hell before the month was out.

He Hadn't Time To Draw His Breath

He found himself awfully dry after listening to Hannyways. He was about to go in the half-door and get a mug of water from the bucket before taking up the tanks of Easy-does-it and Red Scissors. He hadn't time, however, to draw his breath when (damn the bit) he was confronted by a galaxy of his children. There they were – sitting in a ring round the upturned ass-and-car and their faces a comedy of mournfulness. He was already in a foul humour from the insults of Hannyways and this was a sad way to be welcoming their own father back home:

'Father-father-father!' they all began to bawl, led on by his eldest son (Barbaha): 'Listen-listen! Please listen to us! We have been out in the yard all morning – waiting for you to come home and give us the law.'

'Fair play to ye,' said Bohorlody, nodding his head. And again he reminded himself that when things went astray – whenever an argument rose up between any of the household members – it was his job to address the rest of them and give them out the law.

'We'll Go To Law'

'Right, byze, get the chairs out, let ye. We'll go to law.'

He'd listen to all the arguments and (wise man that he was) he'd give his children his verdict. Himself and (if need be) his wife (The Dainty Woman) would administer justice fair-and-square for each one of them to clearly contemplate. It had always been like this. They knew it. There had been times in the past when the law said that the guilty child had to get himself a belting with the razor-strop – times when one of them had to be pelted into the stream – times when another one of them had to get himself the full contents of the bucket of water down on top of his condemned head.

'Fair play to ye again,' said Bohorlody somewhat bemusedly and yet a bit more indifferently this time. His children's greeting hadn't been enough to remove the sourness and sickness that he felt from the disgraceful carry-on of Hannyways. Indeed (had they known it) he was in no mood this morning to listen to any of their childish worries.

Then (as if reading his mind) up spoke the brave Barbaha:

'Father – ye know how we've always needed yeer advice. After trying out our own bouts of the law we find ourselves well and truly beaten – there's nothing for it but to go to law with yer own good self – ye'll surely give us yeer verdict like ye've done in the past – there's no better man on this earth than yeerself.'

In all his born days this was the biggest mouthful of words that Bohorlody had ever heard pouring out of Barbaha's mouth:

'Grand to ye again!' said he, warming to the theme. He was secretly delighted with the high praise that Barbaha had just heaped on him as the leader of the house. His good humour was restored.

He Had His Doubts Still

Like them – he still had one or two little doubts nagging at him about his children's ability to refer to the law in his absence. He recalled the last time they had gone to law before he'd a chance to get home and give them his own final verdict. The misery of it haunted him to this day – how could he forget it? It was no laughing-matter. The hens from Timmy Bellow's Ragwort Field had found themselves a small hole in the briars near his ash-pit: 'Why shouldn't we come in here (they thought) and lay a little egg or two for ourselves in the ash-pit?' And in through the gap they came – more than a dozen of them at a time.

'Why shouldn't we eat a little grain in here, while we're at it (they thought)? Then the little trespassers found their way into Bohorlody's yard and were in the act of eating the oats and spuds from the galavanize tray near the ass-and-car when the children spotted them. They shooshed them up the yard with their hands until they had trapped them inside in The Welcoming Room.

What were they going to do about these thieving hens? Father wasn't home. There was no time to waste. There and then they decided they'd have to go to law and hold a trial. Barbaha kept watch over the hens with the yard-brush and kept them imprisoned inside the half-door. The brothers and sisters sat in a circle on a bench and then solemnly went to law. It was the first time they had done this sort of thing and they felt a bit uncomfortable. However, it didn't take them long before they reached a unanimous verdict and found the hens guilty of trespassing. Though they were none too certain what the penalty for this crime should be, they made a neat little gallows. Then they strung up and hanged every damned one of those chickens before throwing them back into Timmy's field.

As with Adam and Eve, there followed a good deal of shame – a kind of nakedness to their spirits. So they kept themselves away from the yard and the chastising dishcloth of The Dainty Woman. When evening came they were even more ashamed of having hanged Timmy's chickens and they wondered whether it had been right to do so: 'We'll have law a second time as soon as father cooms home,' they said and they each nodded their heads and waited in silence for Bohorlody to come home and be their judge. Whatever it would be, it'd be acceptable to all.

But an hour later – as soon as he came back into the yard after setting his traps and snares on the edge of The Bog Wood – Bohorlody had the rage of a pure madman on him:

'That the Devil may shit on top of ye, ye little ninny-hammers.'

They'd never seen him in such a fury and he stamped his big boots almost through the floor and hastened for the sallyswitch to redden their legs. Then he raised his voice and let a roar out of him:

'I'll now give ye a lengthy epistle, indeed I will – one that ye'll remember for a long while to coom' – and he whaled into them with the sallyswitch till they were black and blue and he banned them from ever again carrying out the law without reporting first to him for his approval or disapproval – whatever the case might be. After that he kicked out from under them the bench on which they'd been sitting and he left them in a tearful pile on top of one another in the yard. Then he stormed out across the stream and went off to drink six good pints of The Black Doctor so as to wash the taste of his children out of his mouth.

The Time For Forgiveness

However, live and let live (he thought). And even before he'd gone off to the creamery this morning he had cooled down a good bit and had felt that the time was ripe to forgive his children and to let them have a share in the law a second time. And now – after hearing the lofty praises so sincerely bestowed on him by Barbaha, he had relaxed even more. Their warm welcome for him when he'd stepped into the yard told him that he should try and give serious attention to whatever was troubling them on this occasion and should attempt to drive their sorrow out of their minds:

'What, tell me, is the reason for wishing me to go to law with ye?'

Barbaha again spoke up on behalf of the others: 'After a great deal of talk we felt that our beloved dog (Rapper) ought to die – and the sooner he dies, the better. He's been killing the sheep for far too long. He's been eating the eggs for far too long. And eggs as ye know, are scarce everywhere since the blasted war. This morning he went a step too far. After biting Arse-and-Pockets in the arse he has pulled the legs of Moll-the-Man's daughter almost out of their sockets and she's lying on her back inside on a bed in The Roaring Town hospital.'

'A terrible thing – a terrible thing,' said Bohorlody, shaking his head and walking round the yard. 'And what kind of death have ye agreed for him in all yeer discussions?'

Again Barbaha spoke up: 'When we found ourselves hanging the hens we did a bad thing – a very bad thing indeed – and we are as sorry as hell over it and ask your forgiveness. And now – we are in need of yeer wise advice, father, since we ourselves are not sure of how the killing of him ought to be done. Only you know how to handle a matter as serious as this one.

You – and only you – have the reins for the hanging of Rapper, father.

You – and only you – have the gun for the bullet to his head.

You – and only you – have the sally-hole in Bog Boundless for the drowning of him.

Father (please! please!) we need you to give us the family law. We need it now. Go on, do – give us the law!'

'What would ye have me do?' said Bohorlody.

'In view of yeer deep love for Rapper from his earliest puppy-eared days, we have made an agreement among ourselves – that is, if you yourself would agree to it – that the bullet to the head would be the best possible thing for him – and the least painful death for him.'

Bohorlody was as pleased as punch with the fine way his children had come to an agreement over Rapper and with their approach to the law and their proposed death-sentence for him. He took the hand of his eldest son in his and he shook it warmly:

'Dammit – ye children have addressed the law more than well. And (mee brave byze) yeer attempt has been a brave one – almost as good as I could have done meeself. Fair play to the lot of ye!'

His wife (The Dainty Woman) was struggling out along the yard with an armful of washing. She stopped at the side of the pighouse and cocked her ear. Rapper himself lay sleeping indifferently in under the ass-and-car. From time to time his tail would flop about like an old broken piece of rope as he dislodged a fly.

Eggs. Eggs. Eggs.

Eggs. Eggs. Eggs. The Dainty Woman was all the time thinking about her eggs. Seemingly no-one had a single egg in the place, thanks to the thievery of Rapper. There wasn't a soul these days, who wasn't pressing hard to get rid of this wretched dog – as much as Bohorlody loved him. In the back of every farmer's head was the hanging rope or the gun or the sack for drowning him.

The lack of eggs had thrown The Dainty Woman's mind back to those earlier days during The Civil Strife when there wasn't an egg to be got. It was a most shameful period (she reflected) in Rookery Rally's history. May God forgive the fighting men: families were at war with each other the length and breadth of Copperstone Hollow – families who had lived amicably enough all their lives. Suddenly they'd become bent on killing one another and the smell of cordite from their guns was everywhere. Some took up the gun for De Valera: other took up the gun for Michael Collins. Above in Kilnamona – a few miles left of Mureeny the battle went on for a whole day. It started at nine in the morning. It died down at four in the evening. No wonder the frightened hens weren't laying their eggs! The cows in their dread would give very little milk either that day. Four young lads, not more than twenty years-of-age (although no-one ever counted birthdays) three of them Free Staters and one for De Valera – had been slaughtered. The women ran out the doors in a heap. They hurried down to the churchyard gate. They saw their dead sons spread out in a line in front of the church door. A pathetic sense of guilt, shame and misery silently filled their hearts. Once more they took off their black aprons as was the custom. They threw them over the faces of their wasted sons. They knelt down together (friend and foe alike) on the bloody ground and they prayed together. Only then (the poor shivering women) did they begin to bawl like a pack of sick donkeys.

The priest at the time (Canon Lofty-Step) came out from the church in his vestments to do the necessary obsequies and administer The Last Sacraments. He handed out several rosary-beads to the women. He blessed each one of them. He told them to go and offer up prayers at Our Lady's Altar – that the killings and the lootings would stop – that all our men would get a stem of sense. Night, noon and morning the women and children were skinning their knees raw and praying in front of The Sacred Heart picture.

A Bit Of A Laughing-stock

It was in those days that the present high-faluting Hannyways had become a bit of a hero and also a bit of a clown in one and the same week- a sort of miracle. He had put on his wife's apron and gone off to the hayshed where for the last three mornings his wife's favourite little guinea-hen (Rosie) was deliriously cackling as she laid her eggs. Hannyways climbed the ladder. He was delighted to find six newlaid eggs. He put them into his apron.

He was coming down the ladder and making his way very carefully – eggs being so precious. Blast the bit – at that precise moment didn't the guns start blazing away at full force. To his eternal credit (and we talked about it for months to come) Hannyways pelted his body off of the last few rungs of the ladder and dived towards the ditch. Mindful of his precious apron-load of eggs, he had the good sense at the very last minute to twist his body away from the metal stanchion of the hayshed whilst he was falling out into space. In that moment of glory he was better than a tomcat in the air and not a single one of the six eggs was smashed. It's sad to say, however, that he collided with the upright stanchion of the iron hayshed and was knocked out cold.

When the firing of the guns was finished and the whole of Rookery Rally rose up from the ground they found the poor fellow lying unconscious (if not dead entirely) on a sop of hay. The news spread quicker than lightning: 'Hannyways has broken his skull in two places: Hannyways has not broken a single one of his eggs'. He was the hero of the hour – indeed he was.

A fortnight later, however, these words of praise were to be rubbed off of his slate: the same fellow utterly disgraced himself by putting his soot-cleaning rods up the chimney with a white sheet on top of them for his enemies to see. Again the news spread fast and this time the old gossips (those Weeping Mollys) were in full pursuit to bring home to us the truth of the matter:

'Hannyways has shown the white feather – he has shown the white feather! Yes he has! Hannyways has played the craven coward!' And from that day onwards, (at least for the next month-and-a-half and until the rest of Rookery Rally had the heart to forgive him) Hannyways was given the royal name of *Captain Shun-the-Battle*.

That Devil-of-a-dog

And now once more we found ourselves with not a single egg to call our own – all thanks to that devil-of-a-dog, Rapper. Being four years old, you'd think that Bohorlody's black-and-white collie would have had a bit more sense in him. Matters were worse: he was not only the destroyer of our women's fine eggs (hen's eggs: duck's eggs: geese's eggs) but added to that – he'd become the killer of Old Sam's lambs.

As A Young Dog

Bohorlody had had the rearing of Rapper ever since Moll-the-Man gave him to him as a puppy. He had gone up to her house to play the forty-five-hand-wheel game of cards. He recalled the evening well. It was during the magical hour of twilight that Rapper was born on a heap of hay in the brilliant green light of Moll's summertime haggart. The wind in the sunshot leaves was rustling delicately above the little pup's new life. The geese and the hens were marching majestically up to see what all the fuss was about. It was a grand and special occasion.

Bohorlody took the little pup home under his warm jacket. He started to feed him on a bran-mash of bread-and-milk with a dash of pepper to keep him trim and healthy. Very soon the two of them became as close to each other as two sides of a sheet, always gazing trustingly into each other's dreamy eyes – and the little fellow with those lugubrious looks that'd break your heart and he all the time wagging his cute little tail. Whichever way Bohorlody came home from Curl 'n' Stripes' drinking-shop with his newspapers and his packages of biscuits – be it the Old Road, The New Road, The Creamery Road or The Open Road – Rapper was sure to come scampering along to meet him, leaping up on him when he was halfways home and his tail thrashing joyfully and his tongue lolling out. Bohorlody couldn't believe it. None of us could. It was enough to make you doubt your own senses. It was as if Rapper had run out of the yard after being pulled towards Bohorlody through the air by some sort of supernatural magnet – as if witchcraft had caused him to come flying through space and time itself – to travel the correctly chosen road and come trotting home gaily by his master's side.

None of us had the brains to fathom out how he, a mere youngster, knew which of these roads his master would be taking home from the shop. Nor was Rapper like any of Bohorlody's other previous dogs – silly little fools, all of them. They would go scampering hare-like ahead of him across The Pool Field. When they saw a rabbit you'd see them cannonading (oh, the frustration) into each other (the hysterical little squeaks out of them) – allowing their quarry to escape and vanish. In contrast, Rapper always had the good sense to follow at Bohorlody's heels. He had always been like his very own shadow, a perfect little dog.

Pure Genius

On those memorable days when Lord and Lady Elegance brought their dogcart out travelling to meet the wind coming down from The Hills-of-the-Past, Rapper would perform acts of pure genius for them. He climbed up onto Easy-does-it's Stile. At Bohorlody's whistle he jumped down and landed on his shoulders. He leapt over his ashplant when he held it three feet in the air. He rolled over at his command and would speak up with the loudest of barks. Then he'd sit on his haunches and put his nose between his front paws to beg subserviently, his brown nose peeping out coyly and flirtingly. He was as good as The Daffy-Duck Circus. And oh, how he made the fine rich lord and his lady shake their dogcart asunder with their fits of polite yet hearty laughter.

At other times, Rapper went scurrying off down the yard and into the haggart, chasing the chickens and their little chicks good-humouredly all around the windy grasses. He almost blew the little creatures away with the harmless heat of his milky body. In between times he sneaked behind the hayreek. Then he sprang out (oh, the prankster that was in him!) and terrorized the ladylike flock of geese as they went marching through the haggart and out as far as the potato-sack on the stick. He was laughter itself as he sent them flapping and squawking in a musical harmony to the top of the dungheap near the far ditch. They were enjoying these games of cat 'n' mouse every bit as much as himself. Of course that was long before he took a liking to ripping open the bellies of lambs and devouring their carcasses.

The Air Of A Young Poet

Time flew by and as the seasons changed there came into Rapper the air of a young poet. For ages, it seemed, he would sit on the ass-and-car at the bottom of the yard. The children could see him watching those aimless fluffy clouds above him as they drifted across the sky on their way to Clare and Galway and on towards The Great Ocean. In an almost dreamlike state he slid down from the cart and dazed himself across the yard, as though mimicking those very same cottony clouds. In and out he wafted amongst the brown and yellow chicks – through the green and rusty docks and the mallows he wafted – without ever hurting a single one of the fowl and ignoring the charms of the sow.

He Became Another Dog

But sadly everything changed and the children knew it. It was as though Rapper had become an unquiet dog – a total stranger. Had he forgotten those days when he'd follow Bohorlody out by the pighouse gap, his nostrils breathing in the raw air of the early morning, his ears listening to the twittering of the little birds in Timmy Bellow's Lane? Had he forgotten those days when just the clink of his master's spoon on his mug of tea, the ring of his knife against the kettle, were enough for him – telling him it was time for him to set off with Bohorlody? Six times a day they had strolled together to the well inside Old Sam's grove for the buckets of spring-well water.

Intoxicated By Wind, Sun And Rain

Those days were now gone. In his heart – in his soul – Rapper had developed an inexplicable exhilaration awaiting to be satisfied – had become intoxicated by the harping of the wind and the sunlight and rain. Like any young poet (the simpleton that he was) he was no longer content to sit moping by the fire with his nose twitching – no longer content to watch the uneven flames flickering up the chimney and listen to the crickets serenading him. He began to run races with imaginary dogs and shadows round and round in The Thistle Field. He fought with the scintillating gleams of the sunlight. He danced with the shadows of the purple and yellow wildflowers.

Rookery Rally Was Too Small For Him

Rookery Rally was soon too small a place to hold a soul like his and to bring him the everlasting happiness he desired. Like many a dog before him he craved for the fairy woods of Lisnagorna and its hidden pathways. He looked to the hills of The Mountainy Men and longed to be up there in The Hills-of-The-Past – up there at the end of our Open Road and Sheep's Cross – up there where the wild dogs lived – dogs bigger than black lions. It was as though they were sending secret messages down to him. He could see in such places unaccountable possibilities for adventure, which we humans could never imagine with our limited eyesight.

What Was Bohorlody To Do?

And now as the lawmakers sat in the yard on their chairs Bohorlody found himself in a state of unhappy contemplation. Himself and The Dainty Woman were like other households in Rookery Rally who had lost a number of their dogs to the call of the wild and had to get rid of them in order to destroy the bad luck that such dogs brought on farms. His sister (Dowager) said it was an ancient curse, which had now come to Bohorlody's doorstep. Moll-the-Man talked of the curse of the *come-hither* having been put on him. Dowager herself called it *the evil eye*. She too had been given a curse when she once found a bag of cattle-bones down near the metal bridge. They had been thrown in over her ditch just below John's Gate – a well–known curse that she called *the pishogues.* Everyone had their suspicion at the time as to which precise fairyman among us had the power of the *come-hither, the evil eye* or *the pishogues.* But they feared to speak out in case the priest might damn them from the altar.

Wild Dogs

Bohorlody now found that Rapper had joined up with a pack of wild dogs that had recently arrived in The Valley of The Pig. This was a new one on him. His dog began to stay out the whole of the night. What was he thinking of (the simpleton)? At four o'clock in the morning hadn't he a warm nest for himself by the side of his own turf fire to warm his tail if he wanted to? In Lisnagorna two newborn lambs had been found frightened out of their lives and then their bellies ripped open. Rapper's name was mentioned. Next day Red Buckles, on his way back from the creamery, reported that there had been a tremendous battle between Rapper and the father of the six young badgers below in The Bog Wood. From that moment on Rapper's right front paw would be crooked and he'd spend the rest of his days limping. He had barely escaped with his life. And yet there was no chastising him. He had lost all his nobility – all his previous goodness. It was clear that his relentless battles with sheep and badgers were not going to be enough for him – that the taste of their blood was not going to be sufficient to calm the bloodlust which had unfortunately risen up inside in his dog-soul.

It Got Worse

It got worse. The old man, Toes-Apart, had two fine sons. They almost killed each other one Sunday afternoon in their efforts to shoot Rapper, who was killing their lambs faster than they could count them. They made an ambush for him at either end of Patsy-Mick's hayshed. They lay in wait – armed with Toes-Apart's two new guns.

Rapper climbed the five-barred gate. They saw him heading towards them up along the lane. From opposite sides of the ditch they let fly their enraged cartridges. They entirely missed killing Rapper but came within an inch of shooting the eyebrows off of one another. The Devil's father was in the soul of that blasted dog (they said).

Some of the pellets sprayed themselves onto Toes-Apart's favourite hen, hitting her in her lower wing. From that day onwards she was one of the comedy turns of Rookery Rally. She'd lost whatever sense of timing – whatever sense of direction and balance – she previously had. When the wind came roaring through Toes-Apart's haggart it blew this young hen off sideways as though she were performing an amusing ballet through the air. And when she landed on her feet she came dancing, dancing, dancing her little tippy-toe steps sideways towards the henhouse, frightening every duck and goose in sight with her strange new dance-steps. Had you a piano, you could waltz the music to it.

Toes-Apart

As a rule Toes-Apart was a very shy man like many of The Mounainy Men. We never heard a word out of him. But this time he needed no fire-bellows to fan the anger, which had risen up in him and which brought him down from his warm fireside above in The Valley of The Pig. He marched straight into Bohorlody's Welcoming Room. Without so much as taking a drop of the holywater at the door he crossed the floor:

'My family is decent, as ye well know,' said he, facing up to Bohorlody. 'But that renegade-of-a-dog must die and die he will'.

There wasn't another word out of him – he being the very shy man. He snatched up his hat and turned back upon Bohorlody from the half-door:

'Either you kill him or I'll do it for you.' And he flung himself out of the yard and back up to The Valley of The Black Cattle. Bohorlody was left looking after him and scratching his head. Enough said.

A Desire For Human Blood

By this time Rapper was doomed to an early death for he and his wickedness had made himself too many enemies to count on ten fingers. In his craze for adventure his madness was running away with him. Eggs and sheep had at last proved a monotonous diet to be trying his teeth on. He had another little thought – a new one. He'd like to try something a bit tastier – he'd like to give his tongue the added taste of human blood. In his dog's mind a man or a woman's rank didn't matter a damn. He'd as soon lay into the britches of Lord Elegance as take a bite out of a tinker's backside. But for the moment – neither his mighty lordship nor the lowly tinker had any need to fear. A day had arrived when Rapper (in an attempt to satisfy his thirst for human blood) would lay his teeth into another poor man's rear quarters – the traveling Jewman, Arse-and-Pockets.

Rank and Order

In the crudity amongst us we knew the order and the ranking of all mankind – or we thought we did. We believed that the literate folk of The Roaring Town were a step or two above us semi-literates here on the hillslopes. The hillslopes in their turn were ranked a step or two above The Mountainy Men in as much as those poor scholars had hardly ever had the chance of getting their nose stuck into a book and devouring the learning therein. They were often miles away from the nearest schoolhouse and, what with tending to their father's several black cattle and horses, they had more than enough to be doing at home. They met the schoolchildren coming home (that's what they said) when they themselves were driving down to the shop for the sacks of flour.

Then there were others below the rest of us. From as early as the first of March we had seen a number of these cross-country travellers rising up amongst us like the new shoots in the fields and coming to our door. There was the polite little pedlar-woman: there were the two heather girls with their good-luck charms: there were the fortune-tellers. We'd give them each a cut of bread soaked in tea as well as a pitcher of milk after first sprinkling some of it in the four corners of The Welcoming Room so as not to give away our good luck. We'd give them a penny or two and they'd retreat backwards out the yard – all the time blessing us and our several ancestors back along. And then there were the rascally tinkers (themselves and their insolence) who from days immemorial had come here to steal away our asses and horses, selling them in neighbouring valleys. We'd meet these rascals with a withering stare and reach for the tongs to pelt it out across the yard after their skedaddling heels. There wasn't one of us that didn't rain down unprintable curses on them when we were saying our prayers at Sunday Mass for they had left us without a yardbrush and they'd take the two eyes out of your head if you let them. More than once we had set the dog onto the seat of their britches. Not a turkey – not a goose (the blackguards!) – was ever safe from the likes of them. They came like the fox just after twilight:

'Ah, there's nothing like a boiled or baked hen (they said).'

When you looked out the window the next day they had made a clean getaway, having slaughtered not one but a dozen hens and possibly having scampered off with a sheep – if not the entire ass himself.

But being a Jew, poor Arse-and-Pockets was cast even below the likes of them – at the bottom of the entire heap by every man, woman and child. The priest didn't have to inform us that it was Arse-and-Pocket's heathen brothers who had nailed Our Blessed Saviour to that big cross on Calvary Hill. We knew how to treat a Jew like Arse-and-Pockets. Shame on us! Be it tinker or Jew, wasn't Ignorance a fine thing here in Rookery Rally?

The Dainty Woman

There was, of course, the exception to any rule. The Dainty Woman was full of sympathy for everyone and she called Arse-and-Pockets the stone that the builder rejected: 'Yes, he's a Jew,' said she. 'And does that mean he's got to be an outcast among the rest of us?' As you might have guessed, The Dainty Woman had been so called because of her daintiness of spirit and she always had this soft spot for Arse-and-Pockets.

The Yearly Routine

It was the same story every year. As soon as the heavy snows were gone away and the new springtime was on its way, you could look out for Arse-and-Pockets trudging up The Creamery Road. This was a sign that the year had truly started. These last seven years this little scarecrow-of-a-man had been appearing amongst us as regular as clockwork. Little children, seeing him for the first time, were frightened to death at the sight of him. To them he was like a white-faced ghost from out of their storybook. Suddenly they'd see him standing in front of them on their flagstones. But he was as harmless as the day he was born.

Where did he come from? Where was he going? Like the rivers all around us, we didn't know for sure. The truth of the matter (said By-Jiggery, his wife nodding) was that he came from the back streets of Limerick. He owned a spanking new pony-and-trap, which he filled to the gills with unpronouncable haberdasheries. Inside in The Roaring Town The Widda-Widda-Woman had a spare room set aside for him above her stables where he slept and rested his sore legs. Each day he rose with the dawn and put on his gaberdine suit and hat. It had a threadbare shine on it from constant wear. He drove his pony-and-trap and his two brown suitcases into the barn of Din-Din-Dinny-the-Stammerer. From there he proceeded to walk the length and breadth of Rookery Rally. For us (as with the children) he was a timeless shade, who came and went from out of the heavens along with our uncertain weather.

He Was Here Again

He was here again now on the flagstones, the sun brightening the yard. His red-raw hands were stretched almost to the ground from the two heavy suitcases he was lugging at his sides with their secret haberdasheries. His oversized arms were like the schoolbook Guy Fawkes on the rack and his raggy raincoat was flapping mournfully in the breeze. The Dainty Woman could see that he was a bit shakier in his limbs this time round, poor man. His gaberdine suit which was once a royal navy in colour was now faded to a light blue.

He stopped at the yard stream and The Dainty Woman ran out eagerly to meet him and see what he had in his suitcases this time round. Barbaha and the other children ran out after her. They marveled at the sight of the two huge suitcases and couldn't understand for the life of them how a small man like himself could carry such a heavy load.

'How are ye, Arse-and-Pockets? Ye're welcome at my door,' said The Dainty Woman.

He made her a polite little bow. He had a list of household goods as long as Tipperary:

'I have ribbons to sell for your fine hair. I have sewing stuffs for your man's socks. I have elastic for your knickers and your garters. I have hairpins for your chignons. I have ointments for the sore jaw. I have secret herbs for the piles on your arse and a few other seldom-mentioned country cures.'

'Stop-stop-stop, will ye! Give us no more of yeer litanies,' said The Dainty Woman, holding her sides and laughing. 'But tell me this, have ye razorblades and have ye shaving soap?'

'I have, ma'am. I have that.'

'And have ye flypapers and have ye boot polish and have ye a scrub-brush?'

'That too, ma'am. And I have cheap watches, in case you might be making the price of a pig!'

'That'll do, that'll do,' said The Dainty Woman good-naturedly and she gave him a wink and a little one of her glowing smiles.

It Was A Glorious Day

The day was glorious, just like those recent days in April. Arse-and-Pockets had always loved the countryside. It reminded him of his warm homeland far away in the east. It had the smell of the new-mown grasses and the air was full of the greenfinches. The crab-trees around Easy-does-it's Stile were beginning to bloom. The ditches were full of blossoms, especially the honeysuckle and the foxgloves on Cheerful Nan's Heights. He could hear the cattle bawling below Old Sam's wire-fence. The nervous little man smiled across the yard at The Dainty Woman.

His Screams

Up untll now other passersby had had the good fortune to escape the savage jaws of Rapper. But on this sad day such was not the fate of poor Arse-and-Pockets. To this day the children awake from their sleep some nights and hear his horrified screams ringing off of the flagstones out at the stream.

And what were the men doing while this was going on? They certainly didn't come hopping over the ditches to see what was happening. Whereas the women always blessed themselves against harm coming to anyone, our fine men (without so much as a blink-of-an-eye) were usually praying that their dog would do his work and tear a chunk out of some tinker's rear quarters. Even the gable-end of the poor man like Arse-and-Pockets would please them. Ah, the cruelty in them – to see the dance-steps of one of their traveling visitors as he went scorching up the road, holding onto his arse for dear life – and they laughing their sides off. Ah, the incivilities of our men and how different their hearts were from most of our gentle women. Wouldn't you like to put a match to their britches!

As if to answer our men's prayers Rapper came out of nowhere and leapt clean over the half-door. There and then he leveled the misfortunate Arse-and-Pockets to the ground and (ah, this evil wretch-of-a-dog) set his teeth firmly into the poor man's britches. He then began to taste the foreign blood of the Jew in earnest. What a terrible sight! Would it ever be forgotten?

His Hidden Parts (Those Private Credentials)

Bohorlody's older daughters were accustomed to whispering jokingly with one another in regard to a certain part of Arse-and-Pockets' secret body-parts. May God forgive them their blushes, the little flippity-jibbits! None of them were strangers to their own brothers' bodies in the overcrowded household, there being so many of them. In previous years these bold girls had given Arse-and-Pockets more than one or two mugfuls of freezing spring-water in the hope that, running silently along inside the ditch, they might see him making his poolie in Timmy Bellows's field before going off on his journey. Whatever their innocent plans, they never found out if he had the special mark of his race on the tip of his private credentials.

The Dainty Woman Ran Into The Yard

With the screams of Arse-and-Pockets ringing in her ears The Dainty Woman ran out into the yard. Barbaha was beside her with the speed of light. Armed with the metal tongs he had brought out a burning sod of turf from The Welcoming Room and, toasting the villainous creature's tail, he relieved Arse-and-Pockets from the dog's teeth. The Dainty Woman picked up the poor misfortunate man and she cradled him in her arms. His cheeks were sunken and yellow. His pained expression had become as vacant as death itself.

'Mercy on us!' screamed The Dainty Woman. 'That basthard-of-a-dog has taken a chunk out of the poor man's arse!'

She Lay Him On The Settlebed

She lay poor Arse-and-Pockets gingerly on the settlebed. Then she boiled up the kettle of water to tend to his wounds. She got down her best goose-wing and she poured out the iodine liberally from her bottle onto it. After she had hushed the children away, who were all gaping at the poor man's agonizing tears, she carefully let down his britches. Gently she eased the iodine onto his upper thigh where the dog had drawn blood from him. She dressed his wounds and soon had him back into middling good shape. She removed his britches from round his boots and sat him by the heat of the fire. With her needle and thread she mended the legs of the britches. She gave him a cup of tea and some soda-bread with jam and sugar on it. Arse-and-Pockets, minus his trousers, drew in the blaze from the fire onto his painful thighs and he began to feel more or less comfortable after that.

To lighten his burden even more, The Dainty Woman took out her purse and she bought from the pile of goods in his suitcases countless little items, which she had no need of and which (worse still) she couldn't afford. She finished off by giving him a dinner fit for Bishop High-Hat himself. She put a little bottle of milk in his sack ('for the journey') after skimming off the top of the cream in case he should run away with her good luck. Wasn't she the noble Samaritan!

His Most Sincere Bow

Abroad in the yard this little scenario came to an end when Arse-and-Pockets gave The Dainty Woman his best and most sincere bow. He showered down innumerable blessings on her and on the rest of the household and on the whole of the Irish race, past and present and to come.

'Stop, will ye!' said the Dainty Woman, her eyes once more full of merry laughter and tears. She couldn't get rid of him out of the yard – so grateful was he as he backed away and kept giving her a string of his foreign blessings. He turned back one more time from the flagstones: 'And may the Lord grant you this, Missus – that you never button an empty arse-pocket from this day forwards!'

That Same Evening

That same evening there was a great deal of commotion at the dinner-table as the children were leathering into their spuds, onions, milk and butter, together with the cabbages and fresh rabbits. They begged their mother to lighten the curiosity of them all – the boys as well as the girls. They were getting on her nerves and, dainty though she was, she had a voice that could sometimes cut like a rasp: 'Ye give me the sick, the whole crew of ye! What in God's name is the matter with ye all? It's Arse-and-Pockets this … and it's Arse-and-Pockets that with ye.' She threw her fork into the potato-champ, which she was stirring onto her plate: 'I'll tell ye this and I'll tell ye no more: I saw his private credentials with mee own two eyes at the fireside. For once and for all, let me tell ye this: Arse-and-Pockets' little privacies are no bigger than an acorn.' And she put her thumb through her middle and fore finger to show the size of it. There was a roar of laughter out of all her daughters. Indeed Bohorlody too – as well as The Dainty Woman and their sons – joined in and they all soon forgot the recent carnage of the poor man's body. And as they golloped down their steaming heap of spuds with their competing forks the girls were constantly interrupted by one or the other of them making the thumb-and-finger gesture. And this was followed by yet another bout of good-natured giggling and laughter all over The Welcoming Room.

But after the dinner the hilarious mood of the household suddenly turned black. They could see the look on Bohorlody's face. It told them that before the week was out there'd be no more Rapper left on this earth – that his hour of execution had arrived.

A Place Called The Sin

Just outside the haggart and on this side of The Thistle Field there was a well-known spot of execution for Rookery Rally dogs. It was a green hollow where strange eyes couldn't see a man performing the dirty deed of killing. This spot was called The Sin. Five noble dogs had already met their death there at the hands of Bohorlody. It was not the hanging-tree behind the cowshed. It was the place for the bullet in the brain. Bohorlody's body shuddered when he thought of the dogs he had killed. Of all the ungracious and savage acts a man could do, this deed – the snatching away of a young dog's life – was almost as fierce as any rape. A dog's death was always dark and dirty. At the moment of death Bohorlody felt an icy misery coming up from The Spirit World. He saw it entering into the dying dog's soul.

It was always the same. Even with the neighbours' dogs – it was Bohorlody, who always had to do the dirty deed. A week ago Growler (Easy-does-it's youngest dog) took the legs of Herald-the-post's daughter from off the ass-and-car and it was Bohorlody, who had dragged him out to The Sin and had the shooting of him. I tell you this: Easy-does-it was never able to hang or shoot or drown one of his dogs. He had three of them in all. He had a dog for the hens: he had a dog for the cows: he had a dog that'd snap its jaws around the britches of any marauding tinkers, who might have a notion of stealing his ass or one or two of his precious cows – a dog that'd clear any young tinker-lad from the half-door if he had the impudence to come back a second time (having already been given one gallon) for a second gallon of milk for his baby brother.

Skinny-Minny

Last week Skinny-Minny's father died. He had been dying for a year-and-a-half. In the end the good woman had almost cursed him into his grave. Those last final stages were filled with his bed being constantly wet and she always turning and twisting him and changing him. And then at last he was laid low (the Lord be good to him) in his shirt in his coffin and his mother's own rosary-beads wrapped round his fist.

We all traipsed up to The Valley of the Pig to pray over him and to lay at her door the respects due to so fine a man. With a shy little curtsy Skinny-Minny came out to meet the droves of us in her yard. She gave us the dignified and customary handshake. One after another we told her how sorry we were for her:

'Sorry for yeer troubles, Skinny-Minny – sorry for yeer troubles,' we kept repeating.

'The same to you – the same to you,' said Skinny-Minny, returning our sympathies, her hands nearly falling off of her from all the fine handshaking we were giving her and she giving back to us. Poor Skinny-Minny! The shy creature had never buried anyone before and she didn't know what words (like *thankyou*) she should have said back to us. Indeed she alarmed us all by offering sympathy to every one of us for our own little troubles when it was she (and no-one else) who had her father lying dead there in the middle of the bed! The litany went on for the rest of the morning: Skinny-Minny giving us her little curtsies (fit for Lady Elegance) and she telling us how sorry she was for troubling us with her father's death. Nobody in living memory had ever said *'sorry for your troubles'* back to the sympathisers and wellwishers at a corpse-house. Some of the rougher women took fits of coughing up their sleeve to stop themselves laughing.

Poor Skinny-Minny. What a state she was in! And now it was all over. She had no man left to reap the corn for her – no man left to mow the hay or plough the soil for her. Where on earth was she going to raise a shilling for herself? And if the troubles of her father's death were not enough for her, when the wake was finally finished and all the fine drinking was over, what do you think lay in store for her? The next blessed night she was herself lying inside in The Roaring Town Hospital on the broad of her back with the print of Rapper's teeth all over her arse and the legs half-chewed out of her sockets where he had dragged her down from her ass-and-car.

Rapper, you wickedest of all dogs ever born – what evil spirit made you do it – made you attack Skinny-Minny this very day when she was about to go down and dig her own father's grave and bury him? Even if it hadn't been Barbaha and his brothers and sisters who had gone to law with their father and pronounced their lawful verdict for his execution, Rapper's vicious attack on Skinny-Minny's legs would have been enough for the rest of us to sentence him to the bullet.

However, it was The Dainty Woman herself (mild-mannered though she was) who proved more forceful than the rest of the household in suggesting that The Family Law now be vigorously enforced on Rapper. Whatever Easy-does-it or Toes-Apart might say about the sheep-killing tactics of Rapper, it was the loss of her eggs (for she hadn't a single egg on the dresser) that put the final curtain on Rapper's fate and handed Bohorlody the rifle.

A Dog Of Pure Indolence

For Bohorlody it was something more than that: it was the realization that Rapper had turned into a dog of pure indolence and self-luxury. To look at him – you'd swear he was three times his age. He no longer concerned himself with the essential job of all our Rookery Rally dogs: the chastising of the foxes. These devils had left us with an almost empty henhouse and there'd soon be not a drop of soup left for us. To see our eggs disappearing by the dozen was one thing. But worse again was the sight of our hens disappearing by the score.

The comical lads below in Curl 'n' Stripes' drinking-shop gave each other the nudge and the wink when they saw Bohorlody coming in the door and the message-bell tinkled after him: 'Bohorlody, coom here a minute, we want you. We hear tell that Simon-not-so-simple has begun painting his manly gander and the rest of his fierce geese with a bright red paint – to confuse the foxes. Blasht you, Bohorlody! Coom on, tell us the truth and don't keep us waiting – what colour are ye painting yeer geese against the invader these days?' Not knowing how to get Rapper to put paid to these devilish foxes, Bohorlody was filled with embarrassment as he hurried away from the drinkers on their barrel-planks and tried to get their laughter out of his ears. Bad cess to you, Rapper! It was time for you to die.

A Time To Die

Bohorlody was inside in The Welcoming Room, helping the Dainty Woman to prepare the dinner. Rapper was lounging across the firelight, half-hidden under the back table. His nose was once more stuck between his paws as he sniffed at the pungency of the burnt-log smoke when he should have been sent hopping out over the half-door with a good sound kick in the arse. Bohorlody, however, was patient. Bohorlody was tolerant – for now.

Such A Mournful Sight

Was there ever so mournful a sight, now that the law of Barbaha and the rest of the children, the law of Bohorlody and the Dainty Woman had sentenced Rapper to die?

Bohorlody was chewing thoughtfully on his pipe:

'Rapper! Rapper! What made ye do it? With the training and the nurturing I gave ye these last four years – what in God's holy name made ye go and steal the scarce eggs of the women of Rookery Rally? Remember Hannyways. Ask him about his hen's eggs. It's as bad as stealing the crutches from the poor cripples outside the hospital gates in town. And what made ye go and tear the arse off of poor Arse-and-Pockets? Rapper! Rapper! – you, who came to Mass behind the horse-and-cart with me each and every Sunday morning – you, who lay across my bed all winter long and banished the fleas and The Boodeemen. Tell me this: what on earth made ye do it?' Poor Bohorlody couldn't get his head round it.

Bohorlody's Reflections

He got up from his chair at the fire. He went on ladling out his mug of goose-soup. He gave another few mugfuls to The Dainty Woman and his children. His mind was elsewhere. He carried on thinking: 'I've been misfortunate in mee dogs – in all of them. I have loved them all – only too well. And they have turned out pure rogues and even worse. I have taught them all their duties: when to be suppliant: when to be the beggar: when to jump the five-barred gate: when to leap the haggart-field singletree. And all for what? – for The Devil to come alive inside each one of them and for all of them to meet with an untimely fate – me, engineering the gallows for a few of them – me, drowning others – me, shooting others here in The Sin behind the Thistle Field.

'Rapper! Rapper! How well ye learnt the art of the clean snap! How well ye learnt the science of pulling the two legs of Skinny-Minny almost out of her sockets! Why was yeer brain unable to learn the skills that would catch those goddamn foxes?

The Slyness Of Bohorlody

From the time the children had agreed on Rapper's execution Bohorlody had befriended his dog like never before. In the planning and the scheming for his coming execution he gave Rapper his sop of milk and bread and his bran-mash whenever his hungry eyes looked into his own eyes – anything to keep him inside in The Welcoming Room and keep him close by. At other times he took him out into the yard and playfully rolled him round amongst the geese and the hens before the two of them came back in again to the turf-fire. He had the entire trust of Rapper (he always had) – now more than ever. Without a bit of cunning to his preparations the planned execution would come to nothing. He knew that Rapper had four fine legs on him – faster than the legs of the tinker (Swallytails) who ran from the pelted tongs of Slipperslapper after he'd spat his tobacco-juice misguidedly into the burner on her hearthstone – faster than Simon-not-so-simple's legs, the time that sympathetic animal-lover ran from Handsome Johnnie's yard when he was about to slit the angry pig's throat as it lay on its back, kicking bits out of the horse-and-cart. To see the speed of Swallytails and Simon-not-so-simple you'd think they were training for the jinnet-race at The Show-Fair. However (given half a chance) Rapper's legs would beat the pair of them hands down.

The Silence

The silence then followed. Bohorlody looked at his dog and he thought to himself: 'Rapper, ye'll never get a chance to throw yeer beautiful legs away from me. It's you (I know) that is practically blind in yer left eye where ye got the fine kicking from Big Blue, the rogue cow. It's at that side (the left) that I'll be sliding up to make a grab for yeer head.'

Tell me, my fine friend-of-a-dog, what is this new occupation of yours? There ye lie, squatting sleepily in under the table, yeer nose tucked comfortably between yeer paws and yeer eyes squinting (almost serenely) before the steady flames of the fire. To look at ye there – a young dog – passing yeer daylight hours the same as an old man of seventy (ye lazy article). It's no wonder that ye're so languid during the sunlit hours when we find ye in the dead of night changing from yeer coat of laziness into newly-sprung life – when ye go off hunting in the starry hills above the Valley of The Black Cattle murdering the geese and the hens of Toes-Apart.'

'I could have saved yeer life before it came to this – before the new law introduced by Barbaha and the rest of them. I should have chastised ye and given ye a few tidy kicks up the arse and sent ye high-jumping over the half-door. Ye'll soon be sent for a far higher highjump than the half-door – sent this blessed afternoon. It's too late – far too late. Up till now Patience hasn't always been my greatest virtue. Ask Hannyways! But I know a trick or two and this is the time for me to be Patience itself. Ye're snoring by the fireside now. But the sky is grey and the dusk will soon be here. I can already smell yer blood on mee hands.

Fairyland Dreams

The fire held everything in its spell and warmth. Fairyland dreams were leaping around inside in the snoring head of Rapper – in behind his eyebrows. Memories of his puppyhood days were filling his brain – fleetingly. Inside in his soul he felt younger by the minute. But then a cautious frown crossed his face. An unearthly feeling of fear – of depression – began to fill his dreams and an utter loneliness came into him. It was a fear of something intangible from far back in his memory – a fear of something his mother had once taught him during those golden days in the green haggart whilst he was still a pup. Inside in the depths of him came an awareness of the forthcoming confrontation with Death. The light of the sun seemed to be dying – or was it the searching light from the fire that was fading, giving up the ghost?

Rapper! Rapper! This is your last hour on earth.

Pictures of his whole life came up before him. Some of them happy, but most of them festered. The latch of the door opened.

'Here come those big boots of my master, Bohorlody (thought Rapper) – his tall man-shadow shouldering itself across my sleepy tail.'

The dreamy Rapper opened one chestnut eye, then two and gave a peep. The drowsy stillness of an early summer's evening was still hanging onto a yellow square of light reflected from the front window. He closed his eyes again, as though to go back to his delightful dreams. This peeping intrusion into his sun-filled solitude irritated and confused him. In spite of himself his ropey tail wagged. The sunlight continued to filter vaguely in through the geraniums on the front windowsill. It surrounded him in a tinsel-like haze – a haze of sadness for the day that would soon be going away into evening. Its glow made a long shadow of the big man coming across The Welcoming Room. Fresh wood smoke began to spiral up the chimney. In his dog's life's dreaming Rapper listened to the delicate sounds of the crackling logs on the fire. His wet nose twitched once more as he smelt the pungency of the burnt logs.

The Ticking Clock

Behold Bohorlody. He was sitting on his chair, rocking to and fro. He sat there a long time. He listened to the clock ticking. He looked at the dog – at the dog he had loved so well. There was an anger and there was a love – both fighting each other inside in the big man's chest: 'By the power of the bellows (said he to himself) the clock is ticking, it's true. It's ticking for you, my lad.'

He got up stealthily. Anxious now to begin his dirty work, he took down the double-barrel gun from the ledge where the horse's collar and haymes were thrown. He took down the box of cartridges from behind the broken jug of sour milk on the press cupboard. He knelt down beside the sleeping dog. For a long time in this eternity of ours he knelt there, whistling silently – sadly – achingly – to himself under his breath, stroking the dog's fur as if to remember it well. He could smell the milkiness of the dog's breath.

'Ye'll be dead in a minute or two, in less time than it takes to skin a cat.'

He took the belt from his britches and slowly, ever so slowly, tied it round the neck of Rapper. The mind inside in the dog was clearly at work now:

'I have been expecting you, even before I saw you,' thought Rapper. 'Here comes Man. Here comes his gun. I must run – I must run faster than the bullets of Man.

It All Happened So Quickly

It all happened so quickly. Rapper cast about him frantically in his mind for an answer to what was happening. Between the man and the dog – between the two palpitating bodies – there was a violent heat – an inexplicable hammering of their feverish hearts. It gave Bohorlody no pleasure: 'How often have we two strayed and hunted in yon greenery,' he thought. He loved his dog, even now, in those fleeting seconds.

Bohorlody shook his head lugubriously. His twisted sweaty face had a pained look to it – as if his boots were pinching his toes. He coughed harshly to clear the lump from his throat. Trying not to work himself up into anger, he dragged the frantic dog out backwards through the half-door and onto the flagstones, knowing he would not be returning with him. He hauled him out by the pighouse gap. A little procession of ducks and geese followed them to the place of execution – The Sin.

The dog began to howl. This was what his mother had warned him about when he was a pup. The fragile hens, not sure of their own fate, ran for cover in underneath the ass-and-car. They set up a tremendous agitation.

'Look at Rapper! Look at Rapper! Look at Rapper!'

They chattered and chattered amongst themselves, as if aware of the dog's fate. From the glassy docks and the haggart parsley the guttural crows flew away to The Thistle Field.

Rapper was whimpering now – dragging at the belt – turning his thin body in sudden jerks. There wasn't a puff of air – not a puff of a cloud – only the shrouding trees – the hidden place of execution behind the haggart – only the threshold of Death and the sinister whisperings of conspiratorial breezes in the dusty gloom and the strange obscure shapes in the black trees.

Bohorlody, his hands sweaty and clammy, was breathing heavily, gritting his teeth and cursing his dog ('get it over with') who wouldn't die gracefully. He tied him to the stake of execution firmly and watched the dog's unseemly indignity as he sat in a pool of his own yellow piss and squinted sadly up at him. There'd be no second chance for him:

'Back! Back! Back ye must go!'

'Back to eternity – back to the source of yeer life, with yeer solitary spirit. Ye're here today. Ye'll be here no longer.'

Bohorlody stepped back. He took up his position.

What was it, Rapper? What was it?

The final realization of the upturned gun-barrel – rattling low to the temples – was the last you heard and the song that sang you into fleecy eternity. Your feet almost jumped out of your skin.

A splintering flash of light. CRACK! CRACK! CRACK!

It filled a dog's simple brain in the hazy afternoon. The last crimson sunset of evening turned shimmering red with the blood of the dog and his unsung death.

Bohorlody blew the smoke from his gun. He looked at the ruby trappings of Rapper's blood. The wind blew cold from River Laughter. He looked into Rapper's terrified eyes – lying there outstretched and crumpled into nothing – no better than a dead chicken's. In the dark pool of quietness, the big man shuddered. He felt rage. And then he felt sorrow.

He Took The Warm Body And Buried It

Dimmed with weariness he went back across the haggart. He took the warm body of his dog down below the laurels. Near the home of the weasel and the rat he dug a mournful hole and he threw Rapper into it. He covered him with the fine black earth from the side of the ash-pit. And at each shovelful he whispered: 'The fine geese and the fine hens that ye ate. The lambs of Toes-Apart that ye ate. The fine eggs from my Dainty Woman that ye ate. Our eggs are all gone. The geese will soon be all gone. The legs of Skinny-Minny are half gone. Why weren't ye a true dog?'

And so the dirge for the funeral of his dog went on and on as Bohorlody tended the grave: 'Why couldn't ye save your fighting for those sly old foxes?'

It was done. It had to be so.

Bohorlody wiped the sweat from his brow. He put away his shovel under the dripping trees. The sun sank into the mauve and amber sky and the breeze sighed sadly. The night would be cold and no longer beautiful. He went back into the house. A black ribbon of smoke came across the sky. The treetops stirred to life as little birds ('We birds are not dead yet!') twittered and chirruped. You cannot see or hear the birds, Bohorlody. Your mind and your kindness are gone – fled elsewhere.

He Closed The Door Behind Him

He closed the door behind him. He rubbed his back against it – for fear the ghost of Rapper might come in and destroy him. Night soon came to him and to his Dainty Woman. The curly black clouds showed where the silhouettes of the tree trunks were. Bohorlody sprinkled holywater on himself and on the foreheads of his wife and family. The children hadn't a word to say – it was all too much for them and the younger ones felt like crying. The big man didn't even bother to light his pipe. He flicked the holywater round the centre of the floor – to guard against The Boodeeman and the wicked spirits that might now bring evil upon him. He threw a mug of water onto the fire, quenching it and he raked out the last embers of the dancing firelight. The heavy stars fiercely swam above his cabin. The moon reflected its slender medals of light in the dark black waters of his yard-stream.

TWELVE

When an angel came into the room of Morning-Glory and called her away.

Sally Gave Birth

Winter had well and truly set in and though the early morning sunlight had put out all the stars and was twinkling through the branches in the haggart, the frost was still covering the Rookery Rally fields as well as the hill-slopes and surrounding pine-forests of Lisnagorna. It was Christmas morning and there was a great bristling amongst everybody – for it was the day-of-all-days when we'd be celebrating the birth of our Saviour (The King of Kings). Not one of us would be behind-hand in our preparations – be it lord, lady or tinkerman. Benbow (son of The Goshling) had his claspknife out, whittling away at a few large turnips and scooping out their insides so as to make lanterns with candles inside them. That was always his style – to welcome any strangers that might be passing their way on Christmas Day. There might be the ghost of Jesus himself walking among them on this most sacred of days. The big man then went off scouring The Bog Wood in search of the biggest log he could find for the centre of the fire. Finally he travelled the lanes for the greenery of mistletoe, the red holly-berries and the velvety ivy as well as a few long branches of the furling cypress-trees that grew round the haggart so as to decorate the walls of his Welcoming Room in honour of The Newborn Christ.

The previous week he had busied himself selecting his best goose – the one he'd been fattening on spuds and oats. And now his wife (Sally) was business itself – ringing its neck, cleaning out the guts and gizzard and saving the feathers for a new bride's pillowcase. She trudged out the pighouse gap and came in with an armful of logs and little bits of twigs. She threw the bits of candlewax in the middle of the heap till it began to glow and soon she had a good fire tearing along musically till the smell of the wood filled every room in their cabin, fogging the windows. All the preparations were made. Peace at last. Had there been children around the place, getting in under their feet, the two of them would have threatened them with a pelt of the reprimanding tongs and sent them scampering out the half-door to go play with the parading ducks and chickens.

The Birth

And then it happened: at midnight Sally knew that the birth of her first baby was imminent. Benbow covered the bed underneath her with large sheets of brown paper to soak up the mess. After the birth he'd burn it all at the back of the hob till it was just a heap of ashes. At three o'clock in the middle of the night Sally had a pain like getting her arm wrenched out of its socket. That was when she gave birth to a little girl. However, when she looked closer at her new baby her heart couldn't stop palpitating with joy and wide-eyed wonder. It was as though there was a shimmering light shining and dazzling from her baby's eyes and a warmth and a wonder pouring from her delicate pink limbs as she slumbered – a glory of the heart and a glory of the soul, which was a match for anything else this happy Christmas Day. And Morning Glory – that's what she became known as. Sally and Benbow would forever remember the dignified serenity of this precious Christmas morning as they blessed her forehead with the holywater.

Early Days

A few years of infancy passed by rapidly – each year wreathed in the poetry of loving-kindness. The child would recall her mother's arms stretching down to take her out of her crib and dandle her in her apron with *how many miles to Banbury – three score and ten – will I be there by candlelight- yes and back again.* She'd recall the feel and shape of her mother's knees (they were big and cumbersome) as the good woman rocked her in rhythm to this little rhyme and many more well-known childhood rhymes and songs.

Early in the day – even before the sun had burnt away the mists – the little girl's father (Benbow) was out on the roads, embracing all sorts of weather – be it hail, rain or snow together with Gus Gilton, Nate Jimmy and Red Buckles. He was a ditch-trimmer and filler of potholes. Together with his three companions they shared a bottle of milk, a few slices of bread-and-jam and some currant cake. They must have cycled and walked the length of north Tipperary. And whilst other small farmers cocked up their noses when asked to do small jobs such as this for The Council Offices, ('what – the likes of *meee* – and I a farmer!') there was no shame in such honest work – at least not for Benbow and his friends. It was regular work. It was safe work. The money was heavy enough too in the pocket and kept them laughing.

The minute he entered The Welcoming Room, Benbow would place his wages on the dresser behind the sour-milk jug. Only then did he hang up his hat on the nail with his usual greeting of 'God save all here!' With his wages he felt as proud as a cat. Sally counted out the heap of coins. She cut them in half. Then she cut them in half again. Finally she cut them once more into yet smaller halves. It was like cutting the playing-cards before the big game. This last small share she gave to Benbow – an eighth of his working wages. Benbow now had enough money to warm his pipe with a squid of Curl 'n' Stripes' tobacco – had enough money for his weekly supply of twelve pints of stout (The Black Doctor) when he cycled his twenty-eight-inch wheeler bike down to the drinking-shop to play cards in pairs alongside that king of cardplayers (Nate Jimmy) at the game of forty-five hand-wheel.

The bond between the little girl and her father and mother was as complete as the wheel and metal rim on their horse-and-cart. In the evening, in between tending to his rabbit-snares and shaping the wire and whittles, the merry-souled Benbow placed his chair in the middle of the floor. With his hobnail boots he beat out a fanfare and beckoned the little girl to come and sit on his kneecaps. The tobacco-pipe stuck in the corner of his mouth, he threw his short, stubby legs out across the floor and lifted Morning Glory slowly into the air: 'Blasht the bit,' he squinted, ' are ye telling me ye still can't see Dublin?' and he'd shake his head confoundedly as higher and higher (the rogue) he lifted her on his shin-bones. The delighted squeals and the panicky excitement of her as she gazed down at his kneecaps (the laughter still echoes to this day) took her breath away and she couldn't help wetting herself down the length of his britches. What the black beetles in the turf-box made of it as they made a frantic run for the half-door – was never recorded.

If The Weather Was Fine

If the weather was fine Benbow took Morning Glory out to listen to the puffing winds and the little birds chirping and to take in the rich smell of the pighhouse dung. Together they fed the hens and turkeys with so much mash from the skillet that the feathered flock could never complain. Suddenly, he would catch his little daughter by one arm and one leg (a *leg-and-a-duck* he called it). Their hearts bursting, he would twirl her round and round (an inch away from the ground) before laying her down gently ('again! again!' – the laughter) in the yard. They were like two roisterous puppies at play and it was as if the rest of the world wasn't there. And all the while Sally and her bread-baking floury fists would be leaning out over the half-door, laughing flush-faced to see the complete love between her little daughter and her own sound man and the threads of love that bound them together, heart and soul. The old fool was like a big child himself (she thought).

At The Schoolhouse

It wasn't long before Morning Glory was seen scurrying off down the road to the schoolhouse in the shadow of The Two Goats Hill with the famed master (Dang-the-skin-of-it) and his musical sister (Big Screech) ready to drive learning into her. In her pockets she carried a few roast spuds and a hard-boiled egg. When she got home Sally made it her business to help the little girl write her homework into her copybook, ensuring that the copperplate curves were the right way slanted and sloped – that the sums were accurately totalled – that *The Lady of Shalott* was rote-learnt little by little each night throughout the year. In the evening when the candles and the lamp were lit and the fire was not only crackling but booming with its sparkling logs, Benbow showed Morning Glory how to draw a rabbit and a crow. He also drew a fighting Freedom-Fighter for her – with the boots, gloves and the rifle. This was in pencil. Fastidiously he went round the outline in Sally's letter-writing ink so as to make the drawing stand out on the page and look more real. He gave it a final touch by adding a cap at a rakish angle, like Rambling Jack's slanting cap. Only then did they get down the playing-cards for a game of *Old Maid* or *Mug and Match 'em* – or else they took the shiny gramophone records out of the bacon-box and, as the records spun round and round, the new school-child had her nose almost buried in the speaker with the music of each song seeping firmly into her.

Spicing Up The Evening

More often than not Benbow (oh, the devil that is inside a man) spiced up his evening talk and accompanied it with a roomful of his spitty-lip pipe smoke. He told Morning Glory a number of entertaining stories which were all outrageously untrue: tales of a gigantic goat in the nearby Yellowstone Quarry: tales of a black-bearded lion that marched in the dead of night from Saddleback Village to the road at Sandy's Cross: tales of how this goat and this lion had between the two of them sent many a man leaping in over the ditch on his way home from Curl 'n' Stripes' drinking-shop. It was enough to give a child's brain indigestion. Sally would stop skinning her rabbit and would laugh her two sides off: 'The only goats and lions left in Ireland – the only goats seen in the dead of night – are fixed to the bottom of a drunken man's glass of The Black Doctor,' she'd say: 'Benbow, avic, if you were squeezed just a little bit more I could get a few better lies out of you and your innocent eyes!' Such a complete storyteller was her lying-hound-of-a-husband. And then her peels of laughter would re-echo off of the four walls.

The Angel

The house itself was neat, small and trim. In between the bouts of laughter and songs there was an air of calmness about it. When the story of Gabriel's

Annunciation to Mary was told in the schoolhouse, Morning Glory understood it almost better than Dang-the-skin-of-it himself. How often did she feel that an angel of one sort or another (maybe one of the lesser ones) was coming unseen to them in through the half-door. She kept her secret inside in her heart.

The angel came: it came in the shape of her new baby brother, Donie. He appeared suddenly while Benbow was away on the roads and Sally was filling the burner with the spuds for the hens and turkeys. Her waters burst at eight o'clock one Friday morning just as Morning Glory was about to run out the door and follow her school-friends down the hill. The little girl ran back into The Welcoming Room and stood beside her screaming mother, whose face had turned the yellow of a quince. On her own the nine-year-old child tended to the agonising birth pains. With her mother's guidance she delivered the baby boy, every bit as cautiously as though she were Doctor Glasses or Black Bess, the nurse with the soot-drop on her jaw.

It was the talk of Rookery Rally. That wasn't all: the little girl washed and cleaned Donie and she presented him to her mother. It was the first time that she had ever missed school. Benbow hurried home. He almost died of shock. He hadn't expected to see this little spark-of-a-son entering the world for at least another month. He stayed beside Sally for the rest of that week. Together with Morning Glory he fussed over his wife. The pair of them fussed Donie almost to death, so affectionately did they coddle him. Next day Morning Glory washed the bloody sheets out at the yard-stream till her childish knuckles were red-raw. Then she hung them on the bushes in the haggart to dry. Inside in The Welcoming Room (with a renewed bout of whispering advices from Sally) she learnt how to make the soda-bread and the yellow-meal cakes, keeping the fire heaped high with turf till the cabin walls glowed. She put further turf-coals on whatever side of the burner-lid ('Turn this bit in nearer the fire . . . put more coals on this side of the lid') her mother requested. Then she took the bread from the burner and put it in a blanket and took it into her mother for her inspection in the bed in The Sick Room.

Each evening when Benbow came back from the ditch-trimming he marvelled at the sight before his eyes – to think the way his young daughter had safely delivered her baby brother and how she had dealt with the afterbirth – burning it at the back of the fire. It was all too much for him to take in. Throughout the birth his little daughter had followed Sally's instructions to the last letter just as she did with the washing of the sheets and the baking of the soda-cake. What a brisk little soul she was! It made Benbow think that a small miracle had taken place in his house – that an angel had indeed come and visited them. The angel was, of course, none other than Morning Glory, his enchanting daughter.

Daily Duties

Each day before going off to school the child continued to do her chores: to fetch water from the well: to bring in the logs: to collect the eggs from amid the nettles and to feed the hens and the gabbling turkeys. With her father she milked her mother's goats on the hill-slopes above the house. Benbow took the goats' milk the two miles into Templeton Fields and The Holy Well. Sally was now getting back enough strength to scrape a bit of blackcurrant jam onto a few cuts of bread – as well as the roasted spuds and hard-boiled eggs – that Morning Glory would need to keep her brains alive and active during her lessons. The little girl kissed her beautiful brother and she ran down the hill towards the schoolhouse.

Herself And Benbow

If Benbow reached home early from work, (the weather preventing the trimming of the ditches or the mending of the potholes) he gave Morning Glory the most unforgettable rides along the slippery roads on the handlebars of his bike. The pure joy and beauty of it all: the breezes piping their serenade softly: the sky-high mountains: the long dark aisles of the perfumed pine-forests in Lisnagorna as if to come walking down to greet them: the scenery and its peacefulness fantastically surrounding them: the schemingly-created pretences (as though the man and the child were about to fall headlong across the road) of her father as he stuttered his rattling bike here and there across the road and threatened to pitch the two of them into the dyke: the child's own playful screams, masking her utter delight and affection for her father as she snuggled into his panting body.

The pipe rarely left Benbow's mouth, not even during these bike rides. He always had a spade and a billhook and a brush strapped onto the crossbar. He carried a billycan for his tea and a few roasted crab-apples and raw tomatoes as well as a slice or two of sodabread wrapped in a wadge of newspapers so that himself and his young daughter could lie down stretch-legged for a while amid the forest's greenery or by the rim of a murmuring river and have what he called a right royal tea for themselves.

Saturday Night

The days were getting shorter. It was of a Saturday night that other men shaved themselves with the cut-throat razor in preparation for next day's Mass. All week long their faces would be hairy and black but at Sunday Mass their jaws were as smooth as a pig's bladder. Benbow was different and shaved whenever he was about to visit the drinking-shop, whatever night of the week he decided to step out. But before he took down his hat and coat from the back of the door he spent an hour of entrancement watching the smiling antics of Donie, the little baby at the breast and the blissful eyes of his dear wife, Sally.

The Hat-box

Most nights Morning Glory brought down the hat-box left behind years ago by her cousins from Yonkers across The Ocean. Then she put on a dramatic display for her bemused parents in front of the dancing firelight. Like a dash of springtime she made a grand entrance, bursting in the doorway to introduce her daunty theatricals. To the encouraging cheers of Benbow and the laughing tears of Sally her first act was a series of introductory cartwheels around the room, over and back. The cat (Whiskers) had enough good sense to run for cover behind the teachest of logs. The dog (Sinister) wagged his ropey tail at the fire. There followed half a dozen dignified posturings and interpretations of the stories in her schoolbooks. The biblical David and Goliath and the ugly sisters from Cinderella were among her favourites.

Sweets From Benbow

She had sweets from Benbow – sweets so rare that no other children knew what they were. By her tenth birthday she had one pure black tooth. It was a marvel to other children who longed to have a tooth like it. The rest of her teeth were a double row of tiny white and even pearls. Of course it was the black tooth that gave her this special charm. She wore three hairclips whereas no other child knew what hairclips were. And, when other children had their hair cross-combed into plaits, she asked for her own hair to be cut in a pudding-basin style like the boys at school. She wanted to vie with the boys – be it in the robbing of orchards, the gathering of hazelnuts, the climbing of trees on The Two Goats Hill, the jumping of rivers or the catching of fish with the bag of flour. She wanted to vie with them in the use of her knuckles too.

Some children carried a small knife with them to school. Like them she raided the turf-shed of any farmer who happened to be in the way of their journey and stole the daily sod of turf so that Dang-the-skin-of-it could warm his extensive bum in front of the blazing fire. After that, she cut herself a fair-sized turnip before wild creatures like the rats got their teeth into them. She spent the day wiping the clay from it onto her sleeve and then eating it raw during recess, for by that time her teeth would be swimming about excitedly in her head at the thought of getting a few juicy mouthfuls of her stolen feast.

One morning she was on her way past Chesty Noolah's house with her newly-snagged turnip when two brave boys leapt out from the ditch in order to steal the turnip-feast she'd just been cleaning. Ah, the little highwaymen! – they who had done none of the work themselves. Away in flight ran Morning Glory, her legs scarcely touching the ground. And then came misfortune as she found herself trapped in the inescapable depths of The Yellowstone Quarry. She was like the rat trapped in the henhouse and awaiting its fate at the hands of Man and his lethal death-bringing hurleystick. She didn't know what on earth she was supposed to do. There was no answer for it but to give the rascals her turnip or have her two eyes bruised and battered.

But the angel came calling on her. He brought into her life a moment of pure inspiration and she ran at the astonished boys, brandishing her knife aloft. She screamed out the old warcry (*hoolah! hoolah!*) at them as she came on. Without a knife of their own to safeguard their skins they lost their bit of foolish schoolboy courage. Morning Glory didn't desist from her attack till she had given the two brave little men an unmerciful pasting with her fists and had turned them into a black and blue painting.

The Month Of Her Tenth Birthday

It was May (the month of her tenth birthday). Bishop High-Hat himself was coming in all his grandeur from his spatial palace over in Clare. It was to be a great and glorious occasion – a bishop with his shepherd's stick and he dressed up in his bright purple robes with the long sleeves and his jovial face as red as a hawberry. It'd be a treat to see him here among us lowly ones and he giving our children The Sacrament of Confirmation. But the children had been warned not to be deceived by his merry looks for he was well able to frighten them with a look from his gandery eye – a good deal more than a tinker pouncing out on them from behind a furze bush. Only the children aged eleven and upwards had been suitably drilled for giving him the answers that filled the doctrinal pages of The Long Catechism – an ongoing task that demanded head-searching memorising of over a hundred questions and answers.

Morning Glory (the clever girl that she was) had been selected by Dang-the-skin-of-it even though she wasn't ten until the end of this month (May) for she knew all the answers forwards and backwards (thanks to her mother) and she could sing them like a song. Father Sensibly was well satisfied with this starry little specimen and so was Sally as she started to make the white confirmation-dress for her daughter. There'd be a photo taken of her in the yard with her long black tresses of hair and her sun-speckled face aglow with happiness and holiness.

The day arrived. Father Sensibly was in his finest black gabardine suit, which the ladies of the parish had bought for him. Dang-the-skin-of-it and his sister (Big Screech) were full of the smell of mothballs. The tea and the cakes and the trimmed ham sandwiches were on display on several trestletables but they were not for the mouths of children – they had to make do with the lemonade and currant bread.

Bishop High-Hat

Bishop High-Hat was particularly interested in the presence of Morning Glory, it being unheard of in Tipperary for so young a child to be selected for her Confirmation. She was seated near the end of the line of children. But before her turn came round for the question-and-answer an almighty commotion was seen rising up. Red Scissor's son (Jackaby) had been at home for the sowing of the potatoes and mangols. He had missed the preparations for this day – missed also the opportunity of selecting a saint's name for his Confirmation. When he was asked what name he had chosen as his new name he could have gone straight through the ground in fright, not knowing what name he was supposed to offer up. Seeing how flummoxed he was, the rascally boys in the row behind him whispered, 'Henry-the-Eighth! Henry-the-Eighth! That's the name that's now the height of fashion!' Whereupon the misfortunate Jackaby gave the answer that these cruel pranksters were hoping for:

'Henry-the-Eighth, your honour.'

Bishop High-Hat almost swooned in his chair and with a crash he dropped the crosier from his hand:

'Put him out! Put that young devil out,' he shouted as the ushers carried the poor misfortunate boy away out of the church and into sad posterity.

All Was Not Lost

Dang-the-skin-of-it, however, was going to be saved any further embarrassment for next in the line was his best scholar, Morning Glory herself. He was as proud as punch of her and he whispered into Father Sensibly's ear that this was the moment for his specially-chosen child to put on her very best performance. The priest passed the message on to the bishop: 'The school's finest scholar,' he smirked.

'And tell me, my child, (said the bishop, his eyes popping expectantly as he looked down at the downcast eyes of the trembling little girl) where will those souls go, who are not of The True Faith – when it's their turn to die?'

He knew it was a more than difficult question – indeed he hadn't quite worked out the answer himself. Without a blink of an eye Morning Glory gave him the school's standard reply:

'To hell, sir.'

There followed a deadly silence.

Unknowingly the poor child had disgraced the entire school. In spite of himself, Dang-the-skin-of-it (for he was normally a gentle soul) sent her back to her place in the church pew with a box to the ear. Morning Glory did not make her Confirmation this year. It simply wouldn't do. It's true – the gentry were not members of what Catholics called The True Persuasion. And yet – it was they that had prevented most households in Rookery Rally from starving to death during the dark days of The Famine. How could any of them ever be going down to hell?

Sally's Rage

Though Sally was the soul of kindliness and calmness, she was a dangerous woman when crossed. On hearing the news she was beside herself with rage. She could picture the wagging tongues and the disgrace her child would have to face opposite everyone in the parish once they found that she hadn't passed the bishop's Confirmation Test and her two eyes filled up with tears. Those old gossips (The Weeping Mollys) would rub their hands gleefully together and spread the news the length and breadth of Copperstone Hollow. There was nothing for it but to stand firm and fight her daughter's corner as any mother should. Up to the gates of the schoolhouse (a thing unheard of before then) she stamped her big boots. She burst in through the door. In front of the open-mouthed children she made a mother's heartrending assault on the ears of Dang-the-skin-of-it:

'And if my child had told that smart-minded bishop in his fancy togs that those who are not of the true faith would have as much right as ourselves (every bit) to enter the gates of heaven – what would his high-and-mightiness have thought about that sort of answer? All our lives we've been taught and have believed that they were a pack of heathens?'

Of course Dang-the-skin-of-it realised that such an alternative answer would have met with an equal rebuke from the bishop. The normally good-humoured master was somewhat ashamed of his previous anger and the slap he'd given to Morning Glory's jaw. The poor man had been caught between two fires: he couldn't help thinking of all the high-falutin' ceremony – the expensive suit – the cakes – the high tea. It had all been grand stuff and meticulously prepared for. Damn it – when all was said and done – he had been made a holy show of by Morning Glory in front of the bishop and his attendants with their long black robes – their red buttons and crimson skullcaps. What was Bishop High-Hat to think – only that the innocent child had given him the answer that Dang-the-skin-of-it had been teaching his children all year long. He'd be lucky if he still had a roof over his head this coming spring and not be sent back to Mayo. He had been handed no alternative but to give the child the clout to her jaw.

Morning Glory Got A Penance

In spite of Sally's nobility in defending her daughter, Morning Glory was to receive a penance and it came quite unexpectedly. She had her father's bag of sweets (the humbugs) and was secretly sharing them with Meg-the-Leg at the back of the classroom. The long schoolhouse had two parts to it: the lower end under the tutelage of Big Screech and her musical piano – the upper end, backing away from it, in the charge of the master. Big Screech was teaching the younger children the virtues of the darning needles whilst Morning Glory and her companions were under the expositions of Dang-the-skin-of-it and his favourite book of romantic poetry. The two girls dug their sticky fingers into the bag of sweets and silently began consuming them where they though no-one could see them in the back row.

Suddenly from behind them streaked the raging torrent that was Big Screech: 'Is this the way ye're teaching yeer children?' she shrieked at Dang-the-skin-of-it. The first (and the last) thing that Morning Glory knew was the mistress's red-and-white point-to-the-map stick dipping expertly into the mouth of the bag of sweets. The bag was sent sailing to the four corners of the universe. The two little heads were clashed fiercely together and the children fell to the ground – unconscious and, as far as the other children could see, stone dead! Seeing stars was a phrase that Morning Glory would later understand only too well.

Sally Drove Her Ass Once More

Before next morning's cockerels had finished crowing Sally found herself once more in a state of incensed rage and she drove her ass-and-car up to the gates of the schoolhouse, all the time framing the severest of curses in her mind. She startled the children with her whirlwind entrance as she raced across the room. She pushed Big Screech up against the wall and threatened to send her packing out of Tipperary: 'Back to the rocky county where ye came from (she roared) – back picking spuds, where ye have always belonged – that's where I'll have ye if ye ever again lay hands on mee child.'

Christmas Came On

The following Christmas came on. Everyone put on their thick coats and scarves. Lady Demurely was as busy as a gnat, taking little gifts to the children all over the hills. Family parcels from The Land of the Silver Dollar and The Land of John Bull had to be delivered and excitedly unwrapped by us. They were so numerous that Herald-the-post came calling on Benbow to help him get the deliveries up into the more remote parts of the hill country – there'd be at least a dozen parcels apiece.

The Christmas season was a great time for postmen. The twelve-mile journey out beyond The Hills-of-The-Past and Bog Boundless and as far as The Last Lookout and Diggledy-goo would leave their two old mares irritable and steaming. Herald and Benbow didn't mind a bit. Wherever they went, they'd be greeted more-then-friendly ('a happy Christmas to the pair of ye') with a bit of bacon, a few slices of Christmas cake and a glass or two of the Mountainy Men's homebrewed whiskey (the rawgut potheen) to take the chill out of their bones.

Benbow's Return

The first night that Benbow returned from his long journey he had difficulty finding his way into the yard and he stumbled about and almost fell in the stream. A tired man – a weary and befuddled man – he finally made his way in the door to Sally and staggered across to the fire. He was as drunk as a mule. It was the first time he'd ever put the raw-gut whiskey past his lips. Sally made a grab at him and pelted him disdainfully into the settlebed. Like the rest of the women in Rookery Rally she had an unnatural hatred of the dreaded Drink. In her eyes it was the greatest curse on earth.

Next time round – even though the twelve-mile journey was a tough one to travel – she felt bound to call on her young daughter to go with the chastened Benbow when he was making his list of postal deliveries. She'd make sure there'd be no back-pedalling ever again on his part. The child followed her mother's instructions to the letter: her father (a lesson well-learnt, fair play to him) did not come home drunk that evening or any other evening for the rest of his life.

When The Flowers Came Back

The following spring the time came for the flowers to return and for Morning Glory to learn how to cycle a bike. Benbow was patience itself. Soon the rest of us saw the bliss of a first morning's cycling when his young daughter and the hollow-sounding rattle of her mudguards came speeding exuberantly out passed our ears. Long before we clapped eyes on her, we'd hear her tingaling-tingaling bell and her singing voice racing down High Straits and frightening everything in her way – goats, horses, pigs and turkeys alike:

'Clear the way, let ye! Here comes a woman from Tipperary!'

In Through The Shop Door

The accident which had occurred to Blue-eyed Jack's brother (Lofty Larry) – the time his brakes gave way and he went tearing around La-de-dah's bend and had half his ear torn off along the slates of the linney lean-to – was a story that all our children knew only too well:

'Remember what happened to poor Lofty,' their mothers would roar after them when first they took to the bike. And then they'd follow this bit of advice up with: 'Test the brakes before setting off down by The Kill'.

Unfortunately the brakes of Morning Glory failed to pass this elementary test. She was halfway down the slope that led to the drinking-shop when she found herself zigzagging across the road. She knew it wasn't an angel but a ringing devil that was coming to visit her this time round. Miraculously she steered the bike (maybe her angel was working for her after all) over the crossroads at Travellers' Rest. Somehow she managed to avoid getting herself killed by the horses racing home from the creamery. She saw the green door of Curl 'n' Stripes' drinking-shop. The door saw her. Her bike went in through the doorway at the speed of an express bullet, knocking half-a-dozen pints of The Black Doctor and several pipes of tobacco skyways from the startled gobs of the faithful drinkers. She (another little miracle) ended up in a bag of flour next to The Gawk and his good friend Gunpowder (a man with a weak backside) – her head ending up the size and shape of a snowman.

Only Half-killed

The cuts to her face told us that she had been only half-killed. That evening several of us came up the hill to visit her and see the results of the accident. The sweets given to her would take a year-and-a-half for her to eat and would surely produce yet another fine black tooth in her mouth.

Curl 'n' Stripes was no fool: he moved his shop-door a few feet further west so that such an accident to his bags of flour would never happen again and that neither his doorway nor his seasoned drinkers would ever again have the discomfort of a mad child and her even madder bike meeting them like a runaway train from Limerick: the next misfortunate child could break her damn skull off of the wall instead. The gospel according to Saint Curl 'n' Stripes!

The Platform Dance

As usual The Platform Dances were held again the following summer on the wooden platforms laid out in the fields. Across from Morning Glory's windows stood one of these platforms amidst the wild goats and the even wilder asses, who must have been highly intrigued by the wild music and the tidy dance-steps of the men in their clattering hobnail boots.

By this time Morning Glory was fourteen years-of-age and a damp heat often filled her body. She was what we called a half-child and a half-woman – at a delicate age – a troublesome time of mood swings for her and other girls of the same age. With her heart pounding she'd spend her evenings kneeling on the stool in her bedroom and peeping forlornly out the moonlit window at the platform and the dancers as they went spinning and swinging around on their skelping feet. She pictured the fun they were having. She could hear the melodions and fiddles rasping away. And as she gazed out over the darkening hillslope, she felt more and more like a prisoner locked in some fairyland tower, unable to reach out and participate in the joy of the heavenly music. The roars of laughter told her that a life of great beauty was out there – a place of mystery – a place of magic. No matter how many times she asked her mother if she'd let her go dancing, it was always the same answer: 'A child is a child and men are but men. They'll take advantage of you and your innocent pink cheeks'. Morning Glory wondered what all this sort of talk meant.

The Night Of Her Escape

The night of her daring escape came on. The hillside fairies tiptoed into her room and wriggled their way into her head. They opened the latch of her bedroom window for her. Tiptoe. Tiptoe. She eased her way carefully out the window and stepped down onto the dewy grass that awaited her eager toes. She patted the dog (Sinister) into silence. With her heart in her mouth she feared none of the nightly ghosts and she hurried across the field to the dance. It was heaven on earth. The flickering stars seemed to fall all round her but she knew them not for she was having the finest time in all her life and she swore the older girls into silence.

Later that evening and before the moon had gone back to sleep behind the clouds she tiptoed home again. She crawled in through her window and into bed. It wasn't a dream. Her mother was never to know what she'd been up to and she repeated the joyful dancing every Saturday night throughout the entire summer till her feet were red-raw from it.

Jay-Jay

It had to happen. A lad called Jay-Jay (the son of Be-Jaypurs) found his way onto the floor. He was a year older than Morning Glory and this was his first year wearing a long britches. He had a swagger that ran throughout his body. He had a smile that would melt the heart of an innocent girl. Midway through the fine dancing he plucked up courage and took Morning Glory behind the ditch. She was the picture (he thought) of a lovely red apple waiting to be picked. But – brave though he was, he didn't know what he was supposed to do once the two of them were alone in an unknown world. He stretched his arms out sideways as though he were about to stop a runaway calf. Morning Glory (the little innocent) repeated the gesture. It was a moment of tender intimate beauty when their two hearts rocked like a ship on the waves. Scarcely breathing, they wrapped their outstretched arms awkwardly round each other. They gave one another one or two shy little pecking kisses from lip to delicate lip.

That Night

On that enchanting night Morning Glory was transfused with happiness. She skipped swimmingly homewards through the silent grasses. She thought she was about to fly out across the Rookery Rally chimneys and off into outer space. Breathlessly she got into her bed and pinned herself in, wrapping the sheets round her like a stuffed mummy in case she might truly fly off to heaven where (she knew) all the happy souls lived. The kisses of Jay-Jay had been as sweet as a jar of treacle.

Then It Happened

Then it happened. It happened without Morning Glory planning a bit of it. It was a sunny Monday morning. The angel came into the house.

The sunshine was blinding her eyes. Her mother was out in the haggart, hanging the sheets out to dry on the bushes. Her daughter was alone in the room, coo-cooing and smiling over the chuckles of her little brother – popping her head now to this side and now to that side of his pram – much to his amusement.

Suddenly she felt an eerie silence entering the room. She was sure it was the angel – coming for her at long last. At first she heard nothing. And then she seemed to see a luminous light. The Welcoming Room was humming with that strange humming noise that those irridescent greenflies make around a heap of dung. The invisible messenger came closer and closer. It whispered in her ear. It told her that the kisses of Jay-Jay at The Platform Dance were not meant for her – told her that she was being saved for a far nobler calling – told her that God in his heaven (the angel's call now seemed deafeningly loud) was beckoning her to come and join him in his heavenly task amongst the poor wretches living in the backstreets of cities far over the seas.

She Caught The Cattle-boat

It wasn't easy for Father Sensibly to persuade her mother to let her go. But the angel was now firmly in control and told Morning Glory what to say. Though she was still very young she packed her small suitcase a week later and caught the cattle-boat across The Herring Pond to the land of John Bull. Poor Benbow – he who throughout her childhood had played those childish games of *leg and a duck* and *can you see Dublin?* – was grief-stricken beyond measure and kept trying to squint his tears away. He had nothing left now except the echoes of her girlish laughter:

'For the love of Christ – she's but a child,' he wept – spitting the words out with as much distain as he could. He thought his heart was going to burst inside his shirt.

He took Morning Glory to The Roaring Town Station. Sally had cried throughout the whole night and was too heartbroken to leave her room. Benbow placed a slice of bread-and-jam and an apple in his daughter's fist. He went off and spent a long time in the station lavatory. He could not bear to look his child in the eye: 'I've a cold in mee eyes,' he kept saying through the midst of his tears. But the tears kept swelling up and rolling down his sad jaws.

Sally And Benbow Waited

The following months Sally and Benbow waited and waited – all the time praying for a return visit from their lovely daughter. Sally dusted The Welcoming Room as never before. Benbow whitewashed the walls. Even the horses's tackling got a magnificent polishing where they lay in a heap on the side of the hob. The whole place shone like a church. There'd be be no sense welcoming their daughter back to an untidy house and having her trip over the buckets, kettle and skillets, would there? In the meantime the nuns had used the hedge-trimmers to sheer off Morning Glory's lovely long hair as was the custom and it lay in a sad heap in a panier-basket in the convent corridor. Then they put a gold ring on her finger and told her she was now a bride of Christ.

Several Trips Home

In due course the saintly damsel made several trips home on the cattle-boat. She being so very young – the nuns had pledged themselves to this so as to soften the sadness in the heart of Benbow and Sally and assure them of their daughter's happiness. As soon as she arrived home, their spirited daughter showed that she was still able to prove herself handy with her fists – the fists that had saved her turnip from the thieving boys those many years ago. And so – whenever a young man came calling at her door in a vain effort to persuade her to give up her ridiculous holy notions (going back to the convent – I ask you! – to marry with Christ and a nun's ring on her finger) she was seen spitting on her fists – leaving them flat on their back and nursing a terrible toothache from the clouting she gave them.

The New Guard

There was a new Guard below in Abbey Cross. He was a dashing young fellow – what we called a modish blade. He had come from Clare. With him he had brought a dazzling new motorbike – a machine that was out of this world. Its equal had never been seen by any of us before – what with our simple ass-and-cars and horse-and-carts. The old folk ran out to get a look at it and marvelled at the shine in it. The men fell into a shock at the speed of it. With its red and its silver and its long mirrors and its intricate pipes that weaved through its middle like the waves in a river it glowed like the tempting sun (said the young girls, the poetry coming out through their ears) and they clasped their hands together: if only they could get a ride on its saddle. The handsome Guard and his wondrous motorbike was the snake from Eden and we were all left scratching our heads: had this fella come down to us from the moon?

He Came Calling

The Guard came calling at Morning Glory's door in the hope that himself and his beautiful machine might pluck so fine a flower and have him for himself. He swore he'd give her the moon and the stars. When he entered the half-door he saw her sitting by the fire – herself and her nun's veil. She was as stunningly beautiful as he'd been told – even more than his bike.

But suddenly – he couldn't believe what his eyes were looking at. She was pulling on a Woodbine fag together with Benbow – the two of them sending hollow smoke-signals up to the rafters. Father and daughter – and they as happy as a king and his queen: a nun and a fag in her fist. Was the likes of it ever heard tell of in all Ireland?

She Took To The Saddle

Without a blush Morning Glory followed him out into the yard. She felt a rush of new excitement. What was her previous old bike with its runaway brakes to her now? How had she ever thought so much of it? She followed his beckoning finger and sat behind him on the saddle. Seconds later – her veil whipping back over her shoulder – her Woodbine fag cocked daintily in the heel of her fist – she found herelf tearing round the windy bend – flying passed the astonished drinkers who had raced out the shop-door to see the sight and hear the roar of the engine. From that day forth Benbow and Sally were down on their bended knees most of the day – crossing their hearts and praying that their daughter wouldn't meet with an untimely death.

Dallying And Languishing

Each day The Guard came dallying and languishing. Himself and Morning Glory and the bike – they flew through the valleys and out over the hills and sped as far as The Roaring Town. For the whole of that summer our heroine smoked fag after fag with her new companion from Clare. She drank bottles of The Black Doctor alongside him on the ditch whenever they took a break from riding his magical machine.

He Couldn't Have Known

But what could a young man have known about the thoughts inside in her saintly head? She was merely acquiring the lower and lesser habits that she'd need to learn if she was ever to work amongst the down-and-outs in the backstreet slums of big cities like London. She knew she'd have to learn (and quickly) what it was like to take on the day-to-day manners of a downtrodden man – knew that her endeavours to match the young Guard in his smoking and drinking would prove a useful weapon when the time came for her to reach inside the minds of those poor and bitter men, none of whom had a hope in hell of making a better life for themselves on the rough streets of the city.

The Summer Ended

The summer ended. Our young heroine went back to the convent and its fragrant rose-garden, her angel once more taking her silently by the hand.

When she was inside the four walls of the nunnery and Mother Superior's back was turned she again showed the wild side of her nature. As though she were a magician she'd sneak out from beneath the folds of her black habit a few bottles of The Black Doctor and a large packet of fags to keep the other nuns company. With the windows wide open she taught some of the wilder ones (the impressionable ones too) her new skills of drinking the odd bottle of The Black Doctor and inhaling the smoke from her fags and putting streams of it out through her nose. To their delight she became the high point of an otherwise dreary beads-clacking day. And all this was in preparation for the boisterous fray when the day would come for her and the rest of them to be sent out into the big bad world.

Down Into South America

The Reverend Mother was a clever old lady and knew the depths of Morning Glory's love for the poor. The following year she sent her far far away – to live among the downtrodden souls in the rainforests of Brazil. A few years later she sent her into the backstreet slums of deepest India where she worked steadily amongst a new wave of poor and unwanted souls. Our heroine always had a pocketful of loose fags in her bib. From time to time she'd give her misplaced beggars one or two of her fags, cutting them into halves – but only if they were good and behaved themselves – only if they stopped cursing her and threatening to kick the brains out of her head for chastising them for their lack of manners to her. Otherwise (she promised) she'd keep her treasure-throve of fags locked firmly in her bib. She was never afraid of these men and in return they loved to see her coming down the street towards them. It wouldn't always be like this. One day there'd come a time when she'd find herself too old and too feeble for this sort of laborious work – a time when she'd have to go back to the nunnery (if God only spared her the health).

She Kept Her Beautiful Unlined Face

The years sped on. Miraculously Morning Glory did not grow old like the rest of us. She kept her beautiful unlined face – the face of the young fifteen year-old damsel, who had once danced the night away and kissed lips with Jay-Jay – who had once smoked her fags in the ashes with her rosy-cheeked father, Benbow. In many ways she was still that selfsame wild young girl, who had sailed her veil away over the back of a young Guard's motorbike, her hands clasping his warm waist for dear life. Her beautiful head of hair was let grow long again, for the convent no longer scalped young girls of their hair as a sign that they were denying the world and its worldly goods.

And another thing – throughout the rest of her days Morning Glory continued to have that rapturous smile – though the scowling bishop had never seen it – a smile that lit up the world around her – a smile that reflected the teachings of Benbow and Sally. She became (and would always be) the apple of Rookery Rally's eye. May her angel (the one that came into her mother's kitchen that washing-day Monday long ago) stay with her forevermore.

THIRTEEN

How Jimbo-the-Go-Boy fought a battle with his bishop but lost it.

Jimbo

Jimbo was the son of Lizzy-the-Herd and Bedad-sez-I. He was the grandson of Tom Jibberish – a memorable character who was our first-remembered gravedigger and whose wife (Tongue-of-all-Tongues) had washed corpses inside in the poorhouse before finally leaving him on a night-to-be-forgotten.

Jimbo was a Go-Boy – an uproarious one – famed among all our long list of Go-Boys. He was as resplendent as any man that ever broke wind and his nimble steps were as high-kicking as the half-castrated jinnet's when it was first carted to Moll-the-Man's ass-and-car. We grown-up mortals enjoyed the antics of him with an almost irreligious reverence and (in short) no broad-winged eagle soared higher on the mountainside.

Meeting Up With Children

Moll-the-Man's children lived a good bit further away from the schoolhouse than most children. They'd three miles of a journey to drag their feet along before reaching the school gates and were up even before the lark's song and out on the road before eight each day. One misty morning as the night-clouds were scurrying away they were coming out over The Difficult Stile from Red Buckles' Meadow and would soon be putting a nice bit of a step on it up along High Straits. They were anxious not to be late for school and get their legs belted by Big Screech. The punishment for latecomers was always the same – the ceremony of being handed the black-handled knife and told go down to the stream and bring back a sally-switch with which to receive the honour of a good thrashing.

An Almighty Shock

What an almighty shock they got when only halfways up High Straits and not another child yet in sight. Down from the branches of a high bush – as though coming out of the clouds – loomed the remarkable shape of Jimbo-the-Go-Boy. They had never seen a Go-Boy up close before. Some of the smaller ones believed that such a person was only a colourful character from the pages of a storybook and their eyes were now bedazzled at the pure sight of Jimbo. They couldn't fathom out what he was wearing or why. For on his head was his grandfather's cocked-hat – with a few pheasant-feathers sticking out at the sides: lower down his body he was wearing not one, but two large pairs of red calico drawers (presumably his mother's): one of these drawers was pulled up over his britches: the other was wrapped garishly round his throat and shoulders like a winter muffler. Both sets of drawers were wide enough to fit a handy-sized cow inside them. On his legs he wore an unrecognisable assortment of footwear – a squelchy wellington on his right foot and a cleeted clog on his other foot and no socks that you'd care to notice.

Hurtling Towards The Children

As he came hurtling towards the children he seemed like a moving blur of redness – right up from his knees to his chin with the appearance of a fine fat pig that had lately been stabbed in the throat. All they could do was blink and stare in disbelief at the garish apparition in front of them. This was almost too much for them to handle at this sleepy hour of the morning and they were rooted to the spot, not knowing which way to turn or whether to lie down on the road and pretend they were dead. Was the whole thing a bad dream? Were they still asleep in their beds? Had they lost all their senses even before they got to the school gate – senses that they'd badly need since their brains were usually knocked out of their heads by the savagery of Big Screech and her fists? One thing was sure: no-one in Tipperary had ever dressed up like this wild man – not even that delirious old madwoman, Slipperslapper. Jimbo must have spent half the night pampering himself and getting ready for the huge effect he knew he'd have on a group of harmless children.

It Was No Laughing Matter

It was no laughing matter – not even for the older ones. If they had been at home in the safe company of their mother, the sight of Jimbo would have been enough to make a cat laugh – especially the red drawers adorning his limbs. But out here in the middle of nowhere they were simply a band of schoolchildren all on their ownsome in the big bad world and as good as abandoned by the rest of mankind. All they could do was wait and see what Jimbo next had in store for them – some sort of Go-Boy performance, no doubt, that they'd yet to witness in their young lives. Some sort of amusement. On the other hand it might be something far more fierce and scary. They didn't know which. This new creature might not be like the hilarious Jack Fart and the melodious bouts of controlled farting from his astonishing arse, which made every child laugh themselves sick for miles around the hills. He might (heaven forbid) turn them into crows: might turn them into little bunny rabbits: might make the pack of them bawl their eyes out for Moll-the-Man to come and rescue them and take them back home to the folds of her matronly apron.

There He Stood

He stood there in the middle of the road. And then – he did what was quite unexpected: he blessed himself religiously and started to do a spellbinding dance for them, weaving this way and that way in the middle of High Straits. He suddenly danced up onto the far ditch. He paused there like a church-statue, looking up at the sun as though he'd never seen it before. With his fingers on his lips he commanded the children's silence (as if they weren't dumbstruck enough already at the absurdity of him). Whereupon he hopped down and with his slithery body began to make a number of slow and twisty steps, pretending to be an old cat tormented in the rain – making strange mewling sounds as if he was in need of a sup of milk. Then *choo-choo-choo* went his pistonlike arms as he made a few laborious steps round the middle of the road as though he were an exhausted train coming into The Roaring Town from Limerick. Not for a minute did he stand still. He crossed again to the far side of the road and placed one foot on the ditch to give himself a bit of a push-off. Then he pelted himself across the gap towards the children – making a number of cartwheels, handsprings and somersaults, the likes of which they'd never seen before. The performing tumblers at The Daffy-Duck Circus would be in the halfpenny-place next to him. No-one in Tipperary could hold a candle to such madcap gaiety when joined to the dazzlement of his colourful drawers. What a tale they'd have to tell their school-friends – if they ever got away from Jimbo with their two fine legs left in one piece.

His Gob-music

By now the craziness in him (not to mention his broken teeth, his hairy jaws, his bulging eyes) had made all their heads run round and round in dizzying circles. But there was more: for then came his gob-music on a dirty bit of paper-and-comb as he played his raucous tunes seemingly for the foxgloves and honeysuckle on the ditch so that the children expected the flowers to spring out on the road and join the mad fellow in his dance.

He ended his entertainment by making a final run into the squealing midst of the children. You'd hear the roars of the younger ones below at River Laughter. Some of them were sure he was going to carry them off in a bag like The Wreck of The Hesperus once threatened them (that is before he settled down with his new wife, The Shy Woman). Even the older ones weren't sure whether his cruel intent all along hadn't been to prevent them reaching the schoolhouse – a place as hateful to him as a jug of sour milk.

And then came his concluding lion-like shouts, the spits flying up from his throat as he called on all the saints in the skies above him – called on all the devils under the earth beneath him – called on his mother and father and all his ancestors (naming them in a long line of unmentionable rudeness back as far as Noah's Flood) to come down from the clouds and bear witness to the beauty and grandeur of his Go-Boy's soul – a soul (he cried) that had a beauty unappreciated by everyone on God's earth other than himself. His words were like a sort of pagan prayer that the children clearly couldn't make head nor tail of. They had never in all their lives heard such rambling talk out of anyone.

He Sprang Back In Over The Ditch

His dazzling show had ended. Jimbo-the-Go-Boy sprang back in over the ditch – gone in a flash back into the clouds where (some of them thought) he had seemingly come from. There was no getting away from it, they were going to be late for Dang-the-skin-of-it's first lesson (*Dictation and Transcription*) and they had visions all over again of the sally-switch on their legs. One or two of the little ones were so alarmed by Jimbo's unreal display that they had finally wet their britches. The older children (now that he'd gone) were able to relax a good bit. They assured one another that they'd nothing to fear from him. They had (they told themselves) seen through his disguise and were smart enough to realise (could they have put it into words) that behind his fanciful clothing he had no more than an unearthly love of gaiety in him – that his adventurous soul was harmlessness itself. To witness the antics of a Go-Boy for the first time in their lives – a Go-Boy with his mother's two pairs of red drawers wrapped round his belly and throat – was (they felt) well worth the pain of a few strokes of the sally-switch when they reached the schoolhouse – was far better sport than all the fine sermons Father Sensibly had in his bag at Sunday Mass.

He Had Never Married

Like the Go-Boys before his time Jimbo was a man of a singular character. In the first place he had never married. Indeed the damsels had never cast so much as an eye in his direction. By now he was well passed the wedding-age and wouldn't see fifty years-of-age again in a hurry. Still – he had the liveliness of a fresh buck-of-a-lad twenty years younger than himself and would have been a fine catch for a pretty rosy-cheeked damsel half his age.

But (as with all Go-Boys) what made him that bit different was another niggling little problem – a problem that would never allow him to catch the eye of a damsel: he needed a small bit of grassland to offer her. Even a man in his youth would have needed the land. We all knew that for a fact. If only Jimbo had been given this little blessing from his father (Bedad-sez-I) – just a small piece of land – just a half-acre haggart with a few appletrees – even a little garden with one or two spindly rosebushes to prune. The only land he'd ever owned (he kept telling everyone) was the bit of earth in his mother's geranium box on her windowsill. The only other thing he owned (apart from his mother's two pairs of drawers) was his father's feathered hat, his faded flannelette shirt and his army frockcoat with the brass buttons reaching down to the toes.

Of course he had something else to offer – what he called *mee musical grace.* Such an unusual turn of speech was proof (said Ned-the-Soldier) that he was only an old windbag with nothing to offer but this sort of useless talk. However – who was Ned-the-Soldier? Wasn't he and his ugly sour puss just that little bit jealous of Jimbo's remarkable turn of character? But that didn't stop the old devil from racing on and on. He'd have you know that Jimbo's so-called *musical grace* and his fairyland dressing-up was a mere cover-up for the old fool having no knowledge of a woman's bed – that the only bed Jimbo had ever known was the one he slept in alongside his smelly old mother before she died on him. Ah, the cruelty of the human tongue!

Be that as it may. From the minute the children met up with Jimbo they were never going to share in Ned-the-Soldier's unworthy regard for him – not even the little ones. They counted themselves the luckiest children ever. No other child had seen the colourful appearance of a true Go-Boy as close up as they had. No other child had ever witnessed his unbelievable cartwheels and somersaults and the power of his spirit sparkling like some sort of magical volcano.

In their heart-of-hearts these young ones had the right air to it. They couldn't put it into words, of course. But we could have told them that Jimbo was simply a remarkable bundle of fun with the unique courage to stamp his personality all over the place – able to stand up and be judged differently from the rest of his fellowmen – able to enrich the days of old and young alike by hopping out ubiquitously from one ditch or another at the most inappropriate of times and give his unsuspecting hosts the entertainment of their lives – that what he lacked (not possessing a few acres of land and not knowing the comforts of the marriage-bed) was more than compensated for by his high-stepping jinks along life's highway. Weren't they the fortunate children to have thus been introduced to Jimbo? Indeed they were. Enough said.

Bedad-sez-I

As for Jimbo's father (Bedad-sez-I) – he had been given his unusual name for always having the habit of prefacing any pronouncement of his by shaking his index finger so as to gain a man's attention and starting off with the words *Bedad-sez-I. . .*

'Bedad-sez-I . . . in all mee life I never saw him looking better,' he sighed whilst gazing down on The Gog's dead body at the wake above in Sheep's Cross.

'Bedad-sez-I . . . wouldn't ye think that the man-in-black would give his tongue a bit of a rest some Sundays,' he'd moan when the Mass went on jawing for longer than twenty minutes.

Jimbo's Inspiration

As far back as anyone could remember it was Bedad-sez-I who had been Jimbo's inspiration. Indeed he was something of a Go-Boy himself and whenever he burst out laughing the folds of his belly wobbled about like wet dung on a shovel. Though he hadn't the fanciful cut of his son's later attire he was still able to win his own bit of fame: it happened on the day of his wedding and would never be forgotten. A few days earlier he had the good fortune to find a pair of discarded wellingtons in Old Tim Bellow's dyke. They'd come in handy for the journey to his imminent wedding (he thought) and he could spare his shiny black brogues till the moment came for him to parade up the church aisle. He'd keep the old wellingtons on his feet till the very last minute and ride his bike right up to the back door of the church before changing into his new shiny brogues.

The Wedding-day

The wedding-day came along and the yard and the bushes were shimmering beneath a passionate sky. Bedad-sez-I's mother (Tongue-of-all-Tongues) dressed him up in a smart sports-jacket and grey flannels and for this special occasion a white shirt with the open-buttoned collar flared out over the coat's own collar. He had a high quiff in his hair as well as his father's best boots to wear (not the wellingtons). He was as shiny going out the door as a fine general and his father (old Tom Jibberish) stood back to take a long look at him. Puffing on his pipe, he asked him (wasn't the old fellow the whimsical wag) how many soldiers he had at his command on the battlefield – so proud was he of his son stepping out to go and get himself married.

It was the season when new flowers were shouldering their way up through the weeds in the fields. The ditches were already swaying with them. The birds all round him were singing cheerily. The meadows were getting into full bloom and the sun was shining down on top of his head. Bedad-sez-I was the soul of merriment as he cycled his way on through the pinetrees and down the hillslope from Lisnagorna. His heart was ablaze like the sun.

Shortly after leaving the yard he had changed into the wellingtons, wrapping his father's boots neatly in a paper bag and strapped onto the handlebars of his bike. I need hardly tell you that his father had stolen these same boots from Red Scissors's grandfather whilst the latter gentleman was having a sleep for himself abroad in Bog Boundless.

His Little Bit Of Comfort

Apart from his First Holy Communion Day his wedding-day was going to be the happiest day in his life. He was on his way to get himself hitched up to Lizzie-the-Herd (*mee little bit of comfort*) and his mind was full of the little squeezes he'd be getting out of her stout arms when he got close up to her in the night and the bedroom tumblings and jostlings would begin to shake the house.

He had started out early enough on the road. Whistling like a boy, he sped along until he reached the stream across The Road-to-the-Hollows. It had never been anything other than a harmless trickle. He suddenly realised that the recent rains had raised the level of the water by something like a foot-and-a-half. Damn the bit – didn't his right-foot wellington have a few small holes in it and it let the stream's icy water into his sock, soaking it.

'Bedad-sez-I . . . I'll have to deal with this confoundedly extraordinary situation,' said Bedad-sez-, who (like his later son Jimbo) was inclined to use a few big words now and then. He hopped down from the bike and put on one of the new boots in place of the leaky wellington. He took a hurried glance at his pocket-watch and found that he had less time to spare than he'd have wished and he pedalled on at top speed until he reached the church door.

By then Lizzie-the-Herd and her entire pack of cousins (and what looked like half of Tipperary) were all seated snugly up at the front and they decked out in their finest fashion. They were beginning to get a bit fidgety. Where on earth was Bedad-sez-I? Was he coming or was he not coming to his own wedding? And in between praying for a satisfactory outcome to the day's wedding one or two of them had begun to curse the poor fellow into the depths of hell.

Meanwhile . . .

Meanwhile what was Bedad-sez-I to do? He was going to be late. He'd be the talk of the whole church – of the entire parish. He reached the churchyard and without giving himself a minute to think he rode his rusty old bike straight through the front door of the church. By this time a few of the sleepy congregation had started to have the odd little romantic dream about the future love-nest of Lizzie and Bedad-sez-I. However – they woke up in an instant when (horror-of-horrors) they beheld the intended groom and his bike cycling furiously up the main aisle – up towards the very altar steps – a wellington full of holes on his right leg and a shiny boot on his left leg. They gasped. They groaned. Confusion hit them like a rock. This was a pure disgrace (the likes of it never having been seen before) – to be seen cycling a bike around inside The House of God and a man dressed out in such outrageous footwear.

Breathlessly Bedad-sez-I threw his bike in a heap next to his bride-to-be and, giving her a sly little wink and a nudge, he cast his merry old soul next to his *little bit of comfort.*

Suddenly the congregation could see a cheerful smile on Father Sensibly's face. It was as though a dark cloud had just flown out the church window. Relieved at last, they got back their senses and the previous hush and their sighs of distaste now turned into bursts of thunderous laughter. Its echoes might well have ruined the dignified composure of the holy place (where such laughter was clearly forbidden) if Father Sensibly hadn't already filled his pockets with a pile of green poundnotes from Lizzie-the-Herd's father. And for days thereafter Bedad-sez-I with his one wellington and his one shiny black boot (and he riding his rusty old bike up along the church aisle) made a laughable story that kept us all in fine form. It travelled not only the length of north Tipperary but (we're told) back as far as Father Sensibly's birthplace in Clare. It had been an exceptional privilege (he told his ancient mother) to marry a man in a wellington and a boot – a privilege that would never again be witnessed in the whole of Ireland.

His Dream Of The Ocean

Long before the birth of Jimbo the only men brave enough to dream about going to see the mighty waves of The Great Ocean had been Bedad-sez-I and his trusty companion, Lowry-with-the-Moustache – the only fellow ever seen with a waxed moustache until our recent schoolmaster (Dang-the-skin-of-it). In their nightly dreams the two would-be adventurers heard this vast amount of water continually calling them – telling them it was simply lying out there on its own and dying to be discovered by us if only we'd pluck up a bit of courage and get up off of our lazy arses.

Unable to stand the ache in their chests Bedad-sez-I and Lowry decided they'd take the ninety-mile trek to the far side of Galway. When they got home they could tell the rest of us that The Great Ocean did in fact truly exist because they themselves had cast their eyes on it – they could then answer everybody's question: was it really a thousand times bigger than Lord Plus-Fours lake? Did it look the same as Old Needle-and-Cork (the schoolmaster of those days) had taught them during his Point-to-The-Map lessons? Up until now (for all anyone knew) The Great Ocean might as well have been a fairytale and a prank in the mind of that hairy old drunkard-of-a-schoolmaster – might as well have been a bit of a dream drummed up at the card-players' winter fireside in Curl 'n' Stripes' drinking-shop. Our two heroes shrugged their shoulders: they had had enough of playing these silly little guessing-games: they were bursting to know what was the truth about The Great Ocean.

Tongue-of-All-Tongues

Bedad-sez-I had another cute reason for wanting to take to the road: he was desperately anxious to get away from his wretched mother (Tongue-of-All-Tongues). Even in those days some of our women were known to have the spiteful powers of Invectiveness and to get themselves into fits of contortion with their fiery eyes and venomous tongues. His cruel mother had this intolerable gift and could spit fire as good as a solicitor. By now she had driven her poor son clean out of his mind with the sizzling spears she kept throwing at him ('sorry am I for the day I gave birth to the likes of you.') Such malevolent talk cut him to the bone, piercing his heart more than any blow of a cudgel. He told everyone that he'd rather be out walking throught the rustling ferns and listening to the chirruping of the birds – or even seen walking through a field of nettles – than listen to his weasel-of-a-mother wearying the life out of him. 'Twould try the patience of Saint Patrick (said he).

Back After Rabbiting

After rabbiting successfully for a few nights with his ferret and nets Bedad-sez-I would sometimes take himself off on a little drinking-spree with Lowry. It was just for a few days (no more than this) that he'd leave his mother and the farm unattended behind him. On his return Tongue-of-All-Tongues would meet him in the haggart even before he tumbled in the door and had time to pelt off his jacket. For a woman with little or no schooling the scornful words she then spat out of her mouth were enough to fill a Bible as she leathered him with the list of his sins:

'Most rakish of all the unsaintly rakes in Ireland – ye're the talk of the whole wide world. Where is yeer decency? Have ye no shame in ye?'

It was the last straw – the one that finally put an end to the patience of Bedad-sez-I – the thousandth time that he'd asked himself the same old question: was she hoping to conquer a grown man like himself – make him bawl like a child and sue her for mercy? He looked away from her. And in spite of himself his eyes filled up with painful tears. Without so much as going to the bucket for a mug of water he turned on his heel, leaving the ghost of his mother to swallow her words back down her throat and stand at the door like a fool.

He belted up the road to meet Lowry and the two of them sat on the ditch. There and then they laid out plans for their unheard-of journey into The Unknown. Yes (he told himself) he'd give his old crone-of-a-mother plenty of reason to be wagging her filthy tongue at him the next time she saw him crossing the haggart. Yes (he again told himself) he'd finally get her wicked words out of his hair and shake the dust of the yard from off of his boots. He'd leave his mother to rot at the doorstep: he'd leave her to milk her own cows and fight with their shitty tails: he'd leave her to chop her own logs and take the splinters out of her eyes. When he finally came back home she'd be good and ready (said he) to kiss his arse. With dreams of adventure filling their heads – himself and Lowry would spend a whole month in Galway. They'd see and breathe into their lungs the heart and soul of The Great Ocean. Lowry then put his two arms round his friend's sad shoulders and gradually brought the smile back onto his face and the life back into his heart until Bedad-sez-I began to feel a good deal better.

At The Crack Of Dawn

The next morning when the dawn sky was just turning white and aware of the sun's arrival, Lowry went into town early and sold his mother's best cow. He had the price of it stuffed teasingly in his hip-pocket. It was a soft mid-summer's day and the two brave byze went off over the fields with the reins and winkers to fetch their horses. They didn't take with them so much as a drop of holywater (the heathens!). Bedad-sez-I was in an unforgiving mood. Nor did he go back to give a wave of the handkerchief to Tongue-of-All-Tongues.

The Spirit Of Great Seafarers

Those dreams and those spirit that made the great seafarers and past explorers sail out over the seven seas now saw our two heroes disappearing out of Tipperary and into the early morning sunrise. Ah, the honeysweet life! Their hearts were full of the brightness of the new fields and hedgerows and not long afterwards they could be seen rattling their way along the road leading towards Galway. It was going to take them weeks of wild carousing along the way before they'd reach Galway itself. In the meantime they were going to help themselves to The Drink in every drinking-shop that stood in their way.

Though they had given themselves a good feed of rabbit-stew with oceans of turnips, carrots and spuds thrown in, they soon found themselves with their bellies hanging out of them and craving with hunger. However- they kept themselves going with a few stolen apples and a pocketful of hazelnuts along the riverbanks. At last they came to a lonely Protestant church in the middle of God-knows-where. They sneaked in through the back door where they found a welcome bottle of altar-wine and a sack of dry communion-wafers. Then the two unholy blackguards (may God forgive them their sin) kept their merry old souls alive by eating half the sack of wafers and feasting on the wine till the bottle ran dry. Had all saintliness faded from the rascals' brains? When the two heathens came home a month later and told yarns about the great adventures they had given themselves it would be hard for anyone in Rookery Rally (even The Weeping Mollys) to believe such damned lies as theirs. Didn't every-one know that to step inside the door of a Protestant church was a sure way of getting yourself struck down by a bolt of God's lightning?

At The Side Of The Ocean

They finally arrived at the side of The Ocean. The poetry of their schoolbooks *('the white-crested foamy sea-horses, the ancient wine-dark waves, the storm-tossed mountainous snarls of the angry salty main')* filled the mind of Bedad-sez-I and his love of the long words. The two of them hadn't put a razor to their jaws all the time they were on the road and by now Bedad-sez-I *(the gingery hairy one* the Galway girls were to call him) had a beard that reached down to his waist if not all the ways down to his ankles.

A Very Strange Couple

And then they were there. With anxious eyes the Galway men came down to look at the two wild men and to ask them what part of the world they came from for they looked a very strange couple. Galway had never seen the likes of two such hairy apes as these two coming to greet them and they asked them if all men elsewhere were now wearing their beards this way. Was it a new kind of fashion that had come down from Dublin? Of course this was said with a bit of a smirk. The children ran down and hid behind the men's wellingtons. As always these little ones wanted to know the truth and in their own way they were just as inquisitive about the two new arrivals. In their eyes the two doughty heroes looked the very same as Saint Peter and Saint Paul in their picture-prayerbooks.

Down To Greet The Mighty Waves

Next morning – even before the first cockerel had begun its crow Bedad-sez-I and Lowry went down to greet the mighty waves – waves that they knew they'd never see again. They were delighted to be the centre of such gay old times. They stripped off their togs (shifts and all) the way they would do when taking their yearly washing in the sally-hole of Bog Boundless. They went leaping into the freezing waters of The Great Ocean. Oh the joy of it! They could scarcely believe it. Tipperary's rivers could go hang!

This was the life for a real man! They soon felt like two young sheepdogs prancing around in the snows of a January field.

They spread out their legs and they fired their piss all round The Great Ocean. They challenged her to put up a bit of a fight and attack them: 'Coom on! Blasht ye! We're here from Tipperary and ready to test yeer metal!' You'd have liked to get inside their heads there and then – for the two fainthearts were in dread of their natural lives lest they got themselves drowned and never got home to their own warm fireside. Nobody in Rookery Rally could swim a stroke barring Spare-Ribs and Matt-with-the-Machinery. Of course they couldn't let on to one another their dread. So – to give themselves a bit of a lift they continued to curse The Great Ocean and to threaten her destruction and to kick her waves up to the heavens. The roars that came out of their mouths must have startled the sleepy sea-nymphs in the depths of the waves! Horses couldn't have done a better job of it.

The Bemused Galway Girls

It was fortunate that their two beards were long enough to cover their bellies and their private credentials – else the bemused Galway girls would have been put to the blush at the sight of their manly private bits. For, on hearing the early morning roars of the two new arrivals, both girls and boys had come down to the edge of the sea to witness such unheard-of commotion:

'A box-camera! Quick! Quick! A box-camera!' shouted one of the Galway men. It was a chance for history to be written as never before – two strange men from Tipperary and they standing in their pelts (*glory to ye, byze!*) without a stitch of clothes on them – without even a coy little blush – and they entertaining the eyes of the whole of Galway. It would be a remarkable photo – a sight never to be seen or heard tell of in Galway again – a sight that Rookery Rally and even Father Sensibly would soon have the privilege to lay their eyes on. As though the one lewd photo wasn't bad enough, there was a second photo taken – with Bedad-sez-I and Lowry turning their brazen bare arses up at the camera for a photo that would have shocked the bespectacled Pope in his palace back in Rome.

Of course our women later on never got so much as a glimpse at these unseemly photos for there was a limit to what the eyes of our prim damsels could be let look at. However, when both sets of photos found their way back to Tipperary a few weeks later and were shown in Curl 'n' Stripes' drinking-shop, the steam could be seen coming out of the heads of our old gossips (The Weeping Mollys). Wouldn't you know it – they were more than a bit envious of all the attention showered on our two manly specimens. Always wanting themselves to be the centre of the news, the old crones told everyone that the photos had been selling like hot cakes right across Galway – that they were bringing in a tidy sum of money for the man with the box-camera – that it was a shame that poor old Lowry and Bedad-sez-I couldn't make a brass farthing out of it. Wouldn't you know how these jealous wretches would make hay out of the two adventurers' lost opportunity – how they'd get in the last gleeful word! Women and their gossiping, I ask you.

He Was In The Worst Possible Wear

When he got back home, Bedad-sez-I was in the worst possible wear and even his own mother kept herself and her tongue a safe distance away from him for his clothes stank to high heavens. Silently she'd have wished she had an eagle's wings and could fly back to Galway with him strapped to her back and pelt him straight into the middle of The Great Ocean in order to scrub the dirt off of him.

As for Lowry, so fierce was his mother's tongue that he didn't dare bring his boots into the yard but crept secretly in over the back ditch of the haggart. He was met, however, with a beautiful surprise – namely the battle for his very life. For his mother had picked out her best few sods-of-turf from the shed. They were rock-hard and with these she greeted his head. Before he could blink his eyes shut, she had blinded him with the first few fine volleys. This she followed up by chastising his two shins with the broken leg-of-the-chair when the poor man (groping his way round the edge of the haystack) was in no fit state to defend himself. The yard-brush on this occasion was not thought fit enough to kill a miserable son (*mee little shitty-arse*) for running away with the price of her best cow in his pocket.

Yet when Lowry had mended his wounds and when Bedad-sez-I had been converted (for a short while) to drinking from the bucket of spring-water and when the two of them had washed away their sins in the depths of River Laughter, not one of us could deny that they were the two best men on the planet and their was laughter and smiles galore as we raised them (almost) to the status of sainthood – heroes above all other heroes – established forever as an unassailable piece of our history. And from that day on, as children sat and smoked their stolen fag butts on the logs in Old Sam's orchard, the magical journey of Lowry and Bedad-sez-I to see The Great Ocean and get their pictures taken without a stitch of clothes on them would often cheer up a sad and rainy afternoon – the way those two brave explorers had stepped into the waves to challenge and frighten the life out of The Great Ocean ninety miles from home. In the children's minds it was as good as having travelled to the moon and back.

A True Go-Boy

Jimbo had inherited that wild energetic nature which his father had manifested in going off to see The Great Ocean. And though Bedad-sez-I wasn't a true Go-Boy in that he had the responsibility of a good bit of land, he had always felt that he was entitled to this name thanks to the merry jinks of himself and his nakedness in The Great Ocean. With his son, however, it was going to be a different story.

This is the way things were: tilling and ploughing the land, rearing the cattle and tending to the horses, were never to be Jimbo's – even though he was the eldest son and was entitled to it. And all this was because of the cursed Drink – the Drink that he'd taken a liking to the minute he left off his schoolday britches. As soon as his father died, his mother (Lizzie) kept pestering and pestering him to give it up till he was sick and tired of hearing her voice singing that same old song. To give her son the farm would (she said) be to sign the last sod of it away to every drinking-shop owner in town. So instead she handed the land to his later-born sister (Molly) and her crafty husband (Pussyfoot) from beyond the mountains. The result was what you might have expected: Jimbo (as soon as he was denied his birthright) was overtaken by an acute ache in his chest – a sorrow akin to the anger and depression which his father had once felt when he turned away from the haggart after the lashing of his mother's cruel tongue.

He Went Out The Half-door

However, having been born with a stout heart and a serene mind, he was not a man to be seen crying in his boots or beaten down into the ground. He turned his back forever on his contemptible mother and sister and went out the half-door without so much as a look back. He flung himself across the yard and set off over the fields to discover the rest of the world for himself – the run of its genial rivers, the heat of its summertime breezes (he'd tell you in those lofty words of his).

Not knowing what else he could turn his hand to other than the job of farming, he realised the depth of his loss. However, his natural instincts told him to throw his mother's disregard for him right back in her face. He'd make the old devil rue the day she took the land from him and he turned his back on the drinking-shops, thereby avoiding his mother's earlier predictions of his imminent downfall and death.

Free At Last

Free at last, he soon saw a glimpse of light ahead of him in his new life. Now that he was landless – now that he was dismantled of even a single field of inheritance – he would follow in the footsteps of Bedad-sez-I and establish himself as an entertainer – as a fully-fledged Go-Boy. But would he have the courage? It would mean turning himself into a brand new individual the likes of whom we hadn't seen before – a man that'd challenge our senses – a man that'd dress himself festively in colourful clothing – a man that'd perform outrageous public acts to send us out of our minds.

He began to like the idea. The thought of it made him laugh out loud. He could see his horrified mother throwing her hands up in the air. He could picture the look of distain on her sad old face – her sheer embarrassment at having brought onto the earth a wretched son for a Go-Boy. Would she ever be able to look another mortal in the eye or show her face outside The Welcoming Room? And Jimbo's laughter was to remain with him for the rest of his days.

The Talents Of A Go-Boy

What are the talents of a Go-Boy? There was many a man who wanted to put up a bit of a fight against conventionality – against the overbearing tongues of their women, against the daily drudgery of tilling the soil, against the pomposity of certain well-meaning clerics who allegedly knew better than others the sort of way we were supposed to arrange our daily lives. They were keen to follow in the wake of Jimbo and let all their past miseries go to blazes. Chief among these lads was Samson from above in Lisnagorna – a tall fella and as straight as a bar – with a nose on him broad enough to be a spade.

Samson

When Samson witnessed the performances of our merry Jimbo his own ardour for the life of a Go-Boy got the better of him. His calling, however, wasn't as pure and honest as Jimbo's. To be fair to him – with his mane of long dark hair he sometimes had the stance and gymp of a Go-Boy. He walked with the hayfork horizontally across the broad of his back and in under his armpits – hoping to advance the upright stance of his manly carriage whenever he came striding through The Valley of The Pig to catch a mouthful of mountainy air. But being a farmer (at least for half the day) he didn't fit the true nature of a Go-Boy – namely a landless entertainer. And try as he might, it was to prove no use for him.

The dance in Gibbet Hill came round. The rage of life was rising in him. He stood before the looking-glass, admiring his newly-shaven face. He oiled and frizzed up his new pair of whiskers. He was wearing his best brown suit and his father's ginger topcoat. It reached down to his boots. He put the soapy water on his long dark locks to stiffen them into a fashionably wavy quiff. He caressed his hobnail boots with half a tin of blacking. He felt he was spotless and ready to demolish any fair damsel who came within his sights. He would entertain her with his style and comely wit. He'd tear the wooden floor of the platform to bits with his dancesteps as soon as he reached The Dance-in-the-fields.

The amorous lad set out. It was a cool evening and the sun was still faintly glowing. He felt almost serene and threw his chest out challengingly. It would be a magnificent occasion. Wouldn't any Go-Boy envy the style of him? Like a young turkeycock he entered the field's gateway where the stewards (big towering lads) were collecting in the fourpence entrance-money from each of the dancers. He threw his coat and jacket in under the first bench he came across. He was stripped down to his shirt and was ready to tear the women apart.

He strolled round the edge of the platform, spitting on his fists and rubbing the palms of his hands together: 'Mee time has come,' he said. 'I'm about to chastise one or two fine young women in their flouncy skirts and lay them in mee clutches'. He was suitably oiled not only in his hair and his red cheeks but also on the inside of his chest with a good few mouthfuls of his father's raw-gut whiskey.

He made a few sidesteps across the floor towards the women seated in a colourful line at the far end of the floor: 'Will ye dance, missee? Will ye dance, mee dearest?'

Was there something wrong with their hearing? He heard not a word back from the giggly girls.

'Will ye dance, blasht ye?' he repeated.

'No, kind sir,' said they in mock imitation of one of their former schoolday rhymes, 'we will not dance with ye.'

Then one of the little hussies put paid to any chance of further conversation: 'We'll not dance with a farmer's son and the smell of cowshit on his clothes.' And the rest of the girls took a fit of laughing at him.

Samson felt as though he'd been struck by lightning. He gave way to a tearful fit of anger and stamped his big boots on the wooden floor, sending splinters into the air. Oh, to be the victim of a bunch of silly women! Like a chastised schoolboy his cheeks turned red and he made up his mind to abandon any further attempts to dance. He'd seek out the bottom of a few glasses of The Black Doctor in Merrymouth's drinking-shop over the road. But before he left the dancefloor he cursed the laughing *mee-damsels* straight into hell.

'At home in Lisnagorna, ye saucy young sour-pusses,' said he, 'I've women of mee own and plenty.'

It was then that the little madams took an even greater fit of laughting, almost doubling themselves in two. It was the best bit of sport they'd had all evening. Little did they know – an even better bout of sport was next to follow.

Samson staggered across the dancefloor, his shoulders now slumped. He felt humbler and less sure of his stride than before. He started looking for his coat and his jacket, trying to remember where he'd put them. These damned women had distracted the brains out of his head. Ah-ha – he found them – in underneath the bench at the entrance to the field. But the bench was no longer empty: it was thronged with a new array of apple-cheeked women, their hair tidily half-plaited and half-loose and they all dressed up in their gaily-printed frills and flounces. Like the previous bunch of women they were having the time of their lives – laughing and giggling in the shiny light of the dancefloor. The older ones were giving the wink and little smiles of invitation from their wet lips to the men seated on benches the other side of the platform. They in turn were giving the glad-eye back to them good-naturedly. A bit of The Devil's brazenness then found its way into one or two of the more experienced young madams. They whispered encouragement to their younger sisters, who still had their hands clasped coyly between their knees. The immodest heathens had crossed their legs and began to show the young men more than a bit of their white thighs and their stocking suspenders – causing uncomfortable embarrassment to the younger lads by revealing also a shade of their mauve knickers and the elastic.

Poor innocent Samson! What an inauspicious end to a night's dancing was about to follow. He reached for his coat and jacket underneath the women's legs, his fingers grasping about in search of them. He made a sudden grab and roughly pulled out his coat, anxious to get away from the women and the smell of their perfume and facepowder and still cursing their entire race under his breath. But they – thinking that he was about to molest them and make a raid on their thighs (the dirty little whoor), frightened the stars round the field with sudden squeals and shrieks. You'd have heard them at the fireside in Merrymouth's drinking-shop across in the village:

'Help! He's making a raid on our legs! Go 'way, ye dirty little devil!' could be heard all round the dancefloor.

In front of them stood the startled Samson with the coat and the jacket in his fists. From out of nowhere stormed the two sturdy gate-stewards to confront this rascal from the mountains and keep some sort of calm and orderliness in the dance. They knew what to do: they'd give him a taste of their medicine. They made a rush at him from behind his back and whipped the two legs from under him:

'Is this the way ye do things above on the mountains?' said one of them.

'Looking up with yeer gawk-eyes to see if ye can spot the colour of a young girl's knickers, is it?' said the other one.

They dragged the poor lad ferociously to his feet and over as far as the door. Some of the dancers said they overplayed their part in order to impress the girls and maybe get a jostle or two from them in the bushes later on. Others said that they were hoping to raise the temper of the mountainy man and hear the profanity of his curses so that they'd have good reason to belt the jaws off of him when they got him outside. Poor artless Samson – with neither a dance for his feet this unholy evening nor the feel of a woman's legs later behind the ditch – was spirited out through the gateway. The stewards pelted him into the darkness – into Oblivion, you might say. His entertainment was not to be got at The Platform Dance in Gibbet Hill. Enough said.

Play-Your-Life-Away

A Go-Boy's life was not going to be the vocation for Samson. A Go-boy has a certain air of capriciousness to his name – a style that Samson could never emulate. There is an unfathomable joy (*play! play! play your life away*) in the heart of a Go-Boy. Indeed Playfulness is his true calling – the very centre of his existence. You'd be sitting on your ass-and-car and see him running at speed a stonethrow from the creamery gates. You'd see him an hour later entering The Roaring Town at a similar gallop and then coming back over the railway bridge with a pound of mutton – that's if you were travelling at the speed of a greyhound. How on earth did he do it?

To keep us on our toes we awoke one morning to see poor Samson's hat and britches ('where did mee britches go to?') perched on top of the church steeple – stolen by Jimbo – placed up there by the same fellow. It was a puzzle that left us scratching our heads for a week-and-a-half. The commotion caused Father Sensibly such a shock that he caught an unusual bout of flu and took to his bed. Even the little birds stopped singing as if they were in mourning over him.

The New Confession

By mid-morning the usual crew of women were outside the confession-box and (unaware of Father Sensibly's illness) were hellbent as usual on telling him their small sins and getting themselves saved from hell. Who was the scoundrel (a needless question), who crept unnoticed into the sacristy and togged himself out in the holy man's cassock and soutan (the mitre and the stoll as well)? Who was it that beat them all to the door of the confession-box? Yes – it was Jimbo, admirably dressed for his new role as a visiting priest (the heathen). In his most subsouciant voice he gently prodded these poor old dames to tell him their harmless few sins: 'Yes – my child! Go on! Go on! That little sin of yours isn't nearly enough of a sin to get you into hell. Come now, don't be shy – you must have a few more serious sins for me to absolve you from.'

For a finish he wheedled out a cartload of intimacies and misdemeanours not only from the shy women but also from two of his own uncles. By midday he had been given such a shock to his system that he could fill an entire book. Of course, when his blasphemous rascality was discovered he didn't dare set foot in the parish for a month-and-a-half as there was an army of four-grained forks waiting for him – to do untold damage to his rear quarters.

Bassy The Terrier

The anger of our men and women, however, was shortlived and we were soon laughing when we heard of Jimbo's next endeavour – his battle with Old Sam's fierce terrier (Bassy). He was heading to the church to buy a heap of religious medals to pin on his jacket as a reminder of his wartime bravery when Bassy (that devil-of-a-dog) leapt out over the ditch and bit him so severely on the seat of his britches that he couldn't sit down at the table and have his dinner. Later that evening he marched into Old Sam's yard. Letting a mighty roar out of him he ran at the terrier and caught him by the tail and the leg. Mindless of Bassy's countless fleas – he proceeded to bend his hind leg back as far as it would go – until the poor creature roared blue murder. Then he sank his savage teeth into the squealing animal's ear till he had it nearly torn off: a sure cure (said he) for any dog that likes to bite humans.

The Winter Sliders

In the snowy winter Jimbo was the first to arrive at the top of Easy-does-it's hillslope – the first to start the downhill sliding on his belly-board. He won the hearts of us all as he took the wooden board down the slope at an unmerciful speed unnatural to man. Without a thought of stopping he hurled himself and his sledge (what we half-expecting) straight into Simon-not-so-simple's ditch, bouncing clean out over it and landing in the briars in a leg-wriggling heap of mock rage. We were left in stitches.

As if that weren't enough – on his next slide he risked breaking his skull as he sped down the course only to end up somersaulting through the air and landing on top of Dowager's cowshed. The talk of Jimbo and his sledging filled us with bouts of amusement that lasted throughout the winter.

August Came Round

August came round. It was the time when most of us were worked off of our feet – what with the mowing and harvesting of the hay – and yet we found time to do a little bit of celebrating here and there. Jimbo managed to keep us on our tippy-toes with more of his whirling antics. It was a Sunday evening and the smoky twilight would soon be arriving on the skyline above the church in Copperstone Hollow. A good crowd of us were out and about in the fresh mountainy air – watching the final of the handball between Towser and Joe Soap in the ball-alley next to the church. Others were sitting inside in Merrymouth's drinking-shop and already well down into the second and third pint of The Black Doctor. Jimbo had been up at the counter with a few old cronies, carousing his gizzard for the past hour at least. But now he was gone out.

Suddenly we heard a commotion down near The Shrine of The Blessed Virgin. It was Jimbo – and he roaring and pawing at the ground like an enraged bull. The news ('come and see Jimbo!') went quickly round. We were bristling with anticipation. The handballers stopped their play and the rest of us emptied the drinking-shop without bothering to finish our drinks. Thirty yards down from the shrine we saw a telegraph-pole propped up against the side of Jimmy Lamplighter's hayshed. There was a reins roped round it. Jimbo was about to make a run at this treacherous obstacle in an effort to knock it down with a belt of his forehead. We looked at the pole. We looked at Jimbo. Were our eyes deceiving us? One of them (the pole or Jimbo) was about to meet its doom and we roared on our encouragement. The suspense was killing us. Shouts of joy rose from the children.

'Hush, let ye!'

'Be quiet yeer mouths!'

Jimbo positioned his arms and legs. He clenched his fists. He was about to make another bit of history – about to make a mad dash at the telegraph-pole and destroy it:

'The heavens to you, Jimbo!'

He was off and away.

We kept a safe distance away from the hayshed in case Jimbo had doctored the pole and it'd fall down on top of our heads and kill a pile of us.

'Molly, avic, will ye look at the whoor!' shouted Towser to his sister.

Such a feat had never been seen before – a duel between a man and a telegraph-pole. Ah, the vanity of the man!

'Ah – me and mee mother,' groaned one or two women and they prayed silently for Jimbo's head and they rattled their rosary-beads.

A minute later we saw that Jimbo had smashed his forehead off of the pole. The Guards and the nurse (Black Bess) came quickly on the scene and carried him away to the hospital. Who were the filthy blackguards who had mixed the potheen and the whiskey – mixed the brandy and rum – into Jimbo's half-empty glass when he was out making his poolie? Didn't they know there'd be no fun in it – that Jimbo would get the thought fixedly into his head that he could fly to the moon – that he could swim The Mighty Shannon River – not that he'd be sure to damn near kill himself?

Training The Young

A week later we found Jimbo restored to his previous state of good health. You couldn't kill an article like him. He set out to encourage the youngsters in their hurling skills. As soon as he arrived in the centre of Old Sam's Field he stood amongst one or two heaps of fresh cowdung. Once more he was wearing one of his mother's colourful drawers – this time as a hurling-togs outside his trousers. He was also wearing his grandmother's dress, stuffed down untidily into the drawers. All he needed now was a bit of powder and paint to set himself off and keep us all in fits of uncontrolable laughter. There was silence. He closed his eyes. More silence. Then he begged the children to hurl the cowdung up into his face – as much as they could muster. They didn't need to be asked twice. Covered in the thick cowdung, the freshening characteristics of Jimbo made a fine portrait of him as he spun round and round the field deliriously. See his laughing face! See his joy! Smell the cowdung all over him! He raced off in the direction of Curl 'n' Stripes' drinking-shop. What a sight he was on entering the shop amidst the startled drinkers and their pints of booze frozen in time – halfways up to their whiskery lips!

The Regatta At Windy-View

'Were ye at the Regatta in Windy-View or were ye sick?' asked The Weeping Mollys? Of course we were all there. Jimbo was once more on show – him and his haughty swaggering after his historic row with the telegraph-pole and his remarkable portraiture in cowdung. The stewards had a roll of chickenwire rigged up around a stretched-out track. By special invitation there was to be a handicap-race between the great man and a broken-legged hare. The crowd gathered round. They stretched out their necks like a pile of young ganders. Several penny-bets were thrown down as to which one would win the race – Jimbo or the hare.

It would soon be time for the race to start.

Jimbo had been drinking a good few drops of the black stuff throughout the morning. He tore off his shirt (the one his father left him) and proceeded to rub a few handfuls of spearmint across his chest.

'*A sure cure for the fleas*,' he laughed.

He began preening his puny body and strutting back and forth, showing us the great man he was. The steward called him to the starting-line. He suddenly turned and glared at us: 'Take a good look at me now – I'm The Star of Paradise, that's who I am – as fine a man as ever blew froth from a pint of The Black Doctor.' What the startled hare thought of this sort of speechifying as he wriggled about in the hands of the starter we dread to think

Jimbo spat on his fists. He stared glassy-eyed at the finishing-tape. He raised his leg and held it a moment in the air. He made a few scurrilous gestures with his backside and let rip one or two squeaky farts before positioning himself alonside the hare.

And then they were off.

To help him on his way the hare had been given a savage dart of a pin up under his tail. Jimbo and the crippled creature made an earnest attempt to get away down the track. Soon enough our Go-Boy was out in front. That's when the real buffoonery took hold. A visiting curate from Clare had a cute little terrier cradled in his arms. He was stroking it thoughtfully. He could see Jimbo heading for the finishing-line where the prize of a pound-of-tea was waiting for him. And then he had a vision. To add to the sport he threw the terrier in over the wire. In the confusion and excitement (if not terror) the eejit-of-a-dog ran straight across Jimbo's path, entangling itself in his wellingtons and leaving him outstretched on the grass with a dent in his nose. It was nothing less than a disgrace. And to the angry shouts of the gamblers (blasht it) the race had to be abandoned there and then. The hare had already reached the finishing-tape – only to be disqualified on the spot and deprived of his one bit of fame, poor thing. Some wily wags said that the exhausted creature was subsequently arrested and thrown in the lock-up and that Father Sensibly had the finest hare-soup ladled out to him from his maidservant the very next evening.

The Hurling

The following week was a major event when The Munster County Hurling Final was to take place in The Showground. Long before any of us came alive or the sun had embraced the mountains Jimbo reached the sleepy town. Hurling for us would be the blue-and-gold jerseys of our Tipperary stone-throwers. Hurling against them would be their mortal enemy – the cherry-shirted Cork hurlers from The River Lee. There was already a festive air to the day: 'It's a good year when we have Cork bate and the hay saved,' would be the phrase on all our lips.

A Real Lady-Dazzler

Jimbo with his white linen shirt and his yellow cross-sash was like the conductor of a Dublin orchestra. With his glistening walking-cane and his white surgeon's gloves he was a man of consummate importance if you didn't know who he was and if you'd come from as far afield as Cork. Today he was about to confront the unsuspecting visitors and bring out the finest notes of his creative madness. They had travelled in droves – what appeared to be the whole population of Cork. He could see them from over the ditch as they came bowling towards him from The Railway Station. He smiled to himself. He placed himself at the crossroads. They'd be sure to pass his way in order to get to the hurling-ground:

'Here they come! Here they come! Stand back!'

With their red rosettes and the screech of their silver whistles and all the hurly-burly that went with it – here was a spectacle for our sore eyes. The visitors stopped at the crossroads, unsure of their direction. Should they take the left road? Should they take the right road?

That's when The Wily Fairies, who always lived on the edge of hell, sped up under Jimbo's feet and lodged themselves deep in his brain. With his raised cane and his officious pair of white gloves he stepped out to greet the Corkmen. With a proud wave of his hand he instructed them (*coom on! coom on!*) to follow on behind him. They turned and followed him like a herd of sheep. Graciously brandishing his cane and waving at the amused townies who had come out to see this exciting pilgrimage, he proceeded to lead them off towards the right, stamping his boots down along Bell Alley and round the corner passed The Barber's Shop. From there he proceeded to lead them off to the left.

Building up steam and raising his voice into something like a military bellow he escorted his Cork guests back along Sky Street. You'd never think he'd have the nerve as he trailed them around the blessed circumference of the town – in along one side and back out the other side. After marching them all over the neighbourhood, he finally led the poor misfortunates to within a stonethrow of where they'd started out – back to the crossroads. And there they parted company. A moment of confusion (a moment of untold mystery) followed and then sheer panic and pandemonium took over. The bedraggled Corkmen turned into a swarm of angry bees: 'The bleddy little fecker!' roared their leader, 'let me get at him till I break every tooth in his head.'

They'd not be seen dead in Tipperary again: 'Why – the little shitty-arse!' screeched others, 'wait till I get my hands on him – he'll not have a testicle to his name when I'm finished with him. The match'll be as good as over by the time we get to see the action.'

Their repeated misuse of poor Christ's name outmatched even our own inventive oaths and swearwords as they heaped curses on Jimbo and his father and mother. Their nostrils flared – sniffing here and sniffing there to see if they could smell out Jimbo anywhere. But our agile hero had fled like a ghost in the night, missing all the commotion. By now he was safe and sound at the lower end of Bell Alley, his heart chuckling merrily and fit to burst. This day had been the finest of outings for Jimbo – a magnificent climax – a day of purest merriment and fun-making – ending up (unlike Samson) in his complete getaway. Lest we forget – it had been cruel indeed to lead our Cork guests astray the way he did – and in such a time-wasting exercise. But the humour of a Go-Boy was always going to be different from everyone else's – a humour all of its own making. Rest assured – Jimbo's mother must have slept uneasily in her bed that night when the men from Cork continually questioned her son's parentage (the basthard! the basthard!) long into the evening.

The Donkey-Derby

Two weeks later the sun was again strong in the sky and driving us all delirious with sweat. Jimbo went to The Daffy-Duck Circus where he entered The Donkey Derby on a very emaciated ass (Raggity). Some lads had cleverly oiled up our hero with a drop or two of the rawgut potheen. The race would soon begin. The pranksters (urged on by Jimbo) stood at either side of Raggity. Jimbo got them to heave him up on the ass's back. He sat there like a delicate egg on a horse's saddle. A moment later we saw his arms flailing the air (the actor that he was). We heard the screams of him as he hung onto the ass's ears for grim life. We saw him wobbling about hysterically – his lungs gasping and his eyes glaring dizzily and his legs jiggling in the air (h*elp me! help me! I'm getting killed*!) – till you'd think his bodily appendages were about to fall off of him.

At his behest the juggling pranksters pelted him up (time and time again) on one side of the bemused Raggity – only for Jimbo to bounce off at the other side and down onto the grass. The rapturous shouts of the men – the radiant faces of the women – defied description (but fulfilled the dreams of Jimbo). After each bit of pitching and pelting there followed a hush – a hush that'd break your heart from trying to stifle the laughter rising up in you. Finally, however, our hero *(no better man! no better man!*) was seated firmly on his saddle and the race could then get underway.

By now Jimbo's face was as red as a lobster's with the sweat dropping off of his nose. The best entertainment was yet to follow when just as the race was about to commence he persuaded one of the women to take the hatpin from her coat and stick it in under the fidgetty ass's tail.

WHOOOOOOOSH!

Away stormed the frightened ass (*make way, lads! make way*!) as though he were a zebra fresh in from Africa. Indeed he almost went out from underneath Jimbo's legs altogether – followed by our flurries of laughter at the sight of our Go-Boy seated firmly back-to-front and his nose up close to the ass's smelly tail and the two of them in sweaty harmony. A second later they were seen levelling to the ground three furious tinkers and two blind pensioners as Jimbo and Raggity headed for the finishing-line and the award of The Big Prize Cup. Fair play to you again, Jimbo!

The Following Week

With The Donkey Derby now behind him and The Daffy-Duck Circus put away till next year, it was time for The Show-Fair. Apart from hurling the slither ball into the upturned milk-tank from twenty yards out and The Carrying-the-squealing-pig-race and The Blindfold-handbarrow-race, there was going to be the famed Mad-Ass-Race. Jimbo's recent ass-racing accomplishment had given him a bit of an edge and he was anxious to visit Moll-the-Man and get her help and encouragement for so famous a venue. In due course the sympathetic Moll gave him her wise advice. He'd be well prepared (she said) when he got to the starting-line.

A Man Among Schoolboys

There were other lads (mere schoolboys, he thought) ready for the jolting gallop. There was Ned Nettles (the son of Big Horse) and Freckles (the son of Eyeless-Tom, who was half-blind from a fall in The Yellowstone Quarry). There was Batty (The Water Diviner's son from Goat's Cross whose grandfather had been a jockey of some fame): 'Why not enter the race and keep up the ould name?' said his proud father. And then there was Bad Organization's one and only son (Handlebars – with his new moustache and not a bit of his mouth in sight). These brave boys were standing up in their stirrups and ready to whip hell out of their skinny old asses, who were already steaming in fear as they staggered their way down the field towards the starting-line.

It wouldn't be long before the real sport began.

With a piece of twine a few pranksters had fixed up a bit of a board on Jimbo's back. Across it was written in red rodden *The Derby Winner*.

'The Derby Winner?

He is in mee arse,' said some of the women.

The day's high point was imminent. On Moll-the-Man's advice (wasn't she the wag) Jimbo called for a spud – a roasting hot spud from the tent. It had a good spiral of steam rising up from it. He then called for those two old sly-boots (Clever Jack and Tenderfoot) and whispered a few soft words in their ear. The devils didn't even raise a smile but produced a stocking and wrapped the hot spud inside it – a spud that was to prove the greatest spur that ever ruled an ass's hooves.

The whistle went for the race to start.

Clever Jack and Tenderfoot stepped forward.

'By the time we're finished they'll think Jimbo's ass is running on electricity,' the two of them smirked.'

They quickly thrust the hot spud straight up into the ass's arse. It was just as Moll-the-Man had advised: for she'd promised Jimbo that no arrow on earth would match the likes of Raggity – that the poor devil would be out the gate like a bolt of lightning – clean out of the town – out over the top of The Mighty Mountain – halfways to the moon before the rest of the eejits had pranced their asses away from the starting-line.

The Derby Winner

The Derby Winner – his eyes ablaze and his hooves flashing like polished gold (and with Jimbo once more seated back-to-front on him) proved faster than the wheels of Doctor Glasses' motorcar ('twas said). A pack of mad dogs could not have set such a pace as this mighty individual. And when the crowd raced from the field to catch a hold of Jimbo and put a stop to the great ass they came back and told how his iron shoes were so hot that you'd fry an egg on them.

Ah-ha – the bone and beauty of an ass and his master!

That's the way to do it, Jimbo! That's the way to do it! You have the blessings of every man-jack-of-us showered down on your head this day. You've earned yourself a handsome feast of The Black Doctor as soon as the evening sun goes down, Fame like yours doesn't often fall on a man's shoulders – and on this memorable day we will drink Jimbo's health till our eyes start smouldering – till we're fuller than ticks on a cow's udder.

The Political Election

Later that afternoon there was more in store for us. Having been given a few mouthfuls of whiskey to revive his head and his heart, Jimbo stepped forth to make the day's final guest appearance. To help things along Clever Jack presented him with a charm to wear round his throat – his father's lucky rat's foot.

Jimbo called for a tarbarrel. He called for a bucket. The crowds were unwilling to leave for home and gathered round him. The same pranksters who'd pelted him onto the ass had been briefed to put Jimbo on top of the upturned tarbarrel when it arrived so that his voice and gesture could he seen and heard all round the field and given their rightful due. We were in for a bout of rare entertainment from our host for the great man was about to deliver his famed Election Speech.

The bucket was finally produced from the nearby drinking-shop. It was hooked upo as a makeshift microphone. Into its depths Jimbo was getting ready to say a few words of condescending wisdom to our own good selves and (if you were fool enough to believe him) to The Irish Nation at large. His two acolytes (Clever Jack and Tenderfoot) tied the bucket onto a long rope. They trailed the rope to some fencing-wire. They entwined the fencing-wire to the telegraph-pole. The new-fangled electricity could now be let loose from the pole to the wire so as to reach Jimbo's mouth. After that – he'd be well and truly connected to The Irish Nation and in a position to give the world his famed broadcast.

The Roars Of The Crowd

We closed in around Jimbo. To hear the roars of the crowd – you'd think (at the very least) a king was being crowned. Clever Jack and Tenderfoot (the sportsmen that they were) lowered the bucket and clamped it firmly on Jimbo's head. Then they belted it with their fists and sticks. Mercy-on-us – to hear the rackety din of the metal bucket. And all this – even before our hero had been given a chance to give out his wise words to The Irish Nation. One or two playful rascals were trying to get the bucket up over Jimbo's sore ears. Others were trying to keep it stuck fast on his head. We stood on tippy-toe (*be-mee-oath, is he still alive*?) to take a good look at him and his famed bucket. Wiping the tears from our eyes, we could scarcely stand up from our fits of laughing at the sight of the frantic Jimbo (the merry actor that he was) struggling above on the tarbarrel. At last – freeing his aching head, he got himself into a seemingly towering rage – the fog steaming out of his head and the froth flurrying from his lips. Though he hadn't yet started his Election Speech his cheeks were as shiny as a pair of buttercups.

One thing more was needed before Jimbo could broadcast his news to the rest of the world. A couple of women hurried back with an army-coat once worn in The Great War. They put it round Jimbo. A couple of expectant men had trimmed the coat with a row of metal buttons – coupled with Jimbo's own religious medals and a few tin saucepan-circles to show how bravely our dapper hero had fought in a number of horrendous battles. Finally they brought out a few coloured flags to hang round him by way of a platform. The scene was set for him to go speechifying full pelt.

He Began To Clear His Throat

'Give us the whole of yeer heart, Jimbo,' we roared.

With head erect he cleared his throat and got ready to give us the full benefit of his wisdom.

'I'll show these simpletons that I'm no sop of hay on the road,' said he to himself.

'I'll give them a deluge of words that they'll not forget in a hurry,' thought he again.

Maybe he'd tell us he'd been appointed the new minister for all the asses in Tipperary – and for asses like ourselves among them. We'd have to wait and see as our hero drove his head deep into the hollow bucket to test it for microphonical effect (himself and his big words again):

'I'm speaking to The Irish Nation this evening,' came the nasally voice out of the depths of the bucket. This was a fine start – better than a Mission – and soon there wasn't a dry eye among us:

'I have been elected as Chief Pig-Surgeon for this region of Tipperary. I tell ye, byze – the price of pigs has gone far too high. Yes – far too high. And worst of all – the hemline of our ladies' dresses has gone far too low. Yes – far too low.'

His voice was already rising like a fountain. Such a hero could outmatch the speech of a priest on the altar, couldn't he?

We kept firing questions up at him: 'What about The Work?' we yelled. 'Coom on, blasht you, what about The Work?'

'What we want is Fair Pay and Fair Play,' said Jimbo, quoting a well-chosen theme that was to become a household saying for days to come.

'We want to know about The Land,' we yelled back at him. 'Tell us about The Land, coom on – what's keeping you?'

After that we wanted to know about The Water.

Then we wanted to know about The Women. And several scurrilities were fired up at him for we wanted to know precisely what we should do with these women of ours. The filthy answer to this question was such that even Jimbo was too shy to give it to us. The ground resounded with stamping feet and echoing bouts of more and more tearful laughter. For it was clear to every man-jack-of-us what we'd like to be doing with *the women* and Jimbo didn't need to befoul the air with forbidden words.

A Little Hush

Then came a little hush when a note of seriousness crept into the festivities. We wanted to know what we should do about The Black North. Heavens above – how Jimbo let us have the full flow of his wisdom!

For the next half-hour his name and his fame ruled over us as he frightened us to death with his fierce fighting talk – his two fists all the time cleaving the air. He asked us for our support, if he was elected. What he wanted (he declared) was Freedom for The Roaring Town. What he wanted was Liberty from John Bull's claim on the six counties in The Black North. He was getting himself more and more light-headed as the minutes went by. His body was full of contortions. His face was full of twists – his neck swelling as he danced on the tarbarrel in mock rage. He could scarcely hide the laughter that was constantly rising up in him – not just this minute but throughout his whole life. But he hid this laughter and hammered his chest and roared out his challenging defiance:

'May God bless Ireland.'

'May we live for the day when our island will be free – all thirty-two counties of it.'

He was now inspired. We should (he said) rise up – one and all. We should (he said) head for the bleddy north. We should (he said) burn out the basthards as soon as we could – that's what we should do. This was met with thunderous applause ringing off of the bucket as we also (hysterical with joy) began to play our part in this make-believe election. Jimbo's rascally words were clearly the result of his long feast of booze following his horrendous race with the ass and the hot spud.

A blaze of patriotism had filled the entire field as we looked up at Jimbo. Yes (we said) – Jimbo's heart was in the right place. Yes (we said) – a quiver of light was shining out of him. We almost expected him to rise up to heaven. Was there ever a Go-Boy like Jimbo – a man that could fill a crowd with laughter and (better still) could laugh at himself and still be alive at the end of this great day? And as he hopped down from the tarbarrel and wiped the sweat from his brow we agreed good-humouredly that our one-and-only Go-Boy should be elected as our next noble candidate and should continue broadcasting whenever the chance came up.

Bishop High-Hat Was Not Amused

There was one amongst us, however, who was not to be amused by our gifted entertainer. And that was Bishop High-Hat. He'd been invited in from Clare to officiate at the next hurling-match in The Showgrounds. It'd be another day of rarity and festival – an honour to have a holy man like him in our midst – he having been invited to throw in the hurling-ball and start the scrimmage at the start of the match.

The day came on. It was time for the ceremony. He threw the ball in between the legs of the hurlers. Then – all hunched up like a hedgehog expecting a shower of rain – he scurried his fat little legs back to the sideline in case he got a belt of the ball on the back of his holy skull.

Shortly afterwards an unholy row was heard filling the air: 'Who is that old bagman at the side of the pitch?' roared the bishop.

Why – it was our own roisterous Jimbo and he full to the gills with drink. He was running up and down the sideline, encouraging the players to shift themselves and put a bit of flogging into it and dent a few more of their opponents' heads.

'Sit down, you silly old fool!' thundered the bishop, his angry face reddened from the whiskey affecting him after his dinnertime reparations. In the eyes of everyone a holy bishop was an authoritative personage next to Almighty God. To be lectured to by a bishop was usually enough to shrivel the stoutest hearts amongst us. But Jimbo turned round and stared at the bishop and the other dignitaries that were grovelling round the holy man like a red rash.

'Go kiss mee arse,' he roared.

The crowd burst out laughing in pure delight. This was better than a circus. It was far more than that, however: it was a sore trial for any bishop – a trial that might well undermine his very power and authority. What was he to do?

Oh Holy Virgin-in-heaven! To have heard such obscenities out of Jimbo's mouth – a perilous thing for you to have done, old friend. Ah – the power that The Drink can have on a man's befuddled mind – for our hero to say such a filthy thing to a bishop of our Holy Mother Church.

And then Jimbo (were our eyes deceiving us?) lowered his britches in front of Bishop High-Hat – for the holy man and his crawling cronies to inspect his true colours – his yellow old arse. The world had finally come to an end – surely it had.

The Following Sunday

Next Sunday we all arrived early for Mass, having got wind of the trouble ahead. Father Sensibly came out on the altar – even before it was time for him to start saying Mass. His mind was made up. There had to be a stop put to our Go-Boy's friskiness. He'd give Jimbo a bludgeoningn he'd not forget in a hurry before he and his likes got a foothold over The Church. He'd give the rest of us an unrehearsed sermon we'd remember for the rest of our lives. The holy priest stood between the tall candles and the vases of flowers. Slowly and solemnly he put on his black hat. He wheeled round and raised his hand, commanding our silence. We could see his stormy face. We could see the grimace round his mouth as his cold glacier eyes penetrated into us.

Then he spoke to us in a very loud and harsh voice and (ah, the noble man that he was) his words were savage indeed: 'I am ashamed – I am absolutely astounded – indeed out of my natural life – to have witnessed what went on at The Showground's hurling-match. Ye were all there and (mother-of-god) the bishop himself was honouring us with his presence. What will his holiness think of me now? Do ye know what he'll say? "Is this the unsaintly way (he'll say) that Father Sensibly has been training his congregation?"

Then our priest wiped an imaginary tear from his eye: 'I can never again look him in the eye – never again sit down to tea and sandwiches with him.'

His fury knew no bounds and his face became as red as a beetroot. It was a fine and tragic performance – even outshining Jimbo's mock Election Speech for he'd worked himself up into a fine old fit – good enough for the Dublin stage. This was so unusual in his nature – so unlike his genial good self with that unctuous flute-like voice of his *(God bless my little lambs)* when we were giving him our fistfuls of coppers every Sunday.

He had to pause and give himself breath before the torrent of words could start again. Finally – he pointed a riveting finger straight down at poor Jimbo as though he were looking at a distorted scarecrow-of-a-man. It was the holy finger of scorn. And with his eyes raised towards heaven and his arms lifted shoulder-high our dutiful priest cursed the now-bedraggled Jimbo from a great height – cursed him and all his descendants (should he ever be fortunate enough to get married and have any). It was nauseating for us to have to sit and listen to him and we bowed our heads. We knew something was wrong. Just like Jimbo – Father Sensibly had gone a step too far in showing off his almightiness in front of us poor scholars.

Jimbo Bowed To His Fate

Jimbo had felt as safe as a nest on a Clare cliff – up till now. We were all mesmerised at Father Sensibly's vengeful words. It was time for our hero to fret. His previous manly confidence – his self-composure – had disappeared in an instant and he no longer felt one bit sure of himself. Instead – he had the look of a tragedian about him and a pair of sorry-looking eyes that we'd never seen before on him – burdensome eyes with not a ray of sunshine left in them.

The now-tainted hero of the Mad-Ass Race was never going to be a match for a man-of-the-cloth – especially here in the church and on foreign ground. He bowed his frightened head at the comeliness of Father Sensibly's refrain. Such a curse – such a priestly prophecy – might turn a man into a goat (his mother once told him) – might even bring back his dead grandmother's ghost on an unsuspecting night to haunt him for his wickedness till the end of his days. He had always had a premonition that something like this might one day happen to him and mar his happy-go-lucky Go-Boy days here in Ireland.

He Hit The Road For John Bull

For the next night or two Jimbo returned forlornly to the loneliness of his sad little cabin. Then came Monday with its cold dawn when the ear-kiss of the birds seemed nowhere to be heard and the gloomy clouds of the half-light seemed to sag heavily on his tired shoulders:

'Tis time (said he) to free meeself from the handles of mee plough.'

He put on a clean white shirt. He put on his best brown suit (his father's wedding-suit) and his father's hat. He took the ashplant from its leaning-place behind the door, not forgetting to pocket his mother's rosary-beads and the lock of her hair that she had wrapped in a prayerbook for him before she died.

It didn't need The Weeping Mollys to tell us (we all knew) that the poor fellow had been well and truly humbled by the prophecies of Father Sensibly – that our priest had frightened him more than any wild sow could ever have done – that the path ahead had been firmly laid out in front of him – that our Go-Boy had lost the heart to remain a Go-Boy amongst us ever again. With a tear in his eye he shut the door behind him. Then his clattering boots bade farewell to the now-dead spirit of Playfulness and Fun and he shook hands with Droopiness and its attendant Dispirited Fairies.

His Few Possessions

He took with him his portmanteau with a few bits of his possessions and a head of raw cabbage and a bit of bacon in case he should starve on his journey.

He headed for the train and the station. He had never in his life even seen a thing called a train. A withered crowd of us gathered on the platform. Our hearts were melting inside in us for the gossamer thread that had bound us to him was about to get broken. Some of us had oiled his throat with a stocious amount of whiskey and a few good glasses of The Black Doctor. There wasn't a soul (barring Ned–the-Soldier) that didn't hate to see him going away – going away for an exciting life above in Dublin's city – a place where there wasn't a trace of cowdung to be seen – and taking with him his colourful life which would surely awaken the dead therein. Perhaps he was heading even further out across The Herring Pond and on towards The Land of John Bull and the city we called Pandemonium.

The Train

In an ominous cloud of smoke and steam the train from Limerick appeared round the bend and lumbered to a stop. Before he entered the carriage-door Jimbo stood on the step. There was a terrible sadness in him – as though we had all neglected him over the years. His heart was as heavy as the train itself as he tearfully gave us a wave of his ashplant. It was his last farewell, almost as though he were about to be executed. There he stood (would we ever forget it?) in his father's wedding-suit. There came a hush. Would he give us a last Election Speech? He cleared his throat and gazed down at us. Then his voice rang out as clear as a blackbird's as he gave us his father's old favourite song – *Sydney Harbour*. He sang it from start to finish – every bit as good as Bedad-sez-I – and nobody left till he was done. The porter had lowered his whistle and had hidden his green flag under his jacket and had taken off his cap as though in memory of a great hero.

Jimbo closed the door tightly *(good luk! good luk!'* we cried time and again) and the cadaverous old train began slowly to edge its rattling wheels away from the platform till it faded into a small pinhole and our hearts went down the track after him. Our Go-Boy was about to plunge through time and space – away (though we didn't know it then) to an uncertain existence in Liverpool – many miles from the rest of us. Never again would our eyes behold him and we waved our hankerchiefs after him and our red eyes wept bucketfuls of tears. For us it was like a death or a wake – like going off to the faraway moon. We knew that Jimbo would never be coming back and could only guess how much he'd miss us all and the woods and the hills and the rivers and everything else that made up his soul and the soul of all of us.

That Evening

After trudging home we spent that evening deep in our bereavement of him and wondering over his whereabouts and whether he'd be making piles of money – wondering in what manner or shape he had greeted his new surroundings. We weren't kept waiting long for an answer and we soon heard the whole tale of it. For inside in The Widda-Widda's drinking-shop The Weeping Mollys had met up with Lowry, the former drinking partner of Bedad-sez-I – the wild man that had once appeared in the naked photographs that had enlivened the citizens of Galway. Though he had left us ten years earlier, Lowry was home for the burial (God be good to her) of his mother below in Abbey Acres Graveyard.

Questions. Questions. Questions. Yes – Jimbo had indeed landed safe and sound in Liverpool. Yes – he had spent the journey entertaining the rest of the passengers with his yarns and his songs. And what of his mothers two pairs of red drawers – the ones that he had dressed up in to entertain the schoolchildren with? As soon as he landed, he had thrown them to the four winds for the Liverpool children to fight over. Wisely he knew that his days of dressing up in a pair of red drawers were over and done with.

Liverpool, How Are You?

But there was a humorous end to Lowry's tale. Jimbo had brought to Liverpool his very own Go-Boy's strides and charm. The minute he landed he could be seen marching up and down the side of the quayside in search of his good friend (Lowry), who had promised to welcome him but was lurking instead (the rascal) behind one of the luggage-vans.

'Blasht ye, lads, have any of ye seen mee ould comrade, Lowry? I've been missing him awfully,' shouted Jimbo to any of the passersby whose coat he could grab a hold of.

You can imagine the look on their faces as they hurried away from him. The desperation in him – you'd think he was taking a casual stroll round The Roaring Town in search of his last stray cow. It was then that we all held our two sides from the fits of laughter we took. Poor innocent Jimbo had no notion of the immense size of a city as big as Liverpool. Nor could he have known that the whereabouts of Lowry (whether he was alive or dead or had even come back down from the moon) was of no interest whatever to the minds and hearts of the millions of people living in an impersonal and soulless spot like Liverpool. Indeed the workers on the quayside must have thought Jimbo was yet another one of those crazed old Irishmen, who came across the sea to annoy the hell out of them. Seemingly Liverpool would be left scratching its head for a good while yet. Indeed Liverpool (whether it was ready or not) was about to see the rebirth of a true entertainer – a true hero in the shape of Jimbo-the-Go-Boy, the son of Lizzie-the-Herd and Bedad-sez-I. And although he had been cursed by Father Sensibly and had disgraced himself opposite Bishop High-Hat, we would always remember Jimbo as the purest bit-of-dazzle amongst the legions of Go-Boys who had ever lived here in Rookery Rally's past. Enough said.

FOURTEEN

How Ellie-May and her quiet man
fell out of love and then back in love again

Tooraloo

Tooraloo was the husband of Norry-What's-Your-Hurry and she was a woman who sometimes took half the day to stagger out of bed. They lived in Cuckoo Haven – halfway between Sack-and-Tack and the little village of Saddleback, a mile beyond Old Gentility's small farm. It was a spot hidden in a huge shadow in a hollow out by The Eagles' Nest. Their lives were peaceful enough – sharing in the milking of their seven cows and going to the well each day for the four buckets of water. Norry was the sister of Hammer-the-Smith, who (apart from I'll-Daze-Ye) was the toughest man in our midst. He had arms and shoulders on him that the mighty boxer Jack Dempsey would have been proud to call his own. Tooraloo himself was a useful pig-killer, next in importance and skill only to Blue-eyed Jack. After wiping the blood of the pig on his trousers he was always sure to tell you that the dead pig never felt a *shnig* – meaning that he had given the poor creature the quickest and most sudden death possible with a belt of his sledgehammer straight into the forehead rather than the traditional slow death of the black-handled knife down the throat.

Norry-What's-Your-Hurry?

Norry-What's-Your-Hurry was his twin soul in that she made from the killed pig the finest sausages imaginable and also those other blood-puddings, both the white and the black. She also had the one and only butter-churn apart from the one on our own Creamery Road. Kind woman that she was, she was never slow to lend her churn to her neighbours. I tell you this – her butter was as good as any sold inside in The Roaring Town. Of course on those days when she was making her churn of butter she was in a good bit more of a hurry to get herself out of bed and for that day at any rate she proved herself untrue to the name that one or two of her unkind neighbours had bestowed on her earlier in life.

He Had The Land

Tooraloo had the land. It was not in too bad a shape for a man from the hills. Norry-What's-Your-Hurry was the lucky damsel, you'd imagine – pretty enough with her fine pink cheeks, her raven hair and her sparkling eyes. She was well able to entice the heartfelt love out of him with a fluttery blink of those coaxing eyes of hers. But if that's what you were thinking, there wasn't a man in Rookery Rally who wouldn't have laughed out loud and shaken their wise old heads: for the thought of Romance and slobbery lovemaking were as foreign to our men and women as the man in the moon. Whatever the life of the romantic heart was like inside in the town, our countrymen were always sensible and practical people. It was only when guests came back from The Land of John Bull or The Land of The Silver Dollar that we saw those silly wet kisses – saw the cuddling and downright coddling and tomfoolery that went on. This alarmed every one of us, for in Rookery Rally we were in mortal fear of all bodily contact, more than a few of us having died from consumption. And we knew that contagion and diseases such as tuberculosis were passed along especially from mouth-to-mouth kisses. As soon as the babies were born they were seldom touched by any of us. The little innocents were changed rapidly when they were wet or soiled and then they were left down on the concrete floor away from the hugs and the kisses and the dangers of diseases. How often, when men saw their sisters returning from abroad and offering them their new foreign babies for a little hug or a little kiss, were the uncouth fellows seen to spit into the fire and say: 'For godsake, woman, will ye give yeer tongue a rest and let the child down on the floor where he can roll round in his piss like we all used to do!' Enough said.

She Knew All This

Norry knew all this. What she needed was the security of the land's income. What Tooraloo needed was a bunch of children to help him look after the land and (later on) to support him in his old age. Norry was prepared, therefore, to tolerate rather than enjoy their bedroom tussles and jostles and to produce for Tooraloo as many children as God deigned to give her. It was a spit-on-your-hands job for the pair of them.

Following on from one of their few bedroom tussles (our men plucked up the courage only when they'd drank enough of Curl 'n' Stripes' medicine in his drinking-shop) the handsome pair proudly realised that they were to become parents for the very first time and that a little gift would soon be born to them. At this stage they were both closer to forty than to thirty years-of-age. It was to be their first and only child and you can imagine their delight.

Ellie-May

As soon as his little daughter could walk she was taught to march from the press cupboard to the half-door and back again with the hurley-stick strapped to her shoulder:

'Left-right! Left-right!' her father would say. 'Who are you going to war with?'

'The British,' came the reply from the child's innocent mouth.

When women saw the little girl marching and drilling with her cute little hurleystick, they'd shake their heads. The child hadn't the foggiest idea who or what the British were. As far as little Ellie-May could make out The British might well be a strange band of robbers about to run off with her father's cattle and sheep. And it wasn't long before the little girl ventured from the half-door and out onto the lane leading down to The Creamery Road. Once more she could be seen marching up and down and pointing her terrifying little hurleystick at the smiling men and their ass-and-cars, who were taking the milk over to the creamery.

'That Heathen, Cromwell'

Tooraloo and Norry's desire to see Ellie-May marching round the yard with her hurleystick for a rifle was nothing new amongst us. Although it was almost three hundred years ago, none of us were allowed to forget the time when Cromwell's soldiers came marching into our country – putting men, women and children to the sword. Long before a single one of his soldiers had set foot in Tipperary there was a great fear of Cromwell and even babies at their mother's knee had it drummed into their skulls that he was a limb-of-Satan and a monster risen up out of hell.

His army had been in an awful hurry to capture Limerick. The only way through was to march across our hills but the steep slopes above Saddleback Village stood in the way of his army's heavy cannons. The foreigners realised that if they were ever to take Limerick by surprise these huge guns would have to be pushed out over the top of the hills so as to take the downward slope and go straight on and raid the city.

But where on earth were the strong local men to help them push the cannons? And another thing – earlier in the day our adolescent girls had made sure to jump in over the ditch in dread of their lives and fearing the lechery of these foreign soldiers. Our men hadn't been slow either and had hidden themselves deep in the woods, knowing that they'd be ordered to push those damn cannons up to the top of the hill. Only the old women had been left behind. Surely none of those foreign blackguards would have it in his heart to humiliate a bunch of old crones and make them come out the door and push such heavy battering guns – as though an Irishman's mother or his grandmother was no better than an old ass to be driven along? Surely these mighty warriors would be strong enough to get down off their tired horses and push their own bleddy cannons – or were they an army of little mice? This sort of talk was no use: the foreign captains forcibly dragged the old women out from their cabin doors. And like you'd drive on sheep or cattle to the market-place, Cromwell's men scornfully whipped the hides of these old ladies till the blood ran down their legs, compelling them to push with every ounce of their strength so that the soldiers could reach the walls of Limerick before daybreak and then commence smashing the inhabitants into surrender. More than one poor old soul died that morning on the hill-slopes above Sack-and-Tack and Saddleback Village, their hearts giving out on them from the constant whipping and the exhaustive pushing.

A Small Bit Of Joy

But, like all stories, there was a small bit of joy (thank God) left at the end. The foreign soldiers had yet to meet with the bravery of the Limerick women, who met them with a less than merry greeting, hurling rock after rock down on top of their heathen heads and keeping them at bay till the rescue would arrive. Thereafter some of the old women had enough breath left in their bodies to tell their children and grandchildren how their hero (Sarsfield) had made an overnight march through the winding hills, reaching Limerick ahead of Cromwell's men and bringing guns and ammunition towards the relief of the besieged city. With much elaboration and admiration his story was talked about over the years and even little Ellie-May's ears were filled with blacker-than-black tales of the enemy forces and whiter-than-white tales of our own brave freedom-fighters. Isn't that always the way?

The Time Of The Troubles

Ellie-May was scarcely out of the schoolhouse of Drool and Hairy-Chin (that is, if she ever spent a day in their school) when she found herself carrying messages to the rebels on the run. It was the time of The Troubles when the light of Freedom beckoned our men. She took them notes hurriedly scribbled on bits of paper all over The Hills-of-The-Past and on through Diddledy-goo and on to the foot of The Mighty Mountain – notes telling the fighters the details of the enemy's whereabouts. From the constant running she was doing she was beginning to build legs on her that would well suit a racehorse – to build lungs on her that would well suit a greyhound. When caught (good child that she was) she made sure she'd swallow the paper messages to avoid getting herself shot and thrown in across the ditch. Her task of course wasn't always an easy one. One freezing

January night she was forced at gunpoint to dig a trench a foot deep across a track where The Tans intended to spring an ambush on our men coming down from Sack-and-Tack with sackfuls of gelignite.

These wartime years greatly disturbed our households and were seldom (if ever) reported across the water in The Land of John Bull. The action of The Tans filled the hearts of our women with fear and embedded hatred in the hearts of our men. One thing was sure – our young boys were not the ones so much at risk as were the blossoming girls. And Ellie-May (though a mere child of fourteen) was a good-looking country girl. One afternoon she fell into the clutches of two merry Tan soldiers. It was then that the sun went out of her life. For these brave boys did unmerciful things to her body. They must have given her an awful gruelling (said Father Sensibly) for they left her clothing floating on the waters of River Laughter and The River Fairies hung their heads in shame and could be heard crying in the woods for many days thereafter.

The Punishment Of The Tans

The rape of a child (she being so very young) was beyond all measure of understanding. The Devil was alive and unsmiling and doing very well for himself. There had to be an answer to this crime. Tooraloo and Hammer-the-Smith spat on the palms of each other's hands and they swore an oath (*mighty* would be too gentle a word for it) that they'd go and seek revenge before the week was over. They were seen carrying two double-barrel guns and a pair of shovels out across the fields. They found the haunts of the two drunken soldiers. They followed their tracks – in the very same way as a weasel might track the one single rabbit and avoid being misled by any other rabbit standing in its path. In short – they caught up with The Tans and shot them in the knees. They shot them in the genitals. They shot them in their faces. Then with their two shovels they buried them in the soft earth of Bog Boundless – but not too deep down: 'Let the wild foxes and the golden eagles come down (they said) and dig them up and feast on their entrails.' Just the briefest of Christian burial rites would do for the likes of them (they said). So they knelt down and said a hurried and mumbled Act of Contrition for the young soldiers' departed souls and they asked the good God-in-heaven to forgive them their own fierce cruelty.

The women, when they heard of this murderous deed, crossed themselves and started to pray for the wellbeing of Tooraloo and Hammer-the-Smith so that God would spare their wicked souls and not fry the two of them inside the bowels of hell. They knew within their hearts that hatred only breeds more hatred – that the brutal way The Tans were killed was unforgiveable.

The men, however, slapped Tooraloo and Hammer-the-Smith on their backs:

'More power to yeer elbows!'

'Ye're the two best men in all Ireland.'

'By the power of the stars, ye're the salt of the bleddy earth!'

Ellie-May Turned Very Strange

The first thing we noticed following this horrendous ordeal was how sad and silent Ellie-May had become, standing there at the half-door and vacantly staring out at the grey-blue glow of the dying day and the impending shadows on The Mighty Mountain. No one could fathom out what sorrows lay in the recesses of her young mind. Some of the women huddled their heads together and they took a big bag of red apples up to her to chew on. Others went round scouring the ditches and made up a fine big nosegay of flowers for her bedroom altar. One and all – they felt a bit sheepish. They didn't know what to say to her. Nor did she know what to say back to them and they quickly came away – a few of them with flushed faces of anger and others weeping.

For the next few weeks she was seen to be acting peculiar. The world seemed very small to her. She no longer ran with her messages to the rebels around The Hills-of-The-Past. Nobody saw her marching to and fro with the other girls on the lanes above The Creamery Road with her hurleystick strapped to her shoulder. She never came down past our doorways to the shop for her mother's bag of messages.

As Though A Thunderstorm Erupted

And then a thunderstorm erupted inside in her chest. Like Slipperslapper in later years, we saw a new woman rising up out of the ashes of poor Ellie-May's soul. She cast The Tans' ransacking of her body to the back of her mind. Whereas women all over the world would have covered themselves in mourning-ashes after such wounds as hers and would have torn their garments into shreds, Ellie-May now replaced her agonies by dressing herself up in her grandmother's cast-off colourful clothes. She let her hair hang down loose like the horse's mane of the tinkers. She found half a dozen rags and tied them into her head like a rag-rope of ringlets. Then as soon as the first shimmering light of morning came on, she hopped out the doorway to greet the fairy-folk – full of exileration and wearing her father's big hobnail boots – the ones with the shamrock studs in them. Her eyes sparkled like the shine in a sweet-gallon tin as she headed for the delicate field-flowers and went on towards the green pinewoods. We couldn't help noticing that her legs had turned as red as ripe cherries from the way The Tans had belted her, making the poor girl look as if she had fallen into a heap of briars. Her cheeks were puffed out like the red radishes in Lord Elegance's garden and she was breathing hard, not knowing or caring where she was heading:

'The poor maddened creature,' sighed Dowager sadly when she saw the state of her.

'All she needs now, thanks to the way them bleddy Tans manhandled her,' said Blue-eyed Jack, scratching his jaw, 'is a pair of honeysuckle trumpets hanging out of her ears.'

Canon Next-to-God

In The Roaring Town Canon-next-to-God heard about the recent tragedy bestowed on Ellie-May. He speedily reported it to Bishop High-Hat. Something had to be done to prevent this young girl from an uncontrolable madness and ending the rest of her days in The House for Nervous Disorders. The holy man drove up The Creamery Road in his motorcar.

Fingering his rosary-beads, he entered the half-door and prayed to God that he would be able to soothe away Ellie-May's cares:

'God bless you, my child,' said he. 'For the good of your health,' he went on, 'and for the good of your Christian soul, it is time for you to go tend to your father's cows – time for you to forget the hatred that all wars bring to mankind.'

He knelt down and said one or two decades of the rosary alongside Ellie-May, Tooraloo and Norry-What's-Your-Hurry. And though he had heard of the savage treatment meted out to the two Tan soldiers by the guns of Tooraloo and Hammer-the-Smith, he never said a single word about their murderous killings. For priest though he was – and with the powers (some of the older folk still believed) to turn all of us into wild goats if he were to put his mind to it – the holy man knew that Tooraloo was as likely to put a bullet in his holy skull as quick as look at him.

She Turned To Her Farm

Ellie-May now spent all her time attending to Tooraloo's farm and his seven cows. Unlike her unhurried mother she continued to be an early riser. Waving her buckets and her green stool in the air she could be seen running across the fields as she came chasing after her cows. At this rate she'd be the first to have her cows milked while the rest of us were still wiping the sleep from our eyes.

However – for the first few weeks things were a good bit difficult. Like any girl learning a new craft, it took her some time to get used to her new role of milkmaid. After a night of boredom in the darkened fields the cows seemed anxious for a little bit of variety – a little bit of enjoyment. So they split up the quiet of their morning by taking a few little runs behind one little bush or another little bush, avoiding Ellie-May and her angry buckets:

'Here, sooky-sooky! Here sooky-sooky!'

It was proving a devil of a job for poor Ellie-May to get her milk. Indeed it took her half-the-day to get it all into her buckets. As a result – an exasperated Tooraloo was often the very last man coming in the gates of the creamery on his ass-and-car. However – so much did his heart grieve for the violation that had been dealt to his one and only child that he hadn't the heart to hear or say a single word of rebuke against her.

The mindless children in Rookery Rally knew nothing of the sorrows in Tooraloo's heart. Just like the cows, they were anxious for a fresh bit of light-hearted amusement. So they headed up to Tooraloo's farm, eager to see for themselves the antics of the new milkmaid. They listened to the repeated calls of Ellie-May to her cows. They stood on the ditch and mimicked her frustrated cries with their own version of *here sooky sooky* simply to annoy Ellie-May and enjoy the curses that she rained down on them and on the mothers that had brought them onto the earth. To add insult to injury, the cows soon became experts in a new milking-game – to such an extent that when all the milk was gone from their udders and the buckets were full to the brim, they took turns to walk slyly over the field and give the buckets a few unmerciful kicks, sending the milk pouring off among the buttercups and daisies. All Ellie-May could do was put her hands over her eyes and sit in the middle of the field, bawling like a banshee:

'Where are all the saints in heaven gone to – the ones I pray to every morning and night? Where is the bespectacled Pope when I need him the most? Where is Canon-next-to-God in my hour of distress?' The list went on and on like a new litany.

Herself And The Cats

Another week went by. One of her four cats had a litter of kittens. Ellie-May soothed away the ache in her heart by refusing to drown them in the tarbarrel and kept half-a-dozen of them lying with her on the upturned ass-and-car. She played with them as a cat with a feather, stroking them playfully. She talked to them as though they were her own children – child that she herself still was in spite of everything that had happened to her. She allowed them to sit with her on top of the breakfast table watching her as she cracked open her two eggs and stirred the salt and butter abstractedly round and round in them with her knife. But The Devil was standing at the half-door and the kittens rewarded Ellie-May for her kindness by eating from the frying-pan the six sausages that Tooraloo (anxious to spoil her) had left for her to feast on after she'd eaten her eggs. Between the kittens and the cows – between the lost sausages and the spilt milk – Life was a trial that no young girl (and she already losing her mind) could be expected to tolerate. Whether sitting in the middle of her yard or sitting in the middle of the field, Ellie-May felt that her nerves were getting the better of her – that she couldn't catch her breath from all the troubles ailing her. Even though she couldn't put it into words, she needed the breath of natural freedom – needed to unbridle her grief. Young as she was (thought Tooraloo and Norry) it would be best for her soon to get herself a good man to look after her. The two of them wouldn't always be around to guard her against the evils of this rotten world.

The Batty Pony

To spoil her even more, Toorlaoo took himself off on a long journey to Monks Abbey. He brought back with him the finest batty pony any of us had ever seen. It had an energetically high step and its speed could give any racehorse (including Jimbo's runaway ass at The Show-Fair) a run for its money. Once again Canon-next-to-God's motorcar came steaming its way up the slopes. Mindful of the fragile state of the violated young girl's disposition he brought with him what looked like yet another gallon of holywater, intent on blessing the three of them – Tooraloo (the wicked Tan-slayer), Norry and Ellie-May. Most of all he had come to bless the legs of the brand-new pony. By this time Ellie-May had named her lovely creature Beauty. For beautiful indeed he was – himself and his foaming white mane.

Years later Norry was to remember this day as if it were yesterday. Unusual for her (the slowcoach) she couldn't fathom out why she had been in such a hurry to get out of bed so early in the morning – why Nature was attracting her eye more than usual – as though the fairy spirits were calling her to come and join them. Maybe it was the guiding hands of her guardian angel for before the clock struck eight she had said her morning prayers, had lit a good fire from the whitethorn hedglings and thorny bushes and bounced out the door. The last thing she was expecting was the arrival of the good canon and his motorcar all over again. At the same time Ellie-May was also awake – looking out over the half-door and dreamily admiring the silvery shine from the morning's first light lying on the pighouse laurels, the ivy at the haggart-stick and the holly bushes at the henhouse. She hadn't long crossed the yard to attend to Beauty's needs when her reveries were interrupted by the holy canon slamming the door of his motorcar. In a flash he saw that Ellie-May had fallen head over heels in love with the grandeur of her pet pony. She couldn't do enough for him. Fair play to you, Tooraloo, thought the canon when he realised what a sacrifice the man must have made out of his meagre savings – how far he must have travelled to bring back so fine a gift to his daughter.

Ellie-May bowed before the holy man. Then, as though he weren't in the yard at all, she began stroking the pony's hooves and forelocks. And though he was already as clean as a new pin she began to currycomb him so unsparingly with the wire brush that you could see your face glistening in his hide. Almost every day (said Tooraloo to the priest) his daughter was seen taking this blessed pony up to Hammer-the-Smith to get yet another pair of unnecessary shoes fitted onto him. The canon smiled.

The Pony Took Flight

A day or two later Madam Misfortune struck a severe blow. At the break-of-day Ellie-May's beloved Beauty decided to take flight, leaving the poor girl profoundly heartbroken and the fat tears rolling down the side of her nose. Where had he gone? And more importantly – why? Had he headed back to where he came from – headed back to rub noses with some other pony – a pony (perhaps) that he simply couldn't live without? No – that was far from the mark

As though it was Springtime, the season of new love, Beauty had been put out of his stride by a new arrival in the shape of a handsome chestnut mare belonging to Lord Elegance's niece (Rowena), a damsel fresh in from a finishing-school in the faraway spa-town of Bath. The graceful mare took one look at Ellie-May's fine young pony. The pony took one look at the charms of Rowena's mare. Ah (the smell and appearance of them) – was ever a love-match so instantly in blossom? In the blink of an eye Beauty forgot the previous day's grooming – forgot the currycombing – forgot the petting and pleasuring and the sugar-lumps he'd been getting from Ellie-

May in the yard. As soon as the angelic mare glided passed, he darted off after his new love – to where his heart had flown – up into the hills.

Dumbfounded, the bereaved Ellie-May sat alone and moped outside the half-door. And just as she did when the cattle laughed at her, she began bawling like a banshee. Would she ever see her beloved Beauty again? Would she ever get him back? And nothing could console her.

Neddy-the-Quiet-Man

And now The Kindly Fates kicked Madam Misfortune aside. Their troop of capricious fairies started weaving their silk-threaded spells on their spiritual loom. For not too far away from the sad scenes in Tooraloo's yard there lived a very shy fellow – Neddy-the-Quiet-Man. Up until now he had lived a life that was free from care or complication. Were he aware of the plans these mischief-making fairies had in store for him, who knows to what corner of the earth he'd have skedaddled to – or whether he'd have allowed himself ever to have been born? In his humble cabin beyond Slack-and-Tack he'd have carried on living his life of peace and quiet till kingdom come – that is if Beauty hadn't arrived unannounced at the turn of the road and begun grazing absentmindedly on the thistles outside his field-gate. As for Rowena's mare – she had vanished from sight and the pages of our history.

Neddy (we are told) had always been good with horses. So he took his reins and winkers and headed towards Beauty. With the patience of a saint he managed to cajole and soothe the pony out of his lovelorn misery. With whispering words of kindness he coaxed him back as far as the haggart. He kept him there till the time was ripe for the amorous creature to grow calm enough to be mounted and ridden back to Ellie-May.

Neddy's Arrival

The second day after his escape Beauty (with the nonchalant Neddy on his back) was seen arriving back in Tooraloo's yard, bringing the light with him. How quickly the sun leaves the clouds behind. For suddenly a grateful Ellie-May had laughter-lines round the corner of her eyes. It was like Christmas all over again. She showered the quiet man with several cups of tea. She filled his plate with ham and buttered soda-cake.

Tooraloo ran back from the hayshed. He opened the bottle of whiskey and warmed Neddy's gizzard with one or two glasses of its fine medicine. The quiet man was enthralled by all these acts of kindnesses. Nor did the exquisitely blue eyes of Ellie-May go amiss on him. In short – she was soon to become his newfound wealth. It was not what Neddy's father had planned for his son ever since his birth. It was not the long step into Clare for this lad to seek out a goodly wife for himself – not The Matchmaker's spit-on-yer-fist and a sealed dowry with a promised woman from back over the hill. Now that he had rescued and returned her lost pony, his world was about to be turned upside-down. In Ellie-May's eyes he had become the saviour sent to her from heaven – the object of her genuine affection henceforth. Before the month was finished the two of them had consummated their lot. With the blessings of Canon-next-to-God and of Holy Mother Church and the whole population their wedding-banns were proclaimed and the graces of The Marriage Sacrament locked the two of them in merry harness – man and wife

And Then The Children came

Time went by quicker than a star and a day came when they spread the news that there was to be an unexpected addition to the household. Ellie-May's joy was unimaginable – especially when not one but three bright-eyed babies made their way into the world beneath the screaming rafters: three children (I ask you) all born from the very first jostle with Neddy on the springs of the marriage-bed. The cat and her kittens could scarcely have done a better job of it. Needless to say – the saintly canon was called back for a third time, triplets never having been heard tell of on this side of Tipperary. He blessed Ellie-May and her three babies with yet another gallon of his precious holywater.

The Wayward Test-me

Sometimes there is a short hop from happiness to sadness. For though the three unnamed-as-yet little ones (their very own Faith, Hope and Charity)

had brought Neddy and Ellie-May a happiness nothing short of delirium, life couldn't be more different at another cabin sixty strides down the lane. Here lived Ellie-May's young cousin – the wayward Test-Me. They shared the same grandmother. Test-Me had given birth to a strapping baby boy almost at the same hour of the morning as Ellie-May. However – there were to be no shouts of joy from her and her sad-eyed parents (Mary and Joseph) – no roaring bursts of celebration – no toasting with the whiskey-glass.

Test-Me was all of seventeen. She was like a delicate young dove, a simple doughy-skinned girl with girlishly long hair. She knew nothing of life's mysteries until they came along and hit her flat in the face. Her baby boy arrived most unexpectedly – a wonder indeed. Was it a Virgin birth? No, it was the shame of the house. It was the talk of Rookery Rally. The little infant was whipped away from under her legs before the poor girl could even catch a glimpse of him or cradle him in her arms or offer him the breast. Before the screaming girl could even give him an honest name he was whisked away to town to be fostered.

The gossipy Weeping Mollys did not have a field day of it this time round and were hushed away from the end of the lane. The moment was far too painful for the rest of us to dwell on – especially for Mary and Joseph, the misfortunate parents of Test-Me. We could only pray that the matter would be quickly put to one side and forgotten like last year's flood – that we could all hold our heads up once more and get on with our lives as though nothing shameful had happened in our midst. The men of course shrugged their shoulders as only men would do. They had seen it all before as soon as their young heifers came into heat. It was (said our soothsayers) an unfortunate accident that could have happened to any young girl when she came into heat:

'It could have happened (they told the women) to any of yeer own daughters, ye high and mighty old hypocrites!'

But, damn the bit (said the women) – what on earth came into Test-Me's slobbery head to have rolled up her skirts yet again and get herself this second child? For she had already delivered her firstborn son only the year before when she was sixteen and scarcely out of her own cradle – at a stage in life when every other sixteen year-old was still walking barefooted round the fields and still wearing their ankle socks – even when going for a frolic to The Platform Dances-in-the-fields.

Canon Next-to-God

Canon-next-to-God was normally a mild and sympathetic man. But on this second occasion he turned himself into Pontius Pilate and was seen to give the poor girl no comfort whatsoever. Setting aside his other duties, he attended to this second tragedy with split-second haste. He purred his motorcar stealthily up The Creamery Road and in along the lane. The wheels of another motorcar followed silently behind him. We had never seen two motorcars together before this day – unless of course in a procession to a funeral. Was there a funeral somewhere today? Perhaps. Blue-eyed Jack watched them passing by:

'Something is in the air, ma'am,' he said to his mother.

On the flagstones stood Test-Me's father, waving down the cars. The following scene was like a Lenten tragedy. Out from the second car hopped two young Guards, looking every bit like the reliable law-enforcers that they were.

A Grey Morning

It was indeed a grey morning – the light falling sadly in between the dripping trees:

'Where are we off to?' said Test-Me. And seeing the official-looking eyes of The Guards and the solemn look of her priest she was filled with alarm"

'On a journey,' said her priest.

'And why are The Guards coming with us?' said she.

'They're driving you to yer grandfather's place in Galway where ye'll be safe from the evil old gossips,' said he. 'Ye wouldn't want those Weeping Mollys constantly standing at the end of the lane or knocking at yeer door, would ye?'

The car plunged out of the yard and on over the hill. From time to time Test-Me looked back beneath the interlacing trees. Then in uncomfortable silence they drove the rest of the way out beyond The Mighty Mountain. In less than an hour they were outside the gloomy walls of a convent. The place looked like a cemetary with the semi-circular sign in black letters over the gate.

The Screams Of Her

Here in Rookery Rally they say that the screams of this misfortunate girl could be heard ringing echoingly back across the Tipperary hills. Test-Me fought her captors as though she was a young tigress – knuckling the skulls of the stout-armed nuns who had come out the gate to drag her away from her weeping father and from the door of the motorcar. Oh, how they pulled at her! Oh, how they viciously dragged at her hair, to try and cast her (as if into hell) inside the walls of their sacred convent. Test-Me proved tougher than a barnacle on a Kerry boat. She wouldn't let go of the car-door handle. It took half-a-dozen of the angry red-faced nuns and their unholy curses (their veils a-flying and their sleeves rolled up to their armpits) to get a proper run in at her. They savagely hacked at her wrists – though some of our more wily and unreliable gossips swore that Test-Me proceeded to take a good few mouthfuls of flesh from their arms with her bare teeth.

To behold her anger – to behold her tears – her Fear – it shook her weak-willed father to his boots. You should have seen the hatred in her eyes as she cursed him into the fires of hell:

'It's for the best, my poor daughter,' cried he.

She was like the pig that refused to leave the pig-house door and parade to the place of slaughter. It took several more minutes to disengage her from the door handles:

'Can't ye pair of eejits do something rather than stand there like open-mouthed fools?' said the frustrated nuns to the hapless Guards. Whereupon one of the Guards (the impudent pup) came up behind Test-Me and gave her a royal kick in the arse, which sent her floundering headlong into the arms of the holy nuns and the job was done.

The Canon Thanked The Father

Canon-next-to-God made the sign-of-the-cross on his chest. He blessed the heroic young Guards. He thanked the good God-in-heaven. He thanked the grieving father. He thanked the nuns. He almost thanked the motorcar – so nervous and ashamed of himself was the holy man. Like a second Judas he was now the unhappiest mortal in the whole of Tipperary (possibly even on God's earth) and would stay that way for many a moon to come. For at heart he had been nothing but a good man before this – himself and his gallons of holywater.

Gone Forever

Test-Me was gone forever. From that day forth (till his dying day) her father would not be allowed to set eyes on her. It was as if her wasted beauty had been buried alive in a grave. The hapless girl had paid the price for her little bit of pleasure behind the ditch. For five-and-forty years she'd slave in the nuns' laundry-room as a knuckle-skinned skivvy – the price of redeeming her soul and getting herself a chance to reach heaven. It was the only way (we were told) of absolving the rest of us in Rookery Rally from the taint of her sinfulness. We had to grin and bear it. Poor Test-Me. Enough said.

It Was A True Love-match

At the other end of the lane Neddy-the-Quiet-Man settled down with his beloved Ellie-May. Their marriage was the exception to the rule in Rookery Rally – it was a True-love match – with his heart inside in her heart and with her heart inside in his heart. No longer did she need to go on nursing her wounds and mourning her afflictions after the savagery of The Tans. Like any young mother she had enough work to do in caring for her three little ones and looking after her new man.

She had turned into a pure saint. Her sanity had been fully restored to her. There was no more running round the countryside in the gladrags of her grandmother. When the day's work was done, she'd sit near the spinning-wheel at the fire. She'd sing her loving-songs (*coo-coo-coo! coo-coo-coo!*) into the ears of her delicate little threesome.

The Jealous Fairies

It was unfathomably strange for us to see how quickly Ellie-May had shed her grief. In Rookery Rally, however, a woman's happiness could never be left alone for too long. The ever-creative niggardly tongues soon got to work. The Jealous Fairies came hopping out over the ditch and they wooed a number of our women into malicious bouts of gossip. How could one single woman have given birth (they whispered) to three separate babies – and all at one and the same time, I ask you? This had never happened before. After all, Ellie-May wasn't a sow – or was she?

It brought more than a sniggering laugh to their eyes when they began telling one another (at the well, at the shop door, at the church gates) that there was a simple reason why the holy canon had been sent for at the time of the babies' births – that he'd never have been summoned unless there was something very wrong indeed. It was clear (they said) that something abnormal had occurred in the life of Ellie-May. They couldn't get to the bottom of it – at least not yet.

Neddy's Tears

Little by little an inkling of what might be the truth began to dribble its way into Neddy-the-Quiet-Man's ears. The fact that three babies had been born meant that only one thing could have happened – there had to be three fathers as well as three babies. What sort of eejity talk was that? Neddy couldn't believe what he was hearing. In his sorrow the poor man was often found sobbing bitter tears abroad in the cowshed. It was rare for our children to see a grown man crying – unless it was a man crying tears of joy when the mare had her beautiful foal. That was understandable. Once or twice they saw a man crying even more when the mare fell down dead in a drain abroad in the field. But Neddy seemed to be weeping for nothing that any of the children could lay their hands on. This was a new one on them. The men were flummoxed too. You'd wonder (they said) why on earth a quiet man like Neddy had never sought the advice of his Confessor – why he had never spoken to Doctor Glasses – why he had never shared a few drinks with Hammer-the-Smith (Ellie-May's uncle) and told him of his worries and the predicament he was in. More than anything else (the quiet man that he was) why hadn't he the gumption to stand in front of Ellie-May herself and ask her to explain herself – ask her to admit to having strayed from the marriage-bed in the company of two other unnamed heathens?

All that Ellie-May could see were the dark clouds that had taken a hold of her husband's spirit. For the life of her she couldn't understand why he was looking so sad and miserable. Maybe it was in the breed of Neddy to turn a sort of sad and mournful as he grew older. It had happened before to a number of our men. But little did she know that her poor husband was going demented at the thought of two scoundrels having had their pleasure with his beloved Ellie-May. Soon his bouts of rage became the devil's-own curse and he swore that if he ever caught up with the two joy-boys that had bedded his wife he'd hang them from the crossbeams outside The Roaring Town's jail.

The Departure Of Shy Dennis

A week since the gossip of those cackling women had trickled its alarm into poor Neddy's ears another bit of stray news reached our ears – even before the creamery carts had started out with the milk: Shy-Dennis had left his outpost – departing for good during the stealth of the night. This was a very strange thing for any of our men to have done. But then we gave ourselves a little thought: Shy-Dennis was an odd sort of creature, wasn't he? Everybody knew that. He was forever tramming his hay in the middle of the night – forever gazing up and counting the millions of stars like a blessed Magi searching for the right star to guide his hayfork – forever riding his aged mule round the fields before the cockerel had a chance to wipe the sleep from its eyes.

We heard that he and his mule had been spotted passing The Engine House in The Roaring Town. Tom Tatters, the town's hobgoblin, said Shy-Dennis was on his way to a convent in Kilkenny (like Soolah Patricia and Kate Solitary before him) and taking with him his whole fortune (a tidy sum of five hundred pounds) stitched inside in his saddle-pack. The news came back that he'd reached the convent gates a week later, by which time he looked an unholy wreck. He told the startled nuns (whether it was true or not) that he had at last come home:

'Who on earth are you?' gasped the nuns.

'What is your business at this hour of the night?' they demanded, looking this strange character up and down and the long black coat he was wearing with the bit of string wrapped round its middle:

'I am Saint Joseph,' replied the poor confused fellow. 'This is my ass.'

Fair play to them, the nuns took him in and gave him a bowl of soup. They were just about to send him swiftly on his way when he produced his fortune from out of his saddle-pack:

'I've brought ye mee fortune'.

You can imagine how their worried faces suddenly changed colour and shone like the blessed sun. All talk of his leaving was thrown up in the air and flung out the window. Shy-Dennis was as welcome as the flowers in May. The nuns must have danced the finest of jigs for the next week-and-a-half.

They Bought The Mansion

For less than the price of a song and at the stroke of a solicitor's pen Neddy and Ellie-May (he hadn't yet told her of his misgivings about the rascals that had helped father their triplets) put their stamp on Shy-Dennis's tumbledown shack – what we scurrilously called *the mansion.* Tooraloo and Norry-What's-Your-Hurry were more than a trifle sad to see the two of them leaving the old homestead and drive off in their ass-and-car. They waved the white handkerchief after them. You'd think that they were bound for The Land of The Silver Dollar even though they were merely travelling a hop and a jump away – to the other side of The Creamery Road.

Within a week the quiet man and his pick-axe and pitchfork had eased away a great deal of his anger and had laid out six excellent drills in his new haggart for his seed potatoes and cabbage shoots. Ellie-May washed the floor of the new Welcoming Room till it shone and glistened like a haystack in the snow. She brought back a big new table from The Roaring Town. When the fire was lit with the whitethorn logs, their new cabin was as good as a palace. Soon Neddy began to forget his troubles. The two of them were like those cosy little lovebirds that you'd see in a cage at The Daffy-Duck Circus.

The Death Of Rahilly

Their newfound joy (isn't it always the way?) was soon tempered with a cutting sorrow. Neddy's beloved father (Rahilly) came to his untimely end. Doctor Glasses had repeatedly warned him that eating out of the burner those big feeds of fat bacon after killing his three yearly pigs would bring him his final reward – that he'd cover his arteries in heaps of grease from the meat and that it'd be the end of him. With the first spasms of pain he knew that our good doctor was only too right. He told Neddy that the sentence was on him – that he'd seen the blessed angels coming down to greet him and fetch him into the clouds.

He got out his best white shirt and his black suit and put them on. He took the rosary-beads from off of the nail. He went and lay down on top of the bed, the rosary-bead neatly twisted in his fingers, looking a bit like the holy Saint Francis. The neighbours knew that something was amiss when there was no morning smoke rising up out of his chimney. They came in the door. There they found him, stone cold dead on top of the bed – laid out neatly in his fine suit-of-clothes and ready for his coffin and his Maker.

Neddy Blinked Out The Candles

Like the ending of a spell, Neddy blinked out the happy-death candles and with just the silence in the room and allowing nobody else in the bedroom door he said farewell to the ghost-of-his-father. He spent the rest of the week grieving over Rahilly. Ellie-May held his tearful cheeks in her hands each evening. She kept repeating: 'God is good! God is great!' But Neddy couldn't make head or tail of it all. His father's death had been so unexpected for he had been as healthy as a snipe throughout his life.

Rahilly's Whiskey-still

No fortune of silver or gold did Rahilly leave behind him and that was to be expected since his farm was small and the land and the cattle were just about middling. But he had bequeathed a far better gift to our quiet man. For behind Rahilly's barn in the depths of his turf-shed was his famed whiskey-still that he'd used for the unlawful brewing of a particular rawgut brew – a brew that knew no bounds. It had the kick of a mule in it. It'd set your lungs on fire. It'd spring the eyes out of your head. It'd produce in you a delicious madness that you'd beg to come and hit you time and time again.

Now Was The Hour

Now was the hour. Neddy found himself the owner not only of the still but of all the green glass bottles, the buckets, kettles and jars, the copper worm and wires, Rahilly's babbling brook – the entire paraphernalia. News in Rookery Rally (need I tell you) travels faster than a motorcar. Overnight Neddy became the most popular man in the whole of Ireland. He inherited a multitude of new friends (and not one single woman among them) from all round The Hill-of-The-Past and out as far as Crown River and Currywhibble. They'd soon be having the merriest of old times throughout the night from belting into his fine mixture and wiping their thirsty parched lips. His newly-inherited still was the constant talk everywhere: he was toasted as the dearest of friends – as the salt of the earth.

Surely matters would be different now.

For Rahilly (it seems) had never been over-anxious in the quantity of his whiskey-making and had attended to it only for the odd few weddings, funerals and wakes. What everyone wanted to know from the start was whether the untested Neddy would be as skilful with his newfound whiskey-still as Rahilly had been in the past? Might he send down for them and give them a little taste or two of his new bottles to see if they were any good? Maybe.

The Birth Of A Master Brewer

There now came a new and unhappy chapter. In less than a week the hopeful expectations of every man-jack-of-us were to be realised when it was found that Neddy (the fine decent man that he was) had a second string to his bow – apart from taming lovesick ponies in their tracks. For within a short while he and his ingenuity bore the men of Rookery Rally a wonderful harvest with his beautiful medicinaries and the smell and the smoke on it. If there were titles to be handed out – if there were diplomas or medals, rosettes or labels to be awarded for the making of fine potheen – Neddy was about to be crowned The Absolute Master Brewer. His potheen was second-to-none and he was seen as the expert for choosing the best spuds, the best barley, the best wheat and rye for the whiskey-droplets that trickled out from his copper wires and into his green bottles.

The First Visitors

The first visitors ran their boots up the hill at breakneck speed. They sniffed and they sniffed. Then they sniffed again. They were as busy as wasps. Neddy waited in silent hope. Slowly and gingerly they gurgled the first few drops. Once they had drained four or five thimblefuls, their tastebuds were beyond any repair that Doctor Glasses might achieve. They couldn't get enough of the blessed stuff. They ran back down the hill even quicker than they'd come up. They told us that the pour of it had rattled the few teeth left in their heads – that it had burnt its way down their throttle like a bird singing lovesongs to them.

Before the month was out a dozen of our younger men had made imaginative excuses to skuttle up the hill to Rahilly's former dwelling-place. By next morning when the sun had cleared away the blue gauze from behind Old Sam's orchard these same young buckos shambled home and completely forgot what day of the week it was and had mouths on them as dry as the parched road. Within the hour they were mountainously asleep and all that could be heard was a loud snoring that could have awakened the dead in Abbey Graveyard. But they'd be alive and kicking in a week or so to buckle back into the work of the farm.

These early adventurers were then followed by a lively trail of older men stepping out fairly lively to shake hands with Neddy and shove into the drink. Like the youngsters they drank so much of Neddy's whiskey that they were seen staggering round The Creamery Road like a bunch of sick cats. For once in their lives The Weeping Mollys' vocabulary wasn't nearly diverse enough to describe what they saw.

The Sadness Of Ellie-May

Ellie-May was seeing far less of Neddy these days. The energy that once went into his nightly bedroom tussles with her was now going into the chemistry of the whiskey-still. She was rightly grieved to see so many men knocking on her door every blessed day of the week and asking her the way to Rahilly's barn.

It was the women of sounder minds than the gossipying Weeping Molly, who were first to plant the seed of worry and doubt into her. They warned her that Neddy (being new to the task) would surely get himself caught by The Guards and taken away from herself and her three little babies – that the four walls of the prison cell would become his new friend and that he might never be let out to see her and the children again.

Poor Ellie-May.

She didn't know what on earth she was supposed to do. She hated to see Neddy returning each day on his ass-and-car and a fistful of green bottles full of the new whiskey – hated to see her Welcoming Room (her yard too) full of strange men – hated to see how Neddy's throat was taking such a fine shine to his own new medicine.

She had no peace of mind. How could she get rid of the whole damn parcel of these wretched layabouts and their boots traipsing all over the place night, noon and morning? She knew that if Neddy didn't stop this whiskey carousing she'd be forced once more to go seek the help of her good friend, Canon-next-to-God.

By this time, however, it was already too late for her to pluck up enough courage to make a stand against Neddy. He was more or less beyond her control. The only arguments that he'd listen to were his own ones and he'd give her that annoying little smile – you know, the one a man give his woman in the middle of receiving a dressing-down from her hostile tongue. It'd break a woman's heart to see the way Neddy went on defending himself. He reminded her of the new coat and the two dresses (the black one and the red one) that he'd recently bought for her from Fanny Farthingale's Dress Shop in town. He reminded her of the hat, the gloves and the lace-up boots, which he had brought back to her from Tipperary Town. He was making hatfuls of money (he reminded her) – even more than the rabbit-poachers and the fishermen who were poaching their salmon from Clashing River and The Mighty Shannon River itself.

The New Men

Before long there arrived cartloads of new faces – polite enough men from outside Ellie-May's known world. These men smacked their lips and taught our men how to get the best out of Neddy's whiskey. They were experienced drinkers. Sip the glass gently (they said). Caress it on the inside of your cheeks like you would a good woman (they said). Take a speculative little pause in between and then come at it again (they said). It was the art of making love to the glass (they said). And our men laughed and went on pouring it down the throttle, their faces getting redder by the minute till they were the rawness of radishes. But the hilarity and the exaggerated mild-mannered ways, which at first came into them with the whiskey, were soon replaced by a dull gloominess and they returned to their wives in the shape of two new men, namely Mister Half-Drunk and Mister Dead-Drunk.

She Knew What To Do

Enough was enough. It was too much for the women (not just for Ellie-May) to put up with anymore. Any fool could see that their men were swimming in Neddy's potheen, so much had they fallen in love with it. And, even though not all of these womanly souls were primed full of virtue, the primitive urge to do what was right and what was just still had a chance to bloom in them. As far as Ellie-May was concerned, nothing short of Pure Rebellion was going to win back their men.

She rolled up her sleeves and spat on her fist. She knew exactly what had to be done and that she was the woman to do. Like the young girl that she once was with the hurleystick strapped to her shoulder (*'Who are you fighting?'* – *'The British'*) she had the answer for dealing with this latest enemy of hers – the ignoble potheen. It was time to strike out.

Saint Stephen's Night

It was Saint Stephens's Night. The Wran-Byze Dance was taking on its usual celebratory course above at the long-house of Din-Din-Dinny-the-Stammerer's, a stonethrow from Neddy's turf-shed and his whiskey-still. With their love of the music and dancing all were having a whale of a time – a-flipping and a-tripping round the cement floor and out into the cobbled yard. There was no dance (not even The Evening Institute Dance or The Platform Dance-in-the-fields), which could compare with this dance (The Dance-of-The-Wran-Byze). It was the time when men threw down the hayfork, the spade and the shovel (the plough too if they had to) so as to get their feet onto the dance-floor. Old and young alike were soon destroying the floor with the cut of their hysterical hobnail boots – that is, in between wiping the sweat from their foreheads and bouncing their broad-shouldered damsels on their knees near the fire.

The dancing was good. The drinking was even better. The whole crowd of men and women were feeling mellow as could be. Then one of the men (we later thought it was Sikey) happened to look out the window to see was there a frost coming on and if the stars were any good. He whispered to the man next to him. In the clear moonlight the two of them could see a few little lanterns listlessly zig-zagging up along the hillside:

'Tis The Guards! Tis the feckin Guards!'

There were a dozen lamplights in all and a group of young law-enforcers in the shape of the town's constabulary. Their shadows swayed across the leafy stream at Moll-the-Man's ditch. They drifted up the hillside towards Neddy's turf-shed. Clearly they were bent on an intensive search for the whereabouts of his still. Being young, however, and with the inexperience of youth behind their ears, they felt a bit fragile as they took their tentative steps through *The Aye Field* (shaped like the letter 'A' with a ditch running across its middle). Their hearts soon began to pound uncertainly, not knowing if the coast was clear or whether in between the bouts of singing and dancing the revellers might get a chance to clear away their glasses of potheen or (more importantly still) whether Neddy might get a chance to hide away the still and its implements.

We knew it! Damn it! We knew it! The little feckers were coming to arrest Neddy. He'd be seeing the inside of the jailhouse this very night and he'd be there at least for a month or two.

And Then We Wondered

And then we began to wonder as we looked out the window: who was the sly little fox that had reported Neddy to The Guards?

Was it the priest?

Was it Ellie-May? No, it couldn't be her.

So, who?

Rahilly's Turf-shed

And now the full light of the moon could be seen behind the high banks of raggy clouds as we watched the smoke coming up from the chimney of Rahilly's turf-shed. Neddy was hard at his work, producing the medicine that our throats craved. Frantically we watched The Guards heading nearer and nearer to the gate of Rahilly's haggart. There was no time to raise the alarm or to warn our good friend. We hadn't so much as a ferret's jingly-bell between us.

The Guards leaped in over the ditch. What was in the back of their minds? Had they no heart for poor Neddy? Surely they had mothers and fathers of their own? The women on the dance-floor stood back. The half-sets and the Clare-battering steps were now gone from us. A dozen of our men reached for their coats. They hurried out across the fields and hid themselves in the stealth of the darkness.

The Guards had beaten them to Rahilly's yard. They surrounded the turf-shed. From their hiding-place our men could see the lanterns clearly – could see the young townies sniffing and whiffing like a pack of hunting-dogs – looking for the smell of the whiskey.

They gave a few raps on the door of the shed. How the hell did they know the place to be looking for? What animal had been bad enough to have told them where to look? It was now the moment of truth and the anger was boiling inside us. Our men couldn't let a bunch of schoolboy Guards draw a curtain over the antics of Neddy without giving them a few belts on their sore heads – a few smacks in their gobs – to take back to town with them.

If only Neddy had been listening to the persistent barking of his two trusty sheepdogs, warning him of the approaching Guards. And then we had a little thought: if Saint Peter had once been brave enough to raise his sword in an effort to protect Jesus, surely not one of our men would be so meek and mild as not to take their own opportunity this very night? Meanwhile – where the hell was Neddy? I'll tell you where – he was inside sitting by the fire – a drunken husk of himself – and so preoccupied with the last of his whiskey-glass as not to hear or take heed of such warnings as a dog's howls.

Maybe The Guards Were Human

Then, as we looked out the window, we had another little thought to ourselves. Maybe The Guards were human after all. Maybe they'd be men enough to step out of line – just this once – and join the rest of us and take in a little of Neddy's pure medicine? Just a few little sips. After all, it was a cold and frosty night. What better way to ward off the ague in a man's limbs than a drop or two of Neddy's fine whiskey?

Maybe.

Perhaps.

But there was no use cajoling ourselves. We knew that these young men were fashioned from different clay than ourselves. They were from a newer school. They had been given their Christian Brotherhood's ethics – had drunk the contents that lay in the good books of Bede, Augustine and Aquinas – had poured it all down their throats at an early age like we were now drinking in the whiskey. We could never have the skills of the tongue to persuade these lads to stay a little while in our company and have a few sups of welcome with us. After all, we were only the poor scholars from the hills – few of us having had the fine chances of the townies to get ourselves into the realms of high-falutin' scholarship. So now – we were at a loss what to do. Why couldn't these Guards go about their real business elsewhere – the business of tracking down a stray horse-and-cart without its lamp or breaking up the odd bout of boxing between a few rival tinkers?

A Time For Action

Enough surmising: it was time for inspiration and action. The women quenched the lamps. The men threw the whiskey-cask out the back window. Then with a few sound sticks they leapt into Rahilly's haggart. In the dark the silence was broken. There was a fight. It was a great bleddy fight. It was nobly done – a beautiful fight as long as it lasted. Our men gave The Guards a right good belting and damn near killed one or two of them as they looked at the blood trickling from their own knuckles. They left two more officers with injuries that would require the repair of a number of careful stitches. They gave the rest of them a few broken ribs and cracked jaws to take back home with them. In despair and when they realised that our men were not play-acting and that they were getting far too rough with them The Guards cocked their pistols towards our men's heads and our men fled like gnats in all directions.

They Found The Medicinaries

Stiff in their limbs, The Guards nevertheless searched the most remote parts of Rahilly's turf-shed as directed by none other than Ellie-May (the devil's horned heathen). They found some of the kettles. They found the still. They found the copper worm. They found the pick and the shovel, which had dug and hidden the entire project. All had been piled neatly in the middle of the dungheap that lay behind the cowshed.

There was an unbelievable sadness in what next happened. With their sledgehammers they smashed into smithereens whatever needed to be smashed. They had found everything except a good few of the jugs and the rest of the kettles – all still full to the gills with the whiskey. These treasures had been buried in God-knows-where. Neddy hadn't been such a dull-witted eejit as not to know that some sneaking little shitty-arse would one day be the cause of his ruination.

Well-satisfied with the results of their sledgehammering and the death of the whiskey-still, The Guards hauled themselves and their wounds back towards The Roaring Town. Along with them they took Neddy. It was a truly terrible sight. How mournful the rest of us felt – to see him hauled along like a common criminal in a pair of handcuffs. From the window we saw the last of the poor devil being dragged down the stumbling hillside by the belt of his greatcoat. The young men were taking him into the jailhouse. It was enough to make a horse cry.

The Little Judas

Hitherto Ellie-May (the little Judas) hadn't dreamt of the damage she'd be doing in reporting Neddy to The Guards. The full extent of it now came home to her when she heard the commotion coming down the hill. She ran out the lane. She saw Neddy being taken along by the scruff of his neck and led away unceremoniously across Adam-and-Eve's field. Her heart leapt up in her throat and filled her with utter sorrow for her poor husband and with bitterness towards the pitiless Guards, who were pushing him along as thought he were a backward sheep.

Oh, if only she could have turned the clock back to yesterday! Oh, if only she had a pair of wings that would fly her through the air and snatch her lovely man back from this miserable crew, who were already lifting Neddy out across the lower stile! She watched the last few traces of him fading away behind the Lisnagorna pinetrees. The heartless moon, which had directed the law-enforcers up here, was ironically departing, having done her dirty work. The sun was already coming up over our misty rivers. By this time The Wran-Byze Dance was inevitably just a bit of history. Would the sunlight ever again stream back into us?

Poor Neddy

Poor Neddy! The penalty was enormous – a total of seventy-five pounds. It was a pure fortune in anyone's eyes. He'd have to stay in jail until it was paid – every blessed shilling of it. Not to be beaten, we all rallied round – even the women. None of us had dreamt that our good friend would have been treated so savagely. We ran raffles by the score. We entertained several card-playing competitions far and near for the traditional pound-of-tea and the plucked goose and turkey. The Yallowboy and his limping wellingtons were persuaded to run a short race (like Jimbo had done) against a captured three-legged hare on a specially constructed wired-in course. Instead of pennies, many poundnotes changed hands to see the outcome of this extraordinary contest. Our renowned hero, Bazeen, was persuaded to bob up and down in his pig's barrel so that we could take money from the spectators to see if their wattles could break open his skull and kill him outright.

We Heaped Up All The Money

In due course we heaped all the money together. We paid the fine down to the last shillings and pence. We decided that we would plan another dance in honour of his imminent homecoming from the jailhouse – a dance which would be the greatest dance of all time – a dance that would beat into a cocked hat even our famed Wran-Byze Dance and send it back into the realms of forgotten memory. It might take us a month-and-a-half to plan it all and send out all the invitations. Even though The Guards had destroyed all our future whiskey-making, they hadn't found the remaining kettles (thanks be to our merciful God-in-heaven) or the jugs and the green bottles. When the time came for the dance we'd have oceans of the medicine to swig down our throats.

It Was Ellie-May

It wasn't long before one of the younger Guards with a loose tongue on him let slip the news that it was Ellie-May (and no-one else) who was the cause of Neddy rotting away inside in the jailhouse. It was all very well for Canon-next-to-God calling her a pure heroine in the battle against the cursed Drink. From that moment onwards the rest of us made sure that the little heathen felt the consequences of her actions. We gave her the full force of our anger and fury. We spat at her feet whenever she passed us by. Eventually the poor confused woman sat at home, afraid to stir out the door. She waited to see the outcome of Neddy's rage when he returned from his trip to the jailhouse. He'd no longer be her quiet man – this she knew. With his fists he'd inflict a full-sized beating on her jaw and rain down the stick on her arse. Our minds were full of the suffering dished out to other women who had informed on their men or had reported to The Tans the whereabouts of their renegade husbands. It would be lucky enough for Ellie-May if Neddy didn't strip her of her clothes and tie her to the gatepost and cover her in tar and feathers as was done to our previous informers. Almost choking with glee at the wretched situation Ellie-May had gotten herself into, the women danced their wretched tongues all over Rookery Rally. It's a wonder they didn't dance their silly heads right off of the earth!

The Hero Came Home

The hero of the spud and the barley duly came home and we all came down as far as the bridge to greet him. There was a hush. We waited with baited breath to see what the outcome would be. It was like that once-in-a-lifetime moment when our forefathers stood outside the gallows at the jailhouse. Neddy descended from Red Scissors' pony-and-trap. He ceremoniously bade his friend farewell. He stepped in across the yard-stream. Ellie-May was gazing out the window. Her man had come home to her. But in his eyes she saw not a trace of warmth.

Neddy did all we could have wished of him. He chastised his wife as any man would have been expected to do: 'My fine decent woman!' he roared. 'Aren't you the little naygar!'

It all happened very quickly after that. Ellie-May didn't run away from him. It was not the thrashing that she had expected with the sparkling stars resulting from his fists. As quick as a bird-on-a-twig he tied a reins round her ankles. He hoisted her up onto the rafters, her skirts falling down round her face, her red calico drawers laid bare for all to see and admire when they'd come in the door.

There she hung like a withered turkey with a cramp in its jaw and her two heels swaying from the rafters. Even then, she didn't say a word. She took her punishment well. She loved her man. She loved her children. She loved her home. She hated the whiskey and the destruction it had brought on the men. She had humiliated Neddy as no man on earth should ever have been humiliated – what with the jail and the handcuffs. She had gone too far and this was his way of punishing her.

In the eyes of the rest of us (even the women) Neddy had been given no other choice. With his wife left swinging on the reins in the air, he went out to the turf-shed and began his own self-inflicted immolation. For the rest of the night he lay down on top of the rough and sharp sods of turf. Their jagged edges left him as sore as hell the next morning. It was as though he had been unable to punish his wife without also adding a further punishment to himself. Meanwhile Ellie-May fell into unconsciousness.

Divine Intervention

With Ellie-May strung up on the rafters and Neddy nursing his sore arse on top of the heap of turf, some sort of divine intervention had to come to the rescue. It arrived from the other end of the lane – from Mary and Joseph's yard. You'd never have expected it to come from there. Ever since poor Test-Me's transportation to the gloomy nunnery they had been unable to stir foot from their half door. They had spent most of the day hiding themselves under the blankets – for shame's sake. Of course the rest of us were left wondering what on earth had happened to Test-Me since the day she went away. Had she really reformed and become a newly-uplifted character? Was it true that she'd gone off and joined up with the holy nuns? Rather than tell a pack of lies and put a mortal sin on their souls her parents had no choice but to hide away from us. Joseph sat in front of the fire (the hearthstone often fireless) and let his Woodbine fag dangle from his lips till the ashes on it were two inches long. Mary was unable to get a wink of sleep throughout the nights and stood looking out the window at the stars, wondering what sort of cruel life Test-Me was now experiencing. It was all too much for the two of them. It was so unjust.

'Why (said Mary) – why-oh-why didn't the young whelp, who'd given her the pleasures of his body, get punished equally alongside her?' It was a good question. Had she the power in her body, she'd have reddened his arse for him. And her eyes filled up with bitter tears.

For The Last Hour Or Two

But that was nothing to the shock and sorrow that was about to inveigle herself and Joseph. For the last hour or two they had been listening to the cries of the little triplets some sixty strides down the lane. It was nothing new. The children cried all the time – often during the night when you didn't want to hear them. But what was Ellie-May doing about it? Seemingly nothing.

With only a dress slung across her shoulders Mary strapped herself into a pair of wellingtons and ran down the lane. She reached Ellie-May's yard and entered The Welcoming Room. Ah me! What a terrible sight met her eyes – Ellie-May and she strapped up by her ankles to the rafters – like a pig that's been newly slaughtered. Never would she forget it. She didn't even know if the poor woman was alive or dead and she let a cry out of her that almost dragged poor Ellie-May out of her state of unconsciousness. With the aid of a carving-knife and an armful of pillows and blankets to protect her sudden fall, the good woman carefully lowered Ellie-May to the ground. She covered her shivering body with a dozen more blankets. She poured a whole cup of whiskey (the drink that Ellie-May had always dreaded) down the misfortunate soul's throat and brought her back into the world.

The Arrival Of Tooraloo

With the summoned arrival of Tooraloo and Norry-What's-Your-Hurry (and she hurrying this time at an alarming speed) they managed (together with Hammer-the-Smith) to carry the hapless Ellie-May home with them, the triplets in tow. And there she would stay as in days of old, delirious and out-of-her-mind. There was no sign of Neddy.

Ellie-May spent the next hour muttering hollowly in her sleep:

'Mee heart is broken.'

'Mee soul is cut in two.'

'Far better had Neddy broken mee jaw than to come to this – the breaking of mee spirit.'

Then up spoke Tooraloo: 'Why didn't Neddy give Ellie-May a few handy taps of the switch across her arse like we all would've loved to do?'

'Yes,' said Hammer-the-Smith, 'a few skelps of the hurleystick across her ribs would have done the trick – a just reward for bringing The Guards on us and landing Neddy in jail.'

For a minute they stood there in stupefied silence, unable to make head or tail of it all.

Then up spoke Tooraloo: 'Why string her up like a pig facing the slaughterman's sledge?' he sighed, continuing the tune of it.

All three of them had a great deal of sympathy for Neddy – to be seen punishing his wife and acting like a true man opposite all the old gossips. The entire population of Rookery Rally had expected a punishment. It was The Family Law. It had to be delivered to Ellie-May and she had to await her fate. Hadn't The Good Book at school explained it to every man-jack-of-us: a man had a right to chastise his wife when the need arose? But – it was the unholy way that Neddy went about it that we all found unforgiveable.

Bright And Early Next Day

Bright and early next morning the three self-appointed grandees and guardians of Ellie-May marched their boots back to Neddy's yard. He staggered out the door to size up the moment. Had they brought their double-barrel guns with them – the guns that they had used to maim and kill the two Tan soldiers? No. Had they brought their shovels with which to bury his dead body? No. What then?

Tooraloo (being Ellie-May's father and the spokesman for the house) spoke up first. There wasn't even an oath or a curse out of him:

'It was right and lawful to chastise your wife, Neddy. But that isn't the end of it.'

Hammer-the-Smith spoke up next:

'The punishment you gave her (the reins and the rafters) showed great imagination – but that isn't the end of it.'

Norry-What's-Your-Hurry spoke up after that:

'The deed has been done. It cannot be undone. But it's time now for you to do your penance.' And there wasn't the trace of a smile in her eye.

The long and the short of it was that the three wise lawmakers had gone to law the previous night (the way it always was with our families) and they'd decided the fate of Neddy within their own four walls. There was no escape for him if he were ever to show his face again – if he were ever to regain his good name in the eyes of Tooraloo, Norry and Hammer-the-Smith – indeed in the eyes of Ellie-May – in the eyes of us all.

Breaking All The Rules

It was unheard of for a wife to have broken her marriage vows – to have taken herself and her children away from the nest. But now we were to see the courage of Ellie-May as she broke the golden rule of Mother Church ('what God has put together let no man pull asunder') and took the road to freedom – a freedom from the oppressive hands of Neddy. It took all her bravery to call the traditional beliefs of the rest of us into question. It'd be the talk of Rookery Rally for years to come. It'd be the talk of The Roaring Town itself. It'd cause ructions in the church in Copperstone Hollow. But perhaps the bespectacled Pope would be soft enough to free Ellie-May from another bout of Neddy's madness? Would he? We wondered.

Neddy's Penance

Neddy put his forlorn arms in the air in surrender to his fate. For his penance he'd have to fight his way back towards Ellie-May's forgiveness. He'd have to learn the new rules of Gentleness. He'd have to earn back his old name of being The Quiet Man. And he bowed his shameful head:

'I'll do whatever it takes to get Ellie-May and the children to come back home and sit round the bright fireside as of old. For what's my life worth without their blessed presence?'

Then up spoke Norry-What's-Your-Hurry once more:

'Ellie-May will not be returning till your punishment has been set and met. Indeed she may never return.'

'What must I do? What must I do?' said Neddy. I'm ashamed of the sudden way I went about chastising her – the way I brought about the harsh humiliation of her. When I left the jail I thought it wasn't half-good-enough for her. I was wrong. I was very wrong. Never again will I do her an ounce of harm – if only she'd come back home to me.'

Then Tooraloo stepped forward:

'Your seven cows are stately creatures (this you know) – all of them except the Kerry-blue, who is so old that she'll soon be making calf-meal below in Monks' Abbey. Your best milker is your favourite cow, Lily (*The Lily-of-The-Valley* as Ellie-May calls her). She gives you gallons of milk each day. Think of all the money – think of all the fine creamery cheques – that her milk has given you over the months.'

He fixed his level gaze on Neddy before continuing:

'Now you must put a reins round Lily's neck. You must bring her out from the halter in the cowshed.'

It was getting more solemn by the minute as Tooraloo went on:

'This is the time to test your love for your wife – the time to ask Ellie-May's forgiveness in the proper manner – the time for your self-inflicted retribution. You are to surrender Lily and hand her over. From now on she'll belong to Ellie-May.'

This sentence was a harsh one on Neddy. His sorrow for the loss of his cow would be great. It would hit him hard in the pocket. As Abraham had once been put to the test and forced to march up the hill to wield the axe over his only son (Isaac), Neddy would be forced to make the ultimate sacrifice – forced to show his hand and demonstrate his love for Ellie-May.

Without so much as the blink of an eye he handed his three judges the lovely Lily. They put the reins round her neck. They marched her down the lane towards their half-door where Ellie-May and the little ones were getting used to their new life. They tied Lily to the haggart-stick. There wasn't a murmur out of the three little ones. Together with their mother they were sleeping blissfully as though they hadn't a care in the world.

A Crestfallen Man

Neddy went in the half-door and opened a bottle of his finest whiskey. In the next three hours he and his salty tears drained it down to the last drop. He ended up in a heap on the floor. It would take him long into the night before he awoke, shivering with the cold and the guilt.

Next Day

Next day came along, her usual flushed and cheerful self, shaking away the night chill. Neddy awoke and wondered was he in heaven or in hell. He heard the chuckling voices of his three little children. He thought it was the sounds of angels in the skies up above. Then into the yard stepped Ellie-May. He couldn't believe his eyes. She was strolling towards him and leading back the gentle whitehead Lily on a reins. Behind her in a procession came Tooraloo, Norry-What's-Your-Hurry and Hammer-the-Smith. In the elbow of their arms they were each carrying one of the three children, the as-yet-unnamed Faith, Hope and Charity.

They Had Cast The Dye

They had cast the dye. The wrongs of The Informer and the wrongs of The Rafter-hanging Neddy and his means of retribution had been gone over again and again in the course of The Family Law that evening. Ellie-May had shed her last tears. They had never been the tears of self-pity. For when she'd found herself hanging from the rafters she remembered the way Jesus had been treated – the way he had been spat at – the way he'd been whipped and crowned with bloody thorns. Not a single word had her Saviour said in his defence. And hadn't he been an example to us all?

True for him! And so she had kept her calm – had kept her counsel. She'd withheld her tears. It was the least she could have done.

When she'd seen Lily being marched down the lane – when she'd heard the immense sacrifice that Neddy was prepared to make – she had realised that her husband was the sorriest man on God's earth – prepared to surrender a man's most precious food – his daily milk – prepared to surrender all the money from the gallons of milk that Lily brought him in the monthly creamery-cheque. She had wept and wept and her heart had come up into her throat – to think of such a noble sacrifice and how her own self-worth had once again been restored to her. She couldn't wait to wash her face and comb out her hair. She couldn't wait to dress the little ones.

And as she now drove Lily into Neddy's yard she was almost bursting with the new love she felt for her man. She felt glorified and uplifted – a woman that was recently dead and now restored to life and on her way back to Happiness.

Neddy came out the door to meet her. He walked across the yard – clumsily at first. The handshakes followed. Then the awkward embrace to seal their newfound friendship. It would have brought a tear from a stone – as though the biblical Ruth and Naomi were smiling down from the clouds on the two of them and repeating all over again their mutual words of trust and love:

'Where you go, I myself will go.'

'Your footsteps will be my own footsteps.'

'Your people and your God will be my own people and my God.'

In suchlike manner the man and the woman were once more joined together as one. Neddy would never again raise his voice or his hands in wrath against Ellie-May. He would never again return to the whiskey-still and the making of his father's whiskey.

He knew he'd be losing many of his so-called friends – the new topers and the heavy drinkers. They could all go rot in hell for all he cared. Ellie-May had lost the respect of many women after the way she had informed on Neddy and the rest of them. They too could go rot in hell for all she cared. The little family were now on their own – forced hereafter to look inwards on themselves – forced to learn the new art of the recluse. The rattling tongues and their wicked old gossip had seen to that. For the next few weeks The Weeping Mollys kept up a heavy head of steam in their efforts at persecution.

Tooraloo Had The Right Air To It

Tooraloo had the right air to it. He comforted Neddy and Ellie-May. He told them that the anger of the rest of the men and women had done them a great and lasting service – that it was a blessing in disguise – that it had forced Neddy and Ellie-May to look back at their foolishness. Indeed it had brought Neddy and Ellie-May closer and closer than ever before. They realised how much they needed each other. They saw once more the beauty in each other's soul.

Life Is Short and Life Is Good

Life is short and Life is good and Life cannot be kept in a dark cave forever. And soon we were all able to take an example from the pair of them. With a speed that beggared belief the dark clouds in Rookery Rally ravelled themselves up into a ball and hurled themselves out across The Great Ocean. And the luminous sun (our long-time harbinger of happiness) came up dazzlingly and glistened our eyes once more. Indeed before the month was out we were in each other's arms all over again – back in our very own heaven as of old.

Once again we saw the kindly spectre of Canon-next-to-God stepping along smartly into our midst. He seemed to be everywhere at once. In his hand he had yet another gallon of holywater. He'd need to lash a good deal of it on us for there had been much to forgive. He blessed Neddy. He blessed Ellie-May. He might well have blessed himself (mindful as he always was of poor Test-Me). Indeed it was a wonder he didn't bless the recently cruel rafters to drive out the wicked old Devil from them!

Up At Dinny's

To celebrate we'd have to have yet another bit-of-a-dance. The House-Dance that followed above at Din-Din-Dinny-the Stammerer's was sure to live up to its name: 'the grandest dance there ever could be'. It was more than beautiful. Men, women and children came out to scrub their faces in every yard-stream – for none of us wanted to look an obstacle. We dug deep around the corners of our Welcoming Rooms to find our most resplendent outfits. We spat on our boots till they were polished like glass. Then we hastened across the fields and arrived in a thundering great heap in Dinny's yard. And before the hour was out even the women were seen whaling into the remains of the whiskey-kettles and the bottles, jugs and jamjars and were soon running like headless chickens round the floor from it. What the silvery moon in the sky or the roosting crows in the rookery thought of all the merriment we shudder to think:

'Down the throttle with it!' was heard again and again.

'Mee belly's on fire!'

'So good a drink (said Neddy) it'd burn a hole in a sod-o-turf.'

In a merry crowd we made several attacks with our rattling hobnails on the sparkling dance-floor till the soles of our feet were raw from the churning of the music.

We danced the evening away.

We danced the night away.

We danced half the next day away.

We toasted Neddy: 'The sound man that ye are!'

We toasted Ellie-May: 'The heroine of the hour after forgiving her man!'

We toasted Peace itself: 'As long as we all shall live!'

Throughout the evening the mild-mannered Creamery Manager had been sitting next to Doctor Glasses in the corner next to the fire. They'd been watching the fine old times and the ringing of the fiddles and flutes and the gaiety of the dancers. They'd been passing the hours warming their shins with the blaze from the turf-sods and imbibing glass after glass of the rawgut whiskey. In the end Doctor Glasses had eyes on him that glittered like a pair of marbles and his flushed cheeks were the colour of red radishes.

We could see that our medical genius was as full as a tick (said some) and as drunk as an owl (said others). We had never seen the poor man like this before for we all knew that he'd never let a drop of strong liquor past his lips until this evening's celebration. He'd be in bed for the rest of the week, his dreams full of all the wild dancing. For once in his life he'd have a head on him as heavy as a sack of flour. And another thing – for the first time in his life he'd find himself placed at the very top of his own surgery's sick-list.

Both himself and the Creamery Manager and the whole pack of us wouldn't have missed this evening's entertainment – not for the world. So merrily had Neddy's whiskey roared insides all of us that not only the next evening but the next night and indeed the rest of the week flitted clean away and disappeared before we heard tell of them or knew they'd arrived or could lift a muscle or an eyebrow. The dance at Dinny's (we all agreed) had been a night-and-a-half – a Rookery Rally dance that we'd take to our grave, every man-jack-of-us. Indeed it had! Enough said.

Postscript

Sadly the logs were now all burnt into perfect crisps and the fire that had accompanied the stories had finally died away on the card-players. It had been yet another great evening for the Rookery Rally storytellers. It was time now for the poachers to nudge into their topcoats, to bless themselves with the holy-water from the font at the door and to wish one another good luck before trudging off on their separate ways across the hills beyond Fort Dangerous.

Blue-eyed Jack spread out the last cinders and he threw a few mugs of water on top of them. He placed his mother's hot jar in her bed down near her feet. Then he himself went off into the Big Cave Room behind the hob, where he said a few weary prayers and hopped in under the damp blankets, rubbing his toes together to bring the warmth of the fire back into them. He was soon asleep like the rest of us.

Yours truly,

Edward Forde Hickey (December 2016)